GOLD

BOOKS BY
Stewart Edward White

FICTION
The Glory Hole

Of the Far West: The Claim Jumpers
Blazed Trail Stories—The Westerners—The Killer
Arizona Nights
The Long Rifle

Of the Far North: Conjuror's House—The Silent
Places—Skookum Chuck—Secret Harbour

Of the Lumber Woods: The Blazed Trail
The Riverman—Blazed Trail Stories
The Rules of the Game

Of California: The Rules of the Game—The Gray
Dawn—Gold—The Rose Dawn—On Tiptoe
Ranchero—Folded Hills

Of Mystery: The Mystery (With Samuel Hopkins Adams)
The Sign At Six

Of Africa: The Leopard Woman—Simba—Back of Beyond

ADVENTURE
THE OUT OF DOORS—EXPLORATION
The Forest—Camp and Trail—The Mountains
The Land of Footprints—The Cabin
African Campfires—The Pass—The Rediscovered
Country—Lions in the Path

HISTORICAL AND PHILOSOPHICAL
The 'Forty-niners
Daniel Boone: Wilderness Scout
Credo—Why Be a Mud Turtle?
Dog Days

JUVENILE
The Magic Forest
The Adventures of Bobby Orde

GOLD

By

STEWART EDWARD WHITE

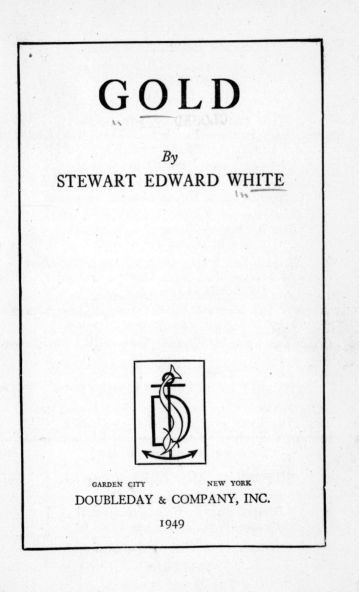

GARDEN CITY   NEW YORK

DOUBLEDAY & COMPANY, INC.

1949

CONTENTS

PART I.—PANAMA

CONTENTS

PART I
PANAMA

GOLD

CHAPTER I

OH, SUSANNAH!

Somewhere in this book I must write a paragraph exclusively about myself. The fact that in the outcome of all these stirring events I have ended as a mere bookkeeper is perhaps a good reason why one paragraph will be enough. In my youth I had dreams a-plenty; but the event and the peculiar twist of my own temperament prevented their fulfilment. Perhaps in a more squeamish age — and yet that is not fair, either, to the men whose destinies I am trying to record. Suffice it then that of these men I have been the friend and companion, of these occasions I have been a part, and that the very lacks and reservations of my own character that have kept me to a subordinate position and a little garden have probably made me the better spectator. Which is a longer paragraph about myself than I had purposed writing.

Therefore I will pass over briefly the various reasons, romantic and practical, why I decided to join the gold rush to California in the year 1849. It was in the air; and I was then of a romantic and adventurous disposition.

The first news of the gold discovery filtered to us in a roundabout way through vessels to the Sandwich Islands, and then appeared again in the columns of some Baltimore paper. Everybody laughed at the rumour; but everybody remembered it. The land was infinitely remote; and then, as now, romance increases as the square of the distance. There might well be gold there; but more authentic were the reports of fleas, rawhides, and a dried-up coast. Minstrel shows made a good deal of fun of it all, I remember. Then, when we were of a broad grin, came the publication of the letter written by Governor Mason to the War Department. That was a sober official document, and had to be believed, but it read like a fairy tale.

"I have no hesitation in saying," wrote the governor, "that there is more gold in the country drained by the Sacramento and San Joaquin rivers than would pay the costs of the late war with Mexico a hundred times over." And he then went on to report in detail big nuggets and big washings, mentioning men, places, dates, in a circumstantial manner that carried conviction.

Our broad grins faded. The minstrels' jokes changed colour. As I look back, it seems to me that I can almost see with the physical eye the broad restless upheaval beneath the surface of all society. The Mexican war was just over, and the veterans — young veterans all — filled with the spirit of adventure turned eagerly toward this glittering new emprise. Out in the small villages, on the small farms, the news was talked over seriously, almost without excitement, as offering a possible means of lifting the burden war had laid. Families strained their resources, mortgaged their possessions, to equip and send their single strongest members to make the common fortune.

OH, SUSANNAH!

Then came the song that caught the popular ear; and the rush was on. Most great movements are done to song, generally commonplace. It was so in this instance. *Oh, Susannah!* or rather a modification of the original made to fit the occasion, first sung in some minstrel show, ran like fire in the tinder of men's excited hopes. From every stage, on every street corner, in every restaurant and hotel it was sung, played, and whistled. At the sound of its first notes the audience always sprang to its feet and cheered like mad.

The desire to go to el-dorado was universal, and almost irresistible. The ability to go was much more circumscribed. For one thing, it cost a good deal of money; and that was where *I* bogged down at the first pull. Then I suppose a majority did have ties of family, business or other responsibilities impossible to shake off. However, we all joined one or more of the various clubs formed for the purpose of getting at least some of their members to California; and discussed heatedly the merits of the different routes; and went into minute and fascinating details as to processes of which we knew less than nothing; and sang *Oh, Susannah!* and talked ourselves into a glorified fever of excitement; and went home with our heads in the clouds. Once in a great while some of these clubs came to something — as a body I mean; for individual members were constantly working themselves up the summit of resolution to rush headlong and regardless down the other side and out of our sight. When a man had reached a certain pitch of excitement he ran amuck. He sold anything, deserted anything, broke through anything in the

5

way of family, responsibility, or financial lacks in order to go. But, as I say, occasionally one of these clubs pooled its individual resources and bought some old tub of a whaler, or outfitted a wagon train, and started off. But generally we got only as far as *Oh, Susannah!* I remember once, in coming out from one of our meetings, finding myself next a solemn and earnest youth originally from my own rural village. He walked by my side for several squares lost in a brown study. Then suddenly he looked up.

"Frank," said he with conviction, "I believe I'll go. I know most of this talk is wildly exaggerated, but I'm sensible enough to discount all that sort of thing and to disbelieve absurd stories. I shan't go with the slightest notion of finding the thing true, but will be satisfied if I do reasonably well. In fact, if I don't pick up more than a hatful of gold a day, I shall be perfectly satisfied."

Which remark sufficiently indicates about where we all were!

CHAPTER II

THE HAMMERLOCK

We had many sorts of men in our club, but nearly all young. One, in especial, early attracted my attention, and held it through all the changing vicissitudes of our many meetings. I say attracted me, though fascinated would be perhaps the better word, for after the first evening of his attendance I used deliberately so to place myself that I could watch him.

He came always in a rather worn military cape, which on entering the door he promptly threw back in such a manner as to display the red lining. This seemed an appropriate envelopment of his flaming, buoyant personality. He walked with his chin up and his back straight, and trod directly on and over the ends of his toes so that he seemed fairly to spring with vigour. His body was very erect and tall and pliant, bending easily to every change of balance. If I were never to have seen his face at all I should have placed him as one of the laughing spirits of the world. His head was rather small, round, well poised, with soft close-set ringlets all over it like a cap, in the fashion of some marble gods I have seen. He had very regular, handsome features, with a clear, biscuit-brown complexion, and a close-clipped, stubby, light moustache. All these things were interesting and attractive, though no more so than are the

7

vigour and beauty of any perfect animal. But the quality of his eyes placed him, at least to me, in a class apart. They were sober, clear eyes, that looked out gray and contemplative on the world about them; so that one got the instant impression of a soul behind them that weighed and judged. Indeed they were not laughing eyes at all, and rather negatived the impression made by the man's general bearing. But somewhere down in them something flickered like a strong burning candle in a brisk wind. Occasionally it was almost out; then again it blazed up clear, so that one thought to see it plainly through the steady brooding look. It always fascinated the beholder, for it was mysterious. Whether it came and went, grew and shrank, following delicately the moods or reflections of the spirit within, or whether it was a purely fortuitous effect of light and refraction, no man was ever able to say. And some men later made some very bad guesses. I myself think it was the devil of genius — a devil behind the steady control of a clear brain. His name, I soon discovered, was Talbot Ward.

At this period I was starting in as an assistant bookkeeper to a large exporting firm. They were enterprising people, and already they were laying plans to capture some of the California trade. The office talk I heard concerning the purchase of ships, the consignment of arms, the engagement of captains and of crews further inflamed my imagination. I received the vast sum of nine dollars per week. As I was quite alone in the world, and possessed no other resources, the saving of the five hundred dollars agreed upon as the least sum with which it was possible to get to California was fairly out of all question.

One evening, after the meeting, to my great surprise, Ward fell into step with me.   We had up to that moment never exchanged a word.

"In New York long?" he demanded.

"About six months," I told him.

"Farm bred, of course?" he remarked.   "Where?"

"Ashbury in Vermont," I replied, without the slightest feeling that he was intrusive.

He stopped short in the street and looked me up and down reflectively, but without comment.

"I've been watching you at these fool meetings," said he, falling into step again.

In spite of myself I experienced a glow of gratification at having been the object of his interest.

"Fool meetings?" I echoed inquiringly.

"Suppose, by a miracle, all that lot could agree, and could start for California to-morrow, in a body — that's what they are organized for, I believe," he countered — "would you go with them?"

"Why not?"

"Martin is why not; and Fowler is why not; and that little Smith runt, and six or eight others.   They are weak sisters. If you are going into a thing, go into it with the strong men. I wouldn't go with that crowd to a snake fight if it was twelve miles away.   Where do you live?"

"West Ninth Street."

"That's not far.   Have you a good big room?"

"I have a very small hall bedroom," I replied wonderingly; "a number of us have the whole of the top floor."

Somehow, I must repeat, this unexplained intrusion of a total stranger into my private affairs did not offend.

"Then you must have a big sitting-room. How many of you?"

"Four."

"Can you lick all the others?"

I stopped to laugh. By some shrewd guess he had hit on our chief difficulty as a community. We were all four country boys with a good deal of residuary energy and high spirits; and we were not popular with the tenants underneath.

"You see I'm pretty big ——" I reminded him.

"Yes, I see you are. That's why I'm with you. Do you think you can lick me?"

I stopped short again, in surprise.

"What in blazes ——" I began.

He laughed, and the devils in his eyes danced right out to the surface of them.

"I asked you a plain question," he said, "and I'd like the favour of a plain answer. Do you think you can lick me as well as your rural friends?"

"I can," said I shortly.

He ran his arm through mine eagerly.

"Come on!" he cried, "on to West Ninth!"

We found two of my roommates smoking and talking before the tiny open fire. Talbot Ward, full of the business in hand, rushed directly at the matter once the introductions were over.

Our arrangements were very simple; the chairs were few and pushed back easily, and we had an old set of gloves.

"Which is it to be?" I asked my guest, "boxing or wrestling?"

"I said you couldn't *lick* me," he replied. "Boxing is a game with rules; it isn't fighting at all."

"You want to bite and gouge and scratch, then?" said I, greatly amused.

"I do not; they would not be fair; a fight's a fight; but a man can be decent with it all. We'll put on the gloves, and we'll hit and wrestle both — in fact, we'll fight."

He began rapidly to strip.

"Would you expect to get off your clothes in a real fight?" I asked him a little sardonically.

"If I *expected* to fight, yes!" said he. "Why not? Didn't the Greek and Roman and Hebrew and Hun and every other good old fighter 'strip for the fray' when he got a chance? Of course! Take off your shirt, man!"

I began also to strip for this strange contest whose rules seemed to be made up from a judicious selection of general principles by Talbot Ward.

My opponent's body was as beautiful as his head. The smooth white skin covered long muscles that rippled beneath it with every slightest motion. The chest was deep, the waist and hips narrow, the shoulders well rounded. In contrast my own big prominent muscles, trained by heavy farm work of my early youth, seemed to move slowly, to knot sluggishly though powerfully. Nevertheless I judged at a glance that my strength could not but prove greater than his. In a boxing match his lithe quickness might win — provided he had the skill to direct it. But in a genuine fight, within the circumscribed and hampering dimensions of our little room, I thought my own rather unusual power must crush him. The only unknown quantity was the spirit or gameness of us two. I had no great doubt of my own determination in that respect — I had been on too many log-drives to fear personal encounter. And certainly Talbot Ward seemed to show nothing but eager interest.

"You don't show up for what you are in your clothes," said he. "This is going to be more fun than I had thought."

My roommates perched on the table and the mantelpiece out of the way. I asked the length of the rounds.

"Rounds!" echoed Talbot Ward with a flash of teeth beneath his little moustache. "Did you ever hear of rounds in a real fight?"

With the words he sprang forward and hit me twice. The blows started at the very toe of his foot; and they shook me as no blows, even with the bare fist, have ever shaken me before or since. Completely dazed, I struck back, but encountered only the empty air. Four or five times, from somewhere, these pile-driver fists descended upon me. Being now prepared, to some extent, I raised my elbows and managed to defend my neck and jaws. The attack was immediately transferred to my body, but I stiffened my muscles thankfully and took the punishment. My river and farm work had so hardened me there that I believe I could have taken the kick of a mule without damage were I expecting it.

The respite enabled my brain to clear. I recovered slowly from the effect of those first two vicious blows. I saw Ward, his eyes narrowed calculatingly, his body swinging forward like a whalebone spring, delivering his attack with nice accuracy. A slow anger glowed through me. He had begun without the least warning: had caught me absolutely unaware. I hit back.

He was so intent on his own assault, so certain of the blinding effect of his first attack, that I hit him. I saw his head snap back, and the blood come from his lips. The blows were weak, for I was still dazed; but they served, together with the slow burn of my anger, greatly to steady me. We were once more on equal terms.

For perhaps two minutes I tried to exchange with him. He was in and out like lightning; he landed on me hard almost every time; he escaped nine out of ten of my return counters. Decidedly I was getting the worst of this; though my heavier body took punishment better than his lighter and more nervous frame. Then suddenly it occurred to me that I was playing his game for him. As long as he could keep away from me, he was at an advantage. My best chance was to close.

From that moment I took the aggressive, and was in consequence the more punished. My rushes to close in were skilfully eluded; and they generally laid me wide open. My head was singing, and my sight uncertain; though I was in no real distress. Ward danced away and slipped around tense as a panther.

Then, by a very simple ruse, I got hold of him. I feinted at rushing him, stopped and hit instead, and then, following closely the blow, managed to seize his arm. For ten seconds he jerked and twisted and struggled to release himself. Then suddenly he gave that up, dove forward, and caught me in a grapevine.

He was a fairly skilful wrestler, and very strong. It was as though he were made of whalebone springs. But never yet have I met a man of my weight who possessed the same solid strength; and Ward would tip the scales at considerably less. I broke his hold, and went after him.

He was as lively as an exceedingly slippery fish. Time after time he all but wriggled from my grasp; and time after time he broke my hold by sheer agility. His exertions must have been to him something terrible, for they required every ounce of his strength at the greatest speed. I could, of course, take it much easier, and every instant I expected to feel him weaken beneath my hands; but apparently he was as vigorous as ever. He was in excellent training. At last, however, I managed to jerk him whirling past me, to throw his feet from under him, and to drop him beneath me. As he fell he twisted, and by a sheer fluke I caught his wrist.

Thus through no great skill of my own the fortunes of war had given me a hammerlock on him. Most people know what that is. Any one else can find out by placing his forearm across the small of his back and then getting somebody else to press upward on the forearm. The Greek statue of "The Wrestlers" illustrates it. As the pressure increases, so does the pain. When the pain becomes intense enough, the wrestler rolls over and the contest is won. Some people can stand it longer than others; but all sooner or later must give up. In fact, skilled wrestlers, knowing that otherwise the inevitable end is a broken arm, save themselves much tribulation by immediately conceding the bout once this deadly hold is gained.

I began to force Talbot Ward's hand slowly up his back.

Very gently, an inch at a time, I pressed. He said nothing. Once he attempted to slip sidewise; but finding me of course fully prepared for that, he instantly ceased struggling. After I had pushed the hand to the hurting point, I stopped.

"Well?" said I.

He said nothing.

Now I was young, and none too well disciplined, heated by contest, and very angry at having been so unexpectedly attacked at the beginning. I was quite willing to hurt him a little. Slowly and steadily, and, I am ashamed to say, with considerable satisfaction, I pressed the arm upward. The pain must have been intense. I could feel the man's body quiver between my knees, and saw the sweat break out afresh. Still he made no sign, but dug his forehead into the floor. "I can stand this as long as you can," said I to myself grimly.

But at last I reached the point where I knew that another inch, another pound, would break the bone.

"Do you give up?" I demanded.

"No!" he gasped explosively.

"I'll break your arm!" I snarled at him

He made no reply.

The blood was running into my eyes from a small scrape on my forehead. It was nothing, but it annoyed me. I was bruised and heated and mad. Every bit of antagonism in me was aroused. As far as I was concerned, it was a very real fight.

"All right," I growled, "I'll keep you there then, damn you!"

Holding the arm in the same position, I settled myself. The pain to the poor chap must have been something fearful, for every muscle and tendon was stretched to the cracking point. His breath came and went in sharp hisses; but he gave no other sign. My heat cooled, though, as I look back on it, far too slowly. Suddenly I arose and flung him from me. He rolled over on his back, and lay, his eyes half closed, breathing deeply. We must have been a sweet sight, we two young barbarians — myself marked and swollen and bloody, he with one eye puffed, and pale as death. My roommates, absolutely fascinated, did not stir.

The tableau lasted only the fraction of a minute, after all. Then abruptly Talbot Ward sat up. He grinned up at me with his characteristic momentary flash of teeth.

"I told you you couldn't lick me," said he.

I stared at him in astonishment.

"Licked? Why, I had you cold!"

"You had not."

"I'd have broken your arm, if I had gone any farther."

"Well, why didn't you?"

I stared into his eyes blankly.

"Would you have done it?" I asked, in a sudden flash of illumination.

"Why, of course," said he, with a faint contempt, as he arose.

"Why did you hit me at first, as you did? You gave me no warning whatever."

"Do you get any warning in a real fight?"

I could not controvert this; and yet uneasily, vaguely, I felt there must be a fallacy somewhere. I had been told and not told, what should, or should not, be done, in an affair that apparently could have no rules, and yet had distinctions as to fair and unfair, some of which were explained and some left as obvious. I felt somewhat confused. But often in my later experience with Talbot Ward I felt just that way, so in retrospect it does not strike me so forcibly as it did at that time.

"But you're a wonder! a perfect wonder!" Ward was saying.

Then we all became aware of a knocking and a rattling at the door. It must have been going on for some time.

"If you don't open, I'll get the police! I promise you, I'll get the police!" the voice of our landlady was saying.

We looked at each other aghast.

"I suppose we must have been making a little noise," conceded Talbot Ward. Noise! It must have sounded as though the house were coming down. Our ordinary little boxing matches were nothing to it.

Ward threw his military cape around his shoulders, and sank back into a seat beneath the window. I put on an overcoat. One of the boys let her in.

She was thoroughly angry, and she gave us all notice to go. She had done that same every Saturday night for a year; but we had always wheedled her out of it. This time, however, she seemed to mean business. I suppose we *had* made a good deal of a riot. When the fact became evident, I, of course, shouldered the whole responsibility. Thereupon she turned on me. Unexpectedly Talbot Ward spoke up from the obscurity of his corner. His clear voice was incisive, but so courteous with the cold finality of the high-bred aristocrat, that Mrs. Simpkins was cut short in the middle of a sentence.

"I beg you, calm yourself, madam," said he; "it is not worth heating yourself over: for the annoyance, such as it is, will soon be removed. Mr. Munroe and myself are shortly departing together for California."

CHAPTER III

THE VOYAGE

If I had any scruples — and I do not remember many —
they were overcome within the next day or two. It was
agreed that I was to go in Ward's employ, he to pay my
passage money and all expenses, I to give him half the gold
I might pick up. This seemed to me, at least, an eminently
satisfactory and businesslike arrangement. Ward bought
the outfits for both of us. It turned out that he was a
Mexican war veteran — hence the military cape — and
in consequence an old campaigner. His experience and
my rural upbringing saved us from most of the ridiculous
purchases men made at that time. We had stout clothes
and boots, a waterproof apiece, picks and shovel, blankets
and long strips of canvas, three axes, knives, one rifle, a
double shotgun, and a Colt's revolver apiece. The latter
seemed to me a wonderful weapon, with its six charges in
the turning cylinder; but I had no opportunity to try it.

Ward decided instantly for the Panama route.

"It's the most expensive, but also the quickest," said he;
'a sailing ship around the Horn takes forever; and across
the plains is ditto. Every day we wait, some other fellow
is landing in the diggings."

Nearly every evening he popped into our boarding house,
where, owing to the imminence of my departure. I had been

restored to favour. I never did find out where he lived. We took our passage at the steamship office; we went to the variety shows and sang *Oh, Susannah!* with the rest; we strutted a bit, and were only restrained from donning our flannel shirts and Colt's revolving pistols in the streets of New York by a little remnant, a very little remnant, of common sense. When the time at last came, we boarded our steamship, and hung over the rail, and cheered like crazy things. I personally felt as though a lid had been lifted from my spirit, and that a rolling cloud of enthusiasm was at last allowed to puff out to fill my heaven.

In two days we were both over being seasick, and had a chance to look around us. Our ship was a sidewheel steamer of about a thousand tons, and she carried two hundred and eighty passengers, which was about two hundred more than her regular complement. They were as miscellaneous a lot as mortal eye ever fell upon: from the lank Maine Yankee to the tall, sallow, black-haired man from Louisiana. I suppose, too, all grades of the social order must have been represented; but in our youth and high spirits we did not go into details of that sort. Every man, with the exception of a dozen or so, wore a red shirt, a slouch hat, a revolver and a bowie knife; and most of us had started to grow beards. Unless one scrutinized closely such unimportant details as features, ways of speech or manners, one could not place his man's former status, whether as lawyer, physician or roustabout. And we were too busy for that. I never saw such a busy place as that splattering old ship slowly wallowing her way south toward the tropical seas. We had fifty-eight thousand things to discuss, beginning with Marshall's first discovery, skipping through the clouds of rumours of all sorts, down to intimate details of climate, outfit, prospects, plans, and the best methods of getting at the gold. And to all these subjects we brought a dozen points of view, each of which was strange to all the others. We had with us men from every stratum of society, and from every point of the compass. Each was a product of his own training and mental upbringing, and was incapable, without great effort, of understanding his neighbour's point of view. Communication and travel were in those days very limited, it must be remembered, and different communities and sections of the country produced strong types. With us discussion became an adventurous exploration into a new country; the man from Maine could not but be interested in finding out what that strange, straight-haired, dark creature from Carolina might think of even the most commonplace subject. Only our subjects were not commonplace.

So my chief impression of that voyage down was of knots of men talking hurriedly and excitedly, as though there were not a moment to waste; and the hum of voices rising and falling far into the night.

Only two things were capable of breaking in on this tense absorption of the men in each other and in their subject — one was dolphins, and the other the meal gong. When dolphins appeared each rushed promptly to the side of the ship and discharged his revolver at the beasts. I never saw any harm come from these fusillades, but they made a wonderful row. Meal times always caught the majority unaware. They tumbled and jostled down the companionways only to find the wise and forethoughtful had preëmpted every chair. Whereupon, with most ludicrous expressions of chagrin or of assumed nonchalance, they trooped back to meet the laughter of the wise, if not forethoughtful, who had realized the uselessness of the rush. After a moment's grumbling, however, the discussions were resumed.

There was some quarrelling, but not much. A holiday spirit pervaded the lot; for they were men cut off from all experience, all accustomed surroundings, all the restraints of training, and they were embarked on the great adventure. I do not now remember many of them individually. They were of a piece with the thousands we were destined to encounter. But I do retain a most vivid mental picture of them collectively, with their red shirts, their slouch hats, their belts full of weapons, their eyes of eagerness, their souls of dreams; brimming with pent energy; theorizing, arguing, disputing; ready at an instant's notice for any sort of a joke or excitement that would relieve the tension; boisterous, noisy, laughing loudly, smothering by sheer weight of ridicule individual resentments — altogether a wonderful picture of the youth and hope and energy and high spirits of the time.

Never before nor since have I looked upon such a variety of equipment as strewed the decks and cabins of that ship. A great majority of the passengers knew nothing whatever about out-of-door life, and less than nothing as to the conditions in California and on the way. Consequently they had bought liberally of all sorts of idiotic patent contraptions. India rubber played a prominent part. And the deck was cumbered with at least forty sorts of machines for separating gold from the soil: some of them to use water, some muscular labour, and one tremendous affair with wings was supposed to fan away everything but the gold. Differing in everything else, they were alike in one thing: they had all been devised by men who had never seen any but manufactured gold. I may add that I never saw a machine of the kind actually at work in the diggings.

Just now, however, I looked on the owners of these contraptions with envy, and thought ourselves at a disadvantage with only our picks, shovels, and axes.

But we had with us a wonderful book that went far toward cheering up the poorly equipped. Several copies had been brought aboard, so we all had a chance to read it. The work was entitled "Three Weeks in the Gold Mines," and was written by a veracious individual who signed himself H. I. Simpson. I now doubt if he had ever left his New York hall bedroom, though at the time we took his statements for plain truth. Simpson could spare only ten days of this three weeks for actual mining. In that period, with no other implement than a pocket knife, he picked out fifty thousand dollars. The rest of the time he preferred to travel about and see the country, picking up only what incidental nuggets he came across while walking. We believed this.

As we drew southward the days became insufferably warm, but the nights were glorious. Talbot and I liked to sleep on the deck; and generally camped down up near the bitts. The old ship rolled frightfully, for she was light in freight in order to accommodate so many passengers; and the dark blue sea appeared to swoop up and down beneath the placid tropic moon.

We had many long, quiet talks up there; but in them all I learned nothing, absolutely nothing, of my companion.

"If you had broken my arm that time, I should not have taken you," he remarked suddenly one evening.

"Shouldn't blame you," said I.

"No! I wouldn't have wanted that kind of a man," he continued, "for I should doubt my control of him. But you gave up."

This nettled me.

"Would you have had me, or any man, brute enough to go through with it?" I demanded.

"Well"— he hesitated —"it was agreed that it was to be *fight*, you remember. And after all, if you had broken my arm, it would have been my fault and not yours."

Two young fellows used occasionally to join us in our swooping, plunging perch. They were as unlike as two men could be, and yet already they had become firm friends. One was a slow, lank, ague-stricken individual from somewhere in the wilds of the Great Lakes, his face lined and brown as though carved from hardwood, his speed slow, his eyes steady with a veiled sardonic humour. His companion was scarcely more than a boy, and he came, I believe, from Virginia. He was a dark, eager youth, with a mop of black shiny hair that he was always tossing back, bright glowing eyes, a great enthusiasm of manner, and an imagination alert to catch fire. The backwoodsman seemed attracted to the boy by this very quick and unsophisticated bubbling of candid youth; while the boy most evidently worshipped his older companion as a symbol of the mysterious frontier. The Northerner was named Rogers, but was invariably known as Yank. The Southerner had some such name as Fairfax, but was called Johnny, and later in California, for reasons that will appear, Diamond Jack. Yank's distinguishing feature was a long-barrelled "pea shooter" rifle. He never moved ten feet without it.

Johnny usually did most of the talking when we were all gathered together. Yank and I did the listening and Talbot the interpellating. Johnny swarmed all over himself like a pickpocket, and showed us everything he had in the way of history, manners, training, family, pride, naïveté, expectations and hopes. He prided himself on being a calm, phlegmatic individual, unemotional and not easily excited, and he constantly took this attitude. It was a lovely joke.

"Of course," said he, "it won't be necessary to stay out more than a year. They tell me I can easily make eleven hundred dollars a day; but you know I am not easily moved by such reports" — he was at the time moving under a high pressure, at least ten knots an hour — "I shall be satisfied with three hundred a day. Allowing three hundred working days to the year, that gives me about ninety thousand dollars — plenty!"

"You'll have a few expenses," suggested Talbot.

"Oh — yes — well, make it a year and a half, just to be on the safe side."

Johnny was eagerly anxious to know everybody on the ship, with the exception of about a dozen from his own South As far as I could see they did not in the slightest degree differ except in dress from any of the other thirty or forty from that section, but Johnny distinguished. He stiffened as though Yank's gunbarrel had taken the place of his spine whenever one of these men was near; and he was so coldly and pointedly courteous that I would have slapped his confounded face if he had acted so to me.

"Look here, Johnny," I said to him one day, "what's the matter with those fellows? They look all right to me. What do you know against them?"

"I never laid eyes on them before in my life, sir," he replied, stiffening perceptibly.

"Take that kink out of your back," I warned him. "That won't work worth a cent with me!"

He laughed.

"I beg pardon. They are not gentlemen."

"I don't know what you mean by gentlemen," said I; "it's a wide term. But lots of us here aren't gentlemen — far, far from it. But you seem to like us."

He knit his brows.

"I can't explain. They are the class of cheap politician that brings into disrepute the chivalry of the South, sir."

Talbot and I burst into a shout of laughter, and even Yank, leaning attentively on the long barrel of his pea rifle, grinned faintly. We caught Johnny up on that word — and he was game enough to take it well. Whenever something particularly had happened to be also Southern, we called it the Chivalry. The word caught hold; so that later it came to be applied as a generic term to the Southern wing of venal politicians that early tried to control the new state of California.

THE VOYAGE

I must confess that if I had been Johnny I should have stepped more carefully with these men. They were a dark, suave lot, and dressed well. In fact, they and a half dozen obviously professional men alone in all that ship wore what we would call civilized clothes. I do not know which was more incongruous — our own red shirts, or the top hats, flowing skirts, and light pantaloons of these quietly courteous gentlemen. They were quite as well armed as ourselves, however, wearing their revolvers beneath their armpits, or carrying short double pistols. They treated Johnny with an ironically exaggerated courtesy, and paid little attention to his high airs. It was obvious, however, that he was making enemies.

Talbot Ward knew everybody aboard, from the captain down. His laughing, half-aloof manner was very taking; and his ironical comments on the various points of discussion, somehow, conveyed no sting. He was continually accepting gifts of newspapers — of which there were a half a thousand or so brought aboard — with every appearance of receiving a favour. These papers he carried down to our tiny box of a room and added to his bundle. I supposed at the time he was doing all this on Molière's principle, that one gains more popularity by accepting a favour than by bestowing one.

CHAPTER IV

THE VILLAGE BY THE LAGOON

In the early morning one day we came in sight of a round high bluff with a castle atop, and a low shore running away. The ship's man told us this was Chagres.

This news caused a curious disintegration in the ship's company. We had heretofore lived together a good-humoured community. Now we immediately drew apart into small suspicious groups. For we had shortly to land ourselves and our goods, and to obtain transportation across the Isthmus; and each wanted to be ahead of his neighbour.

Here the owners of much freight found themselves at a disadvantage. I began to envy less the proprietors of those enormous or heavy machines for the separation of gold. Each man ran about on the deck collecting busily all his belongings into one pile. When he had done that, he spent the rest of his time trying to extract definite promises from the harassed ship's officers that he should go ashore in the first boat.

Talbot and I sat on our few packages and enjoyed the scene. The ship came to anchor and the sailors swung the boat down from the davits. The passengers crowded around in a dense, clamouring mob. We arose, shouldered our effects, and quietly slipped around to the corresponding boat on the other side the ship. Sure enough, that also was being lowered. So that we and a dozen who had made the same good guess, were, after all, the first to land.

The town proved to be built on low ground in a bay the other side the castle and the hill. It must be remembered that I had never travelled. The cane houses or huts, with their high peaked roofs thatched with palm leaves, the straight palms in the background against the sky, the morasses all about, the squawk and flop of strange, long-legged marsh birds, the glare of light, the queer looking craft beached on the mud, and the dark-skinned, white-clad figures awaiting us — all these struck strongly at my imagination.

We beached in the mud, and were at once surrounded by a host of little, brown, clamorous men. Talbot took charge, and began to shoot back Spanish at a great rate. Some of the little men had a few words of English. Our goods were seized, and promptly disappeared in a dozen directions. I tried to prevent this, but could only collar one man at a time. All the Americans were swearing and threatening at a great rate. I saw Johnny, tearing up the beach after a fleet native, fall flat and full length in the mud, to the vast delight of all who beheld.

Finally Talbot ploughed his way to me.

"It's all settled," said he. "I've made a bargain with my friend here to take us up in his boat to Cruces for fifteen dollars apiece for four of us."

"Well, if you need two more, for heaven's sake rescue Johnny," I advised. "He'll have apoplexy."

We hailed Johnny and explained matters. Johnny was somewhat put to it to attain his desired air of imperturbable calm.

"They've got every blistered thing I own, and made off with it!" he cried. "Confound it, sir, I'm going to shoot every saddle-coloured hound in the place if I don't get back my belongings!"

"They've got our stuff, too," I added.

"Well, keep calm," advised Talbot. "I don't know the game down here, but it strikes me they can't get very far through these swamps, if they *do* try to steal, and I don't believe they're stealing anyway; the whole performance to me bears a strong family resemblance to hotel runners. Here, *compadre!*"

He talked a few moments with his boatman.

"That's right," he told us, then. "Come on!"

We walked along the little crescent of beach, looking into each of the boats in the long row drawn up on the shore. They were queer craft, dug out from the trunks of trees, with small decks in bow and stern, and with a low roof of palmetto leaves amidships. By the time we had reached the end of the row we had collected all our effects. Our own boatman stowed them in his craft.

Thereupon, our minds at rest, we returned to the landing to enjoy the scene. The second ship's boat had beached, and the row was going on, worse than before. In the seething, cursing, shouting mass we caught sight of Yank's tall figure leaning imperturbably on his rifle muzzle. We made our way to him.

"Got your boat yet?" Talbot shouted at him.

"Got nothin' yet but a headache in the ears," said Yank.

"Come with us then. Where's your plunder?"

Yank stooped and swung to his shoulder a small bundle tied with ropes.

"She's all thar," said he.

These matters settled, we turned with considerable curiosity to the little village itself. It was all exotic, strange. Everything was different, and we saw it through the eyes of youth and romance as epitomizing the storied tropics.

There were perhaps a couple of hundred of the cane huts arranged roughly along streets in which survived the remains of crude paving. All else was a morass. Single palm trees shot up straight, to burst like rockets in a falling star of fronds. Men and women, clad in a single cotton shift reaching to the knees, lounged in the doorways or against the frail walls, smoking cigars. Pot-bellied children, stark naked, played everywhere, but principally in the mudholes and on the offal dumps. Innumerable small, hairless dogs were everywhere about, a great curiosity to us, who had never even heard of such things. We looked into some of the interiors, but saw nothing in the way of decent furniture. The cooking appeared to be done between two stones. A grand tropical smell hung low in the air. On the thresholds of the doors, inside the houses, in the middle of the treets, anywhere, everywhere, were old fish, the heads of cattle, drying hides, all sorts of carrion, most of it well decomposed. Back of the town was a low, rank jungle of green, and a stagnant lake. The latter had a delicate border of greasy blue mud.

Johnny and I wandered about completely fascinated. Talbot and Yank did not seem so impressed. Finally Talbot called a halt.

"This is all very well; if you kids like to look at yellow fever, blackjack, and corruption, all right," said he. "But we've got to start pretty soon after noon, and in the meantime where do we eat?"

We returned through the town. It was now filled to overflowing with our compatriots. They surged everywhere, full of comment and curiosity. The half-naked men and women with the cigars, and the wholly naked children and dogs, seemed not in the least disturbed nor enlivened.

Talbot's earnest inquiries finally got us to the Crescent Hotel. It was a hut exactly like all the rest, save that it had a floor. From its name I suppose it must have been kept by a white man, but we never got near enough through the crowd to find out. Without Talbot we should have gone hungry, with many others, but he inquired around until we found a native willing to feed us. So we ate on an upturned hencoop outside a native hut. The meal consisted of pork, bread, and water.

We strolled to the beach at the hour appointed with our boatman. He was not there; nor any other boatman.

"Never mind," said Ward; "I'll know him if I see him. I'll go look him up. You fellows find the boat with our things in it."

He and I reëntered the village, but a fifteen minutes' search failed to disclose our man. Therefore we returned to the beach. A crowd was gathered close about some common centre in the unmistakable restless manner of men about a dog fight or some other kind of a row. We pushed our way in.

Johnny and Yank were backed up against the palmetto awning of one of the boats in an attitude of deadly and quiet menace. Not two yards away stood four of our well-dressed friends. Nobody as yet displayed a weapon, except that Yank's long rifle lay across the hollow of his left arm instead of butt to earth; but it was evident that lightnings were playing. The boatman, who had appeared, alone was saying anything, but he seemed to be supplying language for the lot.

Johnny's tense, alert attitude relaxed a little when he saw us.

"Well?" inquired Ward easily. "What's the trouble?"

"Yank and I found our goods dumped out on the beach, and others in their place," said Johnny.

"So you proceeded to reverse matters? How about it?" he inquired pleasantly of the four men.

"I know nothing about it," replied one of them shortly. "We hired this boat, and we intend to have it; and no whipper-snapper is going to keep us from it."

"I see," said Talbot pleasantly. "Well, excuse me

a moment while I talk to our friend." He addressed the man in Spanish, and received short, sullen replies. "He says," Talbot explained to us, "that he never saw us before in his life, and never agreed to take us up the river."

"Well, that settles it," stated the other man.

"How much did you offer to pay him?" asked Talbot.

The man stared. "None of your business," he replied.

"They're askin' twenty dollars a head," volunteered one of the interested spectators.

"Exactly. You see," said Talbot to us, "we got here a little too early. Our bargain was for only fifteen dollars; and now this worthy citizen has made a better rate for himself."

"You should have had the bargain immediately registered before the *alcalde*, señor," spoke up a white-dressed Spaniard of the better class, probably from the castle.

"I thank you, señor," said Talbot courteously. "That neglect is due to my ignorance of your charming country."

"And now if you'll move, young turkey cock, we'll just take our boat," said another of the claimants.

"One moment!" said Talbot Ward, with a new edge to his voice. "This is my boat, not yours; my baggage is in it, my boatman is on the ground. That he is forgetful has nothing to do with the merits of the case. You know this as well as I do. Now you can acknowledge this peacefully and get out, or you can fight. I don't care a continental red copper which. Only I warn you, the first man who makes a move with anything but his two feet will be shot dead."

He stood, his hands hanging idly by his sides, and he spoke very quietly. The four men were not cowards, that I'll swear; but one and all they stared into Ward's eyes, and came individually to the same conclusion. I do not doubt that dancing flicker of refraction — or of devilment — was very near the surface.

"Of course, if you are very positive, I should not dream of doubting your word or of interfering," said the tallest and quietest, who had remained in the background. "We desire to do injustice to no man —— "

Johnny, behind us, snorted loudly and derisively.

"If my knowledge of Spanish is of any value in assisting you to a boat, pray command me," broke in Ward.

The crowd moved off, the boatman with it. I reached out and collared him.

Talbot had turned on Johnny.

"Fairfax," said he icily, "one of the first things you must learn is not to stir things up again once a victory is gained. Those men were sore; and you took the best method possible of bringing on a real fight."

Poor Johnny flushed to the roots of his hair.

"You're right," said he in a stifled voice.

Talbot Ward thawed completely, and a most winning smile illumined his face.

"Why, that's what I call handsome, Johnny!" he

cried. "It's pretty hard to admit the wrong. You and Yank certainly looked bold and warlike when he came along. Where's that confounded *mozo?* Oh, you have him, Frank. Good boy! Come here, my amiable citizen. I guess you understand English after all, or you couldn't have bargained so shrewdly with our blackleg friends."

The flush slowly faded from Johnny's face. Yank's sole contribution to the changed conditions was to spit with great care, and to shift the butt of his rifle to the ground.

"Now," Talbot was admonishing the boatman, "that was very bad. When you make a bargain, stick to it. But I'll tell you what I will do. I will ask all people, *sabe,* everywhere, your people, my people, and if everybody pay twenty dollars, then we pay twenty dollars. *Sabe?* But we no pay twenty dollars unless you get us to Cruces *poco pronto, sabe?* Now we start."

The boatman broke into a torrent of talk.

"Says he's got to find his assistant," Talbot explained to us. "Come on, my son, I'll just go with you after that precious assistant."

We sat on the edge of our boat for half an hour, watching the most comical scenes. Everybody was afflicted with the same complaint — absence of boatmen. Some took possession, and settled themselves patiently beneath their little roofs. Others made forays and returned dragging protesting natives by the arm. These generally turned out to be the wrong natives; but that was a mere detail. Once in a lucky while the full boat's complement would be gathered; and then the craft would pull away up the river to the tune of pistol shots and vociferous yells.

At the end of the period mentioned Talbot and the two men appeared. They were quite amicable; indeed, friendly, and laughed together as they came. The "assistant" proved to be a tremendous negro, nearly naked, with fine big muscles, and a good-natured, grinning face. He wore large brass ear circlets and bracelets of copper. We all pushed the canoe to the very edge of the water and clambered aboard. The negro bent his mighty shoulders. We were afloat.

CHAPTER V

A TROPICAL RIVER

Our *padrone*, as Talbot told us we should call him, stood in front clad in a coloured muslin shirt. The broad sluggish river was alive with boats, all making their way against the current. By the time the lagoon had narrowed, however, they had pretty well scattered.

We entered a tropical forest, and never shall I forget the wonder of it. The banks were lined to the water's edge with vegetation, so that one could see nothing but the jungle. There were great palm trees, which we recognized; and teak trees, which we did not, but which Talbot identified for us. It was a very bald sort of tree, as I remember it. Then there were tremendous sycamores in which were ants' nests as big as beehives; and banana trees with torn leaves, probably the most exotic touch of all; and beautiful noble mangoes like domes of a green cathedral; and various sorts of canes and shrubs and lilies growing among them. And everywhere leaped and swung the vines — thick ropy vines; knotted vines, like knotted cables; slender filament vines; spraying gossamer vines, with gorgeous crimson, purple, and yellow blooms; and long streamers that dipped to trail in the waters. Below them were broad pads of lotus and water lilies; with alligators like barnacled logs, and cormorants swimming about, and bright-eyed waterfowl. The shadows in the forest were light clear green, and the shadows under the hanging jungle near the water were dull green; and the very upper air itself, in that hot steaming glade, seemed delicately green, too. Butterflies were among the vine blossoms, so brilliant of colour that it seemed to me that the flowers were fluttering from their stems. Across the translucent green shadows flashed birds. I recognized little green paroquets. I had never before seen them outside of cages. No man can realize the wonder of finding himself actually part of romantic scenes so long familiar in the pages of books that they have become almost mythical. We sat there absolutely silent, save when calling attention to some new marvel, drinking it in.

Our men paddled steadily ahead. The negro hummed strange minor songs to himself. Suddenly he flashed his teeth at us and broke into full voice:

"Oh, Susannah! don't cry for me!
I'm off to California wid my banjo on my knee."

The accent was queer, but the words and tune were right. Talbot questioned him in Spanish.

"He says all Americans sing it. He has taken many up the river."

"Too many," muttered Johnny. "I wish we'e started three months sooner."

It was growing dusk when we came in sight of a village of bamboo huts on the right bank. To this we headed. Hardly had the boat struck the beach when both of our men leaped ashore and raced madly toward the huts. Pausing only long enough to slide the boat beyond the grip of the river, we followed, considerably mystified. Quick as we were, we found both the *padrone* and his man, together with a dozen others, already seated at a *monte* table. The *padrone* was acting as banker!

We discovered the name of this place to be Gatun. Talbot found us a native hut in which were hammocks we could rent for the night. The hut was a two-storied affair, with a notched pole by which to clamber aloft. I took one look and decided to stay below. My weight seemed sufficient to bring the whole thing down about our ears.

I do not know which had the better of it. My hammock was slung across one corner of the single room. A cooking fire blazed merrily five or six feet away. Some ten or a dozen natives were drinking and talking until nearly morning; and to my personal knowledge some ten or a dozen thousand fleas were doing the same. Six dogs were that hut's allowance. They discovered that my weight sagged my hammock down to a height just suitable for the rubbing of their backs. In vain I smote with boot or pistol barre! They kiyied and departed; but only for a moment. I had not even time to fall into a doze before one of the others was back at it. This amused the drinking natives. I suppose the poor beasts very passionately wanted to scratch their backs. I could sympathize with them; none of them could have had as many fleas as I had, for their superficial area was not as great; but perhaps they had as many per square inch.

In the course of the night it began to rain. I mean really rain, "without going into details as to drops," as somebody has said. Then I ceased envying my friends upstairs; for from all sounds I judged the roof was leaking.

Next morning it was still drizzling. The town was full of sad-eyed, wearied men. I think every one had had about the same experience. The *padrone* was at first a little inclined to delay; but he quickly recognized that our mood was bad, so shortly we were under way.

That day was not an unmitigated joy. It rained, picking the surface of the river up in little spots and rings. The forest dripped steadily. All the butterflies and bright birds had disappeared; and sullen, shifting clouds fairly touched the treetops. It was cold. Wrap ourselves as we would, we became thoroughly chilled. We should have liked to go ashore for a little fire, or at least a tramp about; but there seemed to be no banks, and the vegetation would not let us approach whatever earth there might be. The *padrone* and the big negro thrust their heads through holes cut in the middle of their blankets, and seemed happy. Talbot Ward and Yank took it with the philosophy of old campaigners; but Johnny and I had not had experience enough to realize that things have a habit of coming to an end. We were too wet even to smoke.

That night we spent at a place called Pena Blanca, which differed in no essential from Gatun. We slept there in small sheds, along with twenty or thirty of our ship's companions wedged tightly together. A dozen other similiar sheds adjoined. We were all quarrelsome and disinclined to take much nonsense either from the natives or from each other. Also we needed and wanted food; and we had difficulty in getting it. A dozen incipient quarrels were extinguished because the majority of the crowd would not stand for being bothered by the row. Finally the whole hutful became involved, and it really looked for a moment like a riot. A good deal of bad language flew about, and men seized their weapons. Yank rose to the occasion by appealing to them not "to kick up a muss," because there was "a lady of our own colour in the next room." The lady was mythical, but the riot was averted.

The next day was clearing, with occasional heavy dashing showers, just to keep us interested. The country began more to open up. We passed many grass savannahs dotted with palms and a tree something like our locust. Herds of cattle fed there. The river narrowed and became swifter. Often our men had to lay aside their paddles in favour of the pole or tracking line. Once or twice we landed and walked for a short distance along the banks. At one place we saw several wild turkeys. At another something horrifying, rustling, and reptilian made a dash fairly from between my feet, and rushed *flop* into the water. The boys claimed I jumped straight upward four feet; but I think it was nearer ten. Talbot said the thing was an iguana. I should like very much to be able to describe it accurately, but my observation was somewhat confused. Beyond the evident fact that it snorted actual fire, I am not prepared to go.

Along in the early afternoon we reached bolder shores in which the trap rock descended sheer beneath the surface of the water. Directly ahead of us rose a mountain like a cone of verdure. We glided around the base of it, and so came to Gorgona, situated on a high bluff beyond. This we had decided upon as the end of our river journey. To be sure we had bargained for Cruces, six miles beyond; but as the majority of our ship's companions had decided on that route, we thought the Gorgona trail might be less crowded. So we beached our boat, and unloaded our effects; and set forth to find accommodations for the present, and mules for the immediate future.

CHAPTER VI

THE VILLAGE IN THE JUNGLE

At first there seemed slight chance of getting either. The place was crowded beyond its capacity. The Hotel Française — a shed-and-tent sort of combination with a muddy natural floor — was jammed. The few native huts were crowded. Many we saw making themselves as comfortable as possible amid their effects out in the open. Some we talked with said they had been there for over a week, unable to move because of lack of transportation. They reported much fever; and in fact we saw one poor shaking wretch, wistful-eyed as a sick dog, braced against a tree all alone. The spirit was drained out of him; and all he wanted was to get back.

While we were discussing what to do next, our muslin-clad ex-*padrone*, who had been paid and shaken by the hand some time since, approached smoking a longer cigar than ever. This he waved at us in a most debonair and friendly manner.

"Bread on the water," commented Talbot after a short conversation. "He says we have treated him like a brother and a true comrade in arms; which means that *I* did; you fellows, confound your spiteful souls, wanted to throw him overboard a dozen times. And now he says to follow him, and he'll get us a place to stay."

"Some native pig-sty with fleas," I remarked skeptically, aside, to Johnny.

"You com'," begged the *padrone*, with a flash of teeth.

We came bearing our household goods, because we could nowhere see any one to bear them for us. At that we had to leave the heaviest pieces on the beach. Talbot insisted on lugging his huge bundle of newspapers.

"They may come in handy," he answered us vaguely. "Well, they're mine, and this is my back," he countered to Johnny's and my impatience with such foolishness.

The *padrone* led us through town to the outskirts. There we came to a substantial low house of several rooms, with a veranda and veritable chimneys. The earth in front had been beaten so hard that even the downpour of yesterday had not appreciably softened it. To our summons appeared a very suave and courteous figure—that, it appeared, of the *alcalde* of the place.

"My fren'," explained the *padrone* in English, for our benefit, "they good peepele. They wan' estay. Got no place estay."

The *alcalde*, a portly gentleman with side whiskers and a great deal of dignity, bowed.

"My house is all yours," said he.

Thus, although arriving late, we stopped at the best quarters in the town. The sense of obligation to any one but our boatman was considerably relieved when next day we paid what we owed for our lodging. Also, had it not been for Talbot and Johnny, I am sure Yank and I would have taken to the jungle. There seemed to be required so much bowing, smiling, punctiliousness and elaborate complimenting that in a short time I felt myself in the precise mental attitude of a very small monkey shaking the bars of his cage with all four hands and gibbering in the face of some benign and infinitely superior professor. I fairly ached behind the ears trying to look sufficiently alert and bland and intelligent. Yank sat stolid, chewed tobacco and spat out of the window, which also went far toward stampeding me. Talbot and Johnny, however, seemed right at home. They capped the old gentleman's most elaborate and involved speeches, they talked at length and pompously about nothing at all; their smiles were rare and sad and lingering — not a bit like my imbecile though well-meant grinning — and they seemed to be able to stick it out until judgment day. Not until I heard their private language after it was all over did I realize they were not enjoying the occasion thoroughly.

Toward sunset occurred a welcome break. A mob of natives suddenly burst into view, from the direction of town. They were running madly, led by a very little man and a very big man. The two latter rushed up to the edge of the veranda, on which we were all sitting, and began to talk excitedly, both at once.

"What's the row?" we asked Talbot in a breath.

"Can't make out yet; something about a fight."

The *alcalde* commanded order. Then the matter became clear. The very large man and the very little man had had a fight, and they had come for justice. This much Talbot made plain. Then he chuckled explosively.

"The little man is making his accusation against himself!" he told us. "He is charging *himself* with having assaulted and beaten the other fellow. And the big one is charging *him*self with having licked the little one. Neither wants to acknowledge he got licked; and each would rather pay a fine and have it entered on the records that he won the fight. So much for sheer vanity!"

Each had his desire. The *alcalde*, with beautiful impartiality, fined them both; and nonchalantly pocketed the proceeds.

At dusk millions of fireflies came out, the earth grew velvet black, and the soft, tepid air breathed up from the river. Lights of the town flickered like larger yellower fireflies through the thin screen of palms and jungle; and the various noises, subdued by distance, mingled with the voices of thousands of insects, and a strange booming from the river. I thought it very pleasant; and wanted to stay out; but for some reason we were haled within. There the lamps made the low broad room very hot. We sat on real chairs and the stilted exchange resumed. I have often wondered whether our host enjoyed it, or whether he did it merely from duty, and was as heartily bored as the rest of us.

A half-naked servant glided in to tell us that we were wanted in the next room. We found there our good *padrone* and another, a fine tall man, dressed very elaborately in short jacket and slit loose trousers, all sewn with many silver buttons and ornaments.

"He my fren'," explained the *padrone*. "He have dose *mulas*."

With the gorgeous individual Talbot concluded a bargain. He was to furnish us riding animals at ten dollars each per day; and agreed to transport our baggage at six dollars a hundredweight. The *padrone* stood aside, smiling cheerfully.

"I ver' good fren'? Eh?" he demanded.

"My son," said Talbot with feeling, "you're a gentleman and a scholar; indeed, I would go farther and designate you as a genuine lallapaloozer!"

The *padrone* seemed much gratified; but immediately demanded five dollars. This Talbot gave him. Johnny thought the demand went far toward destroying the value of the *padrone's* kindness: but the rest of us differed. I believe this people, lazy and dishonest as they are, are nevertheless peculiarly susceptible to kindness. The man had started by trying to cheat us of our bargain; he ended by going out of his way to help us along.

At supper, which was served very shortly, we had our first glimpse of the ladies of the establishment. The older was a very dignified, placid, rather fat individual, whose chief feature was her shining dark hair. She bowed to us gravely, said a few words in Spanish, and thereafter applied herself with childlike and unfeigned zest to the edibles. The younger, Mercedes by name, was a very sprightly damsel indeed. She too had shining black hair, over which she had flung the most coquettish sort of lace shawl they call a *rebosa*. Her eyes were large, dark, and expressive; and she constantly used them most provocatively, though with every appearance of shyness and modesty. Her figure, too, was lithe and rounded; and so swathed, rather than clothed, that every curve was emphasized. I suppose this effect was the result of the Spanish mode rather than of individual sophistication; just as the succession of lazy poses and bendings were the result of a racial feminine instinct rather than of conscious personal coquetry. Certainly we fou_ red-shirted tramps were poor enough game. Nevertheless, whatever the motive, the effect was certainly real enough. She was alluring rather than charming, with her fan and her *rebosa*, her veiled glances, her languorous, bold poses, and the single red flower in her hair. And a great deal of this allurement resided in the very fact that no one could tell how much was simple, innocent, and unconscious instinct, and how much was intended. An unpleasing note in both women was furnished by the powder. This so liberally covered their faces as to conceal the skin beneath a dead mat white.

Yank and I were kept out of it, or thought we were, by our ignorance of the language. This did not seem to hinder Johnny in the least. In five minutes he was oblivious to everything but his attempts to make himself agreeable by signs and laughing gestures, and to his trials — with help — at the unknown language. The girl played up to him well. Talbot was gravely and courteously polite. At the close of the meal the women rose suddenly, bowed, and swept from the room. Johnny turned back to us a good deal flushed and excited, a little bewildered, and considerably disappointed. The *alcalde* looked as though nothing unusual were under way. The rest of us were considerably amused.

"You'll see her later," soothed Talbot mockingly.

Johnny gulped down his coffee without reply.

After the meal we went outside. Fires had been built on

opposite sides of the hard beaten earth in front of the house.
Four men with guitars sat chair tilted, backed against the
veranda. Thirty or forty people wandered to and fro.
They were of the usual native class; our host's family, and
one other, consisting of parents and three grown children,
seemed to represent all the aristocracy. These better-class
guests came to join us on the veranda. The older people
did not greatly differ from our host and his wife, except in
cut of masculine whisker, or amount of feminine fat. The
younger members consisted of a young lady, tall and
graceful, a young girl in white, and a man of twenty or
thereabout. He was most gaudily gotten up, for a male
creature, in a soft white shirt, a short braided jacket of blue,
a wide, red-tasselled sash, and trousers slit from the knees
down. The entire costume was sewn at all places, likely
and unlikely, with silver buttons. As he was a darkly
handsome chap, with a small moustache, red lips and a
little flash of teeth, the effect was quite good, but I couldn't
care for his style. The bulk of the villagers were dressed
in white. The women all carried the *rebosa*, and were
thickly powdered. We could see a number of the Americans in the background.

The musicians struck up a strummy, decided sort of
marchlike tune; and the dancers paired off. They performed a kind of lancer figure, very stately and solemn,
seemingly interminable, with scant variation, small pro-
gressions, and mighty little interest to me. We sat in a
stiff row and shed the compliment of our presence on the
scene. It was about as inspiring as a visit to a hospital
ward. What determined the duration of the affair, I

cannot tell you; whether the musicians' fingers gave out, or the dancers' legs, or the official audience's patience. But at last they ceased.

At the beginning of another tune, of much the same solemn character, our young visitor bowed ceremoniously to our host's daughter, and led her down the steps.

"Come on, Johnny, be a sport. Dance this one," said Talbot rising.

"Don't know how," replied Johnny gloomily, his eyes on the receding figure of Mercedes.

"The lady 'll show you. Come along!"

Talbot bowed gravely to the young girl, who arose enchanted. Johnny, with his natural grace and courtesy, offered his arm to the other. She took it with a faintly aloof and indifferent smile, and descended the step with him. She did not look toward him, nor did she vouchsafe him a word. Plainly, she was not interested, but stood idly flirting with her fan, her eyes fixed upon the distance. The dance began.

It was another of the same general character as the first. The couples advanced and retreated, swung slowly about each other, ducked and passed beneath each other's arms, all to the stately strumming of the guitars. They kept on doing these things. Johnny and Talbot soon got hold of the sequence of events, and did them too.

At first Johnny was gloomy and distrait. Then, after he had, in the changes of the dance, passed Mercedes a few times, he began to wake up. I could make out in the firelight only the shapes of their figures and the whiteness of their faces; but I could see that she lingered a moment in Johnny's formal embrace, that she flirted against him in passing, and I could guess that her eyes were on duty. When they returned to the veranda, Johnny was chipper, the visitor darkly frowning, Mercedes animated, and the other girl still faintly and aloofly smiling.

The fandango went on for an hour; and the rivalry between Johnny and the young Spaniard grew in intensity. Certainly Mercedes did nothing to modify it. The scene became more animated and more interesting. A slow, gliding waltz was danced, and several posturing, stamping dances in which the partners advanced and receded toward and from each other, bending and swaying and holding aloft their arms. It was very pretty and graceful and captivating; and to my unsophisticated mind a trifle suggestive; though that thought was probably the result of my training and the novelty of the sight. It must be remembered that many people see harm in our round dances simply because they have not become sufficiently accustomed to them to realize that the position of the performers is meaninglessly conventional. Similarily the various rather daring postures of some of these Spanish dances probably have become so conventionalized by numberless repetitions along the formal requirements of the dance that their possible significance has been long since forgotten. The apparently deliberate luring of the man by the woman exists solely in the mind of some such alien spectator as myself. I was philosophical enough to say these things to myself; but Johnny was not. He saw Mercedes languishing into the eyes of his rival; half fleeing provocatively, her glances sparkling; bending and swaying her body in allurement;

finally in the finale of the dance, melting into her partner's arms as though in surrender. He could not realize that these were formal and established measures for a dance. He was too blind to see that the partners separated quite calmly and sauntered nonchalantly toward the veranda, the man rolling a paper cigarro, the woman flirting idly her fan. His eyes glowing dully, he stared straight before him; a spot of colour mounted on his cheekbones.

With an exclamation Talbot Ward arose swiftly but quietly and moved down the veranda, motioning me to follow. He bent over Johnny's chair.

"I want to speak to you a moment," he said in a low voice.

Johnny looked up at him a moment defiantly. Talbot stood above him, inflexibly waiting. With a muttered exclamation Johnny finally arose from his chair. Ward grasped his arm and drew him through the wandering natives, past the fringe of American spectators, and down the hard moonlit path to the village.

Johnny jerked his arm loose and stopped short.

"Well, sir!" he demanded, his head high.

"You are on your way to California," said Ward, "and you are stopping here over one night. The girl is pretty and graceful and with much charm, but uneducated, and quite empty headed."

"I will thank you to leave all young ladies out of this discussion," broke in Johnny hotly.

"This young lady is the whole of this discussion and cannot be left out."

"Then we will abandon the discussion."

"Also," said Talbot Ward irrelevantly, "did you notice how fat all their mothers are?"

We were wandering forward slowly. Again Johnny stopped.

"I must tell you, sir, that I consider my affairs none of your business, sir; and that I resent any interference with them," said he with heat.

"All right, Johnny," replied Talbot sadly; "I am not going to try to advise you. Only I wanted to call your attention to all the elements of the situation, which you probably had forgotten. I will repeat — and then I am done — she is nothing to you, she is beneath you, you are stopping here but one day, she is charming but ignorant — and her mother is very fat. Now go have your fool fight — for that is what you are headed straight for — if you think it at all worth while."

Johnny's generous heart must have been smiting him sorely, now that his heat and excitement had had time to cool a little. He followed us a few steps irresolutely. We came to the large tree by the wayside. The man with the fever still sat there miserably indifferent to his surroundings.

"Here, this won't do!" cried Talbot. "He mustn't be allowed to sit there all night; he'll catch a chill sure. My friend, give us your arm. We'll find you some sort of a bunk."

The man was dead.

We carried him to the village and raised a number of our compatriots. Not one knew who the man might be, nor even where his belongings had been stored. He had no mark of identification on his person. After a diligent search, we were forced to give it up. The body we buried with all reverence at the edge of the jungle. I wanted to place the matter on an official footing by notifying the *alcalde*, but Talbot negatived this.

"I know this people," said he. "Once let the news of a man's death get abroad, and it's good-bye to any chance of finding his effects to-morrow. And that's our only show to identify him. Best say nothing."

We returned slowly to the *alcalde's* house. The fandango was still in progress. Mercedes flashed her bright eyes at Johnny as we mounted the steps; the Spaniard scowled and muttered an imprecation. Johnny bowed gravely and passed into the house.

We told Yank the circumstances.

"Poor devil," said I. "Like the rest of us, he was so full of hope so short time ago."

Ward nodded.

"And his death was so unnecessary, so utterly and completely useless."

"I don't know," spoke up Talbot musingly. "It seems to us unnecessary, but who can tell? And useless? I don't know. If we hadn't happened to stumble on that poor chap just then, Johnny Fairfax might be in his fix right this minute, and Johnny Fairfax seems to me likely to prove a very valuable citizen."

"And what did the blame critter mean by that?" Yank asked me later.

CHAPTER VII

THE TRAIL

We made desperate efforts next morning to find somebody who knew the man, or at least could point out to us his effects; but in vain. All was confusion, and everybody was too busy getting away to pay us very much attention. This, I am convinced, was not hardheartedness on the part of most; but merely that all men's minds were filled with a great desire. Our own transport men were impatient to be off; and we had finally to abandon the matter. Whether or not the man had a family or friends who would never know what had become of him, we shall never find out. Later in the gold rush there were many scores of such cases.

Having paid the *alcalde* we set forth. Mercedes did not appear. Our good *padrone* was on hand to say farewell to us at the edge of town. He gave us a sort of cup made from coconut husk to which long cords had been attached. With these, he explained, we could dip up water without dismounting. We found them most convenient.

Shortly after we had left town, and before we had really begun our journey in earnest, we passed a most astonishing caravan going the other way. This consisted of sixteen mules and donkeys under sole charge of three men armed with antiquated and somewhat rusty muskets. On either side of each mule, slung in a rope and plain to see, hung a heavy ingot of gold! Fascinated, we approached and stroked the satiny beautiful metal; and wondered that, on a road so crowded with travellers of all grades, so precious a train should be freely entrusted to the three ragged lazy natives. So curious did this seem that Talbot inquired of the leader why it was allowed.

"Whither would a thief run to? How could he carry away these heavy ingots?" the man propounded.

Often around subsequent campfires we have in idle curiosity attempted to answer these two questions successfully, but have always failed. The gold was safe.

Talbot insisted, with a good deal of heavy argument, that our effects should precede us on the trail. The wisdom of this was apparent before we had been out an hour. We came upon dozens of porters resting sprawled out by the side of their loads. I could hardly blame them; for these men carried by means of a bamboo screen and straps across the shoulders and forehead the most enormous loads. But farther on we passed also several mule trains, for whose stopping there could be no reason or excuse except that their natives were lazy. Our own train we were continually overtaking and prodding on, to its intense disgust. Thus Talbot's forethought, or experience with people of this type, assured us our goods. Some of our shipmates were still waiting for their baggage when we sailed to the north.

We now entered a dense forest country. The lofty trees, thick foliage, swinging vines, and strange big leaves undoubtedly would have impressed us under other conditions. But just now we were too busy. The rains had softened the trail until it was of the consistency of very stiff mud. In

this mud the first mule had left his tracks. The next mule
trod carefully in the first mule's footsteps; and all subsequent mules did likewise. The consequence was a succession of narrow, deep holes in the clay, into which an animal's
leg sank halfway to the shoulder. No power on earth, I
firmly believe, could have induced those mules to step
anywhere else. Each hole was full of muddy water.
When the mule inserted his hoof the water spurted out
violently, as though from a squirt gun. As a result we
were, I believe, the most muddied and bedraggled crew on
earth. We tried walking, but could not get on at all.
Occasionally we came to a steep little ravine down and up
the slippery banks of which we slid and scrambled. Yank
and his mule once landed in a heap, plump in the middle of
a stream.

In the course of these tribulations we became somewhat
separated. Johnny and I found ourselves riding along in
company, and much too busy to talk. As we neared a
small group of natives under a tree, three of them started
toward us on a run, shouting something. We stopped, and
drew together.

One of the assailants seized Johnny's animal by the bit,
and another's gesture commanded him to dismount.

"Get out of that!" shouted Johnny threateningly; and
as the men did not obey his emphatic tone, he snatched out
his Colt's pistol. I closed in next him and did the same.

Our threatening attitude caused the men to draw back
a trifle; but they redoubled their vociferations. Johnny
attempted to spur his mule forward; but all three threw
themselves in his way. The rest of the natives, four in

number, joined the group. They pointed at Johnny's animal, motioned peremptorily for him to descend; and one of them ventured again to seize his bridle.

"I don't believe it's robbery, anyhow," said I. "They seem to recognize your mule. Probably you're riding a stolen animal."

"I don't know anything about that," said Johnny, a trifle angrily, "but I know I hired it to go to Panama with: and to Panama I'm going. They can settle their mule question afterward."

But when he gathered his reins again, he was prevented from going on. Johnny reached suddenly forward and struck with his pistol barrel at the head of the man holding his rein. He missed by the fraction of an inch; and the man leaped back with a cry of rage. Everybody yelled and drew near as though for a rush. Johnny and I cocked our weapons.

At this moment we heard Talbot Ward's voice from beyond. "Take 'em from that side!" yelled Johnny excitedly. "Give it to 'em, Tal!"

Talbot shouted again, in Spanish. Every brigand in the lot immediately turned in his direction, shouting perfect fountains of words. After a moment Talbot, afoot, emerged from the jungle and calmly picked his way through the mud toward us.

"Put up your shooting irons," he grinned at us. "These men tell me your saddle pad is on crooked and they want to straighten it for you."

Johnny, and I am sure myself, turned red; then everybody howled with glee. Johnny dismounted, and a dozen eager hands adjusted the harness. We shook hands all around, laughed some more, and resumed our very sloppy journey.

This to me was one of the most terrible days I ever spent. We passed dozens of dead mules, and vultures that sat in trees; and exhausted men lying flat as though dead; and sick men shaken with fever; and one poor wretch, whom we picked up and took with us, who had actually lain down to die. He was half raving with fever, and as near as we could make out had had companions. We twisted him aboard a mule, and took turns walking alongside and holding him on. Beyond the fact that he was a very small individual with light hair and an English accent, we could tell nothing about him. He was suffering from cholera, although we did not know that at the time. That night we spent at a way-side hut, where we left our patient.

Early the next morning we began to ascend a little; and so came to a rocky tableland with palms, and beyond it another ridge of hills. We climbed that ridge and descended the other side. Another elevation lay before us. This we surmounted, only to find a third. After we had put a dozen such ranges behind us, we made the mistake of thinking the next was sure to be the last. We got up our hopes a number of times in this fashion, then fell dully into a despair of ever getting anywhere. The day was fearfully hot. The Indian who had stolidly preceded us as guide at last stopped, washed his feet carefully in a wayside mud hole and put on his pantaloons.

"That looks to me like an encouraging symptom," I remarked.

Shortly after we entered the city of Panama.

CHAPTER VIII

PANAMA

We arrived early in the afternoon, and we were all eyes; for here was a city taken directly from the pages of the Boy's Own Pirate. Without the least effort of the imagination we could see Morgan or Kidd or some other old swashbuckler, cutlass in teeth, pistols in hand, broad sashed, fierce and ruthless rushing over the walls or through the streets, while the cathedral bells clanged wildly and women screamed. Everything about it was of the past; for somehow the modern signs of American invasion seemed temporary and to be blown away. The two-story wooden houses with corridor and veranda across the face of the second story, painted in bright colours, leaned crazily out across the streets toward each other. Narrow and mysterious alleys led up between them. Ancient cathedrals and churches stood gray with age before grass-grown plazas. And in the outskirts of town were massive masonry ruins of great buildings, convent and colleges, some of which had never been finished. The immense blocks lay about the ground in a confusion, covered softly by thousands of little plants; or soared against the sky in broken arches and corridors. Vegetation and vines grew in every crevice; and I saw many full-sized trees rooted in midair. The place was strongly fanciful; and I loved to linger there. To me the jungle seemed like an insidiously beautiful creature enveloping thus, little by little, its unsuspecting prey. The old gray tumbled ruins seemed to be lost in dreams of their ancient days. And through the arches and the empty corridors open to the sky breathed a melancholy air from a past so dead and gone and buried and forgotten that of it remained no echo, no recollection, no knowledge, nothing but squared and tumbled stones.

To tell the truth I generally had these reflections quite to myself. The body of the town was much more exciting. The old dilapidated and picturesque houses had taken on a new and temporary smartness of modernity — consisting mainly of canvas signs. The main street was of hotels, eating houses, and assorted hells. It was crowded day and night, for we found something over a thousand men here awaiting the chance of transportation. Some had been here a long time, and were broke and desperate. A number of American gambling joints did a good business. Native drinking houses abounded. The natives were in general a showy lot, but too lazy even to do a good job at fleecing the stranger within their gates. That was therefore under-taken — and most competently — by the enterprising foreigners of all nations. Foreigners kept two of the three hotels, as is indicated by their names — Hotel Française, Fonda Americano, and the Washington House. Americans ran the gambling joints. French and Germans, mainly, kept the restaurants.

We stopped over one day at the Fonda Americano; and then realizing that we were probably in for a long wait, found two rooms in a house off the main street. These we rented from a native at a fairly reasonable rate. They were in the second story of a massive stone ruin whose walls had been patched up with whitewash. The rooms were bare and geometrically cat-a-cornered and extraordinarily chilly, like vaults; but they gave out on a charmingly unkempt walled garden with a stone fountain in the middle whose features were all rounded by time and blurred with moss, with tall ragged bananas and taller wind-swept palms, and a creeping lush tangle of old plants, and the damp soft greenness of moss and the elfin tinkling of little waters. On our balcony the sun shone strong; so that we could warm our chilled bones gratefully like lizards against a wall.

We tried all the restaurants, one after the other, and found them about equally bad. We also went in — once — for a real Spanish dinner. It consisted of a succession of dishes highly seasoned with the hottest sort of pepper, generally drowned in rich gravy, and composed of such things as cheese, chunks of meat, corn meal, and the like. Any one of these dishes would have been a fine strength test for the average unsophisticated stomach; but your true Spanish dinner consists of a dozen of them. We had horrible indigestion.

In one place, kept by a German, we were treated very disagreeably, and overcharged so badly that Yank vowed he intended to get even. As to just how he was going to do it, he maintained a deep silence; but he advised us he would eat there the following evening. Also he asked four or five other men, with whom we had become friendly, to meet us at the restaurant. We met, ate our meal leisurely, and had a very good time.

"Now," said Yank to us, "when we get up, you fellows all go right out the front door and keep going until you get to the Fonda bar, and there you wait for me. No lingering, now. Do as you are told."

We did as we were told. After about fifteen or twenty minutes Yank sauntered in.

"Now," said Johnny, "I hope you'll explain. We're much obliged for your dinner party, but we want to know what it is all about."

"Well," chuckled Yank, "I just dealt the Dutchman what you might call idle persiflage until you fellows had been gone a few minutes, and then I held him out my dollar. 'What's that?' says he. 'That's a dollar,' says I, 'to pay for my dinner.' 'How about all those other fellows?' says he. 'I got nothing to do with them,' says I. 'They can pay for their own dinners,' and after a while I come away. He was having some sort of Dutch fit, and I got tired of watching him."

Outside the walls of the city was a large encampment of tents in which dwelt the more impecunious or more economical of the miners. Here too had been located a large hospital tent. There was a great deal of sickness, due to the hardships of the journey, the bad climate, irregular living, the overeating of fruit, drinking, the total lack of sanitation. In fact only the situation of the city — out on an isthmus in the sea breezes — I am convinced, saved us from pestilence. Every American seemed to possess a patent medicine of some sort with which he dosed himself religiously in and out of season. A good many, I should think, must have fallen victims to these nostrums.

Each morning regularly we went down to harass the steamship employees. Roughly speaking some three hundred of us had bought through passage before leaving New York: and it was announced that only fifty-two additional to those already aboard could be squeezed into the first steamer. The other two hundred and forty-eight would have to await the next. Naturally every man was determined that he would not be left; for such a delay, in such a place, at the time of a gold rush was unthinkable. The officials at that steamship office had no easy time. Each man wanted first of all to know just when the ship was to be expected; a thing no one could guess. Then he demanded his accommodations; and had a dozen reasons why his claim should be preferred over that of the others. I never saw a more quarrelsome noisy dog-kennel than that steamship office. Why no one was ever shot there I could not tell you.

After bedevilling the officials for a time, our business for the day was over. We had the privilege of sauntering through the streets, of walking down the peninsula or of seating ourselves in any of the numerous bars or gambling halls. All were interesting; though neither the streets nor the gambling places were in full action until late afternoon.

About four o'clock, or half after, when the invariable siesta was over, the main street began to fill with idlers. The natives wore white, with wide soft straw hats, and lounged along with considerable grace. They were a weak, unenergetic, inoffensive race, always ready to get off the sidewalk for other nations provided the other nations swaggered sufficiently. The women, I remember, had wonderful piles of glossy black hair, arranged in bands and puffs, in which they stuck cigars. The streets were very narrow. When a vehicle came along, we all had to make way for it; as also for the gangs of prisoners connected with heavy iron chains around their necks. These were very numerous; and I can hear yet as the leading notes of the place, the clinking of their chains, and the cracked jangling of some of the many cathedral bells.

There was a never-failing joy to us also in poking around the odd places of the town. The dim interiors of cathedrals, the splashed stones of courtyards, the shadows of doorways, the privacies of gardens all lured us; and we saw many phases of native life. Generally we were looked on at first with distrust. There were a number of roughs among the gold seekers; men whose brutal instincts or whose merely ignorant love of horseplay had now for the first time no check. They found that the native could be pushed off the sidewalk, so they pushed him off. I once saw a number of these men light their cigars at altar candles. But Talbot's Spanish and our own demeanour soon gained us admission.

Thus we ran across a most delightful institution. We were rambling in a very obscure portion of town when we came to quite a long wall unbroken save by a little wicket gate. A bell pull seemed to invite investigation; so we gave it a heave. Almost immediately the gate swung open and we entered.

We found ourselves in a wide space paved with smooth great slabs of rocks, wet as though from a recent rain. The space was thickly built up by small round huts of reeds, but without roofs. In the centre was a well, probably ten or twelve feet wide, over which slanted a cross arm and wheel for the drawing of water. No human being was in sight; the gate had been unlatched by an overhead cord.

We shouted. In a minute or so a very irascible old woman hobbled to us from some mysterious lurking place among the reed huts. She spoke impatiently. Talbot questioned her; she replied briefly, then turned and hobbled off as fast as she could go.

"What did she say?" some one asked Talbot curiously.

"She said," replied Ward, "literally this: 'Why don't you take any of them without bothering me? They are all ready.' I imagine she must mean these bird cages; though what they are for I couldn't tell you."

We investigated the nearest. It was divided into two tiny rooms each just big enough to hold a man. In one was a three legged stool; in the other stood two tall graceful jars of red clay, their sides bedewed with evaporation. A dipper made from a coconut lay across the top of one of them.

"Bath house!" shouted Johnny, enchanted.

The water in the porous earthen jars was cold. We took each a hut and poured the icy stuff over us to our heart's content. All except Yank. He looked on the proceedings we thought with some scorn; and departed carrying his long rifle.

"Hey!" shouted Johnny finally, "where's the towels?"

To this inquiry we could find no substantial answer. There were no towels. The old woman declined to come to our yells. She was on hand, however, when we were ready to depart, and took one American dime as payment for the three of us. This was the only cheap thing we found in Panama. We came every day, after the hour of siesta — with towels. Yank refused steadfastly to indulge.

"I'm having hard enough dodging to keep clear of fever'n ager now," he told us. "You don't seem to recollect what neck of the woods I come from. It's a fever'n ager country out there for keeps. They can't keep chickens there at all."

"Why not?" asked Johnny innocently.

"The chills they get shakes all the feathers off'n 'em," replied Yank, "and then they freeze to death."

In the evening the main street was a blaze of light, and the by-ways were cast in darkness. The crowd was all afoot, and moved restlessly to and fro from one bar or gambling hell to another. Of the thousand or so of strangers we came in time to recognize by sight a great many. The journey home through the dark was perilous. We never attempted it except in company; and as Johnny seemed fascinated with a certain game called Mexican *monte*, we often had to endure long waits before all our party was assembled.

One morning our daily trip to the steamship office bore fruit. We found the plaza filled with excited men; all talking and gesticulating. The much tired officials had evolved a scheme, beautiful in its simplicity, for deciding which fifty-two of the three hundred should go by the first ship. They announced that at eleven oclock they would draw lots.

This was all very well, but how did the general public know that the lots would be drawn fairly?

The officials would permit a committee of citizens to be present.

Not by the eternal! Where would you get any one to serve? No member of that committee would dare accept his own ticket, provided he drew one. No one would believe it had been done honestly.

Very well. Then let fifty-two out of three hundred slips of paper be marked. Each prospective passenger could then draw one slip out of a box.

"It's all right, boys," the observers yelled back at those clamouring in the rear.

One of the officials stood on a barrel holding the box, while a clerk with a list of names sat below.

"As I call the names, will each gentleman step forward and draw his slip?" announced the official.

We were all watching with our mouths open intensely interested.

"Did you ever hear of such a damfool way of doing the thing?" said Talbot. "Here, give me a boost up!"

Johnny and I raised him on our shoulders.

"Gentlemen! gentlemen!" he cried a number of times before he could be heard above the row. Finally they gave him attention.

"I'm a ticket holder in this thing; and I want to see it done right. I want to ask that gentleman there what is to prevent the wrong man from answering to a name, from drawing a slip without having any right to?"

"The right man will prevent him," answered a voice. The crowd laughed.

"Well, who's to decide, in case of dispute, which is the

right man and which the wrong man? And what's to prevent any man, after the drawing, from marking a blank slip — or making a new slip entirely?"

"That's right!" "Correct!" shouted several voices.

The officials consulted hurriedly. Then one of them announced that the drawing would be postponed until the following morning. Each was to bring his steamship ticket with him. The winners in the drawing must be prepared to have their tickets countersigned on the spot. With this understanding we dispersed.

This was Talbot Ward's first public appearance; the first occasion in which he called himself to the attention of his fellows assembled in public meeting. The occasion was trivial, and it is only for this reason that I mention it. His personality at once became known, and remembered; and I recollect that many total strangers spoke to him that evening.

By next morning the transportation officials had worked it out. We could not all get into the office, so the drawing took place on the Plaza outside. As each man's name was called, he stepped forward, showed his ticket, and was allowed to draw a slip from the box. If it proved to be a blank, he went away; if he was lucky, he had his ticket *viséd* on the spot. Such a proceeding took the greater part of the day; but the excitement remained intense. No one thought of leaving even for the noon meal.

Yank drew passage on the first steamer. Talbot, Johnny, and I drew blanks.

We walked down to the shore to talk over the situation.

"We ought to have bought tickets good on this particular ship, not merely good on this line," said Johnny.

"Doesn't matter what we *ought* to have done," rejoined Talbot a little impatiently. "What are we *going* to do? Are we going to wait here until the next steamer comes along?"

"That's likely to be two or three months — nobody knows," said Johnny.

"No; it's in six weeks, I believe. They tell me they've started regular trips on a new mail contract."

"Well, six weeks. If we stay in this hole we'll all be sick; we'll be broke; and in the meantime every ounce of gold in the country will have been picked up."

"What's the alternative?" I asked.

"Sailing vessel," said Talbot briefly.

"That's mighty uncertain," I objected. "Nobody knows when one will get in; and when it does show up it'll be a mad scramble to get to her. There's a mob waiting to go."

"Well, it's one or the other. We can't walk; and I don't see that the situation is going to be much better when the next steamer does get here. There are a couple of hundred to crowd in on her — just counting those who are here and have tickets. And then there will be a lot more."

"I'm for the sailing vessel," said Johnny. "They come in every week or two now; and if we can't make the first one, we'll have a good chance at the second or the third."

Talbot looked at me inquiringly.

"Sounds reasonable," I admitted.

"Then we've no time to lose," said Talbot decisively, and turned away toward the town.

Yank, who had listened silently to our brief discussion, shifted his rifle to his shoulder and followed. Shortly he fell behind; and we lost him.

We accompanied Talbot in some bewilderment, for there was no ship in sight nor in prospect, and we could not understand any reason for this haste. Talbot led the way directly to the steamship office.

"I want to see Brown," he asserted, naming the chief agent for the company.

The clerk hesitated: Brown was an important man and not to be disturbed for trivial matters. But Talbot's eye could be very assured.

"What is your business with Mr. Brown?" asked the clerk.

"It is with Mr. Brown," said Talbot firmly, "and I may add that it is to Mr. Brown's own interest to see me. Tell him just that, and that Mr. Talbot Ward of New York City desires an immediate interview."

The clerk was gone for some moments, to the manifest annoyance of a dozen miners who wanted his attention. When he returned he motioned us to a screened-off private office in the rear.

"Mr. Brown will see you," said he.

We found Brown to be a florid, solidly built man of fifty, with a keen eye and a brown beard. He nodded to us briefly and looked expectant.

"We three men," said Talbot directly, "hold three tickets on your line. We were not fortunate enough to get passage on the next steamer, and our business will not permit us to wait until the one after. We want our money back."

Brown's face darkened.

"That is a matter for my clerks, not for me," he said curtly. "I was told your business was to my advantage. I have nothing to do with tickets."

"One minute," said Talbot. "There are between two and three hundred men in this town each one of whom bought a ticket from your company in New York in the expectation, if not under the understanding, that they were to get through passage immediately."

"No such thing was expected or guaranteed," interposed Brown abruptly.

"Not guaranteed, nor expected by you — by us, yes."

"I cannot argue that matter. I have no further time for you. Good-day." And Brown once more reached his hand toward his bell.

"Suppose," said Talbot softly, leaning forward. "I should put it into the heads of those three hundred men that they ought to get their passage money back?"

Brown's hand stopped in midair.

"They are large, violent, armed men; and they are far from pure home influences," went on Talbot mockingly. "Here's a sample of them," said he indicating my huge frame. "And there are a thousand or so more, not directly interested but dying for excitement."

"Are you trying to intimidate me, sir?" demanded Brown.

"I am just stating conditions."

"You are threatening me."

"Ah, that is different," said Talbot Ward.

Brown sat lost in thought for some moments. Then he reached forward and at last struck the bell.

"Let me have your tickets," he commanded us shortly.

He endorsed them and handed them to the clerk, together with a written order. We all sat in absolute silence for perhaps five minutes. Then the clerk returned with a handful of gold. This Brown counted over and shoved across to Talbot. The latter also counted it, and thrust it in his pocket.

"Now," said Brown, with something approaching geniality, "I am counting on your honour to say nothing of this outside. I am gambling on your evident class in life at home."

"You have our promise, and it will be kept," said Talbot rising. "But undoubtedly within two days you will think I am the biggest liar unhung. There will be many more who will think of this same simple plan of getting a refund on their tickets and who will blab it out to every one on the street. You would do well to make your plans now as to how you intend to deal with them. But remember, I, nor my friends, will have had nothing to do with it."

"I understand that there will be plenty making your same demand," said Brown, "but I doubt any of them will think of urging that demand."

We left. As a matter of interest, Talbot's prediction was correct; as, indeed, Brown had immediately recognized it would be. Talbot had only the advantage of thinking a little quicker than the next man, of acting immediately, and of allowing no time for reflection to the other. The steamship office had a strenuous time. Talbot's threat had this much of real significance: that there was, lacking him, no organized demonstration. Each man went for himself and demanded his money back. In a few rare cases he got it; but was generally bluffed out, or blandly referred back to the New York offices, or reasoned out. The situation came near to riot, but in some difficult manner it was tided over. A few settled down to wait for the next steamer. The majority decided for sailing ships, and pocketed their steamer tickets in hopes of future reimbursement. One score of fanatics and ignoramuses, in dense ignorance as to the nature of the journey, actually started out to row to San Francisco in an open boat! They were never heard of again. One or two parties modified this plan by proceeding in fishing boats to the extremity of the peninsula of Lower California, and thence marched overland to San Diego. Their sufferings in that arid region were great, but they managed to arrive many months later.

We returned to our lodgings, congratulating Talbot on the promptitude of his action, for already we saw determined looking men hurrying across the plaza toward the offices.

At our place we found that Yank had not returned. At first we thought nothing of this; but about dusk we found that all his belongings had disappeared.

CHAPTER IX

NORTHWARD HO!

We could not understand this sudden departure, except on the possible ground that Yank, realizing that now the party must split forces, had decided to seek new companions among those lucky enough to sail on the first steamer.

"Even then he needn't have been in such a hurry," complained Johnny a trifle bitterly. "And he needn't have thought we'd be in his way."

"Has he paid his share of the lodgings?" it occurred to me to ask.

We felt quite bitter against Yank, and we carefully avoided his usual haunts, for we did not want to meet him. Then we began to think it strange we had not run across him somewhere on the streets. Then we began to look for him. We found that Yank had disappeared!

At that, a little alarmed, we set ourselves to a serious search and inquiry. A few remembered to have seen him, but were vague as to when and where. The authorities moved sluggishly, and with little enthusiasm. Men were dying every day; and disappearing underground, leaving no trace of themselves behind. One more or less seemed unimportant.

In the meanwhile we spent much of our time by the shore, together with a comfortable majority of our fellow argonauts, awaiting the sighting of a vessel. We had engaged, and paid daily, a boatman to be in readiness to take us off; and we settled our lodgings account a week ahead.

"There's going to be a scramble for that blessed ship," said Talbot; "and we'll just be prepared."

To that end we also kept our effects packed and ready for instant removal.

The beach was not a bad place. It ran out the peninsula in a long gentle curve; and the surges broke snow white on yellow sands. Across deep blue water was an island; and back of us palm trees whipped in the trade winds. We sat under them, and yarned and played cards and smoked. In bad weather — and it rained pretty often — we huddled in smoky little huts; those of us who could get in. The rest tried to stick it out; or returned with rather a relieved air to the town.

The expected ship came, of course, on one of these dull gray days; and those who had thought themselves unlucky in being crowded out of the huts were the first to sight her. They sneaked down very quietly and tried to launch two of the boats. Of course the native boatmen were all inside; trust them! As a high surf was running, and as none of the men were in any sense good boatmen, they promptly broached to and filled. The noise brought us to the door.

Then there was a fine row. One of the two boats commandeered by the early birds happened to be ours! All our forethought seemed to have been in vain. The bedraggled and crestfallen men were just wading ashore when we descended upon them. Talbot was like a raving lunatic.

"You hounds!" he roared. "Don't you dare try to

sneak off! You catch hold here and help empty these boats! You would, would you?" He caught one escaping worthy by the collar and jerked him so rapidly backward that his heels fairly cracked together. Johnny flew to combat with a chuckle of joy. I contented myself by knocking two of them together until they promised to be good. The four we had collared were very meek. We all waded into the wash where the boat lay sluggishly rolling. It is no easy matter to empty a boat in that condition. Water weighs a great deal; is fearfully inert, or at least feels so; and has a bad habit of promptly slopping in again. We tugged and heaved, and rolled and hauled until our joints cracked; but at last we got her free.

In the meantime forty other boats had been launched and were flying over the waves halfway between the shore and the ship.

Talbot was swearing steadily and with accuracy; Johnny was working like a crazy man; I was heaving away at the stern and keeping an eye on our involuntary helpers. The boatman, beside himself with frantic excitement, jabbered and ran about and screamed directions that no one understood. About all we were accomplishing now was the keeping of that boat's head straight against the heavy wash.

It seemed as though we tugged thus at cross purposes for an hour. In reality it was probably not over two or three minutes. Then Talbot regained sufficient control to listen to the boatman. At once he calmed down.

"Here, boys," said he, "ease her backward. You, Johnny, stand by at the bow and hold her head on. Frank and I will give her a shove at the stern. When the time comes, I'll yell and you pile right in, Johnny. *Vamos,* Manuel!"

We took our places; the boatman at the oars, his eyes over his shoulder watching keenly the in-racing seas.

The four dripping culprits looked at each other uncertainly, and one of them started to climb in the boat.

"Well, for *God's* sake!" screeched Talbot, and made a headlong bull rush for the man.

The latter tumbled right out of the boat on his back in the shallow water. His three companion's fled incontinently up the beach, where he followed them as soon as he could scramble to his feet.

Manuel said something sharply, without looking around.

"Shove!" screeched Talbot. "Pile in, Johnny!"

We bent our backs. The boat resisted, yielded, gathered headway. It seemed to be slipping away from me down a steep hill.

"Jump in!" yelled Talbot.

I gave a mighty heave and fell over the stern into the bottom of the boat. Waters seemed to be crashing by; but by the time I had gathered myself together and risen to my knees, we were outside the line of breakers, and dancing like a gull over the smooth broad surges.

Ships could anchor no nearer than about a mile and a half offshore. By the time we had reached the craft she was surrounded by little boats bobbing and rubbing against her sides. She proved to be one of that very tubby, bluff-bowed type then so commonly in use as whalers and freighters. The decks swarmed black with an excited crowd.

We rowed slowly around her. We were wet, and beginning to chill. No way seemed to offer by which we could reach her decks save by difficult clambering, for the gang ladder was surrounded ten deep by empty boats. A profound discouragement succeeded the excitement under which we had made our effort.

"To hell with her!" snarled Johnny, "There's no sense going aboard her. There's enough on deck now to fill her three times over. Let's get back where its warm."

"If I run across any of those fellows in town I'll break their necks!" said I.

"What makes me mad —— " continued Johnny.

"Oh, for heaven's sake shut up!" cried Talbot.

If he had been a little less cold and miserable we probably would have quarrelled. As it was, we merely humped over, and motioned the astonished Manuel to return to the shore. Our boat's head turned, we dropped down under the bow of the ship. In order to avoid the sweep of the seas Manuel held us as closely as possible under the bowsprit. We heard a hail above us. Looking up we saw Yank bending over the rail.

We stared at him, our mouths open, so astonished that for a moment we did not even think to check the boat. Then we came back in a clumsy circle. Yank yelled at us; and we yelled back at him; but so great was the crash of waters and the whistling of wind that we could make out nothing. Then Yank motioning us to remain where we were, disappeared, to return after a short interval, with a speaking trumpet.

"Have you got your baggage with you?" he roared.

We shook our heads and waved our arms.

"Go get it!" he ordered.

We screamed something back at him.

"Go get it!" he repeated; and withdrew his head entirely.

We rowed back to town; it was no longer necessary to return to the exposed beach where we had waited to sight the ships. Johnny and I indulged in much excited speculation, but Talbot refused to show curiosity.

"He's there, and he's evidently engaged us passage; and he wants us aboard to claim it," said he, "and that's all we can know now; and that's enough for me."

On our way we met a whole fleet of boats racing their belated way from town. We grinned sardonically over the plight of these worthies. A half-hour sufficed us to change our clothes, collect our effects, and return to the water front. On the return journey we crossed the same fleet of boats inward bound. Their occupants looked generally very depressed.

Yank met us at the top of the gangway, and assisted us in getting our baggage aboard. Johnny and I peppered him with questions, to which he vouchsafed no answer. When we had paid off the boatman, he led the way down a hatch into a very dark hole near the bows. A dim lantern swayed to and fro, through the murk we could make out a dozen bunks.

"They call this the fo'cas'le," said Yank placidly. "Crew sleeps here. This is our happy home. Everything else full up. We four," said he, with a little flash of triumph, "are just about the only galoots of the whole b'iling at Panama that gets passage. She's loaded to the muzzle with men that's come away around the Horn in her, and the only reason she stopped in here at all is to get a new thing-um-a-jig of some sort that she had lost or busted or something."

"Well, I don't like my happy home while she wobbles so," said Johnny. "I'm going to be seasick, as usual. But for heaven's sake, Yank, tell us where you came from, and all about it. And make it brief, for I'm going to be seasick pretty soon."

He lay down in one of the bunks and closed his eyes.

"You'd much better come up on deck into the fresh air," said Talbot.

"Fire ahead, Yank! Please!" begged Johnny.

"Well," said Yank, "when I drew that steamer ticket, it struck me that somebody might want it a lot more than I did, especially as you fellows drew blank. So I hunted up a man who was in a hurry, and sold it to him for five hundred dollars. Then I hired one of these sail-rigged fishing boats and laid in grub for a week and went cruising out to sea five or six miles."

Johnny opened one eye.

"Why?" he demanded feebly.

"I was figgerin' on meeting any old ship that came along a little before the crowd got at her," said Yank. "And judgin' by the gang's remarks that just left, I should think I'd figgered just right."

"You bet you did," put in Talbot emphatically.

"It must have been mighty uncomfortable cruising out there in that little boat so long," said I. "I wonder the men would stick."

"I paid them and they had to," said Yank grimly.

"Why didn't you let us in on it?" I asked.

"What for? It was only a one-man job. So then I struck this ship, and got aboard her after a little trouble persuading her to stop. There wasn't no way of making that captain believe we'd sleep anywheres we could except cash; so I had to pay him a good deal."

"How much?" demanded Talbot.

"It came to two hundred apiece. I'm sorry."

"Glory be!" shouted Talbot, "we're ahead of the game. Yank, you long-headed old pirate, let me shake you by the hand!"

"I wish you fellows would go away," begged Johnny.

We went on deck. The dusk was falling, and the wind with it; and to westward an untold wealth of gold was piling up. Our ship rolled at her anchor, awaiting the return of those of her people who had gone ashore. On the beach tiny spots of lights twinkled where some one had built fires. A warmth was stealing out from the shore over the troubled waters. Talbot leaned on the rail by my side. Suddenly he chuckled explosively.

"I was just thinking," said he in explanation, "of us damfools roosting on that beach in the rain."

Thus at last we escaped from the Isthmus. At the end of twenty-four hours we had left the island of Tobago astern, and were reaching to the north.

PART II
THE GOLDEN CITY

CHAPTER X

THE GOLDEN CITY

We stood in between the hills that guarded the bay of San Francisco about ten o'clock of an early spring day. A fresh cold wind pursued us; and the sky above us was bluer than I had ever seen it before, even on the Isthmus. To our right some great rocks were covered with seals and sea lions, and back of them were hills of yellow sand. A beautiful great mountain rose green to our left, and the water beneath us swirled and eddied in numerous whirlpools made by the tide.

Everybody was on deck and close to the rail. We strained our eyes ahead; and saw two islands, and beyond a shore of green hills. None of us knew where San Francisco was located, nor could we find out. The ship's company were much too busy to pay attention to our questions. The great opening out of the bay beyond the long narrows was therefore a surprise to us; it seemed as vast as an inland sea. We hauled to the wind, turning sharp to the south, glided past the bold point of rocks.

Then we saw the city concealed in a bend of the cove. It was mainly of canvas; hundreds, perhaps thousands of tents and canvas houses scattered about the sides of hills. The flat was covered with them, too, and they extended for some distance along the shore of the cove. A great dust, borne by the wind that had brought us in, swept across the city like a cloud of smoke. Hundreds and hundreds of vessels lay at anchor in the harbour, a vast fleet.

We were immediately surrounded by small boats, and our decks filled with men. We had our first sight of the genuine miners. They proved to be as various as the points of the compass. Big men, little men, clean men, dirty men, shaggy men, shaven men, but all instinct with an eager life and energy I have never seen equalled. Most wore the regulation dress — a red shirt, pantaloons tucked into the tops of boots, broad belts with sometimes silver buckles, silk Chinese sashes of vivid raw colours, a revolver, a bowie knife, a floppy old hat. Occasionally one, more dignified than the rest, sported a shiny top hat; but always with the red shirt. These were merchants, and men permanently established in the town.

They addressed us eagerly, asking a thousand questions concerning the news of the outside world. We could hardly answer them in our desire to question in return. Were the gold stories really true? Were the diggings very far away? were the diggings holding out? What were the chances for newcomers? And so on without end; and the burden always of gold! gold! gold!

We were answered with the enthusiasm of an old-timer welcoming a newcomer to any country. Gold! Plenty of it! They told us, in breathless snatches, the most marvellous tales — one sailor had dug $17,000 in a week; another man, a farmer from New England, was taking out $5,000 to $6,000 daily. They mentioned names and places. They pointed to the harbour full of shipping.

"Four hundred ships," said they, "and hardly a dozen men aboard the lot! All gone to the mines!" And one man snatching a long narrow buckskin bag from his pocket, shook out of its mouth to the palm of his hand a tiny cascade of glittering yellow particles — the Dust! We shoved and pushed, crowding around him to see this marvellous sight. He laughed in a sort of excited triumph, and tossed the stuff into the air. The breeze caught it and scattered it wide. A number of the little glittering particles clung to my rough coat, where they flashed like spangles.

"Plenty more where that came from!" cried the man; and turned away with a reckless laugh.

Filled with the wine of this new excitement we finally succeeded in getting ashore in one of the ship's boats.

We landed on a flat beach of deep black sand. It was strewn from one end to the other by the most extraordinary wreckage. There were levers, cogwheels, cranks, fans, twisted bar, and angle iron, in all stages of rust and disintegration. Some of these machines were half buried in the sand; others were tidily laid up on stones as though just landed. They were of copper, iron, zinc, brass, tin, wood. We recognized the genus at a glance. They were, one and all, patent labour-saving gold washing machines, of which we had seen so many samples aboard ship. At this sight vanished the last remains of the envy I had ever felt for the owners of similar contraptions.

We looked about for some sort of conveyance into which to dump our belongings. Apparently none existed.

Therefore we piled most of our effects neatly above high tide, shouldered our bundles, and started off up the single street.

On either side this thoroughfare stood hundreds of open sheds and buildings in the course of construction. Goods of all sorts, and in great quantity, lay beneath them, wholly or partially exposed to the dust and weather. Many unopened bales had been left in the open air. One low brick building of a single story seemed to be the only substantial structure in sight. We saw quantities of calicos, silks, rich furniture, stacks of the pieces of knock-down houses, tierces of tobacco, piles of all sorts of fancy clothing. The most unexpected and incongruous items of luxury seemed to have been dumped down here from the corners of the earth, by the four hundred ships swinging idly at anchor in the bay.

The street was, I think, the worst I have ever seen anywhere. It was a morass of mud, sticky greasy mud, of some consistency, but full of water-holes and rivulets. It looked ten feet deep; and I should certainly have ventured out on it with misgivings. And yet, incongruously enough, the surface ridges of it had dried, and were lifting into the air in the form of dust! This was of course my first experience with that common California phenomenon, and I was greatly astonished.

An attempt had been made to supply footing for pedestrians. Bags of sand had been thrown down, some rocks, a very few boxes and boards. Then our feet struck something soft and yielding, and we found we were walking over hundred pound sacks of flour marked as from Chili.

There must have been many hundred of them. A man going in the opposite direction sidled past us.

"Cheaper than lumber," said he briefly, seeing our astonishment.

"I'd hate to ask the price of lumber," remarked one of our ship's companions, with whom — and a number of others — we were penetrating the town. This man carried only a very neat black morocco satchel and a net bag containing a half dozen pineapples, the last of a number he had brought from the Isthmus. The contrast of that morocco bag with the rest of him was quite as amusing as any we saw about us; though, of course, he did not appreciate that.

We walked on flour for a hundred feet or so, and then came to cook stoves. I mean it. A battalion of heavy iron cook stoves had been laid side by side to form a causeway. Their weight combined with the traffic over them had gradually pressed them down into the mud until their tops were nearly level with the surface. Naturally the first merry and drunken joker had shied the lids into space. The pedestrian had now either to step in and out of fire boxes or try his skill on narrow ledges! Next we came to a double row of boxes of tobacco; then to some baled goods, and so off onto solid ground.

We passed many people, all very intent on getting along safely. From the security of the shed stores the proprietors and an assorted lot of loafers watched proceedings with interest. The task of crossing the street from one side to the other, especially, was one not lightly to be undertaken! A man had to balance, to leap, to poise; and at last probably, to teeter back and forth trying to keep his balance like a small boy on a fence rail, until, with an oath of disgust, he stepped off into the slime.

When we had gained the dry ground near the head of the street we threw down our burdens for a rest.

"I'll give you ten dollars for those pineapples!" offered a passerby, stopping short.

Our companion quickly closed the bargain.

"What do you think of that?" he demanded of us wide-eyed, and in the hearing of the purchaser.

The latter grinned a little, and hailed a man across the street.

"Charley!" he yelled. "Come over here!"

The individual addressed offered some demur, but finally picked his way across to us.

"How do you like these?" demanded the pineapple purchaser, showing his fruit.

"Jerusalem!" cried Charley admiringly, "where did you get them? Want to sell 'em?"

"I want some myself, but I'll sell you three of them."

"How much?"

"Fifteen dollars."

"Give 'em to me."

The first purchaser grinned openly at our companion.

The latter followed into the nearest store to get his share of the dust weighed out. His face wore a very thoughtful expression.

We came shortly to the Plaza, since called Portsmouth Square. At that time it was a wind-swept, grass-grown,

scrubby enough plot of ground. On all sides were permanent buildings. The most important of these were a
low picturesque house of the sun-dried bricks known as
adobes, in which, as it proved, the customs were levied; a
frame two-story structure known as the Parker House, and
a similar building labelled "City Hotel." The spaces
between these larger edifices was occupied by a dozen or so
of smaller shacks. Next door to the Parker House stood a
huge flapping tent. The words *El Dorado* were painted
on its side.

The square itself was crowded with people moving to
and fro. The solid majority of the crowd consisted of red
or blue shirted miners; but a great many nations and
frames of minds seemed to be represented. Chinese
merchants, with red coral buttons atop their stiff little
skullcaps, wandered slowly, their hands tucked in capacious
sleeves of the richest brocade. We had seen few of this
race; and we looked at them with the greatest interest,
examining closely their broad bland faces, the delicate
lilacs and purples and blues of their rich costumes, the
swaying silk braided queues down their backs. Other
Chinese, of the lower castes, clad in blue canvas with
broad bowl-shaped hats of straw on their heads, wormed
their way through the crowd balancing baskets at the ends
of poles. Rivalling the great Chinese merchants in their
leisure, strolled the representatives of the native race, the
Spanish Californians. They were darkly handsome men,
dressed gloriously in short velvet jackets, snowy ruffles,
plush trousers flaring at the bottom, and slit up the side of
the leg, soft leather boots, and huge spurs ornamented with

silver. They sauntered to and fro smoking brown-paper cigarettos. Beside these two, the Chinese and the Californians, but one other class seemed to be moving with any deliberation. These were men seen generally alone, or at most in pairs. They were quiet, waxy pale, dressed always neatly in soft black hat, white shirt, long black coat, and varnished boots. In the face of a general gabble they seemed to remain indifferently silent, self-contained and aloof. To occasional salutations they responded briefly and with gravity.

"Professional gamblers," said Talbot.

All the rest of the crowd rushed here and there at a great speed. We saw the wildest incongruities of demeanour and costume beside which the silk-hat-red-shirted combination was nothing. They struck us open-mouthed and gasping; but seemed to attract not the slightest attention from anybody else. We encountered a number of men dressed alike in suits of the finest broadcloth, the coats of which were lined with red silk, and the vests of embroidered white. These men walked with a sort of arrogant importance. We later found that they were members of that dreaded organization known as *The Hounds*, whose ostensible purpose was to perform volunteer police duty, but whose real effort was toward the increase of their own power. These people all surged back and forth good-naturedly, and shouted at each other, and disappeared with great importance up the side streets, or darted out with equal busyness from all points of the compass. Every few minutes a cry of warning would go up on one side of the square or another. The crowd would scatter to right and left, and down through the opening would thunder a horseman distributing clouds of dust and showers of earth.

"Why doesn't somebody kill a few of those crazy fools!" muttered Talbot impatiently, after a particularly close shave.

"Why, you see, they's mostly drunk," stated a bystander with an air of explaining all.

We tacked across to the doors of the Parker House. There after some search was made we found the proprietor. He, too, seemed very busy, but he spared time to trudge ahead of us up two rickety flights of raw wooden stairs to a loft where he indicated four canvas bunks on which lay as many coarse blue blankets.

Perhaps a hundred similar bunks occupied every available inch in the little loft.

"How long you going to stay?" he asked us.

"Don't know; a few days."

"Well, six dollars apiece, please."

"For how long?"

"For to-night."

"Hold on!" expostulated Talbot. "We can't stand that especially for these accommodations. At that price we ought to have something better. Haven't you anything in the second story?"

The proprietor's busy air fell from him; and he sat down on the edge of one of the canvas bunks.

"I thought you boys were from the mines," said he. "Your friend, here, fooled me." He pointed his thumb at Yank. "He looks like an old-timer. But now I look at you, I see you're greenhorns. Just get here to-day? Have a smoke?"

He produced a handful of cigars, of which he lit one.

"We just arrived," said Talbot, somewhat amused at this change. "How about that second story?"

"I want to tell you boys a few things," said the proprietor, "I get sixty thousand dollars a year rent for that second story just as she stands. That tent next door belongs to my brother-in-law. It is just fifteen by twenty-five feet, and he rents it for forty thousand."

"Gamblers?" inquired Talbot.

"You've guessed it. So you see I ain't got any beds to speak of down there. In fact, here's the whole layout."

"But we can't stand six dollars a night for these things," expostulated Johnny. "Let's try over at the other place."

"Try ahead, boys," said the proprietor quite good-naturedly. "You'll find her the same over there; and everywhere else." He arose. "Best leave your plunder here until you find out. Come down and have a drink?"

We found the City Hotel offered exactly the same conditions as did the Parker House; except that the proprietor was curt and had no time for us at all. From that point, still dissatisfied, we extended our investigations beyond the Plaza. We found ourselves ankle deep in sandhills on which grew coarse grass and a sort of sage. Crazy, ramshackle huts made of all sorts of material were perched in all sorts of places. Hundreds of tents had been pitched, beneath which and in front of which an extremely simple housekeeping was going on. Hunt as we might we could find no place that looked as though it would take lodgers. Most of even the better looking houses were simply tiny skeletons covered with paper, cloth or paint. By painstaking persistence we kept at it until we had enquired of every building of any pretensions. Then, somewhat discouraged, we picked our way back to the shore after our heavier goods.

The proprietor of the Parker House greeted us with unabated good nature.

"I know how you boys feel," said he. "There's lots in your fix. You'd better stick here to-night and then get organized to camp out, if you're going to be here long. I suppose, though, you're going to the mines? Well, it'll take you several days to make your plans and get ready. When you get back from the mines you won't have to think about these things."

"There's plenty of gold?" ventured Johnny.

"Bushels."

"I should think you'd be up there."

"I don't want any better gold mine than the old Parker House," said he comfortably.

We paid him twenty-four dollars.

By now it was late in the afternoon. The wind had dropped, but over the hills to seaward rolled a soft beautiful bank of fog. The sun was blotted out behind it and a chill fell. The crowds about the Plaza thinned.

We economized our best at supper, but had to pay some eight dollars for the four of us. The bill was a la carte and contained such items as grizzly steak, antelope, elk, and wild duck and goose. Grizzly steak, I remember, cost a dollar and a quarter. By the time we had finished, it had grown dark. The lamps were alight, and the crowds were beginning to gather. All the buildings and the big tent next door were a blaze of illumination. The sounds of music and singing came from every side. A holiday spirit was in the air.

Johnny and I were crazy to be up and doing, but Talbot sternly repressed us, and Yank agreed with his decision by an unusually emphatic nod.

"It is all a lot of fun, I'll admit," said he; "but this is business. And we've got to face it. Sit down here on the edge of this veranda, and let's talk things over. How much money have you got, Yank?"

"Two hundred and twenty dollars," replied Yank promptly.

"You're partners with me, Frank, so I know our assets," said Talbot with tact. "Johnny?"

"Hanged if I know," replied that youth. "I've got quite a lot. I keep it in my pack."

"Well, go find out," advised Talbot.

Johnny was gone for some time. We smoked and listened to the rather blatantly mingled strains of music, and watched the figures of men hurrying by in the spangled darkness.

Johnny returned very much excited.

"I've been robbed!" he cried.

"Robbed? Is your money all gone?"

"No, there's a little left, but —— "

Talbot laughed quietly.

"Sit down, Johnny, and cool off," he advised. "If anybody had robbed you, they'd have taken the whole kit and kaboodle. Did you come out ahead on those *monte* games?"

Johnny blushed, and laughed a little.

"I see what you're at, but you're away off there. I just played for small stakes."

"And lost a lot of them. I sort of look-out your game. But that's all right. How much did the 'robbers' leave you?"

"Twelve dollars, besides what I have in my clothes—twenty-one dollars in all," said Johnny.

"Well, that's pretty good. You beat Frank and me to death. There's our total assets," said Talbot, and laid a ten-dollar gold piece and a dime on his knee.

"We'll call that dime a curiosity," said he, "for I notice a quarter is the smallest coin they use out here. Now you see that we've got to talk business. Frank and I haven't got enough to live on for one more day."

"There's enough among us——" began Yank.

"You mean you already have your share of the partner-ship finances," corrected Talbot, quickly. "If we're going to be partners—and that's desired and understood, I suppose?" We all nodded emphatic agreement. "We must all put in the same amount. I move that said amount be two hundred and twenty dollars apiece. Yank, you can loaf to-morrow; you've got your share all made up. You can put in the day finding out all about getting to the mines, and how much it costs, and what we will need."

"All right; I'll do it," said Yank.

"As for the rest of us," cried Talbot, "we've got to rustle up two hundred and twenty dollars each before to-morrow evening!"

"How?" I asked blankly.

"How should I know? Out there" he waved his hand abroad at the flickering lights. "There is the Golden City, challenging every man as he enters her gates. She offers opportunity and fortune. All a man has to do is go and take them! Accept the challenge!"

"The only way I could take them would be to lift them off some other fellow at the point of a gun," said Johnny gloomily.

CHAPTER XI

I MAKE TWENTY–FIVE DOLLARS

We talked the situation over thoroughly, and **then** turned in, having lost our chance to see the sights. Beneath us and in the tent next door went on a tremendous row of talking, laughing, and singing that for a little while prevented me from falling asleep. But the last month had done wonders for me in that way; and shortly I dropped off.

Hours later I awakened, shivering with cold to find the moonlight pouring into the room, and the bunks all occupied. My blanket had disappeared, which accounted for my dreams of icebergs. Looking carefully over the sleeping forms I discerned several with two blankets, and an equal number with none! At first I felt inclined to raise a row; then thought better of it, by careful manipulation I abstracted *two* good blankets from the most unprotected of of my neighbours, wrapped them tightly about me, and so slept soundly.

We went downstairs and out into the sweetest of mornings. The sun was bright, the sky clear and blue, the wind had not yet risen, balmy warmth showered down through every particle of the air. I had felt some May days like this back on our old farm. Somehow they were associated in my mind with Sunday morning and the drawling, lazy clucking of hens. Only here there were no hens, and **if it** was Sunday morning — which it might have been — nobody knew it.

The majority of the citizens had not yet appeared, but a handful of the poorer Chinese, and a sprinkling of others, crossed the Plaza. The doors of the gambling places were all wide open to the air. Across the square a number of small boys were throwing dust into the air. Johnny, with his usual sympathy for children, naturally gravitated in their direction. He returned after a few moments, his eyes wide.

"Do you know what they are doing?" he demanded.

We said politely that we did not.

"They are panning for gold."

"Well, what of it?" I asked, after a moment's pause; since Johnny seemed to expect some astonishment. "Boys are imitative little monkeys."

"Yes, but they're getting it," insisted Johnny.

"What!" cried Talbot. "You're crazy. Panning gold — here in the streets. It's absurd!"

"It's not absurd; come and see."

We crossed the Plaza. Two small Americans and a Mexican youth were scooping the surface earth into the palms of their hands and blowing it out again in a slant-wise stream. When it was all gone, they examined eagerly their hands. Four others working in partnership had spread a small sheet. They threw their handfuls of earth into the air, all the while fanning vigorously with their hats. The breeze thus engendered puffed away the light dust, leaving only the heavier pieces to fall on the canvas. Among these the urchins searched eagerly and carefully their heads close together. Every moment or so one of the them would wet a forefinger to pick up carefully a speck of something which he would then transfer to an old buckskin sack.

As we approached, they looked up and nodded to Johnny in a friendly fashion. They were eager, alert, precocious gamins, of the street type and how they had come to California I could not tell you. Probably as cabin boys of some of the hundreds of vessels in the harbour.

"What are you getting, boys?" asked Talbot after a moment.

"Gold, of course," answered one of them.

"Let's see it."

The boy with the buckskin sack held it open for our inspection, but did not relax his grip on it. The bottom of the bag was thickly gilded with light glittering yellow particles.

"It looks like gold," said I, incredulously.

"It *is* gold," replied the boy with some impatience. "Anyway, it buys things."

We looked at each other.

"Gold diggings right in the streets of San Francisco," murmured Yank.

"I should think you'd find it easier later in the day when the wind came up?" suggested Talbot.

"Of course; and let some other kids jump our claim while we were waiting," grunted one of the busy miners.

"How much do you get out of it?"

"Good days we make as high as three or four dollars."

"I'm afraid the diggings are hardly rich enough to tempt

us," observed Talbot; "but isn't that the most extra-ordinary performance! I'd no notion —— "

We returned slowly to the hotel, marvelling. Yesterday we had been laughing at the gullibility of one of our fellow-travellers who had believed the tale of a wily ship's agent to the effect that it was possible to live aboard the ship and do the mining within reach ashore at odd hours of daylight! Now that tale did not sound so wild; although of course we realized that the gold must occur in very small quantities. Otherwise somebody beside small boys would be at it. As a matter of fact, though we did not find it out until very much later, the soil of San Francisco is not auriferous at all. The boys were engaged in working the morning's sweepings from the bars and gambling houses which the lavish and reckless handling of gold had liberally impregnated. In some of the mining towns nearer the source of supply I have known of from one hundred to three hundred dollars a month being thus "blown" from the sweepings of a bar.

We ate a frugal breakfast and separated on the agreed business of the day. Yank started for the water front to make inquiries as to ways of getting to the mines; Talbot set off at a businesslike pace for the hotel as though he knew fully what he was about; Johnny wandered rather aimlessly to the east; and I as aimlessly to the west.

It took me just one hour to discover that I could get all of any kind of work that any dozen men could do, and at wages so high that at first I had to ask over and over again to make sure I had heard aright. Only none of them would bring me in two hundred and twenty dollars by evening. The further I looked into that proposition, the more absurd, of course, I saw it to be. I could earn from twenty to fifty dollars by plain day-labour at some jobs; or I could get fabulous salaries by the month or year; but that was different. After determining this to my satisfaction I came to the sensible conclusion that I would make what I could.

The first thing that caught my eye after I had come to this decision was a wagon drawn by four mules coming down the street at a sucking walk. The sight did not impress me particularly; but every storekeeper came out from his shop and every passerby stopped to look with respect as the outfit wallowed along. It was driven by a very large, grave, blond man with a twinkle in his eye.

"That's John A. McGlynn," said a man next my elbow.

"Who's he?" I asked.

The man looked at me in astonishment.

"Don't know who John McGlynn is?" he demanded. "When did you get here?"

"Last night."

"Oh! Well, John has the only American wagon in town. Brought it out from New York in pieces, and put it together himself. Broke four wild California mules to drag her. He's a wonder!"

I could not, then, see quite how this exploit made him such a wonder; but on a sudden inspiration I splashed out through the mud and climbed into the wagon.

McGlynn looked back at me.

"Freightin'," said he, "is twenty dollars a ton; and at that rate it'll cost you about thirty dollars, you dirty hippopotamus. These ain't no safe-movers, these mules!"

Unmoved, I clambered up beside him.

"I want a job," said I, "for to-day only."

"Do ye now?"

"Can you give me one?"

"I can, mebbe. And do you understand the inner aspirations of mules, maybe?"

"I was brought up on a farm."

"And the principles of elementary navigation by dead reckoning?"

I looked at him blankly.

"I mean mudholes," he explained. "Can you keep out of them?"

"I can try."

He pulled up the team, handed me the reins, and clambered over the wheel.

"You're hired. At six o'clock I'll find you and pay you off. You get twenty-five dollars."

"What am I to do?"

"You go to the shore and you rustle about whenever you see anything that looks like freight; and you look at it, and when you see anything marked with a diamond and an H inside of it, you pile it on and take it up to Howard Mellin & Company. And if you can't lift it, then leave it for another trip, and bullyrag those skinflints at H. M. & Co.'s to send a man down to help you. And if you don't know where they live, find out; and if you bog them mules down I'll skin you alive, big as you are. And anyway, you're a fool to be working in this place for twenty-five dollars a day, which is one reason I'm so glad to find you just now."

"What's that, John?" inquired a cool, amused voice.

"McGlynn and I looked around. A tall, perfectly dressed

figure stood on the sidewalk surveying us quizzically. This was a smooth-shaven man of perhaps thirty-five years of age, grave faced, clean cut, with an air of rather ponderous slow dignity that nevertheless became his style very well. He was dressed in tall white hat, a white winged collar, a black stock, a long tailed blue coat with gilt buttons, an embroidered white waistcoat, dapper buff trousers, and varnished boots. He carried a polished cane and wore several heavy pieces of gold jewellery — a watch fob, a scarf-pin, and the like. His movements were leisurely, his voice low. It seemed to me, then, that somehow the perfection of his appointments and the calm deliberation of his movement made him more incongruous and remarkable than did the most bizarre whims of the miners.

"Is it yourself, Judge Girvin?" replied McGlynn, "I'm just telling this young man that he can't have the job of driving my little California canaries for but one day because I've hired a fine lawyer from the East at two hundred and seventy-five a month to drive my mules for me."

"You have done well," Judge Girvin in his grave, courteous tones. "For the whole business of a lawyer is to know how to manage mules and asses so as to make them pay!"

I drove to the beach, and speedily charged my wagon with as large a load as prudence advised me. The firm of Howard Mellin & Company proved to have quarters in a frame shack on what is now Montgomery Street. It was only a short haul, but a muddy one. Nearly opposite their store a new wharf was pushing its way out into the bay. I could see why this and other firms clung so tenaciously to their locations on rivers of bottomless mud in preference to moving up into the drier part of town.

I enjoyed my day hugely. My eminent position on the driver's seat — eminent both actually and figuratively — gave me a fine opportunity to see the sights and to enjoy the homage men seemed inclined to accord the only wagon in town. The feel of the warm air was most grateful. Such difficulties as offered served merely to add zest to the job. At noon I ate some pilot bread and a can of sardines bought from my employers. About two o'clock the wind came up from the sea, and the air filled with the hurrying clouds of dust.

In my journeys back and forth I had been particularly struck by the bold, rocky hill that shut off the view toward the north. Atop this hill had been rigged a two-armed semaphore, which, one of the clerks told me, was used to signal the sight of ships coming in the Golden Gate. The arms were variously arranged according to the rig or kind of vessel. Every man, every urchin, every Chinaman, even, knew the meaning of these various signals. A year later, I was attending a theatrical performance in the Jenny Lind Theatre on the Plaza. In the course of the play an actor rushed on frantically holding his arms outstretched in a particularly wooden fashion, and uttering the lines, "What means this, my lord!"

"A sidewheel steamer!" piped up a boy's voice from the gallery.

Well, about three o'clock of this afternoon, as I was about delivering my fifth load of goods, I happened to look up just as the semaphore arms hovered on the rise. It seemed that every man on the street must have been looking in the same direction, for instantly a great shout went up.

"A sidewheeel steamer! The *Oregon!*"

At once the streets were alive with men hurrying from all directions toward the black rocks at the foot of Telegraph Hill, where, it seems, the steamer's boats were expected to land. Flags were run up on all sides, firearms were let off, a warship in the harbour broke out her bunting and fired a salute. The decks of the steamer, as she swept into view, were black with men; her yards were gay with colour. Uptown some devoted soul was ringing a bell; and turning it away over and over, to judge by the sounds. I pulled up my mules and watched the vessel swing down through the ranks of the shipping and come to anchor. We had beaten out our comrades by a day!

At five o'clock a small boy boarded me.

"You're to drive the mules up to McGlynn's and unhitch them and leave them," said he. "I'm to show you the way."

"Where's McGlynn?" I asked.

"He's getting his mail."

We drove to a corral and three well-pitched tents down in the southern edge of town. Here a sluggish stream lost its way in a swamp of green hummocky grass. I turned out the mules in the corral and hung up the harness.

"McGlynn says you're to go to the post-office and he'll pay you there," my guide instructed me.

The post-office proved to be a low adobe one-story building, with the narrow veranda typical of its kind. A line of men extended from its door and down the street as far as the eye could reach. Some of them had brought stools or boxes, and were comfortably reading scraps of paper.

I walked down the line. A dozen from the front I saw Johnny standing. This surprised me, for I knew he could not expect mail by this steamer. Before I had reached him he had finished talking to a stranger, and had yielded his place.

"Hullo!" he greeted me. "How you getting on?"

"So-so!" I replied. "I'm looking for a man who owes me twenty-five dollars."

"Well, he's here," said Johnny confidently. "Everybody in town is here."

We found McGlynn in line about a block down the street. When he saw me coming he pulled a fat buckskin bag from his breeches pocket, opened its mouth, and shook a quantity of its contents, by guess, into the palm of his hand.

"There you are," said he; "that's near enough. I'm a pretty good guesser. I hope you took care of the mules all right; you ought to, you're from a farm."

"I fixed 'em."

"And the mud? How many times did you get stuck?"

"Not at all."

He looked at me with surprise.

"Would you think of that, now!" said he. "You must have loaded her light."

"I did."

"Did you get all the goods over?"

"Yes."

"Well, I'll acknowledge you're a judgematical young man; and if you want a job with me I'll let that lawyer go I spoke to the judge about. He handed it to me then, didn't he?" He laughed heartily. "No? Well, you're right. A man's a fool to work for any one but himself. Where's your bag? Haven't any? How do you carry your dust? Haven't any? I forgot; you're a tenderfoot, of course." He opened his buckskin sack with his teeth, and poured back the gold from the palm of his hand. Then he searched for a moment in all his pockets, and produced a most peculiar chunk of gold metal. It was nearly as thick as it was wide, shaped roughly into an octagon, and stamped with initials. This he handed to me.

"It's about a fifty-dollar slug," said he, "you can get it weighed. Give me the change next time you see me."

"But I may leave for the mines to-morrow," I objected.

"Then leave the change with Jim Recket of the El Dorado."

"How do you know I'll leave it?" I asked curiously.

"I don't," replied McGlynn bluntly. "But if you need twenty-five dollars worse than you do a decent conscience, then John A. McGlynn isn't the man to deny you!"

Johnny and I left for the hotel.

"I didn't know you expected any mail," said I.

"I don't."

"But thought I saw you in line —— "

"Oh, yes. When I saw the mail sacks, it struck me that there might be quite a crowd; so I came up as quickly as I could and got in line. There were a number before me, but I got a place pretty well up in front. Sold the place for five dollars, and only had to stand there about an hour at that."

"Good head!" I admired. "I'd never have thought of it. How have you gotten on?"

"Pretty rotten," confessed Johnny. "I tried all morning to find a decent opportunity to do something or deal in something, and then I got mad and plunged in for odd jobs. I've been a regular errand boy. I made two dollars carrying a man's bag up from the ship."

"How much all told?"

"Fifteen. I suppose you've got your pile."

"That twenty-five you saw me get is the size of it."

Johnny brightened; we moved up closer in a new intimacy and sense of comradeship over delinquency. It relieved both to feel that the other, too, had failed. To enter the Plaza we had to pass one of the larger of the gambling places.

"I'm going in here," said Johnny, suddenly.

He swung through the open doors, and I followed him.

The place was comparatively deserted, owing probably to the distribution of mail. We had full space to look about us; and I was never more astonished in my life. The outside of the building was rough and unfinished as a barn, having nothing but size to attract or recommend. The interior was the height of lavish luxury. A polished mahogany bar ran down one side, backed by huge gilt framed mirrors before which were pyramided fine glasses and bottles of liquor. The rest of the wall space was thickly hung with more plate mirrors, dozens of well-executed oil paintings, and strips of tapestry. At one end was a small raised stage on which lolled half-dozen darkies with banjos and tambourines. The floor was covered with a thick velvet carpet. Easy chairs, some of them leather upholstered, stood about in every available corner. Heavy chandeliers of glass, with hundreds of dangling crystals and prisms, hung from the ceiling. The gambling tables, a half dozen in number, were arranged in the open floor space in the centre. Altogether it was a most astounding contrast in its sheer luxury and gorgeous furnishing to the crudity of the town. I became acutely conscious of my muddy boots, my old clothes, my unkempt hair, my red shirt and the armament strapped about my waist.

A relaxed, subdued air of idleness pervaded the place. The gamblers lounged back of their tables, sleepy-eyed and listless. On tall stools their lookouts yawned behind papers. One of these was a woman, young, pretty, most attractive in the soft, flaring, flouncy costume of that period. A small group of men stood at the bar. One of the barkeepers was mixing drinks, pouring the liquid, at arm's length from one tumbler to another in a long parabolic curve, and without spilling a drop. Only one table was doing business, and that with only three players. Johnny pushed rapidly toward this table, and I, a little diffidently, followed.

The game was roulette. Johnny and the dealer evidently recognized each other, for a flash of the eye passed between them, but they gave no other sign. Johnny studied the board a moment then laid twenty-two dollars in coin on one of the numbers. The other players laid out small bags of gold dust. The wheel spun, and the ball rolled. Two of the men lost; their dust was emptied into a drawer beneath the table and the bags tossed back to them. The third had won; the dealer deftly estimated the weight of his bet, lifting it in the flat of his left hand; then spun several gold pieces toward the winner. He seemed quite satisfied. The gambler stacked a roll of twenty-dollar pieces, added one to them, and thrust them at Johnny. I had not realized that the astounding luck of winning off a single number had befallen him.

"Ten to one — two hundred and twenty dollars!" he muttered to me.

The other three players were laying their bets for the next turn of the wheel. Johnny swept the gold pieces into his pocket, and laid back the original stake against *even*. He lost. Thereupon he promptly arose and left the building.

CHAPTER XII

TALBOT DESERTS

I followed him to the hotel somewhat gloomily; for I was now the only member of our party who had not made good the agreed amount of the partnership. It is significant that never for a moment did either Johnny or myself doubt that Talbot would have the required sum. Johnny, his spirits quite recovered, whistled like a lark.

We arrived just in time for the first supper call, and found Talbot and Yank awaiting us. Yank was as cool and taciturn, and nodded to us as indifferently, as ever. Talbot, however, was full of excitement. His biscuit-brown complexion had darkened and flushed until he was almost Spanish-black, and the little devils in his eyes led a merry dance between the surface and unguessed depths. He was also exceedingly voluble; and, as usual when in that mood, aggravatingly indirect. He joked and teased and carried on like a small boy; and insisted on ordering an elaborate dinner and a bottle of champagne, in the face of even Johnny's scandalized expostulations. When Johnny protested against expenditure, it was time to look out!

"This is on me! This is my party! Dry up, Johnny!" cried Talbot. "Fill your glasses. Drink to the new enterprise; the Undertakers' Mining Company, Unlimited."

"Undertakers?" I echoed.

"Well, you all look it. Call it the Gophers, then. Capital stock just eight hundred and eighty dollars, fully subscribed. I suppose it is fully subscribed, gentlemen?" He scrutinized us closely. "Ah, Frank! I see we'll have to take your promissory note. But the artistic certificates are not yet home from the engravers. Take your time. Maybe a relative will die."

"Talbot," said I disgustedly, "if I hadn't happened to smell your breath before supper I'd think you drunk."

"I *am* drunk, old deacon," rejoined Talbot, "but with the Wine of Enchantment — do you know your Persian? No? Well, then, this:

> "Drink to me only with thine eyes,
>   And I'll not ask for wine!"

"A woman!" grumbled the literal Yank.

"The best, the most capricious, the most beautiful woman in the world," cried Talbot, "whose smile intoxicates, whose frown drives to despair."

"What *are* you drivelling about?" I demanded.

"The goddess fortune — what else? But come," and Talbot rose with a sudden and startling transition to the calm and businesslike. "We can smoke outside; and we must hear each other's reports."

He paid for the dinner, steadfastly refusing to let us bear our share. I noticed that he had acquired one of the usual buckskin sacks, and shook the yellow dust from the mouth of it to the pan of the gold scales with quite an accustomed air

We lit our pipes and sat down at one end of the veranda, where we would not be interrupted.

"Fire ahead, Yank," advised Talbot.

"There's two ways of going to the mines," said Yank: "One is to go overland by horses to Sutter's Fort or the new town of Sacramento, and then up from there into the foothills of the big mountains way yonder. The other is to take a boat and go up river to Sacramento and then pack across with horses."

"How much is the river fare?" asked Talbot.

"You have to get a sailboat. It costs about forty dollars apiece."

"How long would it take?"

"Four or five days."

"And how long from here to Sutter's Fort by horse?"

"About the same."

"Depends then on whether horses are cheaper here or there."

"They are cheaper there; or we can get our stuff freighted in by Greasers and hoof it ourselves."

"Then I should think we ought to have a boat."

"I got one," said Yank.

"Good for you!" cried Talbot. "You're a man after my own heart! Well, Johnny?"

Johnny told his tale, a little proudly and produced his required two hundred and twenty dollars.

"You had luck," said Talbot non-committally, "and you ran a strong risk of coming back here without a cent, didn't you? I want to ask you one question, Johnny. If you had lost, would you have been willing to have taken the consequences?"

"What do you mean?" asked Johnny blankly.

"Would you have been willing to have dropped out of this partnership?"

Johnny stared.

"I mean," said Talbot kindly, "that you had no right to try to get this money by merely a gambler's chance unless you were willing to accept the logical result if you failed. It isn't fair to the rest of us."

"I see what you mean," said Johnny slowly. "No; I hadn't thought of it that way."

"Well, as I said, you had luck," repeated Talbot cheerfully, "so we needn't think of it further." It was characteristic that Johnny took this veiled rebuke from Talbot Ward in a meek and chastened spirit; from any one else his high temper could never stand even a breath of criticism. "How about you, Frank?" Talbot asked me.

I detailed my experiences in a very few words and exhibited my gold slug.

"That's the best I can do," I ended, "and half of that does not belong to me. I can, however, in a few days scrape up the full amount; there is plenty to do here. And barring bull luck, like Johnny's, I don't see much show of beating that, unless a man settled down to stay here."

Talbot stared at me, ruminatively, until I began to get restive. Then he withdrew his eyes. He made no comment.

"I suppose you have your money," suggested Yank to him, after a pause.

"Oh — yes," said Talbot as though awaking from profound reverie.

"Well, tell us about it. How did you get it? How long did it take you?"

"About half an hour. I figured that everybody in a place like this would be wanting news. So I sorted out that bundle of old newspapers you fellows were always laughing at, and I went out and sold them. Lucky I got busy with them early; for I don't doubt the arrival of the *Oregon* broke the market."

"How much did you get for them?" asked Johnny.

"A dollar apiece for most, and fifty cents for the rest. I came out two hundred and seventy dollars ahead all told. That, with Frank's and my ten dollars, gave me sixty dollars above the necessary amount."

Johnny arose and kicked himself solemnly.

"For not guessing what newspapers were good for," he explained. "Go on! What next? What did you do with the rest of the day?"

Talbot leaned forward, and all the animation of the dinner table returned to his manner and to his face.

"Boys," said he earnestly, "this is the most wonderful town that has ever been! There has been nothing like it in the past; and there will never be anything like it again. After I had sold out my papers I went wandering across the Plaza with my hands in my pockets. Next the El Dorado there is a hole in the ground. It isn't much of a hole, and the edges are all caving in because it is sandy. While I was looking at it two men came along. One was the owner of the hole, and the other said he was a lawyer. The owner offered to rent the hole to the lawyer for two hundred and fifty dollars a month; and the lawyer was inclined to take him up. After they had gone on I paced off the hole, just for fun. It was twelve feet square by about six feet deep! Then I walked on down toward the water front, and talked with all the storekeepers. They do a queer business. All these goods we see around came out here on consignment. The local storekeepers have a greater or lesser share and sell mainly on commission. Since they haven't any adequate storehouses, and can't get any put up again, they sell the stuff mainly at auction and get rid of it as quickly as possible. That's why some things are so cheap they can make pavements of them when a ship happens to come in loaded with one article. I talked with some of them and told them they ought to warehouse a lot of this stuff so as to keep it over until the market steadied. They agreed with that; but pointed out that they were putting up warehouses as fast as they could — which wasn't very fast — and in the meantime the rains and dust were destroying their goods. It was cheaper to sell at auction."

"And a heap more exciting," put in Johnny. "I went to one of them."

"Well, I wandered down to the shore, and looked out over the bay. It was full of shipping, riding high at anchor. I had an idea. I hired a boat for five dollars, and rowed out to some of the ships. Believe me or not, most of them were empty; not even a watchman aboard! I found some of the captains, however, and talked with each of them. They all told the same story."

"Crews skipped to the mines, I suppose?" said Yank.

"Exactly. And they *couldn't* get any more. So I offered to hire a few of them."

"The captains?" I inquired.

"No; the ships."

"The *what?*" we yelled in chorus.

"The ships."

"But if the captains can't get crews——"

"Oh, I don't want to sail them," went on Talbot impatiently. "It was hard work getting them to agree; they all cherished notions they could get crews and go sailing some more—good old salts! But I hired four, at last. Had to take them for only a month, however; and had to pay them in advance five hundred apiece."

"I beg pardon," said Johnny softly, "for interrupting your pleasing tale; but the last item interested me. I do not know whether I quite heard it right."

"Oh, shut up, Johnny," said Yank; "let the man tell his story. Of course he didn't have the money in his pocket. How did you get it, Tal?"

Ward shot him a grateful glance.

"I told them I'd pay them at four o'clock which gave me plenty of time."

"Two thousand dollars—oh, of course!" murmured Johnny.

"So then," continued Talbot, "I hustled ashore; and went to see some of my merchant friends. In two hours I had contracts with twelve of them that totalled six thousand dollars."

"Why didn't some of them go out and hire ships on their own account?" asked Yank shrewdly.

"Because I didn't mention the word 'ship' until I had their business," said Talbot. "I just guaranteed them storage, waterproof, practically fireproof, dustproof, and within twenty-four hours. I guess most of them thought I was crazy. But as it didn't cost them anything, they were willing to take a chance."

"Then you didn't raise your ten thousand dollars from them in advance payments!" I marvelled.

"Certainly not. That would have scared off the whole lot of them. But I got their agreements; I told you it took me two hours. Then I walked up the street figuring where I'd get the money. Of course I saw I'd have to divide the profits. I didn't know anybody; but after a while I decided that the best chance was to get some advice from honest and disinterested man. So I asked the first man I met who ran the biggest gambling place in town. He told me Jim Recket."

"Jim Recket?" I echoed. "He's the man I was to leave change for my gold slug with."

"Recket keeps the El Dorado, next door in the tent. He impressed me as a very quiet, direct, square sort of a fellow. The best type of professional gambler, in matters of this sort, generally is.

"'I am looking for a man,' said I, 'who has a little idle money, some time, no gold-mining fever, plenty of nerve, and a broad mind. Can you tell me who he is?'

"He thought a minute and then answered direct, as I knew he would.

"'Sam Brannan,' he said.

"'Tell me about him.'

"'To take up your points,' said Recket, checking off his fingers, 'he came out with a shipload of Mormons as their head, and he collected tithes from them for over a year; that's your idle money. He has all the time the Lord stuck into one day at a clip; that's your "some time." He has been here in the city since '48 which would seem to show he doesn't care much for mining. He collected the tithes from those Mormons, and sent word to Brigham Young that if he wanted the money to come and get it. That's for your nerve. As for being broad minded — well, when a delegation of the Mormons, all ready for a scrap, came to him solemnly to say that they were going to refuse to pay him the tithes any more, even if he was the California head of the church, he laughed them off the place for having been so green as to pay them as long as they had.'

"I found Sam Brannan, finally, at the bar in Dennison's Exchange."

"What was he like?" asked Johnny eagerly. "I'll bet I heard his name fifty times to-day."

"He is a thickset, jolly looking, curly headed fellow, with a thick neck, a bulldog jaw, and a big voice," replied Talbot. "Of course he tried to bully me, but when that didn't work, he came down to business. We entered into an agreement.

"Brannan was to furnish the money, and take half the profits, provided he liked the idea. When we had settled it all, I told him my scheme. He thought it over a while and came in. Then we rowed off and paid the captains of the ships. It was necessary now to get them warped in at high tide, of course, but Sam Brannan said he'd see to that — he has some sort of a pull with the natives, enough to get a day's labour, anyway."

"Warp them in?" I echoed.

"Certainly. You couldn't expect the merchants to lighter their stuff off in boats always. We'll beach these ships at high tide, and then run some sort of light causeway out to them. There's no surf, and the bottom is soft. It'll cost us something, of course; but Sam and I figure we ought to divide three thousand clear."

"I'd like to ask a question or so," said I. "What's to prevent the merchants doing this same hiring of ships for themselves?"

"Nothing," said Talbot, "after the first month."

"And what prevented Brannan, after he had heard your scheme, from going out on his own hook, and pocketing *all* the proceeds?"

"You don't understand, Frank," said Talbot impatiently. "Men of our stamp don't do those things."

"Oh!" said I.

"This," said Johnny, "made it about two o'clock, as I figure your story. Did you then take a needed rest?"

"Quarter of two," corrected Talbot, "I was going back to the hotel, when I passed that brick building — you know, on Montgomery Street. I remembered then that lawyer and his two hundred and fifty dollars for a hole in the ground. It seemed to me there was a terrible waste somewhere. Here was a big brick building filled up with nothing but goods. It might much better be filled with people. There is plenty of room for goods in those ships;

but you can't very well put people on the ships. So I just dropped in to see them about it. I offered to hire the entire upper part of the building; and pointed out that the lower part was all they could possibly use as a store. They said they needed the upper part as storehouse. I offered to store the goods in an accessible safe place. Of course they wanted to see the place; but I wouldn't let on, naturally, but left it subject to their approval after the lease was signed. The joke of it is they were way overstocked anyway. Finally I made my grand offer.

"'Look here,' said I, 'you rent me that upper story for a decent length of time — say a year — and I'll buy out the surplus stock you've got up there at a decent valuation.' They jumped at that; of course they pretended not to, but just the same they jumped. I'll either sell the stuff by auction, even if at a slight loss, or else I'll stick it aboard a ship. Depends a good deal on what is there, of course. It's mostly bale and box goods of some sort or another. I've got an inventory in my pocket. Haven't looked at it yet. Then I'll partition off that wareroom and rent it out for offices and so forth. There are a lot of lawyers and things in this town just honing for something dignified and stable. I only pay three thousand a month for it."

Johnny groaned deeply.

"Well," persisted Talbot, "I figure on getting at least eight thousand a month out of it. That'll take care of a little loss on the goods, if necessary. I'm not sure a loss is necessary."

"And how much, about, are the goods?" I inquired softly.

"Oh, I don't know. Somewhere between ten and twenty thousand, I suppose."

"Paid for how, and when?"

"One third cash, and the rest in notes. The interest out here is rather high," said Talbot regretfully.

"Where do you expect to get the money?" I insisted.

"Oh, money! money!" cried Talbot, throwing out his arms with a gesture of impatience. "The place is full of money. It's pouring in from the mines, from the world outside. Money's no trouble!"

He fell into an intent reverie, biting at his short moustache. I arose softly to my feet.

"Johnny," said I, in a strangled little voice, "I've got to give back McGlynn's change. Want to go with me?"

We tiptoed around the corner of the building, and fell into each other's arms with shrieks of joy.

"Oh!" cried Johnny at last, wiping the tears from his eyes. "Money's no trouble!"

After we had to some extent relieved our feelings we changed my gold slug into dust — I purchased a buckskin bag — and went to find McGlynn. Our way to his quarters led past the post-office, where a long queue of men still waited patiently and quietly in line. We stood for a few moments watching the demeanour of those who had received their mail, or who had been told there was nothing for them. Some of the latter were pathetic, and looked fairly dazed with grief and disappointment.

The letters were passed through a small window let in the adobe of the wall; and the men filed on to the veranda at one end and off it at the other. The man distributing mail was a small, pompous, fat Englishman. I recognized McGlynn coming slowly down with the line, and paid him half the dust in my bag.

As McGlynn reached the window, the glass in it slammed shut, and the clerk thrust a card against it.

"*Mails close at 9 p. m.*"

McGlynn tapped at the glass, received no attention, and commenced to beat a tattoo. The window was snatched open, and the fat clerk, very red, thrust his face in the opening.

"What do you want?" he demanded truculently.

"Any letters for John A. McGlynn?"

"This office opens at 8:30 A. M." said the clerk, slamming shut the window.

Without an instant's hesitation, and before the man had a chance to retire, McGlynn's huge fist crashed through the glass and into his face.

The crowd had waited patiently; but now, with a brutal snarl, it surged forward. McGlynn, a pleasant smile on his face, swung slowly about.

"Keep your line, boys! Keep your line!" he boomed. "There's no trouble! It's only a little Englishman who don't know our ways yet."

Inside the building the postal force, white and scared yet over the menacing growl of the beast they had so nearly roused, hastened to resume their tasks. I heard later that the last man in line reached the window only at three, o'clock in the morning. Also that next day McGlynn was summoned by Geary, then postmaster, to account for his share in the row; and that in the end Geary apologized and was graciously forgiven by McGlynn! I can well believe it.

We found Yank and Talbot still at the edge of the hotel veranda.

"Look here, Tal!" said Johnny at once. "How are you going to finish all this business you've scared up, and get off to the mines within a reasonable time? We ought to start pretty soon."

"Mines?" echoed Talbot, "I'm not going to the mines! I wouldn't leave all this for a million mines. No: Yank and I have been talking it over. You boys will have to attend to the mining end of this business. I'll pay Frank's share and take a quarter of the profits, and Frank can pay me in addition half his profits. In return for the work I don't do, I'll put aside two hundred and twenty dollars and use it in my business here, and all of us will share in the profits I make from that amount. How does that strike you?"

"I don't like to lose you out of this," said Johnny disappointedly.

"Nor I," said I.

"And I hate to lose the adventure, boys," agreed Talbot earnestly. "But, honestly, I can't leave this place now even if I want to; and I certainly don't want to."

I turned in that night with the feeling that I had passed a very interesting day.

CHAPTER XIII

UP-RIVER

Two days later Yank, Johnny, and I embarked aboard a small bluff-bowed sailboat, waved our farewells to Talbot standing on the shore, and laid our course to cross the blue bay behind an island called Alcatraz. Our boatman was a short, swarthy man, with curly hair and gold rings in his ears. He handled his boat well, but spoke not at all. After a dozen attempts to get something more than monosyllables out of him, we gave it up, and settled ourselves to the solid enjoyment of a new adventure.

The breeze was strong, and drove even our rather clumsy craft at considerable speed. The blue waters of the bay flashed in the sun and riffled under the squalls. Spray dashed away from our bows. A chill raced in from the open Pacific, diluting the sunlight.

We stared ahead of us, all eyes. The bay was a veritable inland sea; and the shores ahead of us lay flat and wide, with blue hazy hills in the distance, and a great mountain hovering in midair to our right. Black cormo rants going upwind flapped heavily by us just above the water, their necks stretched out. Gulls wheeled and screamed above us, or floated high and light like corks over the racing waves. Rafts of ducks lay bobbing, their necks furled, their head close to their bodies. A salt tang stirred our blood; and on the great mountain just north of the harbour entrance the shadows of cañons were beginning most beautifully to define themselves.

Altogether it was a pleasant sail. We perched to windward, and smoked our pipes, and worked ourselves to a high pitch of enthusiasm over what we were going to see and do. The sailor too smoked his pipe, leaning against the long, heavy tiller.

The distant flat shores drew nearer. We turned a corner and could make out the mouth of a river, and across it a white line that, as we came up on it, proved to be the current breaking against the wind over a very solid bar. For the first time our sailor gave signs of life. He stood on his feet, squinted ahead, ordered us amidships, dropped the peak of the mainsail, took the sheet in his hand. We flew down against the breakers. In a moment we were in them. Two sickening bumps shook our very vertebræ. The mast swayed drunkenly from side to side as the boat rolled on her keel, the sail flopped, a following wave slopped heavily over the stern, and the water swashed forward across our feet. Then we recovered a trifle, staggered forward, bumped twice more, and slid into the smoother deep water. The sailor grunted, and passed us a dipper. We bailed her out while he raised again the peak of his sail.

Shortly after this experience we glided up the reaches of a wide beautiful river. It had no banks, but was bordered by the tall reeds called tules. As far as the eye could reach, and that was very far when we climbed part way up the mast to look, these tules extended. League after league they ran away like illimitable plains, green and brown and beautiful, until somewhere over the curve of the earth straight ahead they must have met distant blue hills. To the southeast there seemed no end but the sky.

From the level of the boat, however, we saw only a little way into the outer fringe. The water lay among the stalks, and mud hens with white bills pushed their way busily into intricate narrow unguessed waterways. Occasionally the hedge of the tules broke to a greater or lesser opening into a lagoon. These were like shallow lakes, in which sometimes grew clumps of grasses. They were covered with waterfowl. Never have I seen so many ducks and geese of all kinds. They literally covered the surface of the water, and fairly seemed to jostle each other as they swam busily to and fro, intent on some business of their own. Their comfortable, low conversational clucking and quacking was a pleasure to hear. When, out of curiosity, we fired a revolver shot, they rose in the air with a roar like that of a great waterfall, and their crossing lines of flight in the sky was like the multitude of midges in the sun. I remember one flock of snow-white geese that turned and wheeled, alternately throwing their bodies in shadow or in the sunlight, so that they flashed brilliantly.

As the sun declined, the wind fell. Fortunately the current in the river was hardly perceptible. We slipped along on glassy waters. Thousands upon thousands of blackbirds dipped across us uttering their calls. Against a saffron sky were long lines of waterfowl, their necks outstretched. A busy multitudinous noise of marsh birds rose and fell all about us. The sun was a huge red ball touching the distant hills.

At last the wind failed us entirely, but the sailor got out a pair of sweeps, and we took turns rowing. Within a half hour we caught the silhouette of three trees against the sky, and shortly landed on a little island of solid ground. Here we made camp for the night.

All next day, and the days after, being luckily favoured by steady fair winds, we glided up the river. I could not but wonder at the certainty with which our sailor picked the right passage from the numerous false channels that offered themselves. The water was beautifully clear and sweet; quite different from the muddy currents of to-day. Shortly the solid ground had drawn nearer; so that often we passed long stretches of earth standing above the tule-grown water. Along these strips grew sycamore and cottonwood trees of great size, and hanging vines of the wild grape. The trees were as yet bare of leaves, but everything else was green and beautiful. We could see the tracks of many deer along the flats, but caught no sight of the animals themselves. At one place, however, we did frighten a small band of half a dozen elk. They crashed away recklessly through the brush, making noise and splashing enough for a hundred. Yank threw one of his little pea bullets after them; and certainly hit, for we found drops of blood. The sailor shook his head disparagingly over the size of the rifle balls, to Yank's vast disgust. I never saw him come nearer to losing his temper. As a matter of fact I think the sailor's contention had something in it; the long accurate weapon with its tiny missile was probably all right when its user had a chance to plant the bullet exactly in a fatal spot, but not for such quick snap shooting as this. At any rate our visions of cheap fresh meat vanished on the hoof.

The last day out we came into a wide bottomland country with oaks. The distant blue hills had grown, and had become slate-gray. At noon we discerned ahead of us a low bluff, and a fork in the river; and among the oak trees the gleam of tents, and before them a tracery of masts where the boats and small ships lay moored to the trees. This was the *embarcadero* of Sutter's Fort beyond; or the new city of Sacramento, whichever you pleased. Here our boat journey ended.

We disembarked into a welter of confusion. Dust, men, mules, oxen, bales, boxes, barrels, and more dust. Everything was in the open air. Tents were pitched in the open, under the great oaks, anywhere and everywhere. Next, the river, and for perhaps a hundred yards from the banks, the canvas structures were arranged in rows along what were evidently intended to be streets; but beyond that every one simply "squatted" where he pleased. We tramped about until we found a clear space, and there dumped down our effects. They were simple enough; and our housekeeping consisted in spreading our blankets and canvas, and unpacking our frying pan and pots. The entire list of our provisions consisted of pork, flour, salt, tea, coffee, sugar, tobacco, and some spirits.

After supper we went out in a body to see what we could find out concerning our way to the mines. We did not even possess a definite idea as to where we wanted to go!

GOLD

In this quest we ran across our first definite discouragement. The place was full of men and they were all willing to talk. Fully three quarters were, like ourselves, headed toward the mines; and were consequently full of theoretical advice. The · less they actually knew the more insistent they were that theirs was the only one sure route or locality or method. Of the remainder probably half were the permanent population of the place, and busily occupied in making what money they could. They were storekeepers, gamblers, wagon owners, saloonkeepers, transportation men. Of course we could quickly have had from most of these men very definite and practical advice as to where to go and how to get there; but the advice would most likely have been strongly tempered with self-interest. The rest of those we encountered were on their way back from the mines. And from them we got our first dash of cold water in the face.

According to them the whole gold-fable was vastly exaggerated. To be sure there was gold, no one could deny that, but it occurred very rarely, and in terrible places to get at. One had to put in ten dollars' worth of work, to get out one dollars' worth of dust. And provisions were so high that the cost of living ate up all the profits. Besides, we were much too late. All the good claims had been taken up and worked out by the earliest comers. There was much sickness in the mines, and men were dying like flies. A man was a fool ever to leave home but a double-dyed fool not to return there as soon as possible. Thus the army of the discouraged. There were so many of them, and they talked so convincingly, that I, for one, felt my golden dream dissipating; and a glance at Johnny's face showed that he was much in the same frame of mind. We were very young; and we had so long been keyed up so high that a reaction was almost inevitable. Yank showed no sign; but chewed his tobacco imperturbably.

We continued our inquiries, however, and had soon acquired a mass of varied information. The nearest mines were about sixty miles away; we could get our freight transported that far by the native Californian *cargadores* at fifty dollars the hundredweight. Or we could walk and carry our own goods. Or we might buy a horse or so to pack in our belongings. If we wanted to talk to the *cargadores* we must visit their camp over toward the south; if we wanted to buy horses we could do nothing better than to talk to McClellan, at Sutter's Fort. Fifty dollars a hundred seemed pretty steep for freighting; we would not be able to carry all we owned on our backs; we decided to try to buy the horses.

Accordingly next morning, after a delicious sleep under the open sky, we set out to cover the three or four miles to Sutter's Fort.

This was my first sight of the California country landscape, and I saw it at the most beautiful time of year. The low-rolling hills were bright green, against which blended the darker green of the parklike oaks. Over the slopes were washes of colour where the wild flowers grew, like bright scarves laid out in the sun. They were of deep orange, or an equally deep blue, or, perhaps, of mingled white and purple. Each variety, and there were many of them, seemed to grow by itself so that the colours were massed. Johnny muttered something about "the trailing glory — banners of the hills"; but whether that was a quotation or just Johnny I do not know.

The air was very warm and grateful, and the sky extraordinarily blue. Broad-pinioned birds wheeled slowly, very high; and all about us, on the tips of swaying bushes and in the tops of trees, thousands of golden larks were singing. They were in appearance like our meadow-larks back east, but their note was quite different; more joyous and lilting, but with the same liquid quality. We flushed many sparrows of different sorts; and we saw the plumed quail, the gallant, trim, little, well-groomed gentlemen, running rapidly ahead of us. And over it all showered the clear warmth of the sun, like some subtle golden ether that dissolved and disengaged from the sleeping hills multitudinous hummings of insects, songs of birds, odours of earth, perfumes of flowers.

In spite of ourselves our spirits rose. We forgot our anxious figurings on ways and means, our too concentrated hopes of success, our feverish, intent, single-minded desire for gold. Three abreast we marched forward through the waving shimmering wild oats, humming once more the strains of the silly little song to which the gold seekers had elected to stride:

> "I soon shall be in mining camps,
>   And then I'll look around,
>   And when I see the gold-dust there,
>   I'll pick it off the ground.

> "I'll scrape the mountains clean, old girl,
>   I'll drain the rivers dry;
>   I'm off for California.
>   Susannah, don't you cry!"

Even old Yank joined in the chorus, and he had about as much voice as a rusty windmill, and about the same idea of tune as a hog has of war.

> "Oh, Susannah! don't you cry for me!
> I'm off to California with my washbowl on my knee!"

We topped a rise and advanced on Sutter's Fort as though we intended by force and arms to take that historic post.

PART III
THE MINES

Sutter's Fort was situated at the edge of the live-oak park. We found it to resemble a real fort, with high walls, bastions, and a single gate at each end through which one entered to a large enclosed square, perhaps a hundred and fifty yards long by fifty wide. The walls were not pierced for guns; and the defence seemed to depend entirely on the jutting bastions. The walls were double, and about twenty-five feet apart. Thus by roofing over this space, and dividing it with partitions, Sutter had made up his barracks, blacksmith shop, bakery, and the like. Later in our investigations we even ran across a woollen factory, a distillery, a billiard room, and a bowling alley! At the southern end of this long space stood a two-story house. Directly opposite the two-story house and at the other end of the enclosure was an adobe corral.

The place was crowded with people. A hundred or so miners rushed here and there on apparently very important business, or loafed contentedly against the posts or the sun-warmth of adobe walls. In this latter occupation they were aided and abetted by a number of the native Californians. Perhaps a hundred Indians were leading horses, carrying burdens or engaged in some other heavy toil. They were the first we had seen, and we examined them with considerable curiosity. A good many of them were nearly naked; but some had on portions of battered civilized apparel. Very few could make up a full suit of clothes; but contented themselves with either a coat, or a shirt, or a pair of pantaloons, or even with only a hat, as the case might be. They were very swarthy, squat, villainous-looking savages, with big heads, low foreheads, coarse hair, and beady little eyes.

We stopped for some time near the sentry box at the entrance, accustoming ourselves to the whirl and movement. Then we set out to find McClellan. He was almost immediately pointed out to us, a short, square, businesslike man, with a hard gray face, dealing competently with the pressure. A score of men surrounded him, each eager for his attention. While we hovered, awaiting our chance, two men walked in through the gate. They were accorded the compliment of almost a complete silence on the part of those who caught sight of them.

The first was a Californian about thirty-five or forty years of age, a man of a lofty, stern bearing, swarthy skin, glossy side whiskers, and bright supercilious eyes. He wore a light blue short jacket trimmed with scarlet and with silver buttons, a striped silk sash, breeches of crimson velvet met below by long embroidered deerskin boots. A black kerchief was bound crosswise on his head entirely concealing the hair; and a flat-crowned, wide, gray hat heavily ornamented with silver completed this gorgeous costume. He moved with the assured air of the aristocrat. The splendour of his apparel, the beauty of his face and figure, and the grace of his movements attracted the first glance from all eyes. Then immediately he was passed over in favour of his companion.

The latter was a shorter, heavier man, of more mature years. In fact his side whiskers were beginning to turn gray. His costume was plain, but exquisitely neat, and a strange blend of the civil and the military. The jacket for example, had been cut in the trim military fashion, but was worn open to exhibit the snowy cascade of the linen beneath. But nobody paid much attention to the man's dress. The dignity and assured calm of his face and eye at once impressed one with conviction of unusual quality.

Johnny stared for a moment, his brows knit. Then with an exclamation, he sprang forward.

"Captain Sutter!" he cried.

Sutter turned slowly, to look Johnny squarely in the face, his attitude one of cold but courteous inquiry. Johnny was approaching, hat in hand. I confess he astonished me. We had known him intimately for some months, and always as the harum-scarum, impulsive, hail fellow, bubbling, irresponsible. Now a new Johnny stepped forward, quiet, high-bred, courteous, self-contained. Before he had spoken a word, Captain Sutter's aloof expression had relaxed.

"I beg your pardon for addressing you so abruptly," Johnny was saying. "The surprise of the moment must excuse me. Ten years ago, sir, I had the pleasure of meeting you at the time you visited my father in Virginia."

"My dear boy!" cried Sutter. "You are, of course the

son of Colonel Fairfax. But ten years ago — you were a very young man!"

"A small boy, rather," laughed Johnny.

They chatted for a few moments, exchanging news, I suppose, though they had drawn beyond our ear-shot. In a few moments we were summoned, and presented; first to Colonel Sutter, then to Don Gaspar Martinez. The latter talked English well. Yank and I, both somewhat silent and embarrassed before all this splendour of manner, trailed the triumphal progress like two small boys. We were glad to trail, however. Captain Sutter took us about, showing us in turn all the many industries of the place.

"The old peaceful life is gone," said he. "The fort has become a trading post for miners. It is difficult now to get labour for my crops, and I have nearly abandoned cultivation. My Indians I have sent out to mine for me."

He showed us a row of long troughs outside the walls to which his Indian workmen had come twice a day for their rations of wheat porridge. "They scooped it out with their hands," he told us "like animals." Also he pointed out the council circle beneath the trees where he used to meet the Indians. He had great influence with the surrounding tribes; and had always managed to live peacefully with them.

"But that is passing," said he. "The American miners, quite naturally, treat them as men; and they are really children. It makes misunderstanding, and bloodshed, and reprisals. The era of good feeling is about over. They still trust me, however, and will work for me."

Don Gaspar here excused himself on the ground of business, promising to rejoin us later.

"That trouble will come upon us next," said Captain Sutter, nodding after the Spaniard's retreating form. "It is already beginning. The Californians hold vast quantities of land with which they do almost nothing. A numerous and energetic race is coming; and it will require room. There is conflict there. And their titles are mixed; very mixed. It will behoove a man to hold a very clear title when the time comes."

"Your own titles are doubtless clear and strong," suggested Johnny.

"None better. My grant here came directly from the Mexican government itself." The Captain paused to chuckle, "I suspect that the reason it was given me so freely was political — there existed at that time a desire to break up the power of the Missions; and the establishment of rival colonies on a large scale would help to do that. The government evidently thought me competent to undertake the opening of this new country."

"Your grant is a large one?" surmised Johnny.

"Sixty miles by about twelve," said Captain Sutter. We had by now finished our inspection, and stood by the southern gate.

"I am sorry," said Captain Sutter, "that I am not in a position to offer you hospitality. My own residence is at a farm on the Feather River. This fort, as no doubt you are aware, I have sold to the traders. In the changed conditions it is no longer necessary to me."

"Do you not regret the changed conditions?" asked

Johnny after a moment. "I can imagine the interest in building a new community — all these industries, the training of the Indians to work, the growing of crops, the raising of cattle."

"One may regret changed conditions; but one cannot prevent their changing," said Captain Sutter in his even, placid manner. "The old condition was a very pleasant dream; this is a reality."

We walked back through the enclosure. Our companion was greeted on all sides with the greatest respect and affection. To all he responded with benign but unapproachable dignity. From the vociferating group he called the trader, McClellan, to whom he introduced us, all three, with urbane formality.

"These young men," he told McClellan, who listened to him intently, his brows knit, "are more than acquaintances, they are very especial old friends of mine. I wish to bespeak your good offices for what they may require. They are on their way to the mines. And now, gentlemen, I repeat, I am delighted to have had this opportunity; I wish you the best of luck; and I sincerely hope you may be able to visit me at Feather River, where you are always sure of a hearty welcome. Treat them well, McClellan."

"You know, Cap'n, friends of your'n are friends of mine," said McClellan briefly.

At the end of half an hour we found ourselves in possession of two pack-horses and saddles, and a load of provisions.

"Look out for hoss thieves," advised McClellan. "These

yere Greasers will follow you for days waitin' for a chance to git your stock. Don't picket with rawhide rope or the coyotes are likely to knaw yore animiles loose. Better buy a couple of ha'r ropes from the nearest Mex. Take care of yoreselves. Good-bye." He was immediately immersed in his flood of business.

We were in no hurry to return, so we put in an hour or so talking with the idlers. From them we heard much praise for Sutter. He had sent out such and such expeditions to rescue snow-bound immigrants in the mountains; he had received hospitably the travel-worn transcontinentals; he had given freely to the indigent; and so on without end. I am very glad that even at second hand I had the chance to know this great-hearted old soldier of Charles X while in the glory of his possessions and the esteem of men. Acre by acre his lands were filched from him; and he died in Washington vainly petitioning Congress for restitution.

CHAPTER XV

THE GOLD TRAIL

We loaded our pack-horses, and set off next morning early on the trail up the American River. At last, it seemed to us, we were really under way; as though our long journeyings and many experiences had been but a preparation for this start. Our spirits were high, and we laughed and joked and sang extravagantly. Even Yank woke up and acted like a frisky colt. Such early way-farers as we met, we hailed with shouts and chaffing; nor were we in the least abashed by an occasional surly response, or the not infrequent attempts to discourage our hopes. For when one man said there was no gold; another was as confident that the diggings were not even scratched.

The morning was a very fine one; a little chilly, with a thin white mist hanging low along the ground. This the sun soon dissipated. The birds sang everywhere. We trudged along the dusty road merrily.

Every little while we stopped to readjust the burdens to our animals. A mountaineer had showed us how to lash them on, but our skill at that sort of thing was *miner's*, and the packs would not hold. We had to do them one at a time, using the packed animal was a pattern from which to copy the hitch on the other. In this painful manner we learned the Squaw Hitch, which, for a long time, was to be the extent of our knowledge. However, we got on well enough, and mounted steadily by the turns and twists of an awful road, following the general course of the river below us.

On the hills grew high brush, some of it very beautiful. The buckthorn, for example, was just coming out; and the dogwood, and the mountain laurel. At first these clumps of bush were few and scattered; and the surface of the hills, carpeted with short grass, rolled gently away, or broke in stone dikes and outcrops. Then later, as we mounted, they drew together until they covered the mountainsides completely, save where oaks and madrone kept clear some space for themselves. After a time we began to see a scrubby long-needled pine thrusting its head here and there above the undergrowth. That was as far as we got that day. In the hollow of a ravine we found a tiny rill of water, and there we camped. Johnny offered some slight objections at first. It was only two o'clock of the afternoon, the trees were scrubby, the soil dusty, the place generally uncomfortable. But Yank shook his head.

"If we knew how they played this game, it might be all right to go ahead. But we don't," said he. "I've been noticing this trail pretty close; and I ain't seen much water except in the river; and that's an awful ways down. Maybe we'll find some water over the next hill, and maybe we won't. But we *know* there's water here. Then there's the question of hoss thieves. McClellan strikes me as a man to be believed. I don't know how they act; but you bet no hoss thief gets off with my hoss and me watchin'.

But at night it's different. I don't know how they do
things. But I *do* know that if we tie our hosses next us,
they won't be stolen. And that's what I aim to do. But
if we do that, we got to give them a chance to eat, hain't
we? So we'll let them feed the rest of the afternoon, and
we'll tie em up to-night."

This was much talk for Yank. In fact, the only time
that taciturn individual ever would open up was in explanation of or argument about some expedient of wilderness life or travel. It sounded entirely logical. So we
made camp.

Yank turned the two horses out into a grass meadow,
and sat, his back against an oak tree, smoking his pipe
and watching them. Johnny and I unrolled the beds,
sorted out the simple cooking utensils, and started to
cook. Occasional travellers on the road just above us
shouted out friendly greetings. They were a miscellaneous lot. Most were headed toward the mountains.
These journeyed in various ways. Some walked afoot
and unencumbered, some carried apparently all their
belongings on their backs, one outfit comprising three
men had three saddle horses and four packs — a princely
caravan. One of the *cargadore's* pack-trains went up the
road enveloped in a thick cloud of dust — twenty or
thirty pack-mules and four men on horseback herding
them forward. A white mare, unharnessed save for a
clanging bell, led the way; and all the mules followed her
slavishly, the nose of one touching the tail of the other,
as is the mule's besotted fashion. They were gay little
animals, with silver buttons on their harness, and yellow

sheepskin linings to their saddles. They carried a great
variety of all sorts of things; and at the freighting rates
quoted to us must have made money for their owners.
Their drivers were a picturesque quartette in sombreros,
wide sashes, and flowing garments. They sat their animals
with a graceful careless ease beautiful to behold.

Near sundown two horsemen turned off the trail and
rode down to our little trickle of water. When they drew
near we recognized in one of them Don Gaspar Martinez.
He wore still his gorgeous apparel of the day before, with
only the addition of a pair of heavy silver ornamented
spurs on his heels, and a brace of pistols in his sash. His
horse, a magnificent chestnut, was harnessed in equal gor-
geousness, with silvered broad bit, silver chains jangling
therefrom, a plaited rawhide bridle and reins, a carved
leather, high-pommelled saddle, also silver ornamented,
and a bright coloured, woven saddle blanket beneath.
The animal stepped daintily and proudly, lifting his
little feet and planting them among the stones as though
fastidiously. The man who rode with Don Gaspar was
evidently of a lower class. He was, however, a straight
handsome young fellow enough, with a dark clear complexion, a small moustache, and a pleasant smile. His
dress and accoutrements were on the same general order
as those of Don Gaspar, but of quieter colour and more
serviceable material. His horse, however, was of the same
high-bred type. A third animal followed, unled, packed
with two cowhide boxes.

The Spaniard rode up to us and saluted courteously;
then his eye lit with recognition.

"Ah," said he, "the good friends of our Capitan Sutter! This is to be well met. If it is not too much I would beg the favour of to camp."

"By all means, Don Gaspar," said Johnny rising. "The pleasure is of course our own."

Again saluting us, Don Gaspar and his companion withdrew a short distance up the little meadow. There the Spaniard sat down beneath a bush and proceeded to smoke a cigaretto, while his companion unsaddled the horses, turned them loose to graze, stacked up their saddles, and made simple camping arrangements.

"Old Plush Pants doesn't intend to do any work if he catches sight of it first," observed Johnny.

"Probably the other man is a servant?" I suggested.

"More likely a sort of dependent," amended Johnny. "They run a kind of patriarchal establishment, I've been told."

"Don't use them big words, Johnny," complained Yank, coming up with the horses

"I meant they make the poor relations and kid brothers do the hustling," said Johnny.

"Now I understand you," said Yank. "I wish I could see what *they* do with their hosses nights. I bet they know how. And if I was a hoss thief, I'd surely take a long chance for that chestnut gelding."

"You might wander over later and find out," I suggested.

"And get my system full of lead — sure," said Yank.

The two camps did not exchange visits. We caught the flicker of their little fire; but we were really too tired to be curious, and we turned in early, our two animals tied fast to small trees at our feet.

The next day lifted us into the mountains. Big green peaks across which hung a bluish haze showed themselves between the hills. The latter were more precipitous; and the brush had now given way to pines of better size and quality than those seen lower down. The river foamed over rapids or ran darkling in pools and stretches. Along the roadside, rarely, we came upon rough-looking log cabins, or shacks of canvas, or tents. The owners were not at home. We thought them miners; but in the light of subsequent knowledge I believe that unlikely — the diggings were farther in.

We came upon the diggings quite suddenly. The trail ran around the corner of a hill; and there they were below us! In the wide, dry stream bottom perhaps fifty men were working busily, like a lot of ants. Some were picking away at the surface of the ground, others had dug themselves down waist deep, and stooped and rose like legless bodies. Others had disappeared below ground, and showed occasionally only as shovel blades. From so far above the scene was very lively and animated, for each was working like a beaver, and the red shirts made gay little spots of colour. On the hillside clung a few white tents and log cabins; but the main town itself, we later discovered, as well as the larger diggings, lay around the bend and upstream.

We looked all about us for some path leading down to the river, but could find none; so perforce we had to continue on along the trail. Thus we entered the camp of Hangman's Gulch; for if it had been otherwise I am sure we would have located promptly where we had seen those red-shirted men.

The camp consisted merely of a closer-knit group of tents, log shacks, and a few larger buildings constructed of a queer combination of heavy hewn timbers and canvas. We saw nobody at all, though in some of the larger buildings we heard signs of life. However, we did not wait to investigate the wonders of Hangman's Gulch, but drove our animals along the one street, looking for the trail that should lead us back to the diggings. We missed it, somehow, but struck into a beaten path that took us upstream. This we followed a few hundred yards. It proceeded along a rough, boulder-strewn river-bed, around a point of rough, jagged rocks, and out to a very wide gravelly flat through which the river had made itself a narrow channel. The flat swarmed with men, all of them busy, and very silent.

Leading our pack-horses we approached the nearest pair of these men, and stood watching them curiously. One held a coarse screen of willow which he shook continuously above a common cooking-pot, while the other slowly shovelled earth over this sieve. When the two pots, which with the shovel seemed to be all the tools these men possessed, had been half filled thus with the fine earth, the men carried them to the river. We followed. The miners carefully submerged the pots, and commenced to stir their contents with their doubled fists. The light earth muddied the water, floated upward, and then flowed slowly over the rim of the pots and down the current. After a few minutes of this, they lifted the pots carefully, drained off the water, and started back.

"May we look?" ventured Johnny.

The taller man glanced at us, and our pack-horses, and nodded. This was the first time he had troubled to take a good look at us. The bottom of the pot was covered with fine black sand in which we caught the gleam and sparkle of something yellow.

"Is that gold?" I asked, awed.

"That's gold," the man repeated, his rather saturnine features lighting up with a grin. Then seeing our interest, he unbent a trifle. "We dry the sand, and then blow it away," he explained; and strode back to where his companion was impatiently waiting.

We stumbled on over the rocks and débris. There were probably something near a hundred men at work in the gulch. We soon observed that the pot method was considered a very crude and simple way of getting out the gold. Most of the men carried iron pans full of the earth to the waterside, where, after submerging until the lighter earth had floated off, they slopped the remainder over the side with a peculiar twisting, whirling motion, leaving at last only the black sand — and the gold! These pan miners were in the great majority. But one group of four men was doing business on a larger scale. They had constructed what looked like a very shallow baby-cradle on rockers into which they poured their earth and water. By rocking the cradle violently but steadily, they spilled the mud over the sides. Cleats had been nailed in the bottom to catch the black sand.

We wandered about here and there, looking with all our eyes. The miners were very busy and silent, but quite friendly, and allowed us to examine as much as we pleased the results of their operations. In the pots and cradles the yellow flake gold glittered plainly, contrasting with the black sand. In the pans, however, the residue spread out fan-shaped along the angle between the bottom and the side, and at the apex the gold lay heavy and beautiful all by itself. The men were generally bearded, tanned with working in this blinding sun, and plastered liberally with the red earth. We saw some queer sights, however; as when we came across a jolly pair dressed in what were the remains of ultra-fashionable garments up to and including plug hats! At one side working some distance from the stream were small groups of native Californians or Mexicans. They did not trouble to carry the earth all the way to the river; but, after screening it roughly, tossed it into the air above a canvas, thus winnowing out the heavier pay dirt. I thought this must be very disagreeable.

As we wandered about here and there among all these men so busily engaged, and with our own eyes saw pan after pan show gold, actual metallic guaranteed gold, such as rings and watches and money are made of, a growing excitement possessed us, the excitement of a small boy with a new and untried gun. We wanted to get at it ourselves. Only we did not know how.

Finally Yank approached one of the busy miners.

"Stranger," said he, "we're new to this. Maybe you can tell us where we can dig a little of this gold ourselves."

The man straightened his back, to exhibit a roving humorous blue eye, with which he examined Yank from top to toe.

"If," said he, "it wasn't for that eighteen-foot cannon you carry over your left arm, and a cold gray pair of eyes you carry in your head, I'd direct you up the sidehill yonder, and watch you sweat. As it is, you can work anywhere anybody else isn't working. Start in!"

"Can we dig right next to you, then?" asked Yank, nodding at an unbroken piece of ground just upstream.

The miner clambered carefully out of his waist-deep trench, searched his pockets, produced a pipe and tobacco. After lighting this he made Yank a low bow.

"Thanks for the compliment; but I warn you, this claim of mine is not very rich. I'm thinking of trying somewhere else."

"Don't you get any gold?"

"Oh, a few ounces a day."

"That suits me for a beginning," said Yank decidedly. "Come on, boys!"

The miner hopped back into his hole, only to stick his head out again for the purpose of telling us:

"Mind you keep fifteen feet away!"

With eager hands we slipped a pick and shovels from beneath the pack ropes, undid our iron bucket, and without further delay commenced feverishly to dig.

Johnny held the pail, while Yank and I vied with each other in being the first to get our shovelfuls into that receptacle. As a consequence we nearly swamped the pail first off, and had to pour some of the earth out again.

Then we all three ran down to the river and took turns
stirring that mud pie beneath the gently flowing waters
in the manner of the "pot panners" we had first watched.
After a good deal of trouble we found ourselves possessed
of a thick layer of rocks and coarse pebbles.

"We forgot to screen it," I pointed out.

"We haven't any screen," said Johnny.

"Let's pick 'em out by hand?" suggested Yank.

We did so. The process emptied the pail. Each of us
insisted on examining closely; but none of us succeeded in
creating out of our desires any of that alluring black
sand.

"I suppose we can't expect to get colour every time?"
observed Johnny disappointedly. "Let's try her again."

We tried her again: and yet again; and then some more;
but always with the same result. Our hands became
puffed and wrinkled with constant immersion in the water,
and began to feel sore from the continual stirring of the
rubble.

"Something wrong," grunted Johnny into the abysmal
silence in which we had been carrying on our work.

"We can't expect it every time," I reminded him.

"All the others seem to."

"Well, maybe we've struck a blank place; let's try
somewhere else," suggested Yank.

Johnny went over to speak to our neighbour, who
was engaged in tossing out shovelfuls of earth from an
excavation into which he had nearly disappeared. At
Johnny's hail, he straightened his back, so that his head
bobbed out of the hole like a prairie dog.

"No, it doesn't matter where you dig," he answered Johnny's question. "The pay dirt is everywhere."

So we moved on a few hundred feet, picked another unoccupied patch, and resumed our efforts. No greater success rewarded us here.

"I believe maybe we ought to go deeper," surmised Yank.

"Some of these fellows are taking their dirt right off top of the ground," objected Johnny.

However, we unlimbered the pickaxe and went deeper; to the extent of two feet or more. It was good hard work, especially as we were all soft for it. The sun poured down on our backs with burning intensity; our hands blistered; and the round rocks and half-cemented rubble that made the bar were not the easiest things in the world to remove. However, we kept at it. Yank and I, having in times past been more or less accustomed to this sort of thing, got off much easier than did poor Johnny. About two feet down we came to a mixed coarse sand and stones, a little finer than the top dirt. This seemed to us promising, so we resumed our washing operations. They bore the same results as had the first; which was just the whole of nothing.

"We've got to hit it somewhere," said Johnny between his teeth. "Let's try another place."

We scrambled rather wearily, but with a dogged determination, out of our shallow hole. Our blue-eyed, long-bearded friend was sitting on a convenient boulder near at hand, his pipe between his teeth, watching our operations.

"Got any tobacco, boys?" he inquired genially. "Smoked my last until to-night, unless you'll lend."

Yank produced a plug, from which the stranger shaved some parings.

"Struck the dirt?" he inquired. "No, I see you haven't." He stretched himself and arose. "You aren't washing this stuff!" he cried in amazement, as his eye took in fully what we were about.

Then we learned what we might have known before — but how should we? — that the gold was not to be found in any and every sort of loose earth that might happen to be lying about, but only in either a sort of blue clay or a pulverized granite. Sometimes this "pay dirt" would be found atop the ground. Again, the miner had to dig for it.

"All the surface diggings are taken up," our friend told us. "So now you have to dig deep. It's about four feet down where I'm working. It'll probably be deeper up here. You'd better move back where you were."

Yank, stretched himself upright.

"Look here," he said decidedly; "let's get a little sense into ourselves. Here's our pore old hosses standing with their packs on, and we no place to stay, and no dinner; and we're scratchin' away at this bar like a lot of fool hens. There's other days comin'."

Johnny and I agreed with the common sense of the thing, but reluctantly. Now that we knew how, our enthusiasm surged up again. We wanted to get at it. The stranger's eyes twinkled sympathetically.

"Here, boys," said he, "I know just how you feel. Come with me."

He snatched up our bucket and strode back to his

own claim, where he filled the receptacle with some of the earth he had thrown out.

"Go pan that," he advised us kindly.

We raced to the water, and once more stirred about the heavy contents of the pail until they had floated off with the water. In the bottom lay a fine black residue; and in that residue glittered the tiny yellow particles. We had actually panned our first gold!

Our friend examined it critically.

"That's about a twelve-cent pan," he adjudged it.

Somehow, in a vague way, we had unreasonably expected millions at a twist of the wrist; and the words, "twelve cents," had a rankly penurious sound to us. However, the miner patiently explained that a twelve-cent pan was a very good one; and indubitably it was real gold.

Yank, being older and less excitable, had not accompanied us to the waterside.

"Well, boys," he drawled, "that twelve cents is highly satisfactory, of course; but in the meantime we've lost about six hundred dollars' worth of hoss and grub."

Surely enough, our animals had tired of waiting for us, and had moved out packs and all. We hastily shouldered our implements.

"Don't you want to keep this claim next me?" inquired our acquaintance.

We stopped.

"Surely!" I replied. "But how do we do it?"

"Just leave your pick and shovel in the hole."

"Won't some one steal them?"

"No."

"What's to prevent?" I asked a little skeptically.

"Miners' law," he replied.

We almost immediately got trace of our strayed animals, as a number of men had seen them going upstream. In fact we had no difficulty whatever in finding them for they had simply followed up the rough stream-bed between the cañon walls until it had opened up to a gentler slope and a hanging garden of grass and flowers. Here they had turned aside and were feeding. We caught them, and were just heading them back, when Yank stopped short.

"What's the matter with this here?" he inquired. "Here's feed, and water near, and it ain't so very far back to the diggings."

We looked about us, for the first time with seeing eyes. The little up-sloping meadow was blue and dull red with flowers; below us the stream brawled foam flecked among black rocks; the high hills rose up to meet the sky, and at our backs across the way the pines stood thick serried. Far up in the blue heavens some birds were circling slowly. Somehow the leisurely swing of these unhasting birds struck from us the feverish hurry that had lately filled our souls. We drew deep breaths; and for the first time the great peace and majesty of these California mountains cooled our spirits.

"I think it's a bully place, Yank," said Johnny soberly, "and that little bench up above us looks flat."

We clambered across the slant of the flower-spangled meadow to the bench, just within the fringe of the pines. It proved to be flat, and from the edge of it down the hill seeped a little spring marked by the feathery bracken.

THE GOLD TRAIL

We entered a cool green place, peopled with shadows and the rare, considered notes of soft-voiced birds. Just over our threshold, as it were, was the sunlit, chirpy, buzzing, bright-coloured, busy world. Overhead a wind of many voices hummed through the pine tops. The golden sunlight flooded the mountains opposite, flashed from the stream, lay languorous on the meadow. Long bars of it slanted through an unguessed gap in the hills behind us to touch with magic the very tops of the trees over our heads. The sheen of the precious metal was over the land.

CHAPTER XVI

THE FIRST GOLD

We arose before daylight, picketed our horses, left our dishes unwashed, and hurried down to the diggings just at sun-up carrying our gold pans or "washbowls," and our extra tools. The bar was as yet deserted. We set to work with a will, taking turns with the pickaxe and the two shovels. I must confess that our speed slowed down considerably after the first wild burst, but we kept at it steadily. It was hard work, and there is no denying it, just the sort of plain hard work the day labourer does when he digs sewer trenches in the city streets Only worse, perhaps, owing to the nature of the soil. It has struck me since that those few years of hard labour in the diggings, from '49 to '53 or '54, saw more actual manual toil accomplished than was ever before performed in the same time by the same number of men. The dis-couragement of those returning we now understood. They had expected to take the gold without toil; and were dis-mayed at the labour it had required. At any rate, we thought we were doing our share that morning, especially after the sun came up. We wielded our implements man-fully, piled our débris to one side, and gradually achieved a sort of crumbling uncertain excavation reluctant to stay emptied.

About an hour after our arrival the other miners began to appear, smoking their pipes. They stretched themselves lazily, spat upon their hands, and set to. Our friend of the day before nodded at us cheerfully, and hopped down into his hole.

We removed what seemed to us tons of rock. About noon, just as we were thinking rather dispiritedly of knocking off work for a lunch — which in our early morning eagerness we had forgotten to bring — Johnny turned up a shovelful whose lower third consisted of the pulverized bluish clay. We promptly forgot both lunch and our own weariness.

"Hey!" shouted our friend, scrambling from his own claim. "Easy with the rocks! What are you conducting here? a volcano?" He peered down at us. "Pay dirt, hey? Well, take it easy; it won't run away!"

Take it easy! As well ask us to quit entirely! We tore at the rubble, which aggravatingly and obstinately cascaded down upon us from the sides; we scraped eagerly for more of that blue clay; at last we had filled our three pans with a rather mixed lot of the dirt, and raced to the river. Johnny fell over a boulder and scattered his panful far and wide. His manner of scuttling back to the hole after more reminded me irresistibly of the way a contestant in a candle race hurries back to the starting point to get his candle relighted.

We panned that dirt clumsily and hastily enough; and undoubtedly lost much valuable sand overside; but we ended each with a string of colour. We crowded together comparing our "pans." Then we went crazy. I suppose we had about a quarter of a dollar's worth of gold between us, but that was not the point. The long journey with all its hardships and adventures, the toil, the uncertainty, the hopes, the disappointments and reactions had at last their visible tangible conclusion. The tiny flecks of gold were a symbol. We yapped aloud, we kicked up our heels, we shook hands, we finally joined hands and danced around and around.

From all sides the miners came running up, dropping their tools with a clatter. We were assailed by a chorus of eager cries.

"What is it, boys?"   "A strike?"   "Whereabouts is your claim?"   "Is it 'flour' or 'flake'?"   "Let's see!"

They crowded around in a dense mob, and those nearest jostled to get a glimpse of our pans. Suddenly sobered by this interest in our doings, we would have edged away could we have got hold of our implements.

"Wall, I'll be durned!" snorted a tall state of Maine man in disgust. "This ain't no strike! This is an insane asylum."

The news slowly penetrated the crowd. A roar of laughter went up. Most of the men were hugely amused; but some few were so disgusted at having been fooled that they were almost inclined to take it as a personal affront that we had not made the expected "strike."

"You'd think they was a bunch of confounded Kesky-dees," growled one of them.

The miners slowly dispersed, returning to their own diggings. Somewhat red-faced, and very silent, we gathered up our pans and slunk back to the claim. Our neighbour stuck his head out of his hole. He alone had not joined the stampede in our direction.

"How do you like being popular heroes?" he grinned.

Johnny made as though to shy a rock at him, whereupon he ducked below ground.

However, our spirits soon recovered. We dumped the black sand into a little sack we had brought for the purpose. It made quite an appreciable bulge in that sack. We did not stop to realize that most of the bulge was sack and sand, and mighty little of it gold. It was something tangible and valuable; and we were filled with a tremendous desire to add to its bulk.

We worked with entire absorption, quite oblivious to all that was going on about us. It was only by accident that Yank looked up at last, so I do not know how long Don Gaspar had been there.

"Will you look at that!" cried Yank.

Don Gaspar, still in his embroidered boots, his crimson velvet breeches, his white linen, and his sombrero, but without the blue and silver jacket, was busily wielding a pickaxe a hundred feet or so away. His companion, or servant, was doing the heavier shovel work.

"Why, oh, why!" breathed Johnny at last, "do you suppose, if he *must* mine, he doesn't buy himself a suit of dungarees or a flannel shirt?"

"I'll bet it's the first hard work he ever did in his life," surmised Yank.

"And I'll bet he won't do that very long," I guessed.

But Don Gaspar seemed to have more sticking power than we gave him credit for. We did not pay him much further attention, for we were busy with our own affairs; but every time we glanced in his direction he appeared to be still at it. Our sack of sand was growing heavier; as indeed were our limbs. As a matter of fact we had been at harder work than any of us had been accustomed to, for very long hours, beneath a scorching sun, without food, and under strong excitement. We did not know when to quit; but the sun at last decided it for us by dipping below the mountains to the west.

We left our picks and shovels in our pit; but carried back with us our pans, for in them we wished to dry out our sand. The horses were still at their picket ropes; and we noticed near the lower end of the meadow, but within the bushes, three more animals moving slowly. A slim column of smoke ascended from beyond the bushes. Evidently we had neighbours.

We were dog tired, and so far starved that we did not know we were hungry. My eyes felt as though they must look like holes burned in a blanket. We lit a fire, and near it placed our panful of sand. But we did not take time to cook ourselves a decent meal; we were much too excited for that. A half-made pot of coffee, some pork burned crisp, and some hard bread comprised our supper. Then Yank and I took a handful of the dried sand in the other two pans, and commenced cautiously to blow it away. Johnny hovered over us full of suggestions, and premonitions of calamity.

"Don't blow too, hard, fellows," he besought us; "you'll blow away the gold! For heaven's sake, go easy!"

We growled at him, and blew. I confess that my heart went fast with great anxiety, as though the stakes of my correct blowing were millions. However, as we later discovered, it is almost impossible to blow incorrectly.

There is something really a little awing about pure gold new-born from the soil. Gold is such a stable article, so strictly guarded, so carefully checked and counted, that the actual production of metal that has had no existence savours almost of the alchemical. We had somewhat less than an ounce, to be sure; but that amount in flake gold bulks considerably. We did not think of it in terms of its worth in dollars; we looked on it only as the Gold, and we stared at the substantial little heap of yellow particles with fascinated awe.

CHAPTER XVII
THE DIGGINGS

The following days were replicas of the first. We ate hurriedly at odd times; we worked feverishly; we sank into our tumbled blankets at night too tired to wiggle. But the buckskin sack of gold was swelling and rounding out most satisfactorily. By the end of the week it contained over a pound!

But the long hours, the excitement, and the inadequate food told on our nerves. We snapped at each other impatiently at times; and once or twice came near to open quarrelling. Johnny and I were constantly pecking at each other over the most trivial concerns.

One morning we were halfway to the bar when we remembered that we had neglected to picket out the horses. It was necessary for one of us to go back, and we were all reluctant to do so.

"I'll be damned if I'm going to lug 'way up that hill," I growled to myself. "I tied them up yesterday, anyway."

Johnny caught this.

"Well, it wasn't your turn yesterday," he pointed out, "and it is to-day. I've got nothing to do with what you chose to do yesterday."

"Or any other day," I muttered.

"What's that?" cried Johnny truculently. "I couldn't hear. Speak up!"

We were flushed, and eying each other malevolently.

"That'll do!" said Yank, with an unexpected tone of authority. "Nobody will go back and nobody will go ahead. We'll just sit down on this log, yere, while we smoke one pipe apiece. I've got something to say."

Johnny and I turned on him with a certain belligerency mingled with surprise. Yank had so habitually acted the part of taciturnity that his decided air of authority confused us. His slouch had straightened, his head was up, his mild eye sparkled. Suddenly I felt like a bad small boy; and I believe Johnny was the same. After a moment's hesitation we sat down on the log.

"Now," said Yank firmly, "it's about time we took stock. We been here now five days; we ain't had a decent meal of vittles in that time; we ain't fixed up our camp a mite; we ain't been to town to see the sights; we don't even know the looks of the man that's camped down below us. We've been too danged busy to be decent. Now we're goin' to call a halt. I should jedge we have a pound of gold, or tharabouts. How much is that worth, Johnny? You can figger in yore head."

"Along about two hundred and fifty dollars," said Johnny after a moment.

"Well, keep on figgerin'. How much does that come to apiece?"

"About eighty dollars, of course."

"And dividin' eighty by five?" persisted Yank.

'Sixteen."

"Well," drawled Yank, his steely blue eye softening to a twinkle, "sixteen dollars a day is fair wages, to be sure; but nothin' to get wildly excited over." He surveyed the two of us with some humour. "Hadn't thought of it that way, had you?" he asked. "Nuther had I until last night. I was so dog tired I couldn't sleep, and I got to figgerin' a little on my own hook."

"Why, I can do better than that in San Francisco — with half the work!" I cried.

"Maybe for a while," said Yank, "but here we got a chance to make a big strike most any time; and in the meantime to make good wages. But we ain't going to do it any quicker by killin' ourselves. Now to-day is Sunday. I ain't no religious man; but Sunday is a good day to quit. I propose we go back to camp peaceable, make a decent place to stay, cook ourselves up a squar' meal, wash out our clothes, visit the next camp, take a look at town, and enjoy ourselves."

Thus vanished the first and most wonderful romance of the gold. Reduced to wages it was somehow no longer so marvellous. The element of uncertainty was always there, to be sure; and an inexplicable fascination; but no longer had we any desire to dig up the whole place immediately. I suppose we moved nearly as much earth, but the fibres of our minds were relaxed, and we did it more easily and with less nervous wear and tear.

Also, as Yank suggested, we took pains to search out our fellow beings. The camper below us proved to be Don Gaspar, velvet breeches and all. He received us hospitably, and proffered perfumed cigarettos which we did **not** like, but which we smoked out of politeness. Our common ground of meeting was at first the natural one of the gold diggings. Don Gaspar and his man, whom he called Vasquez, had produced somewhat less flake gold than ourselves, but exhibited a half-ounce nugget and several smaller lumps. We could not make him out. Neither his appearance nor his personal equipment suggested necessity; and yet he laboured as hard as the rest of us. His gaudy costume was splashed and grimy with the red mud, although evidently he had made some attempt to brush it. The linen was, of course, hopeless. He showed us the blisters on his small aristocratic-looking hands.

"It is the hard work" he stated simply, "but one gets the gold."

From that subject we passed on to horses. He confessed that he was uneasy as to the safety of his own magnificent animals; and succeeded in alarming us as to our own.

"Thos' Indian," he told us, "are always out to essteal; and the *paisanos*. It has been tole me that Andreas Amijo and his robbers are near. Some day we loose our horse!"

Our anxiety at this time was given an edge by the fact that the horses, having fed well, and becoming tired of the same place, were inclined to stray. It was impossible to keep them always on picket lines — the nature of the meadow would not permit it — and they soon learned to be very clever with their hobbles. Several mornings we put in an hour or so hunting them up and bringing them in before we could start work for the day. This wasted both time and temper. The result was that we drifted into partnership with Don Gaspar and Vasquez. I do not remember who proposed the arrangement; indeed, I am inclined to think it just came about naturally from our many discussions on the subject. Under the terms of it we appointed Vasquez to cook all the meals, take full care of the horses, chop the wood, draw the water, and keep camp generally. The rest of us worked in couples at the bar. We divided the gold into five equal parts.

Our production at this time ran from five to seven ounces a day, which was, of course, good wages, but would not make our fortunes. We soon fell into a rut, working cheerfully and interestedly, but without excitement. The nature of our produce kept our attention. We should long since have wearied of any other job requiring an equal amount of work, but there was a never-ending fascination in blowing away the débris from the virgin gold. And one day, not far from us, two Hollanders — "Dutch Charleys," as the miners called that nationality — scooped from a depression in the bedrock mixed coarse gold thirty odd pounds in weight — over $5,000! That revived our interest, you may be sure.

Most of the miners seemed content to stick to panning. Their argument was that by this method they could accumulate a fair amount of dust, and ran just as good chances of a "strike" as the next fellow. Furthermore, they had no tools, no knowledge and no time to make cradles. Those implements had to be very accurately constructed.

We discussed this matter almost every evening. Yank was a great believer in improving the efficiency of our equipment.

"It'll handle four or five times the dirt," said he "and that means four or five times the dust."

"There's no lumber to be had anywhere," I objected

"I know where there's three good stout boxes made of real lumber that we can get for forty dollars," said Yank

"You can't cut that stuff up with an axe."

"John Semple has a saw, a plane, and a hammer; he's a carpenter."

"You bet he is!" agreed Johnny. "I was talking to him last night. He won't lend his tools; and he won't hire them. He'll come with them for fifty dollars a day."

"All right," said Yank, "let's hire him. I'm pretty handy, and I'll stay right in camp and help him. Vasquez can go dig instead of me. We can get 'em cut out and fitted in two days, anyway. We've got the money!"

I think none of us was very enthusiastic on this subject except Yank; but he finally carried the day. Vasquez, somewhat to his chagrin, I thought, resumed his shovel. Yank and John Semple tinkered away for the allotted two days, and triumphantly produced two cradles at a cost of a round one hundred and fifty dollars.

Although we had been somewhat doubtful as to the advisability of spending this sum, I am bound to state that Yank's insistence was justified. It certainly made the work easier. We took turns shovelling the earth and pouring in the water, and "rocking the baby." Our production jumped two or three ounces a day.

CHAPTER XVIII

BEGINNINGS OF GOVERNMENT

Our visit to the town we postponed from day to day because we were either too busy or too tired. We thought we could about figure out what that crude sort of village would be like. Then on Saturday evening our neighbour with the twinkling eye —whom we called McNally, without conviction, because he told us to — informed us that there would be a miners' meeting next day, and that we would be expected to attend.

Accordingly we visited the town. The street was full of men idling slowly to and fro. All the larger structures were wide open, and from within could be heard the sounds of hurdy-gurdies, loud laughter and noisy talk. At one end of the street a group was organizing a horse race; and toward this Don Gaspar took his immediate departure. A smaller group surrounded two wrestlers. At one side a jumping match was going on.

Among the usual incongruities we saw some that amused us more than ordinarily. The Indians, for example, were rather numerous, and remarkable. One wore as his sole garment an old dress coat: another had tied a pair of trousers around his waist; a third had piled a half dozen hats atop, one over the other; and many had on two or more coats. They were, to a man, well drunken.

Their squaws, fat and unattractive, squatted outside the single store of the place. We saw also a dozen or so white men dressed very plainly and shabbily, tall, lank, and spindly, rather weakly in general appearance, their faces sallow, their eyes rather childish but crafty and treacherous, their hair thin and straight. The points in common were pointed, nearly brimless hats, like small extinguishers, and that they were the only men to use suspenders. They were from Pike County in Missouri; and in our experience with them we found their appearance a close indication of their character. They were exceedingly skilful with both axe and rifle, were expert backwoodsmen, but without physical strength, very childish and ignorant, vindictive, narrow, and so extremely clannish and tenacious of their own opinions that they were always an exasperating element to be reckoned with, in any public matter. We saw also a compact little group of dark small men, with bright eyes and quick manners. They held close together and chattered like a lot of magpies. McNally, who had spotted us from afar, informed us that these were "keskydees," and that they always did stick close together.

"What are 'keskydees'?" I asked him.

"That's what everybody calls them," said McNally. "I suppose it's because they always say it, 'Keskydee, keskydee,' like a lot of chickadees."

"French!" cried Johnny, suddenly enlightened. "*Q' estce qu'il dit.*"

"Yes, that's it," agreed McNally; "keskydee. What does it mean, anyway?"

"What is he saying," translated Johnny.

At this time there were a great many French in California; and for a number of years I could not quite understand why. Then I learned that most of them were prize winners in a series of lotteries, called the Lotteries of the Golden Ingot. The prizes were passages to California, and the lotteries were very popular. The French, or keskydees, as they were universally called, always went about in gangs, while the other nationalities were more inclined to amalgamate with the rest of the community. We saw, also, several "Dutch Charleys" who had struck it rich. They were moon-faced, bland, chuckle-headed looking men, generally with walrus moustaches, squat and heavy, with fatuous, placid smiles. I suppose they had no real idea of values, but knew only the difference between having money and not having money. These prosperous individuals carried two or even more watches at the ends of long home-made chains constructed of gold nuggets fastened together with lengths of copper wire. The chains were looped around their necks, about their shoulders and waists, and hung down in long festoons. We had three apparently, of these Dutch Charleys, all deadly rivals in magnificence. They paraded slowly up and down the street, quite satisfied with themselves, and casting malevolent glances at each other when they passed.

The two gambling places and saloons were hard at it. The low rooms were full of smoke, and crowded with slowly jostling men. In contrast to the deadly quiet of such places in San Francisco, these were full of noise and hubbub. The men moved restlessly, threw down their little bags of dust impatiently, and accepted victory or defeat with very audible comments The gamblers, dressed in black, pale, sat steady-eyed and silent behind their layouts. I suppose the life must already have developed, if not a type, at least a uniform mental attitude that showed itself in outward expression. That was, first of all, an intent, quiet watchfulness; and, secondly, an iron resolution to meet whatever offered. The gambler must be prepared instantly to shoot; and at the same time he must realize fully that shooting is going to get him in trouble. For the sympathy of a mining camp was generally strongly against him when it came to a question of this sort. We treated ourselves to a drink at the bar, and went outside.

Already the drift of miners was toward the end of the street where a good sized crowd had gathered. We fell in. Under a large oak tree had been placed a barrel and several boxes from the store, and on these latter our friend John Semple, the carpenter, was mounting.

"John's the *alcalde*," McNally explained to us. "He's the most level-headed man in these diggings."

Most of the miners sat down on the ground in front, though some remained afoot. Semple rapped sharply on the barrel with the muzzle of his revolver.

"This is a miners' meeting," he stated briefly. "And we have several things to talk about. Most important thing, 'cordin' to my notion, is this row about that big nugget. Seems these yere three men, whose names I dis-remember, is partners and is panning down there in the lower diggings, and while one of them is grubbing around with a shovel getting ready to fill the company pan, he sees this yere nugget in the shovel, and annexes it. Now he claims it's his nugget, and the rest of 'em claim it belongs to all of them as partners. How about it?"

Two men sprang to their feet and began to talk.

"You set down!" Semple ordered them. "You ain't got nothing to do with decidin' this. We'll let you know what to do. If the facts ain't right, as I stated 'em, say so; but we don't want no theories out of you. *Set down!* I say."

They subsided, and a silence fell which no one seemed inclined to break.

"Well," said Semple impatiently, "come on! Speak up! Whar's all this assorted lot of theories I been hearing in the say-loons ever since that nugget was turned up?"

A man with the most extraordinarily ragged garments got to his feet and began to speak in a pleasant and culti-vated voice.

"I have no solution to offer this company," said he, "but I am, or was, a New York lawyer; and if my knowledge of partnerships will help any, this is the New York law." He sketched briefly the New York rulings on partnerships, and sat down.

"Much obliged, I'm sure," said Semple cordially. "We're glad to know how they've figgered it out down thar. Only trouble, as far as I see, is that they ain't usually findin' many nuggets down that neck of the woods; so they ain't precisely fitted the case. Anybody know any-thing nearer to home?"

"I panned in Shirttail Bar last two months," blurted

a hoarse and embarrassed individual, without rising, "and down thar they had a reg'lation that airy nugget that weighs over a half ounce that is found before the dirt is thrown in the cradle belongs to the man that finds it, and not to the company. Of course this here is a pan, and not a cradle."

"That's more like business. Anybody know if anywhar they do it the other way around?"

Apparently nobody did.

"Anybody got any idees as to why we shouldn't follow Shirttail in this matter? Dog-gone you! *Set down!* You ain't got nothin' to say here."

The man appealed to the crowd.

"Ain't I got a right to be heard in my own case?" he demanded.

"This ain't your case," persisted John Semple stoutly; "it's decidin' what the policy of this camp is goin' to be regardin' nuggets. Your dog-gone case is mighty unimportant and you're a prejudiced party. And if you don't set down, I'll come down there and argue with you! If none of you other fellows has anything to say, we'll vote on it."

We then and there decided, almost unanimously, to follow Shirttail.

"Now," resumed Semple, after this matter had been disposed of, "there's a bunch of these yere keskydees around throwin' assorted duckfits all this morning; and as near as I can make out they say somebody's jumped their claim or their camp, or something. Jim, supposin' you and your tin star saunter down and eject these jumpers."

A very tall, quiet, slow moving man arose, aimed his tobacco juice at a small tree, drawled out the words, "All right, Jedge," and departed, trailed by a half dozen jabbering keskydees, to whom he paid not the slightest attention.

"Now," said Semple, "we got a couple of Greasers yere caught stealin.' Buck Barry and Missouri Jones caught them at it, so there ain't much use hearin' witnesses as to the fact. Question is: what do we want to do with them?"

"What did they steal?" demanded a voice.

"They just nat'rally didn't steal *nothin'*," said a heavy built, square-jawed, clean-shaven man whom I guessed to be Buck Barry. "Not while I was around."

"Yes," persisted the other, "but what was they after."

"Oh, an extry pair of boots, and a shirt, and some tobacco, et cetery," replied Buck Barry contemptuously.

"Let's see them," shouted several voices.

After a moment's delay two ragged and furtive Mexicans were dragged before the assembly. A contemplative silence ensued. Then an elderly man with a square gray beard spoke up.

"Well," said he deliberately, "airy man so low down and shif'less and miserable as to go to stealin' boots and shirts and tobacco in this camp is shore outside my corral. He sure must be a miserable person. Why'n hell didn't Buck and Missou give him a few lifts with the toes of their boots, and not come botherin' us with them?"

Both Barry and Jones started to reply, but Semple cut them short.

"They was going to do just that," he announced, "but I persuaded them to bring this matter up before this meetin' because we got to begin to take some measures to stop this kind of a nuisance. There's a lot of undesirables driftin' into this camp lately. You boys all recall how last fall we kep' our dust under our bunks or most anywhere, and felt perfectly safe about it; but that ain't now. A man has to carry his dust right with him. Now, if we can't leave our tents feeling our goods is safe, what do you expect to do about it? We got to throw the fear of God into the black hearts of these hounds."

At this juncture Jim, the sheriff, returned and leaned nonchalantly against a tree, chewing a straw.

Accepting the point of view advanced by the chair, the miners decided that the two thieves should be whipped and banished from camp. A strong feeling prevailed that any man who, in this age of plenty, would descend to petty thieving, was a poor, miserable creature to be pitied. Some charitably inclined individual actually took up a small collection which was presented to the thieves after they had received their punishment.

"And now, *vamos*, git!" advised Semple. "And spread the glad tidings. We'll do the same by any more of you. Well, Jim?" he inquired of the sheriff.

Jim shifted his straw from the right corner of his mouth to the left.

"That outfit don't eject worth a cuss," said he laconically.

"How many of them is there?" asked Semple.

"Two — and a shotgun," stated Jim.

"I reckon we'll eject them if we say 'eject'!" cried some one truculently; and several others growled assent.

Jim cast a humorous eye in that direction.

"Oh, I reckon I'm ekal to the job," said he, "and is you say 'eject' again, why out they go. Only when I looked that outfit over, and saw they was only two of them and six of these jabbering keskydees, why, I jest nat'rally wondered whether it was by and according to the peace and dignity of this camp to mix up in that kind of a muss. I should think they ought to be capable of doin' their own ejecting."

A discussion arose on this point. The sentiment seemed unanimous that the Frenchmen ought to have been able to protect themselves, but was divided on the opinion as to how far the camp was now committed to action.

"They'll think they've bluffed us out, if we drop her now," argued one side.

"It ought not to be the policy of this camp to mix up with private quarrels," argued the other.

John Semple decided the question.

"It looks like we're in the hole," he admitted, "and have got to do something. Now, I tell you what I'm going to do: I'm going to have Jim here give these keskydees blank warrants that they can serve themselves, and to suit themselves."

This ingenious solution was very highly commended.

"Unless somebody else has something to bring up, I guess that's about all," announced Semple.

"No inquests?" some one asked.

"Nary an inquest. This camp is gettin' healthy. Adjourned!" And the meeting was brought to a formal conclusion by a tap of the pistol on the empty barrel.

CHAPTER XIX

SUNDAY AT HANGMAN'S GULCH

It was now about four o'clock. The crowd dispersed slowly in different directions, and to its different occupations and amusements. We wandered about, all eyes and ears. As yet we had not many acquaintances, and could not enter into the intimate bantering life of the old-timers. There was enough to interest us, however. A good many were beginning to show the drink. After a long period of hard labour even the most respectable of the miners would have at times strange reactions. That is another tale, however; and on this Sunday the drinking was productive only of considerable noise and boasting. Two old codgers, head to head, were bragging laboriously of their prowess as cooks. A small but interested group egged them on.

"Flapjacks?" enunciated one laboriously; "flapjacks? Why, my fren', *you* don't know nothin' about flapjacks. I grant you," said he, laying one hand on the other's arm, "I grant ye that maybe, *maybe*, mind you, you may know about mixin' flapjacks, and even about *cookin'* flapjacks. But wha' do you know about *flippin' flapjacks?*" He removed his hand from the other's arm. "Nawthin!" said he. "Now *I* am an exper'; a real exper'! When I want to flip a flapjack I just whirl

h.r up through the chimney and catch her by holdin'
the frying pan out'n the window!"

I found at another point a slender, beardless young
chap, with bright black eyes, and hectic cheeks, engaged
in sketching one of the miners who posed before him.
His touch was swift and sure, and his faculty at catching a
likeness remarkable. The sketch was completed and paid
for in ten minutes; and he was immediately besieged by
offers from men who wanted pictures of themselves or their
camps. He told me, between strokes of the pencil, that
he found this sort of thing more remunerative than the
mining for which he had come to the country, as he could
not stand the necessary hard work. Paper cost him two
dollars and a half a sheet; but that was about all his
expense. Alongside the street a very red-faced, bulbous-
nosed and ancient ruin with a patriarchal white beard was
preparing to give phrenological readings. I had seen
him earlier in the day, and had been amused at his impressive glib patter. Now, however, he had become
foolishly drunk. He mounted the same boxes that had
served as the executive desk, and invited custom. After
a moment's hesitation a burly, red-faced miner shouldered
his way through the group and sat down on the edge of the
boxes.

In the earlier and soberer part of the afternoon
the phrenologist had skilfully steered his way by the
safe stars of flattery. Now, as he ran his hands uncertainly
through the miner's thick hair, a look of mystification
crept into his bleary eyes. He felt again more carefully.

"Most 'xtraor'nary!" he muttered. "Fren's," said he.

still feeling at the man's head, "this person has the most extraor'nary bump of 'quisitiveness. Never felt one like it, 'xcept on th' cranium of a very celebrated thief an' robber. His bump of benev'lence 's a reg'lar hole. Bump of truthfulness don' somehow seem to be there at all. Bump of cowardice is 's big 's an egg. This man, fren's," said he, dropping the victim's head and advancing impressively, "is a very dangerous character. Look out for 'm. He's a liar, an' a thief, an' a coward, an' a ——"

"Well, you old son of a gun!" howled the miner, rising to his feet.

He seized the aged phrenologist, and flung him bodily straight through the sides of a large tent, and immediately dove after him in pursuit. There came from that tent a series of crashes, howls of rage and joy, the sounds of violent scuffling, and then there burst out through the doorway the thoroughly sobered phrenologist, his white beard streaming over one shoulder, his pop eyes bulging out, his bulbous nose quite purple, pursued by the angry miner and a score of the overjoyed populace interrupted in their gambling. Everybody but the two principals was gasping with laughter. It looked as though the miner might do his victim a serious injury, so I caught the pursuer around the shoulders and held him fast. He struggled violently, but was no match for my bulk, and I restrained him until he had cooled down somewhat, and had ceased trying to bite and kick me. Then all at once he laughed, and I released him. Of the phrenologist nothing remained but a thin cloud of dust hanging in the still air.

Yank and I then thought of going back to camp, and

began to look around after Johnny, who had disappeared, when McNally rolled up, inviting us to sup with him.

"You don't want to go home yet," he advised us. "Evening's the time to have fun. Never mind your friend; he's all right. Now you realize the disadvantage of living way off where you do. My hang-out is just down the street. Let's have a drink."

We accepted both his invitations. Then, after the supper, pipes alight, we sauntered down the street, a vast leisure expanding our horizons. At the street corner stood a tall, poetic-looking man, with dreamer's eyes, a violin clasped under his chin. He was looking straight past us all out into the dusk of the piney mountains beyond, his soul in the music he was producing. They were simple melodies, full of sentiment, and he played as though he loved them. Within the sound of his bow a dead silence reigned. Men stood with eyes cast down, their faces sobered, their eyes adream. One burly, reckless, red-faced individual, who had been bullying it up and down the street, broke into a sob which he violently suppressed, and then looked about fiercely, as though challenging any one to have heard. The player finished, tucked his violin and bow under his arm, and turned away. For a moment the crowd remained motionless, then slowly dispersed. This was John Kelly, a famous wandering minstrel of the camps, a strange, shy, poetic man, who never lacked for dust nor for friends, and who apparently sought for neither.

Under the softening influence of the music the crowd led a better life for about ten minutes.

We entered the gambling rooms, of which there were two, and had a drink of what McNally called "42 calibre whiskey" at the bar of each. In one of them we found Johnny, rather flushed, bucking a faro bank. Yank suggested that he join us, but he shook his head impatiently, and we moved on. In a tremendous tent made by joining three or four ordinary tents together, a very lively fiddle and concertina were in full blast. We entered and were pounced upon by a boisterous group of laughing men, seized by the shoulders, whirled about, and examined from behind.

"Two gentlemen and a lady!" roared out one of them. "Gentlemen on that side; ladies on this. See-lect your pardners for the waltz!"

There was a great rushing to and fro in preparation. Men bowed to each other with burlesque dancing school formality, offered arms, or accepted them with bearlike coyness. We stood for a moment rather bewildered, not knowing precisely what to do.

"You belong over that side," McNally instructed us. "I go over here; I'm a 'lady.'"

"Why?" I asked.

"Ladies," explained McNally, "are those who have patches on the seats of their pants."

As in most social gatherings, we saw that here too the fair sex were in the majority.

Everybody danced very vigorously, with a tremendous amount of stamping. It seemed a strenuous occupation after a week of hard work, and yet it was great fun. Yank pirouetted and balanced and "sasshayed" and tom-fooled in a manner wonderful to behold. We ended flushed and uproarious; and all trooped to the bar, which, it seemed, was the real reason for the existence of this dance hall.

The crowd was rough and good natured, full of high spirits, and inclined to practical jokes of a pretty stiff character. Of course there was the inevitable bully, swaggering fiercely and truculently back and forth, his belt full of weapons. Nobody took him very seriously; but, on the other hand, everybody seemed to take mighty good care not to run definitely counter to him. In the course of his wanderings he came to our end of the bar, and jostled McNally aside. McNally was at the moment lighting his pipe, so that in his one hand he held a burning match and in the other a glass of whiskey. Without the slightest hurry or excitement, his blue eyes twinkling as humorously as ever, McNally dumped the whiskey over the bully's shock head with his left hand and touched the match to it with his right. The alcohol sizzled up in a momentary blue flame, without damage save for a very singed head of hair.

"Man on fire! Man on fire!" yelled McNally. "Put him out!"

The miners rose to the occasion joyously, and "put him out" in the most literal fashion; so that no more was seen of that bully.

About ten o'clock we were getting tired; and probably the reaction from the "42 calibre whiskey" was making us drowsy. We hunted up Johnny, still at his faro game; but he positively and impatiently declined to accompany us.

SUNDAY AT HANGMAN'S GULCH

He said he was ahead — or behind — I forget which. I notice both conditions have the same effect of keeping a man from quitting. We therefore left him, and wandered home through the soft night, wherein were twinkling stars, gentle breezes, little voices, and the silhouettes of great trees.

CHAPTER XX

THE GOLD WASHERS

Johnny did not return at all that night, but showed up next morning at the diggings, looking blear-eyed and sleepy. He told us he had slept with a friend, and replied rather curtly that he was a "little behind the game." I believe myself that he was cleaned out; but that was none of our business. Every night we divided the dust into five parts. Don Gaspar and Vasquez got two of these. The remainder we again divided into four. I took charge of Talbot's share. We carried the dust always with us; for the camp was no longer safe from thieves.

In order to effect this division we had to have some sort of scales. I went up to the single store to see what I could do. The storekeeper was a drawling, slow, down-east Yankee, perpetually chewing a long sliver or straw, talking exclusively through his nose, keen for a bargain, grasping of the last cent in a trade, and yet singularly interesting and agreeable. His sense of dry humour had a good deal to do with this. He had no gold scales to lend or to hire, but he had some to sell. The price was fifteen dollars for an ordinary pair of balances worth not over a dollar and a half.

"And you'll find that cheap, if the miners keep coming

in as fast as they do," said he. "In two weeks they'll be worth fifty."

We bought them, and obtained from them great satisfaction. Vasquez used to weigh his gold at night, and again in the morning, in hopes, I suppose, that it had bred overnight.

Certainly the storekeeper's statement as to the influx of miners was justified. They came every day, in droves. We began to feel quite like old-timers, and looked with infinite scorn on these greenhorns. They were worse than we had been; for I have seen them trying to work in the moonlight! The diggings were actually getting crowded.

It was no longer feasible to dig wherever we pleased to do so. We held many miners' meetings, adopting regulations. A claim was to be fifteen feet square; work must begin on it within ten days; and so forth. Each of the five members of our party staked out two claims each, on which we worked in turn. All the old-timers respected these regulations, but some of the newcomers seemed inclined to dispute them; so that many meetings and much wrangling ensued. The truth of the matter was that none of us had the slightest permanent interest in the place. We intended merely to make our piles and to decamp. Each was for himself. Therefore there was no solidarity. We regulated only when we were actually forced to it; so that with what we called "private affairs" we declined to interfere. A man could commit any crime in the decalogue if so it pleased him. His victims must protect themselves. Such things as horse stealing, grand larceny, claim jumping, and mining regulations we dealt with; but other things were not our affair. We were too busy, and too slightly interested in what little public welfare a temporary mining camp might have. Even when, in a few cases, turbulence resulted in shooting, we rarely punished; although, strangely enough, our innate Anglo-Saxon feeling for the formality of government always resulted in a Sunday "inquest." We deliberated solemnly. The verdict was almost invariably "justifiable self-defence," which was probably near enough, for most of these killings were the result of quarrels. Murders for the purpose of robbery, later so frequent, were as yet almost unknown. Twice, however, and in both instances the prisoner was one of the gamblers, we pronounced judgment. One of these men was banished, and the other hanged. All in all a very fair semblance of order was kept; but I cannot help now but feel that our early shirking of responsibility — which was typical of all California — made necessary later great upheavals of popular justice.

About this time, also, the first of the overland wagon trains began to come through. Hangman's Gulch was not on the direct route; but some enterprising individual had found our trail fairly practicable for wagons and ten miles shorter than the regular road. After that many followed, and soon we had a well-cleared road. They showed plainly the hardships of a long journey, for the majority of them were thin, sick looking and discouraged. Few of them stopped at the diggings, although most had come west in hopes of gold, but pushed on down to the pastures of the Sacramento. They were about worn out and needed to recuperate before beginning anything new. Some were out of provisions and practically starved. The Yankee storekeeper sold food at terrible rates. I remember that quinine — a drug much in demand — cost a dollar a grain! We used to look up from our diggings at the procession of these sad-faced, lean men walking by their emaciated cattle, and the women peering from the wagons, and be very thankful that we had decided against the much-touted overland route.

One day, however, an outfit went through of quite a different character. We were apprised of its approach by a hunter named Bagsby. He loped down the trail to the river level very much in a hurry.

"Boys!" he shouted, "quit work! Come see what's coming down the trail!" with which he charged back again up the hill

His great excitement impressed us, for Bagsby, like most of the old-time Rocky Mountain men, was not ordinarily what one would call an emotional individual. Therefore we dropped our tools and surged up the hill as fast as we could go. I think we suspected Indians.

A train of three wagons drawn by strong oxen was lurching slowly down the road. It differed little from others of its kind, save that the cattle were in better shape and the men walking alongside, of the tall, competent backwoodsman type, seemed well and hearty. But perhaps a hundred yards ahead of the leading wagon came a horse — the only horse in the outfit — and on it, riding side-saddle, was a girl. She was a very pretty, red-cheeked girl, and she must have stopped within a half mile or so of the camp in order to get herself up for this impressive entrance. Her dress was of blue calico with a white yoke and heavy flounces or panniers; around her neck was a black velvet ribbon; on her head was a big leghorn hat with red roses. She rode through the town, her head high, like a princess; and we all cheered her like mad. Not once did she look at us; but I could see her bosom heaving with excitement beneath her calico, and her nostrils wide. She was a remarkably pretty girl; and this was certainly the moment of her triumph.

We fell into sanity as respects our hours of work and the way we went at it. Often we took as much as an hour and a half off at noon; or quit work early in the day. Then it was pleasant to sit with other miners under the trees or in the shade by the stream swapping yarns, doing our mending or washing, and generally getting acquainted. As each man's product was his own, no one cared how much or how little the others worked. Simply when he quit, his share ceased. This does not mean that we shirked our work, however; we merely grew to be a little sensible.

Some of our discussions were amusing, and several of them most illuminating. Thus, one day, John Semple summed up a long talk in which the conversation had swung wildly among the ideas of what each would do when he had dug "enough" gold. That had led us to consider what amount we thought would be "enough" for each of us. John settled it.

"Enough," said he, "is always a little more than a man has."

The political situation was fruitful of much idle discussion also. California had not been formally placed on any footing whatever by the United States Congress. Whatever any community did in the way of legislation or regulation was extra-legal and subject to ratification. I have heard grave discussions as to whether even murder could be considered a crime, since in this no-man's land there was no real law forbidding it!

A good many Chinese drifted in about this time, and established a camp of their own a short distance downstream. We took some pride in them as curiosities, with their queer, hatchlike hats, their loose blue clothing, their pigtails wound tight around their heads, and their queer yellow faces. They were an unobtrusive people, scratching away patiently, though spasmodically, on the surface of the ground. We sometimes strolled down to see them. They were very hospitable, and pleased at the interest they excited.

We made from fourteen to seventeen ounces of gold dust a day for some weeks, working our two cradles something like eight hours a day. With gold at the then current rate of fourteen dollars an ounce this was a good return, and we were quite happy. Besides, we were always hoping for a big strike. One day, as I was in the very act of turning my shovelful of dirt into the cradle, my eye caught a dull gleam. I instantly deflected the motion to dump the dirt on the stones alongside, fished about, and dug out a nugget that weighed three and three-quarter ounces. This was by far the largest single nugget found in these diggings — for most of the gold here came in flakes — and it attracted much attention. It belonged to me, individually, because I had not yet dumped it into the cradle.

About this time we had to come to some sort of a decision, for our provisions were about exhausted. We had no desire to replenish our stock from that of the local storekeeper. We were doing pretty well in the diggings, but we had also fairly healthy appetites, and I am convinced that at the prices that man charged we should have no more than kept even. Williams, the storekeeper, was levying double profits, one from us, and one from the overland immigrants. Don Gaspar proposed we send out Vasquez with all the horses to restock at Sutter's Fort. We were a trifle doubtful as to whether Vasquez would ever come back, but Don Gaspar seemed to have confidence in his man. Finally, though a little doubtfully, we came to the plan. Don Gaspar sent out also to McClellan for safe-keeping his accumulations of gold dust; but we did not go quite that far. In view of probable high prices we entrusted him with eighteen ounces for the purchase of goods.

While he was away we came to another decision. It had been for some weeks preparing. The diggings were becoming overcrowded. Almost every foot of the bar was occupied, and more men were coming in every day. No longer could the newcomer be sure of his colour the afternoon of his arrival; but was forced to prospect here and there up and down the river until he found a patch of the pay dirt. Most trusted simply to luck, but some had systems on which they worked. I have seen divining rods used. The believers in chance seemed to do as well as any one else.

But, also, our own yield was decreasing. The last week we had gained only nineteen ounces all told. This might be merely a lean bit of misfortune, or it might mean that we had taken the best from our ten claims. Since the human mind is prone to changes, we inclined to the latter theory. We were getting restless. No miner ever came to California who did not believe firmly that he would have done much better had he come out one voyage earlier; and no miner ever found diggings so rich that he had not a sneaking suspicion that he could do even better "a little farther on."

Our restlessness was further increased by the fact that we were now seeing a good deal of Sam Bagsby, the hunter. He and Yank had found much in common, and forgathered of evenings before our campfire.

Bagsby was a man of over fifty, tall and straight as a youngster, with a short white beard, a gray eye, and hard, tanned flesh. He was a typical Rocky Mountain man, wearing even in the hottest weather his fur cap with the tail hanging behind, his deerskin moccasins, and his fringed buckskin hunting shirt. Mining possessed no interest for him whatever. He was by profession a trapper, and he had crossed the plains a half-dozen times.

"No mining for me!" he stated emphatically. "I paddled around after the stuff for a while, till my hands swelled up like p'ison, and my back creaked like a frozen pine tree in the wind. Then I quit, and I stayed quit. I'm a hunter; and I'm makin' a good livin', because I ain't very particular on how I live."

He and Yank smoked interminable pipes, and swapped

yarns. Johnny and I liked nothing better than to keep quiet and listen to them. Bagsby had come out with Captain Sutter; and told of that doughty soldier's early skirmishes with the Indians. His tales of the mountains, the plains, and the game and Indians were so much romance to us; and we both wished heartily that fate could have allowed us a chance at such adventures.

"But why don't you fellows branch out?" Bagsby always ended. "What do you want to stick here for like a lot of groundhogs? There's rivers back in the hills a heap better than this one, and nobody thar. You'd have the place plumb to yoreselves. Git in where the mountains is really mountainous."

Then he would detail at length and slowly his account of the great mountains, deep cañons, the shadows of forests, ridges high up above the world, and gorges far within the bowels of the earth through which dashed white torrents. We gathered and pieced together ideas of great ice and snow mountains, and sun-warmed bars below them, and bears and deer, and a high clear air breathing through a vast, beautiful and solitary wilderness. The picture itself was enough to set bounding the pulses of any young man with a drop of adventure in his veins. But also Bagsby was convinced that there we should find richer diggings than any yet discovered.

"It stands to reason," he argued, "that the farther up you git, the more gold there is. All this loose stuff yere is just what washed down from the main supply. If you boys reely wants rich diggings, then you want to push up into the Porcupine River country."

THE GOLD WASHERS

But with this glowing and vivid impression we gathered another: that of a trackless wilderness, fearful abysses down which to find a way, labyrinthine defiles, great forests. None of us knew how to cope with these things. Yank, the best woodsman of us all, had had no experience in mountains. None of us knew anything of Indian warfare. None of us had the least idea that we could find Porcupine River, even if we were to be given accurate directions on how to get there.

Nevertheless the idea with us had been growing. Some of the bolder spirits among our acquaintances used to talk it over with us at odd times — McNally, Buck Barry, and his partner, Missouri Jones. We did not discuss it as a plan, hardly as a possibility, merely as a pleasant theme. We found, and advanced any amount of objections — the uncertainty of finding any gold at all, the expense of such a journey, the danger from Indians. the fact that we could find other proved diggings much nearer, and a half hundred others. The moment one of us had advanced one of these objections he was at once himself the most eager to demolish it. Thus we gradually worked ourselves toward enthusiasm.

"If Sam Bagsby would join us, it might be worth trying," we came to at last.

But Sam Bagsby scouted any such idea.

"I ain't that kind of a tom-fool," said he. "If I want to paddle my hands blue I'd do it yere. I couldn't make more'n a living anyway. I tell you I ain't got no use for yore pra'rie dog grubbing!"

Then McNally had an inspiration.

"Will you go, Sam, if we pay you for going?" he asked.

"Sure," replied the trapper at once. "I'm a labouring man, I'll go anywhar I'm paid to go."

It came out that Bagsby's ideas of proper compensation were his supplies, fifteen dollars a week in gold, and a drink of whiskey twice a day! In all this gold country he was the only man I met who genuinely despised money. I really think we were hurried to our decision by this unexpected reasonableness on his part. At any rate we decided definitely to go.

CHAPTER XXI

WE LEAVE THE DIGGINGS

There were nine of us — Bagsby, Yank, Johnny Fairfax, myself, Don Gaspar, Vasquez, McNally, Buck Barry, and Missouri Jones. We possessed, in all, just nine horses. Yank, Vasquez, Bagsby, and Jones drove eight of them out again to Sutter's Fort for provisions — Don Gaspar's beautiful chestnut refused to be a pack-horse on any terms. We took the opportunity of sending our accumulations of gold dust to Talbot for safekeeping. I do not know just how much my companions forwarded. Of course I could compute their shares; but had no means of telling just what deductions to allow for the delights of Hangman's Gulch. For Talbot I laid aside as his share of our entire product of four hundred and eighty-six ounces a total of one hundred and ten ounces. This included the half of my own share, as agreed. Roughly speaking, the value of a partnership third, after Don Gaspar's portion had been deducted, was a trifle over a thousand dollars for six weeks' work. There seemed to us also an excellent chance to realize something on the two cradles. I went about among the miners, and without trouble got bids for a hundred dollars each. Johnny was by no means satisfied with this. He insisted that late in the afternoon we drag the formidable engines up the trail to the town, where he deposited them in the middle of the street. There he proceeded to auction them; attracting the crowd by the simple expedient of firing his Colt's revolver. The bidding was sluggish at first, but Johnny's facetious oratory warmed it. The first cradle was knocked down at one hundred and sixty dollars. The second was about to go for approximately the same amount, when Johnny held up his hand.

"Gentlemen," said he impressively, "I do not think you quite realize that for what you are bidding. This is no ordinary cradle, like the other. This is the very identical warranted genuine cradle into which that enormous lump of gold, weighing three and three-quarter ounces — the finest nugget ever unearthed at Hangman's Gulch — was *about to be* shovelled by that largest and most enormous lump of a lad, the gentleman at my right, when seized upon and claimed as private property in accordance with the laws of these diggings. This is the very identical historical cradle! Now, how much am I bid!"

The crowd laughed — but it bid! We got two hundred and forty dollars for it.

Our purveyors returned the second day after. They reported prices very high at Sutter's Fort, and a great congestion of people there; both of those ascending the river from San Francisco, and of overlanders. Prices had consequently gone up. Indeed, so high were all provisions that our hard-headed partners had contented themselves with buying only some coffee, dried beef, and flour. They had purchased also a further supply of powder and balls, and a rifle apiece for such of us as already had none. The weapons were very expensive; and we found that our savings had been much eaten into. We collected our effects, packed them, as many of them as we were able, and sunk to sleep in a pleasing tingle of excitement.

Bagsby got us up long before daylight. The air was chilly, in contrast to the terrific heats to be expected later in the day, so we hastened to finish our packing, and at dawn were off.

Bagsby struck immediately away from the main road toward the north. The country we traversed was one of wide, woody bottoms separated by rocky hills. The trapper proved to be an excellent guide. Seemingly by a sort of instinct he was able to judge where a way would prove practicable for our animals down into or up out of the numerous cañons and ravines. It was borne in on me very forcibly how much hampered we should have been by our inexperience had we tried it alone. The country mounted gradually. From some of the higher points we could see out over the lowlands lost in a brown heat-haze. Deer were numerous, and a species of hare, and the helmeted quail. The sun was very hot; but the air was curiously streaked with coolness and with a fierce dry heat as though from an opened furnace door. All the grass was brown and crisp. Darker and more abrupt mountains showed themselves in the distance, with an occasional peak of white and glittering snow.

Until about three o'clock we journeyed through a complete solitude. Then we came upon some men digging in a dry wash. They had piled up a great heap of dirt from a hole. We stopped and talked to them; and discovered that they were working what they called "dry diggings." The pay dirt they excavated from wherever they found it piled it in a convenient place, and there left it until the rains should permit its washing. They claimed their dirt would prove to be very rich; but I thought myself that they were labouring in great faith. Also we learned what Bagsby had known right along, but which he had not bothered to tell us; that we were now about to cross the main Overland Trail.

We stopped that night near the road, and at a wayside inn or road house of logs kept by a most interesting man. He served us an excellent meal, including real eggs, and afterward joined us around the fire. He was an Italian, short, strongly built, with close curly hair, a rollicking, good-natured face, and with tiny gold rings in his ears. Johnny and he did most of the talking, while we listened. No part of the civilized world seemed to have been un- visited by this pair. Johnny mentioned Paris, our host added an intimate detail as to some little street; London appeared to be known to them from one end to the other; Berlin, Edinburg, St. Petersburg even; and a host of other little fellows whose names I never knew before and cannot remember now. They swapped reminiscences of the streets; the restaurants, and the waiters and proprietors thereof; the alleys and byways, the parks and little places. I knew, in a general way, that Johnny had done the grand tour; but the Italian with his gold earrings and his strong, brown, good-humoured peasant face puzzled me completely. How came he to be so travelled? so intimately travelled? He was no sailor; that I soon determined.

The two of them became thoroughly interested; but

after a time the native courtesy of the Italian asserted
itself. He evidently thought we might feel left out of it;
though I think the others were, like myself, quite fascinated.

"You lika music?" he smiled at us engagingly. "I getta
my Italian fiddle? No?"

He arose at our eager assent, pushed aside a blanket
that screened off one end of the log cabin, and produced
his "Italian fiddle" — a hand-organ!

At once the solution of the wide wandering among the
many cities, the intimate knowledge of streets and of
public places burst upon my comprehension. I could see
our host looking upward, his strong white teeth flashing
in an ingratiating fascinating smile, his right arm revolving
with the crank of his organ, his little brown monkey with
the red coat and the anxious face clambering ——

Next morning we crossed the Overland Trail, and plunged
into a new country of pines, of high hills, of deep cañons,
and bold, rocky ridges. The open spaces we had left behind,
and the great heats. Water flowed in almost every ravine,
and along its courses grew green grass and wild flowers.
Every little while we would come upon openings in the
forest, clear meadows spangled with blossoms; or occasionally we would skirt high bald knobs of rock around
which was stiff brush. For some miles we could journey
at ease through clear woods, then would encounter a gash
in the earth into which, at some expense of trial, we would
have to find a way. At first every stream bed was dotted
with the red shirts of miners. They became fewer as we
advanced, until finally the last pair had been left behind.
We camped that night at the edge of one of the meadows,

beneath pine trees. The air turned very chilly. We built
ourselves a fire of dried branches from the trees. In the
meadow the horses cropped eagerly at the lush green feed,
their bells tinkling pleasantly.

Nothing more remote could be imagined. Nevertheless
Bagsby, Don Gaspar, and Vasquez were not satisfied.
They consulted at length and apart; then Bagsby announced
that sentries must stand watches. We grumbled at this,
but Bagsby was firm, and as we had agreed to obey his
commands we did so now. Don Gaspar explained to us
later that the Mexican thieves would trail a party like ours
for days, awaiting the chance to make off with the horses.
Bagsby also chose the sentinels, selecting himself, Yank,
Vasquez, and Missouri Jones. Once wrapped in my warm
blanket I found myself selfishly glad that my experience
had not been considered worth trusting.

The third day we occupied in surmounting a tremendous
ridge of mountains. We climbed for hours, working our
way up by zigzag and long slants through the pines, the
rocky outcrops, the ledges, and the stiff brush that made
up the slope. It was hard work; and it seemed to have no
end. We arrived at last on a knife-edge summit. Here
the trees were fewer. We looked abroad over the country
we had traversed, and that which lay before us — a succession of dark, dim, undulating ridges with cañons and
valleys between, slanting from the great ranges at the right
to brown rolling hills and the heat-covered, half-guessed
plains. Immediately below us, very far down, was a toy-
like valley, with low hills, and flat places, and groves of elfin
trees, and a twisting bottle green river with white rapids.

WE LEAVE THE DIGGINGS

"Thar's the Porcupine," Bagsby told us briefly.

We took a look, then plunged into the tangles and difficulties of the descent. Just at sundown, our knees bending under us, we came off that terrific slant to a grateful wide flat, grown with scattered oaks, and covered with fine brown grass. A little spring stream wandered through the meadow toward the river on the other side of the valley.

We camped right there, dumping the packs from the horses almost anyhow. After a hearty meal, we rolled ourselves immediately into our blankets and fell into a grateful sleep to the tune of the distant river murmuring over the shingle.

CHAPTER XXII

THE STRIKE

We awoke next morning to a bright day. The helmeted quail were calling; the bees were just beginning a sun-warmed hum among the bushes; a languorous warmth hung in the air, and a Sunday stillness. It was as though we awakened to a new world, untrodden by men; which was, indeed, a good deal the case.

While we ate breakfast we discussed our plans. The first necessity, of course, was to find out about gold. To that end we agreed to separate for the day, prospecting far and wide. Bagsby kept camp, and an eye on the horses. He displayed little interest in the gold proposition; but insisted strongly that we should carry both our rifles and revolvers.

It would be difficult to describe the thrill of anticipation with which I set off up the valley. The place was so new, so untouched, so absolutely unknown. The high ridges on either side frowned down austerely on the little meadows that smiled back quite unabashed. As I crossed the brown dry meadow toward the river a covey of quail whirred away before me, lit, and paced off at a great rate. Two big grouse roared from a thicket.

The river was a beautiful, clear stream, with green wavery water whirling darkly in pools, or breaking white among the stones. As my shadow fell upon it, I caught a glimpse of a big trout scurrying into the darkness beneath a boulder. Picking my way among the loose stones I selected a likely place on the bar and struck home my pick.

I have since repeated the sensations of that day — on a smaller scale of course — in whipping untried trout waters; same early excitement and enthusiasm, same eager sustained persistence in face of failure, same incredulous slowing down, same ultimate discouragement, disbelief and disgust. All that day I shovelled and panned. The early morning freshness soon dissipated. Between the high mountain walls the heat reflected. All the quail stood beneath the shade of bushes, their beaks half open as though panting. The birds that had sung so sweetly in the early morning had somewhere sought repose. I could occasionally catch glimpses of our horses dozing under trees. Even the chirping insects were still. As far as I could make out I was the only living thing foolish enough to stay abroad and awake in that suffocating heat. The sweat dripped from me in streams; my eyes ached from the glare of the sun on the rocks and the bleached grasses. Toward the close of the afternoon I confessed sneakingly to myself that I was just a little glad I had found no gold and that I hoped the others had been equally unfortunate. The thought of working day after day in that furnace heat was too much for me.

My hopes were fulfilled. All came in that night tired, hot, dirty, and discouraged. Not one of the eight of us had raised a sign of colour.

"Well," said Bagsby philosophically, "that's all right.

We've just got to go higher. To-morrow we'll move up-stream."

Accordingly next day we turned at right angles to our former route and followed up the bed of the cañon ten or twelve miles toward the distant main ranges. It was, in general, rather hard scrabbling for the horses, though we footmen did well enough. Sometimes we crossed wide flats, resembling the one we had just left; again, where the cañon narrowed, we had actually to stumble in the rocks of the stream bed. Twice we forded, and twice we had to make great climbs up and down again in order to get by points that came boldly down to the river. It was curious to see the nature of the country change. The pines on the mountains to our right and left seemed to push down nearer to our level; the grass turned green; the stream narrowed and became swifter; the sky seemed to turn bluer; and from the ranges breathed a cool, refreshing wind.

About four o'clock we camped. The flat was green; little clumps of cedar pushed out across it; the oaks had given place to cottonwoods; we had now to make acquaint-ance with new birds. But what particularly interested us was the fact that at this point the high cañon walls at either side broke into rounder hills that opened out widely, and that from among them descended many ravines, barrancas, and dry washes.

The following morning we went prospecting again. My instructions were for the dry washes in the sides of the hills. Accordingly I scrambled up among the boulders in the nearest V-shaped ravine. I had hardly to look at all.

THE STRIKE

Behind a large boulder lay a little cuplike depression of stones in which evidently had stood a recently evaporated pool of water, and which, in consequence, was free from the usual dusty rubble. In the interstices between the stones my eye caught a dull glitter. I fell on my knees, dug about with the point of my bowie knife, and so unearthed small nuggets aggregating probably a half ounce in weight.

Although mightily tempted to stay for more, I minded our agreement to report promptly the first discovery, and started back to camp. Why I did not come a header in that fearful, boulder-strewn wash I cannot tell you. Certainly I took no care of my going, but leaped recklessly from rock to rock like a goat. When I reached the flat, I ran, whooping like an Indian. From the river I could see Johnny and Buck Barry running, too, and had sense enough to laugh as it occurred to me they must think us attacked by Indians. Far down the stream I could just make out figures I knew to be Yank and McNally. They too seemed to be coming to camp, though I could not imagine that my shouts had carried so far.

I burst in on Bagsby, who was smoking his pipe and leisurely washing the breakfast dishes, with a whoop, lifted him bodily by the shoulders, whirled him around in a clumsy dance. He aimed a swipe at me with the wet dish cloth that caught me across the eyes.

"You tarnation young grizzly b'ar!" said he.

I wiped the water from my eyes. Johnny and Buck Barry ran up. Somehow they did not seem to be anticipating an Indian attack after all. Johnny ran up to thump me on the back.

"Isn't it *great!*" he cried. "Right off the reel! First pop! Bagsby, old sport, you're a wonder!" He started for Bagsby, who promptly rushed for his long rifle.

"I'm going to kill the first lunatic I see," he announced.

Johnny laughed excitedly, and turned back to thump me again.

"How did you guess what it was?" I asked.

"Didn't. Just blundered on it."

"What!" I yelled. "Have you struck it, too?"

"First shovel," said Johnny. "But you don't mean——"

I thrust my three nuggets under his eyes.

"Say," broke in Buck Barry, "if you fellows know where the whiskey is, hide it, and hide it quick. If I see it, I'll get drunk!"

Yank and McNally at this moment strolled from around the bushes. We all burst out on them.

"See your fool nuggets and 'colour,' and raise you this," drawled Yank, and he hauled from his pocket the very largest chunk of virgin gold it has ever been my good fortune to behold. It was irregular in shape, pitted and scored, shaped a good deal like an egg, and nearly its size. One pound and a tiny fraction that great nugget balanced — when we got around to weighing it. And then to crown the glorious day which the gods were brimming for us, came Don Gaspar and Vasquez, trailed by that long and saturnine individual, Missouri Jones. The Spaniards were outwardly calm, but their eyes snapped. As soon as they saw us they waved their hats.

"Ah! also you have found the gold!" cried Don Gaspar,

sensing immediately the significance of our presence. "We, too. It is of good colour; there above by the bend." His eye widened as he saw what Yank held. "*Madre de dios!*" he murmured.

McNally, who had said and done nothing, suddenly uttered a resounding whoop and stood on his hands. Missouri Jones, taking aim, spat carefully into the centre of the fire, missing the dishpan by a calculated and accurate inch.

"The country is just *lousy* with gold," he pronounced.

Then we blew up. We hugged each other, we pounded each other's backs, we emulated McNally's wild Irish whoops, finally we joined hands and danced around and around the remains of the fire, kicking up our heels absurdly. Bagsby, a leathery grin on his face, stood off one side. He still held his long-barrelled rifle, which he presented at whoever neared him.

"I tell you, look out!" he kept saying over and over. "I'm shootin' lunatics to-day; and apparently there's plenty game to choose from."

CHAPTER XXIII

THE CAMP ON THE PORCUPINE

We should all have liked to start right in digging, but Bagsby strenuously opposed this.

"You-all have a rich diggings yere," said he; "and you want to stay a while and git the most there is out of them. And if you're going to do that, you've got to get a good ready. You've got make a decent camp, and a stockade for the hosses at night; and if you want yore grub to last you more than a month there's got to be some reg'lar hunting and fishing done."

"That'll take a week!" cried Johnny impatiently.

"Or more," agreed Bagsby with entire complacence. "You can bull at it and go to t'aring up the scenery if you want to; but you won't last long."

Unpalatable as this advice seemed, with all the loose gold lying about, we ended by adopting it. Indeed, we added slightly to our self-imposed tasks by determining on the construction of cradles. Yank had figured out a scheme having to do with hollowed logs and canvas with cleats that would obviate the need of lumber. We deputed Johnny to help him. Bagsby and Vasquez were to hunt and fish for the general benefit, while the rest of us put up a stockade, or corral, and erected a cabin.

I must confess the labour was pleasant. We had plenty

of axes, and four of us were skilled in their use. Personally I like nothing better than the exercise of swinging
a keen blade, the feeling of skillful accuracy and of nicely
adjusted effort. We felled dozens, hundreds, of tall young
pines eight inches to a foot in diameter, and planted them
upright in a trench to form a stockade. Then we ran up
a rough sort of cabin of two rooms. Yank, somewhat
hampered by Johnny, finished his cradles, and turned in to
help us. Bagsby and Vasquez brought in several deer and
an elk, and trapped many quail and hares. We fared
royally, worked healthfully in the shade of our trees, and
enjoyed huge smokes and powwows around our fire of an
evening. Every night we drove the horses within the
enclosure; and slept heavily.

Always in the background of consciousness lay the
gold, the incredibly abundant gold. It coloured our dreams,
it gilded our labour. As we drew to the end of our construction work, I really believe we experienced a slight,
a very slight, feeling of regret that this fine flavour of
anticipation was so nearly at an end. However, I noticed
that though we completed the house at three of the afternoon, we none of us showed any disposition to wait for the
morrow. We promptly lugged one of Yank's log cradles
to the border of the stream and put in two hours washing.

The results were most encouraging, for we gained in
that short time nearly two ounces of flake gold.

That evening we reviewed our situation carefully. The
older heads of the party — Yank, Bagsby, Don Gaspar,
and Missouri Jones — overruled our young desire to
jump into things headlong.

"If this camp is going to get on right," said Yank, "we got to make some provision for working right. Somebody's got to be in camp all the time, that's sure — to cook some decent meals, do the odd chores, and keep an eye on the stock." Bagsby nodded emphatically at this. "And somebody's got to rustle game and fish. Yere's nine husky men to eat. If we leave one man in camp and two to hunt, we have six left for gold washing. That's three to a cradle, and that's just right."

We came to that, too; and so settled into our routine. Bagsby was the only permanent office-holder among us. He was unanimously elected the official hunter. The rest of us agreed to take turn about at the other jobs. It was further agreed to increase our chances by utilizing the cradles at two totally different kinds of diggings. One we located on the bar to wash out the shingle. The other we carried to a point opposite the dry ravine in which I had found my three little nuggets.

Don Gaspar had worked like a nailer at the construction although he was utterly unskilled. Now at the end of the week he was worn out, although he stoutly maintained he was as good as ever. This high-bred, energetic gentleman we had all come to admire, both for his unfailing courtesy and his uncomplaining acceptance of hardships to which evidently he had never been accustomed. Exactly why he underwent the terrible exertions incidental to gold finding I have never quite fathomed. I do not believe he needed money; and I never saw one of his race fond of hard physical work. Indeed, he was the only member of his class I ever met who would work. The truth of the matter probably lies somewhere between an outcropping of the old adventurous *conquistadore* spirit and the fascination of the golden metal itself, quite apart from its dollars-and-cents value. Unanimously we voted in Don Gaspar as camp keeper for the first week. We wanted to give him a rest; but I do not think we pleased him. However, he bowed to our decision with his usual gracious courtesy. As hunting companion for Bagsby we appointed Missouri Jones, with the understanding that every two days that office was to have a new incumbent. Johnny, McNally, and I took charge of the dry wash, and the rest of the party tackled the bar. Of course we all — except Bagsby — were to share equally.

Unless the wash should prove very productive we would have the worst end of it, for we had to carry the pay dirt down to the stream's edge. For the purpose we used the pack-sacks — or *alforjas*, as the Spaniards call them. Each held about sixty or seventy pounds of dirt. We found this a sweaty and stumbly task — to stagger over the water-smoothed boulders of the wash, out across the shingle to the edge of the stream. There one of us dumped his burden into the cradle; and we proceeded to wash it out. We got the "colour" at once in the residuary black sand.

All morning we laboured manfully, and discovered a brand new set of muscles. By comparison our former toil of mere digging and washing seemed light and pleasurable exercise.

"If this stuff don't run pretty high," grunted McNally, wiping the sweat from his eyes, "it's me voting for the bar. We can't stand all day of this."

He heaved the contents of his pack-sack into the cradle and shook it disgustedly. Suddenly his jaw dropped and his eye widened with so poignant an expression that we both begged him, in alarm, to tell us what was the matter.

"Now, will you look at that!" he cried.

We followed the direction of his gaze, but saw only the meadow, and the horses feeding in it, and the thin smoke beyond, where Don Gaspar was bending his proud Castillian spirit to attend to fried steak and flapjacks.

"Look at those horses!" cried McNally with growing indignation.

"What's the matter with them?" cried Johnny and I in a breath.

"Matter with them! Nothing!" cried McNally with comical disgust. "The matter's with us." He rapped his knuckles on his head. "Solid, all the way through!" said he. "Why, save from nat'ral born human imbelicity, should horses be living like gentleman while gentlemen are working like horses!"

We took the hint. That afternoon we saddled the pack-horses and led them, laden with the dirt, back and forth between the ravine and the cradle.

All of us worked until rather later in the day than usual. . . . The hunters, too, did not return until dark. We weighed the results of our labour with eager interest. From our cradle we had taken eleven ounces, while those working the bar had gained just over nine. That was a good day's work, and we were much elated.

"And most any time," exulted Johnny, "we'll run into a big pocket with thousands."

CHAPTER XXIV

THE INDIANS

Although we did not immediately run into the expected thousands, nor did the promise of that first glorious day of discovery quite fulfil itself, nevertheless our new diggings turned out to be very rich. We fell into routine; and the days and weeks slipped by. Bagsby and one companion went out every day to hunt or to fish. We took turns at a vacation in camp. Every night we "blew" our day's collection of sand, weighed the gold, and packed it away. Our accumulations were getting to be very valuable.

For a month we lived this idyllic life quite unmolested, and had gradually come to feel that we were so far out of the world that nothing would ever disturb us. The days seemed all alike, clear, sparkling, cloudless. It was my first experience with the California climate, and these things were a perpetual wonder to my New England mind.

Then one day when I was camp keeper, at the upper end of our long meadow, a number of men emerged from the willows and hesitated uncertainly. They were too far away to be plainly distinguishable, but I believed in taking no chances, so I fired my revolver to attract the attention of my companions. They looked up from their labour, saw the men, and promptly came into camp.

The group still hesitated at the edge of the thicket.

Then one of them waved something white. We waved in return; whereupon they advanced slowly in our direction.

As they neared we saw them to be Indians. Their leader held before him a stick to which had been tied a number of white feathers. As they approached us they began to leap and dance to the accompaniment of a weird rising and falling chant. They certainly did not look very formidable, with their heterogeneous mixture of clothing, their round, black, stupid faces and their straight hair. Most of them were armed simply with bows and arrows, but three carried specimens of the long Spanish musket.

Buck Barry promptly sallied out to meet them, and shook hands with the foremost. They then advanced to where we were gathered and squatted on the ground. They were certainly a villainous and dirty looking lot of savages, short, thickset, round faced, heavy featured, with coarse, black, matted hair and little twinkling eyes. A more brutish lot of human beings I had never seen; and I was almost deceived into thinking them too stupid to be dangerous. The leaders had on remnants of civilized clothing, but the rank and file were content with scraps of blanket, old ragged coats, single shirts, and the like. The oldest man produced a long pipe from beneath his blanket, filled it with a few grains of coarse tobacco, lighted it by means of a coal from our fire, puffed twice on it, and passed it to me. I perforce had to whiff at it also, though the necessity nearly turned my stomach. I might next have given it to one of our own party, but I did not want to deprive him of my own first hand sensation, so I handed it back to another of the visitors for fresh inoculation, as it were. Evidently I had by accident hit on acceptable etiquette, as deep grunts of satisfaction testified. After we had had a whiff all around, the chief opened negotiations in Spanish. Most of us by now had learned enough of it from our intercourse with Don Gaspar and Vasquez to understand without interpretation.

The Indians said they wanted to trade.

We replied that we saw nothing they might trade with us.

In return they produced some roots and several small bags of pine nuts.

We then explained that we were reduced in ammunition and had little food.

Don Gaspar here interpolated hastily, saying that in his judgment it would be absolutely necessary that we made some sort of a present to avoid the appearance of intending an affront. Buck Barry and Jones seemed instantly to accept this necessity.

"Give them two or three of the saddle blankets," suggested Barry, after a moment's thought. "We will have several light hosses going out; and if we have to pad the saddles we can git along with skins or something."

We gave our visitors the blankets, therefore. They seemed well pleased, arose, and shortly made a primitive sort of a camp a short distance outside our stockade. We did no more washing that day. About five o'clock our hunters came in with the best meat of a blacktail deer. Bagsby listened attentively to our account of the interview. Then he took a hindquarter of the newly killed buck and departed for the Indians' camp, where he stayed for an hour.

"I don't think they are out for meanness," he announced when he returned. "They tell me this yere is on a sort of short cut from some of the Truckee lakes down to their villages. But we got to keep a sharp eye on our horses; and we got to stand guard to-night."

Very early in the morning, when we were just up, several of the elders came over to tell us that some of the young men would stay to work for us, if we so desired. We replied that we had no goods with which to pay for work. Shortly after, the whole tribe vanished down river.

For two nights Bagsby insisted on standing guard, and on having some of us take turns at it. Then we declined flatly to do so any longer. The Indians had gone far downstream, as their trail indicated to our hunters, and had shown no signs of even hesitating on the way. We fell into our old routine, and laughed at Bagsby when he shook his head.

About this time Johnny and McNally, scrambling of a Sunday for the sake of a view, stumbled on a small ravine that came nearer realizing our hoped-for strike than anything we had yet seen. After "puddling out" a few potfuls of the pay dirt, we decided to move the cradles. It was not over a half mile from camp, but was out of sight of the stockade. The move was the occasion for a hot discussion. Babgsby wanted to reorganize, and we were reluctant.

"Thar ought to be two men in camp," said he, "and

thar ought never to be less'n three together out hunting. And that's my idee — that ye're paying me money for."

"That leaves us only four men to work the cradles," I objected. "Four men out of nine working."

"Well, thar won't be *no* men out of nine a-workin' if you don't watch out," predicted Bagsby. "You-all forgit this is a self-supportin' community. We got to work for our living, as well as for gold."

"The hunters might go out less," suggested McNally.

"The miners might eat less, then," replied Bagsby grimly. "This ain't what you'd call the best sort of a game country."

We came to it, of course, though with much grumbling. It seemed an almost excuseless waste of good energy; a heavy price in economic efficiency to pay for insurance against what seemed a very remote peril. But we did not know, and our uncertainty gave way.

"But hang it!" cried Johnny, "here's more gold than a hundred men could begin to handle, and we're wasting more than half our resources."

"It do seem so," agreed Yank with his accustomed slow philosophy. "But we can put in longer hours because we rest oftener."

A week passed, and we had almost forgotten our chance visitors. One day the two Spaniards, Buck Barry and I were at the cradle; Bagsby, Yank, and McNally were the hunters for the day. Johnny and Missouri Jones kept camp.

We had had a most successful morning, and were just stacking our tools preparatory to returning to camp for dinner. Buck Barry was standing near some small sage bushes at the upper end of the diggings. He was just in the act of lighting a freshly filled pipe, when he stopped as though petrified, the burning match suspended above the bowl of his pipe. Then he turned quickly toward the sage brush; and as he did so a bow twanged and an arrow sang past his head so close as actually to draw blood from the lobe of his ear. With a roar of anger Buck Barry raised his pickaxe and charged into the bush. We saw a figure rise from the ground, dash away, stumble flat. Before the man could get up again Buck Barry was upon him, and the pickaxe descended. At the same instant we heard a series of whoops and two shots in rapid succession from the direction of camp. Buck Barry came bounding out of the sage brush, and seized his rifle from under the bush where we had kept them.

"Come on!" he panted. "Let's get out of this!"

We ran as hard as we could go for a hundred yards, or until we had reached the flat of the river bottom. Then we paused, uncertain as to just what next to do.

"Wait a minute," said I. "I'll just take a look," and hurried up a little spur-knoll to the right. From that elevation I instantly caught sight of a crowd of Indians coming up the valley at full speed. Most of them were on horseback, but a number loped along on foot, keeping up with the animals. One look was enough. I raced down to my companions again; and we hastily took refuge in the only cover near enough to conceal us — a little clump of willows in a small, damp watercourse. There we crouched, rifles ready.

I was terribly excited. The patter of the horses was now plainly audible, though, owing to the inequalities of the ground, they could not become visible farther than a hundred yards away. I trembled violently, and cursed myself for a coward, though I really do not think I was frightened. At any rate, I became deadly cool the moment the first savage appeared; and I drew a steady bead and toppled him off his horse before any one else had got in action. The shot brought them to a stand. They had, I think, expected to find us in our ravine, and were surprised. Immediately I dropped the butt of my rifle to the ground and began reloading. A shower of arrows flew toward us, but were deflected by the criss-cross of the willows. In fact, this lacework of stout branches seemed to be an excellent sort of armour against arrows. In the meantime my companions had each dropped his man; though Vasquez had better luck than skill, as his savage was only clipped in the leg. I fired once more, and elicited a howl. There could be no missing at the distance, unless a man quite lost his head; and personally I was too scared for that. Another shower of arrows rattled in the willows; then the band broke to right and left and raced away up the hills like mad. They had no courage, and lost stomach for the fight at once when they found us prepared.

We were astonished and delighted, for we had fully expected to be ridden down. As soon as we were quite certain this sudden retreat was not a ruse, we came out from our shelter. How many wounded had made off — if any — we could not tell. Three dead bodies lay on the ground. To them we paid no attention, but, with many forebodings, hurried back to camp.

When we appeared in sight Missouri Jones ran out to meet us, his rifle over his arm.

"Where's Johnny?" I cried.

"He was down at the river a-getting water," said Jones, "and I ain't seen him since."

We all ran down to the edge of the river pool whence we drew our supply. For a moment our hearts stood still, for no Johnny was in sight. Then he arose dripping from the middle of the pool.

"This water's cold," he remarked conversationally. "I think I'll come out. Anybody hurt?"

He waded ashore, and shook himself like a dog.

"I didn't hear 'em until they were right on top of me; and I couldn't get away without being seen," said he; "so I just waded out and imitated a rock with my head."

We roared with laughter by way of relief.

"It isn't the first time, Johnny," said I.

"That's all right," put in Missouri Jones. "This is no joke. They got three of our hosses."

Then he told us his experience.

"I was just a-browning of the venison," he explained, "when I happened to look up, and thar was three of our hosses running off, tails up, and a half dozen Injuns a hoss-back driving 'em. I let drive with old Betsey and Johnny's gun, but they was about out of range. While I was looking after them about forty Injuns went past sky-hootin'. I suppose they thought the first lot had all the hosses, and so they didn't stop. The rest of the hosses, luckily, was asleep behind the cottonwoods. You bet I didn't call their attention to myself."

He exhibited the greatest satisfaction when he learned that we had accounted for four.

"That's something like Injun fighting," he observed, "though these are a pore, spiritless lot. The whole bag ain't worth more than one of them good hosses."

We did no more gold washing that day, but remained close in camp, consumed with anxiety for our companions. From time to time we fired a rifle, with the idea of warning them that something was amiss. The remaining half-dozen horses we ran into the corral.

Night fell and still the hunters did not return. We were greatly alarmed and distressed, but we could not think of anything to do, for we had not the least idea in what direction to look.

"Bagsby and Yank are old hands," speculated Missouri Jones consolingly. "And the fact that Injuns is abroad would make them slow and careful."

None of us felt like turning in. We all sat outside on the ground around a little fire.

Toward midnight we heard voices; and a moment later Yank and Bagsby strode in out of the darkness.

"Where's McNally?" Yank instantly demanded. "Hasn't he come in yet?"

We told him we had seen nothing of the missing man.

"Well, he'll drift in pretty soon," said Bagsby. "We lost him in the darkness not two hours back."

They set to frying some venison steak. Excitedly and in antiphony Johnny and I detailed the day's adventure.

Both the backswoodsmen listened in silence, but without suspending their cooking.

"They didn't bother McNally," Bagsby decided. "They'd drive those hosses away five or six miles before they'd stop; and McNally was with us just a little piece back. He'll be in by the time the venison is cooked."

But he was not; nor by an hour later. Then we decided that we must go out to look for him.

"We can't see nothin' till daylight," said Bagsby, "but we can get started back for the last place we saw him."

It was now about one o'clock in the morning. Bagsby appointed Vasquez, Missouri Jones, Buck Barry, Yank and myself to accompany him. Don Gaspar was suffering from a slight attack of malarial fever; and Johnny, to his vast disgust, was left to hold him company. We took each a horse, which we had to ride bareback and with a twisted rope "war halter."

Bagsby led the way, and we followed closely nose to tail. It was an interesting and wonderful experience, had I had more attention to give it, for we rode mysteriously neck deep in velvet darkness over strange hills, and awful shapes rose mysteriously, and the sky silvered with stars like the glittering of little waves. But my mind was filled with dread and foreboding, and a great anxiety for our merry, blue-eyed companion, and a very considerable wonder as to how our guide managed to find his way.

He did not hesitate, however, as to direction; only occasionally he had to stop and cast back and around for a way through. Often, at a low command from him, we dismounted and led our animals.

We proceeded thus for a long time — five or six miles, I should think. By the undefined feeling of dark space at either hand I judged we must be atop a ridge. Bagsby halted.

"It was somewhere on this ridge we left him," said he. 'I reckon now we'd just better set down and wait for dawn."

Accordingly we dismounted and drew together in a little group. Over the top of the great ranges a gibbous moon rose slowly. By her dim light I could make out the plunge on either side our ridge, and the other dark ridges across the way. Behind us our horses occasionally stamped a hoof or blew softly through their noses.

I lay flat on my back, and idly counted the stars. Happening to glance sidewise, I caught the flicker of a distant light.

"Bagsby," I whispered, "there's a fire not more than a half mile away."

He too lay down in order to get my angle of view.

"It's not McNally," he pronounced after a moment's careful inspection, "for it's too big a fire, and it's a lot more than half a mile away. That's a good big fire. I think it's Injuns."

"Probably the same gang that lifted our hosses!" cried Buck.

"Probably," agreed Bagsby. He sat upright and peered at us through the dim moonlight. "Want to get after them?" he inquired.

"You bet!" said Buck emphatically. "They may have McNally, and if they haven't, they've got our horses."

GOLD

"There's six of us and we can shore make it interesting for that lot," agreed Yank. "Can we get to where they are?"

"I think so," said Bagsby.

We rode for another hour, slanting down the mountain-side toward the flickering fire. Every time a horse rolled a rock or broke a dried branch it seemed to me that the mountains reverberated from end to end. I don't believe I allowed myself to weigh over six ounces all told. Finally we left the slope for the bottom of the valley.

"I'd rather be below their camp than above it. It's going to be hard to get out this way," complained Bagsby, "but it's the best we can do." He dismounted us, and we crept forward another half mile, leading our animals.

"This is as close as I dare take the hosses," whispered Bagsby. "Vasquez, you stay here with them," he said in Spanish, "and when I yell twice quick and sharp, you answer so we'll know where to find you. Come on!"

We stole forward slowly. The fire leaped and flared beneath the widespread branches of a tree. Around it lay a half dozen or so recumbent shapes wrapped in blan-kets. How many more might be lying beyond the light circle we could not tell. Beyond them we saw dimly the forms of dozing horses. Obeying a signal from the old trapper, we circled the camp until we were on the same side as the animals. They raised their heads and blew softly at us; but we lay still, and shortly they quieted down.

"Now," breathed Bagsby, "when I give the word, fire. And each man grab a horse by the picket rope, stampede the rest, and hustle back to Vasquez. Ready!"

We raised our pieces, but before the command to fire was given, one of the sleepers threw aside his blanket, stretched himself and arose. It was a white man!

I confess that for a moment I turned physically sick.

"Hello!" called Bagsby, quite unmoved.

The white man seized his rifle, and the recumbent forms leaped to life.

"Who are you?" he demanded sharply. "Speak quick!"

"Keep yore ha'r on!" drawled the trapper, advancing into the light. "We're perfectly respectable miners, out looking for a lost man; and we saw yore fire."

The rest of us uttered a yell of joy and relief. One of the men who had been sleeping around the fire was McNally himself.

We drew together, explaining, congratulating. The strangers, six in number, turned out to be travellers from the eastern side of the ranges. They listened with interest and attention to our account of the Indian attack. McNally explained that he had been uncertain of his route in the dark; so that when he had caught sight of the fire he had made his way to it. We were still engaged in this mutual explanation when we were struck dumb by a long-drawn-out yell from the direction of our own horses.

"It is Vasquez," explained Barry. "He wants to let us know where he is," and he answered the yell.

But at that moment one of our own horses dashed up to the bunch of picketed animals and wheeled, trembling. Its rope bridle dangled broken from its head. Sam Bagsby darted forward to seize the hanging cord.

"It's cut!" he cried. "Quick! Out across the valley, boys!"

We followed him into the moonlight, grasping our rifles. A moment later a compact band swept toward us at full speed, our horses in the lead, their rope halters dangling, a dozen Indians on horseback following close at their heels and urging them on.

"Shoot, boys!" yelled Bagsby, discharging his own piece.

Our rifles cracked. It was impossible to take aim; and I am sure we hit nothing. But the horses swerved aside from the long fiery flashes, and so ran into the picketed lot and stopped. The Indians flew on through our scattered line without stopping, pursued by a sputter of shots from our Colt's revolvers.

"A while ago I was sorry we had to stop above camp," said Bagsby with satisfaction; "but it was a lucky thing for us. They had to come by us to git out."

"And Vasquez?" Yank struck across our exultation.

CHAPTER XXV

BATTLE

We had a good deal of trouble finding the exact spot where we had left him, for we could get no answer to our calls. He was down in a heap, covered with blood, and quite dead. The savages had scalped him. In our long companionship we had grown very fond of him, for he was a merry, good-natured, willing soul.

"God!" cried Bagsby, deeply moved. "I'll put a ball through the next one of those devils I meet!"

We returned slowly to the fire, carrying the body, which we laid reverently one side and covered with a blanket. In all our hearts burned a fierce, bitter anger. Sullenly we turned to prepare ourselves a meal from the supplies our hosts offered us.

The latter were the father and five sons of a backwoods family from the northwest — Pine, by name. They were all tall, heavily built men, slow moving, slow speaking, with clear, steady eyes, a drawling way of talking, and the appearance always of keeping a mental reservation as to those with whom they conversed. I suppose they were ignorant enough men, as far as education goes, but they always impressed me as being somehow a superior type. Possibly it was because of the fact that they perfectly corresponded to their environment, which was the wilderness.

GOLD

In detail, the old man was upward of sixty, his beard long and grizzled, his hair about his shoulders. The oldest son would count about thirty, and the others went down in stepladder fashion to the youngster, a fine, big, smooth-faced boy of sixteen. They were named after old Pine's favourite heroes, evidently. There was David Crockett Pine, and Governor Boggs Pine, and President Tyler Pine, and Daniel Boone Pine, and Old Hickory Pine, the youngest, an apparent contradiction in terms. They were called by their odd first names — Governor, President, Old — without the least humour.

Just now they stood tall and grim behind us as we ate; and the gray dawn and the rose dawn grew into day. Nobody said anything until we had finished. Then Yank rose to his full height and faced the attentive men.

"I want vengeance," he announced in an even voice, stretching forth his long, lean arm. "Those devils have harried our stock and killed our pardner; and I'm not going to set quiet and let them do it." He turned to us: "Boys," said he, "I know you're with me thar. But I'm going to git our friends yere to go with us. Old man," he said to Pine, "you and yore sons help us with this job, and we'll locate you on the purtiest diggings in these hills."

"You bet!" agreed McNally.

"You don't need to make my boys no offer," replied Pine slowly. "Those divils were after our hosses too; and they'd have got them if you hadn't come along. We'd been told by a man we believe that there warn't no Injuns in this country, or you wouldn't have seen us sleeping es close to our fire. Whar do you-all reckon to come up with them?"

Our old trapper interposed.

"Their rancheree is down the valley somewhars," said Bagsby, "and we'll have to scout for it. We must go back to camp first and get a ready."

McNally and I murmured against this check to immediate action, but saw the point after a moment. The Pines packed their slender outfit; we bound the body of our poor friend across his horse, and mournfully retraced our steps.

We arrived in camp about ten o'clock, to find Johnny and Don Gaspar anxiously on the alert. When we had imparted our news, their faces, too, darkened with anger. Of us all, Vasquez had been the only man who never lost his temper, who had always a flash of a smile for the hardest days. Hastily we threw together provisions for several days, and arranged our affairs as well as we could. We all wanted to go; and Don Gaspar, in spite of the remains of his malarial fever, fairly insisted on accompanying the expedition.

"Señores," he said with dignity, "this was my own man from my own people."

Nevertheless somebody had to stay in camp, although at first some of us were inclined to slur over that necessity.

"There's a strong chance that Injuns will drift by and take all our supplies," Bagsby pointed out.

"Chances are slim — in only a day or so; you must admit that," argued Johnny. "Let's risk it. We can scratch along if they do take our stuff."

"And the gold?"

That nonplussed us for a moment.

"Why not bury it?" I suggested.

Bagsby and Pine snorted.

"Any Injun would find it in a minute," said Pine.

"And they know gold's worth something, too," put in Yank.

"This is a scout, not a house-moving expedition," said Bagsby decidedly, "and somebody's got to keep camp."

"I'll stay, fer one," offered old man Pine, his eyes twinkling from beneath his fierce brows. "I've fit enough Injuns in my time."

After some further wrangling we came to drawing lots. A number of small white pebbles and one darker were shaken up in a hat. I drew in the fourth turn, and got the black!

"Hard luck, son!" murmured old man Pine.

The rest were eager to be off. They leaped upon their horses, brandishing their long rifles, and rode off down the meadow. Old man Pine leaned on the muzzle of his gun, his eyes gleaming, uttering commands and admonitions to his five sons.

"You Old," he warned his youngest, "you mind and behave; and don't come back yere without'n you bring a skelp!"

We spent the next two days strictly in defence, for we dared not stay long from the stockade. I was so thoroughly downcast at missing the fight that I paid little attention to Pine's well-meant talk. My depression was enhanced by the performance of the duty the others had left to our leisure. I mean the interment of poor Vasquez. We buried him in a grassy little flat; and I occupied my time hewing and fashioning into the shape of a cross two pine logs, on the smoothed surface of which I carved our friend's name. Then I returned to the stockade, where old man Pine, a picturesque, tall figure in his fringed hunter's buckskin, sat motionless before the cabin door. From that point of vantage one could see a mile down the valley, and some distance upstream; and one or the other of us occupied it constantly.

About three o'clock of the second day Pine remarked quietly:

"Thar they come!"

I was instantly by his side, and we strained our eyesight in an attempt to count the shifting figures. Pine's vision was better and more practised than mine.

"They are all thar," said he, "and they're driving extry hosses."

Ten minutes later the cavalcade stopped and the men dismounted wearily. They were, as the old man had said, driving before them a half dozen ponies, which Governor Boggs herded into the corral. Nobody said a word. One or two stretched themselves. Johnny seized the cup and took a long drink. Yank leaned his rifle against the wall. Old man Pine's keen, fierce eye had been roving over every detail, though he, too, had kept silent.

"Well, Old," he remarked, "I see you obeyed orders like a good sojer."

The boy grinned.

"Yes, dad," said he.

And then I saw what I had not noticed before: that at

the belt of each of the tall, silent young backwoodsmen hung one or more wet, heavy, red and black soggy strips. The scalping had been no mere figure of speech! Thank heaven! none of our own people were similiarly decorated!

So horrified and revolted was I at this discovery that I hardly roused myself to greet the men. I looked with aversion, and yet with a certain fascination on the serene, clear features of these scalp takers. Yet, since, in the days following, this aversion could not but wear away in face of the simplicity and straightforwardness of the frontiersmen, I had to acknowledge that the atrocious deed was more a product of custom than of natural barbarity.

Old Pine, of course not at all affected, bustled about in the more practical matter of getting coffee and cutting meat; and after a moment I aroused myself to help him. The men lay about on the ground exhausted. They drank the coffee and ate the meat, and so revived, little by little, arrived at the point of narration.

"It's sure one hell of a ride down there," remarked McNally with a sigh.

"Good deal like the foothills of th' Snake Range, pop," put in President Tyler Pine.

"We been riding purty nigh every minute sence we left here," agreed Bagsby. "That rancheree was hard to find."

Little by little the tale developed. No one man, in the presence of all the others, felt like telling us the whole story. We gathered that they had ridden the cañon for several hours, past our first camping grounds, and finally out into the lower ranges. Here they lost the trail left by the Indians when they had first visited our camp; but in casting in circles for it had come on fresher pony tracks. These they had followed persistently for many miles.

"*I* couldn't see the sign of a track for a mile at a time, on that hard ground," interpolated Johnny.

At length the tracks had struck into a beaten trail.

"And then we knew we were on the way to the rancheree," said Bagsby.

The village they found located in a flat by the side of a stream, and they halted to determine just what to do. It was finally decided that while an attack on horseback would undoubtedly strike more instant terror, yet the difficulty of shooting accurately from a gallop would more than offset this effect. Therefore nine of the party crept up afoot, leaving three to lead forward the horses some distance in the rear.

"I was one of them," said Johnny. "They evidently have seen me shoot. I seem to be always out of it."

The men had wormed their way to within a hundred yards of the flimsy huts, or tepees, when they were discovered by the dogs. The Indians immediately rushed out pell-mell, in a crowd, and were met by a deadly volley from the white men's rifles. Caught absolutely by surprise, they turned and fled. Some few loosed random arrows. Their horses coming up at a run in convoy of the rear guard, each man threw himself into his saddle and started in pursuit, shooting right and left with the Colt's revolvers whenever they caught up with the fugitives. Johnny told admiringly how the backwoodsmen had reloaded their rifles while galloping.

"All I could do to shoot mine off, let alone loading!" he confessed.

There was no resistance, and little mortality after the first volley. The Indians bolted like rabbits into the brush. The white men then returned leisurely to the village, which they proceeded to burn to the ground.

"It made a grand bonfire," interrupted Johnny. "Went up like gunpowder. And the Indians yelled and howled at us from the sidehills all the time."

The raiders had fired a few defiant and random shots in the direction of the howling, and then, after collecting the ponies that had not stampeded, rode slowly back the way they had come.

"Didn't see anything of our three horses?" I asked.

"Nary hoss," said Buck Barry. "I figger they jest nat'rally stampeded off when the row started."

"Are you sure those were the same Indians?" I asked.

A long silence fell.

"Well, what if they wasn't — and that's by no means sure," demanded Buck Barry at last, a little defiantly. "The whole lot is thieves and murderers; and if they'd had a chance at us, you bet they'd have taken it. And we showed the red devils they can't monkey with us!"

I looked toward the cross over Vasquez, murdered as wantonly as ever man was murdered for plunder, and could find nothing to say. Whatever the eternal equities of the case may be — and long since I have given up trying to guess what they are — the cold, practical fact remains, that never during our stay on the Porcupine did any Indian come near us again. And I am convinced that if the initial stealing of horses and murder had gone without reprisal, we should have been a second time and more boldly attacked. But if that was the wrong village, what a train of reprisals and reprisals again in turn we may have laid!

"Only we didn't start it, and never would have!" persisted Johnny stoutly.

CHAPTER XXVI
WE SEND OUT OUR TREASURE

Though these Indian troubles had nothing to do with it, nevertheless they marked the beginning of our change of luck. We suffered no definite misfortunes; but things did not go well. The slight malarial attack of Don Gaspar was the first of an annoying series. I suppose we had all been inoculated on the marshes of the Sacramento, and the disease had remained latent in our systems. The hard work in the open air had kept us healthy; but the fever only awaited the favourable moment of depression or of over-work. The combination of ice cold water around our legs and burning sun on our heads was not the best in the world. Fortunately Yank, who came from an ague country, had had foresight enough to bring a supply of quinine. For two months one or the other of us was ailing; and once for a few days five of us were down!

Then, too, I think the zest of the game was palling on us a little, strange as it may seem. We could dig gold from the soil almost at will. It would seem that this single fact would keep normally acquisitive men keyed to a high pitch of endeavour all the time; but it was not so. I suppose we needed a vacation. We began to discuss what we would do when we should see the city again. No one for a moment dreamed that we should quit these rich diggings. We were here to make our fortunes; and the fortunes seemed to be ready for the making. Only the novelty having passed, it had become hard work, just like the making of any other kind of a fortune.

The Pine family camped below us, used our corral, at our invitation, and set placidly to work. They were typical frontiersmen, and settled down in the well-built cabin which they quickly ran up as though they meant to make of it a permanent home. For two months, which brought us up to the end of July, they lived a regular and leisurely life. Then one morning, without any warning at all, they rode over to our cabin, leading their horses, fully packed. Old man Pine explained, while his five tall, steady-eyed sons sat their horses quite immobile in the background, that they had dug enough gold for their necessities, and that they were now going down to the lower country to pick out some good land. These men were the very first I happened to meet who had come into the country with a definite idea of settling.

After the departure of this strong force, began our discussions as to the safeguarding of our gold. It had now reached a very considerable sum — somewhere near thirty-five thousand dollars, as I remember it. Bagsby was very uneasy at its presence in camp.

"The Injuns are beginning to know it's wuth something," he pointed out. "They don't know yet how much, but they know it will buy beads and buttons and paint and whiskey and everything else an Injun wants. And they know that's what we're yere for; and that we must have a lot of it. I don't calc'late that lot we licked will bother us ag'in; but they'll spread the news we're yere. And there's lots of bandits and scoundrels glad to take a chance at us. And while we come out all right before, they'll git us in the long run if we keep at it. I'd like to git rid of the stuff."

Don Gaspar agreed with him, as did also Yank, Buck Barry, and Missouri Jones. McNally, Johnny, and I inclined to the belief that we would do better to keep our wealth by us until we finally left the diggings, maintaining always a proper guard. We could not quite see how the sending out of the gold would much reduce the likelihood of attack; but the others seemed to think the gold would then be safe anyhow, and that the news of its delivery at Sutter's Fort would soon spread abroad.

About this time the discussion took a more practical turn from the fact that our provisions had run so low that we had put ourselves on half rations. As we did not believe it desirable nor healthy to drop down to an exclusively game diet, it would soon become necessary to go for more flour and coffee.

Buck Barry now brought up again strongly the advisability of sending our treasure out to a safe place. His argument was given point by the arrival in camp one evening of three evil-looking Mexicans, shabbily clothed, but well-armed, and mounted on beautiful horses. We fed them well, but saw to the caps of our revolvers and the security of our corral before turning in for the night. In the morning they departed before we were stirring, without so much as a word of thanks. These mysterious visitors had given us no faintest inkling of their business or destination. Don

Gaspar stated flatly that they had come to spy us out, having heard of our presence in the valley from the Indians.

"And I told them," said he triumphantly, "that essoon we would be sen' out for the food."

He went on to argue that thus he had prepared their minds for the fact that pack-horses would soon be going out. By distributing the gold its presence would be unsuspected.

I suggested a strong guard, but both Bagsby and Don Gaspar opposed me.

"There's enough of these yere robbers to git us anyhow, even if we all went," said Bagsby, "and that's why I want to send the stuff out now. The place they'll tackle will be right yere, if they tackle anything at all ——"

I will not weary you with the pros and cons. At the time I thought, and I still think, the whole arrangement most ill advised; but against me was the united opinion of nearly the whole camp, including the most level-headed members of my own party. It was finally agreed that Yank, Buck Barry, and Don Gaspar should take out the gold.

They started very early in the morning, carrying the treasure in saddle-bags and across the horns of the saddle. I argued that Yank rode much the lightest and had the strongest horse, and managed to get the others to confide to him a full half of the metal. At the last moment we had modified the original plan to suit everybody. The horsemen encumbered by pack-animals were to push on as rapidly as possible in order to reach by nightfall the settlement where dwelt the Italian friend. Once there they could feel themselves reasonably safe. Johnny, Missouri Jones and I would ride with them until noon as a sort of escort for the uninhabited portion of the journey. By that hour we figured we should have reached the outskirts of the regular diggings, where, our experience told us, our companions would be safe.

Accordingly we pushed our mounts hard. Unhampered by pack-animals, and aided by knowledge of the route, we made great progress. By noon we had passed the meadow of our night's camp. After a hasty lunch we accompanied our men a few miles farther, then said farewell and godspeed, and hurried back in order to reach home before sunset.

CHAPTER XXVII

THE ROBBERY

We cooked ourselves a meal, and built ourselves a fire. About midnight we heard the sounds of horses rapidly approaching. Immediately we leaped from our bunks and seized our rifles, peering anxiously into the darkness. A moment later, however, we were reassured by a shrill whistle peculiar to Buck Barry, and a moment later he and Don Gaspar rode into camp.

We assailed them with a storm of questions — why had they returned? what had happened? where was Yank? had there been an accident?

Don Gaspar, who appeared very weary and depressed, shook his head sadly. Barry looked at us savagely from beneath his brows.

"The gold is gone; and that's an end of it!" he growled.

At these words a careful, dead silence fell on us all. The situation had suddenly become too serious for hasty treatment. We felt instinctively that a wrong word might do irreparable damage. But in our hearts suspicion and anger and dull hatred leaped to life full grown. We tightened our belts, as it were, and clamped our elbows to our sides, and became wary, watching with unfriendly eyes. Johnny alone opened his lips.

"Lost? I don't believe it!" he cried.

Barry cast an ugly look at him, but said nothing. We all saw that look.

"Where's Yank?" I asked.

"Dead by now, I suppose," flung back Barry.

"Good God!" I cried; and under my breath, "Then you've murdered him!"

I don't know whether Barry heard me or not, and at the time I did not much care. His sullen eye was resting on one after the other of us as we stood there in the firelight. Every face was angry and suspicious. Barry flung himself from his horse, tore the pad from its back, slapped it on the flank, and turned away, reckless of where it went. He cut himself a steak and set to cooking his food, an uncompromising shoulder turned in our direction; nor did he open his mouth to utter another word until the general discussion later in the evening. Don Gaspar, who owned the only riding saddle, unharnessed his horse, led it to water, knee haltered it, and turned it loose to graze. While he was gone no one spoke, but we glanced at each other darkly. He returned, sat down by the fire, rolled himself a cigaretto, and volunteered his story.

"My fren'," said he, with a directness and succinctness utterly foreign to his everyday speech, "you want to know what happen'. Ver' well; it was like this."

He told us that, after we had left them, they hurried on as fast as possible in order to reach the settled country. Owing to the excellence of his animal he was generally some distance in advance. At one point, stopping on a slight elevation to allow them to catch up, he looked back in time to see two men on horseback emerge from the chaparral just behind his companions. Don Gaspar shouted and leaped from his saddle; but before the warning had reached the others, a riata from the hand of one of the men had fallen with deadly accuracy around Yank's arms and body, jerking him violently from the saddle. The thrower whirled his horse to drag his victim, Don Gaspar fired, and by great good luck shot the animal through the brain. It fell in a heap, pinning its rider beneath it. In the meantime Barry had leaped to the ground, and from behind the shelter of his horse had shot the first robber through the body. Our two companions now drew together, and took refuge behind some large rocks, preparing to receive the charge of a band of half dozen who now appeared. The situation looked desperate. Don Gaspar fired and missed. He was never anything of a marksman, and his first shot must have been a great piece of luck. Barry held his fire. The robbers each discharged his rifle, but harmlessly. Then just as they seemed about to charge in, they whirled their horses and made off into the brush.

"We could not tell the why," observed Don Gaspar.

The two men did not speculate, but ran out to where Yank lay, apparently dead, his arms still bound close to his body by the noose of the riata. Barry cut the rope with his bowie knife, and they rolled him over. They found he still breathed, but that, beside the shock of his violent fall, he had been badly trampled by the horses. After a moment he came to consciousness, but when they attempted to lift him upright, they found that his leg was broken.

At this moment they heard the sound of voices, and,

looking up, saw coming from the other direction a band of a dozen men, half of whom were on horseback, and all of whom were armed. This looked serious.

"We got behind the rock," said Don Gaspar, "but we think to ourself our goose is cook."

The newcomers, however, proved to be miners, who had heard the shots, and who now came hurrying up. Evidently the robbers had caught sight or sound of their approach. They were much interested in the state of affairs, examined the horse Don Gaspar had killed, searched for and found the body of the robber Barry had shot. It proved to be a Mexican, well known to them all, and suspected to be a member of Andreas Aijo's celebrated band. They inquired for the dead horse's rider.

"And then, for the first time," said Don Gaspar, "we think of him. He went down with his horse. But now he was gone; and also the horse of Señor Yank. But I think he crawl off in the chaparral; and that the horse of Señor Yank run away with the other horse of the dead man."

And then, I must confess, to our disbelief in the tale, Don Gaspar told us that the miners, their curiosity satisfied, calmly prepared to return to their diggings, quite deaf to all appeals for further help.

"They say to us," narrated Don Gaspar evenly, "that they wash much gold, and that they cannot take the time; and when I tell them our friend is dying, they laugh, and essay that we ought to be glad they come and essave *our* lives; and that we get along all right."

We did not believe this, though we could see no object in Don Gaspar's deceiving us on the point. Three months had passed while we had been isolated in the valley of the Porcupine; and we had not yet been taught what a difference three months can make in a young country. In that time thousands had landed, and the diggings had filled. All the world had turned to California; its riffraff and offscourings as well as its true men. Australia had unloaded its ex-convicts, so that the term "Sydney duck" had become only too well known. The idyllic time of order and honesty and pleasant living with one's fellowmen was over. But we were unaware of that; and, knowing the average generous-hearted miner, we listened to Don Gaspar with a certain surprised skepticism.

"But I follow them," said Don Gaspar, "and I offer them to pay; and after a while two of them come back with me, and we make a litter of branches with many blanket; and we carry Señor Yank down to the town. There is a town there now. And by good chance," concluded Don Gaspar with a little show of quiet racial pride, "we find a California man and his wife, and they do their bes' for Señor Yank, who is very essick, and I think he is now dead from the tramp of the horses. And we borrow the fresh horse and come back."

It was indeed, as I think of it, a wonderful ride in the darkness; but at the time my mind was full of our poor friend. The others, however, thought only of the gold.

"We have left," replied Don Gaspar to the rudely expressed shower of questions, "just the one half. It is well known to all that Señor Yank carried the most of the gold."

"Yes, and we have Munroe to thank for that," snarled Missouri Jones.

"As far at that is concerned, I was against sending out the gold from the very start," I retorted. "If you'd listened to me, it would have all been safe right here."

"If we'd had a decently strong guard, we'd have been all right," growled McNally.

We all saw the futility of our first instinctive flare of suspicion. It was obvious that if Don Gaspar and Buck Barry had intended treachery they would never have returned to us. I think that, curiously enough, we were unreasonably a little sorry for this. It would have been satisfactory to have had something definite to antagonize. As it was, we sat humped around our fire until morning. For a long period we remained sullenly silent; then we would break into recriminations or into expressions of bitter or sarcastic dissatisfaction with the way things had been planned and carried out. Bagsby alone had the sense to turn in. We chewed the cud of bitter disappointment. Our work had been hard and continuous; we were, as I have pointed out, just ready for a reaction; and now this catastrophe arrived in the exact moment to throw us into the depths of genuine revulsion. We hated each other, and the work, and the valley of the Porcupine, and gold diggings, and California with a fine impartiality. The gray morning light found us sitting haggard, dejected, disgusted, and vindictive around the dying embers of our fire.

CHAPTER XXVIII

THE BULLY

With daylight we began to get a grip on ourselves a little. I felt strongly that I should see to Yank, and so announced. Johnny at once offered to accompany me. While we were talking over the future prospects, McNally came over to us, saying:

"The boys are pretty well agreed that we ought to divide up what gold is left, and let each man take care of his own share. Are you agreeable?"

We instantly assented. The scales were brought out, and the division began. It consumed most of the morning, and was productive of much squabbling, in which, however, we took no part. Our share, including Yank's — with which we were intrusted — came to about thirty-one pounds: a value of about seven thousand dollars. We were impatient to be off, and now wanted nothing so much as to be done with the whole affair. Yank had ridden one of our horses; the other had been stolen in the Indian raid. We approached Don Gaspar, who had his own saddle horse and that of Vasquez, not to speak of the remaining pack-animals. To our surprise and delight he offered to accompany us; and Bagsby, too, decided to leave. McNally, Buck Barry, and Missouri Jones, however, could not be persuaded out of their intention of

255

remaining to dig fresh gold; nor, I am afraid, were we very cordial in our insistence. We considered them foolhardy; but in our then mood we did not greatly care.

By noon we had packed our goods, and by night we had broken the back of our return journey.

We found a full-grown town where we had left a few tents and miners' cabins. Its main street ran either side the deep dust of the immigrant trail, and consisted of the usual shanties, canvas shacks, and log structures, with rather more than the customary allowance of tin cans, old clothes, worn-out boots, and empty barrels kicking around. The diggings were in the gulch below the road: but the streets of the town, and especially the shady sides of the buildings, were numerously furnished with lounging men. Some of these were employees or owners of the gambling halls, saloons, and boarding-houses; but most were plain "loafers" — a class never wholly absent from any mining camp, men who washed just enough gold to keep themselves fed and pickled in drink. Many of them were evil-looking customers, in fact about as tough a lot as a man would care to see, unshaven generally, but not always, dirty, truculent and rough, insolent in manner. In our passage of the main street I saw just three decent looking people — one was evidently gambler, one a beefy, red-faced individual who had something to do with one of the hotels, and the third was a tall man, past middle age, with a clean shaven, hawk face, a piercing, haughty, black eye, and iron gray hair. He was carefully and flawlessly dressed in a gray furred "plug" hat, tailed blue coat with brass buttons, a buff waistcoat, trousers of the same shade, and a frilled shirt front. Immaculate down to within six inches or so of the ground, his nether garments and boots were coated thickly with the inevitable red dust. He strode slowly down the street, looking neither to right nor left.

Don Gaspar led the way for a short distance along the wagon road. On the outskirts of the settlement he turned aside to a small log cabin supplemented by a brush lean-to. A long string of bright red peppers hung down the face of it. To our knock came a very fat, rather dirty, but exceedingly pleasant-faced woman with glossy black hair, parted smoothly, and soft black eyes. She opened the door only the fraction of an inch at first, but instantly recognized Don Gaspar, and threw it wide.

To our great relief we found Yank very much alive. He greeted us rather feebly, but with satisfaction. We found that he had been kindly cared for, and that the surface wounds and bruises from the horses' hoofs had been treated with some skill.

"But I reckon I'm hurt some inside," he whispered with difficulty, "for I can't breathe easy; and I can't eat nothin' but soup. And my leg is hell."

The broken leg too had been bound up after a fashion, but it was badly swollen above and below the bandages.

"He ought to have a doctor," said I positively. "There's no doubt of that. There must be some among the miners — there generally is. I'm going to see if I can find one."

I returned to town, and hunted up the beefy, red-faced hotel keeper, who had impressed me as being an honest man.

"Yes, there's a doctor," said he, "a mighty good one.

He went by here a little while ago. Name's Dr. Rankin.
I'll rustle him out for you. Oh, you Pete!" he shouted
into the interior of the building.

A moment's shuffling about preceded the appearance
of a negro boy of twelve or fourteen.

"Yes, sah."

"Go find Dr. Rankin and bring him here right away.
Tell him a gentleman wants him."

"You've got a mighty sudden sort of camp here,"
said I, as we settled ourselves to wait. "Three months
ago I went through here, and there was practically nothing."

"Looks to be a thousand years, though," agreed the
hotel man. "Where you been?"

"Oh, just prospecting," I replied vaguely.

"Strike it?"

"Just fair," I evaded; "not rich enough to keep me
from coming back, you see. Any finds here?"

"The diggings are rich as mud," replied the hotel
man dispassionately. "It's a prosperous camp all right."

"You don't 'wash' yourself?" I asked.

"Not I! I make more than my 'ounce a day' right
here." He jerked his thumb at his hotel.

"A good many 'loafers,'" I suggested.

He looked at me steadily, hesitated for a moment, then
evidently changed his mind.

"Quite a few," he agreed.

At this moment the negro boy appeared, closely followed by the man with the blue coat and white beaver hat
whom I had taken for an eccentric gambler. This man
walked slowly up to face me.

"Well, sir?" he demanded. "I am told I can be of service. In what way?"

His piercing black eye held mine with a certain high arrogance.

"Professionally, doctor," I replied. "A friend of mine is lying badly hurt in a nearby hut."

For a barely appreciable instant his eye held mine after I had ceased speaking, as though he was appraising me. Then he bowed with old-fashioned courtesy.

"At your service, sir," said he. "Pete, you black rascal, get my bag, and get it quick."

The little negro, who had stood by obviously worshipping, broke into a grin and darted into the hotel, almost instantly reappearing with a regulation professional satchel.

"At your service, sir," repeated Dr. Rankin.

We took our stately progress up the street, through the deep red dust. The hot sun glared down upon us, reflecting from the surface of the earth in suffocating heat. Hard as I was, I flushed and perspired. The doctor never turned a hair. As we passed one of the saloons a huge, hairy man lurched out, nearly colliding with us. He was not drunk, but he was well flushed with drink. His mood was evidently ugly, for he dropped his hand to the butt of his revolver, and growled something truculent at me, glaring through bloodshot eyes. Dr. Rankin, who had stepped back to avoid collision, spoke up:

"Malone," said he, "I told you a week ago that you have to stop drinking or come to me. I repeat it."

He turned his keen black eyes upon the big man, and stepped forward. The big man muttered something and moved aside.

Arrived at the hut of the Moreñas, for that it seemed was the name of our host and hostess, Dr. Rankin laid aside his furry beaver hat, walked directly to the side of the bunk on which Yank lay, and began his examination, without vouchsafing anything or anybody else the slightest glance. Nor did he seem to pay more attention to Yank as a human being, but prodded and pulled and hauled and manipulated him from top to toe, his gray, hawk face intent and absorbed. Occasionally, as he repeated some prod, he looked up keenly into Yank's face, probably for some slight symptom of pain that escaped us, for Yank remained stoical. But he asked no questions. At the end of ten minutes he threw the blanket over our friend's form and stood erect, carefully dusting the ends of his fingers against one another.

"Broken leg, badly set," said he; "two broken ribs; severe surface bruises; and possibility of internal bruises in the region of the spleen. Neglected too long. Why wasn't I sent for before?"

I explained. Dr. Rankin listened attentively, but made no comment. His eyes travelled slowly over us all — the fat, pleasant, brown California woman, her bearded husband, who had come in from the diggings, Bagsby's tall, wiry old form, the worn remains of Don Gaspar's finery, and lingered a moment on Johnny's undisguisable air of high spirit and breeding.

"How many of you belong here?" he demanded. "I

can't waste time on the rest of you. Those who are not directly concerned, kindly step outside."

"Johnny and I will take care of this," I told the others hastily, before they had time to say anything.

"Now," cried Dr. Rankin, removing his blue coat, and turning back the frills of his shirt, "hot water!"

We assisted at the rather dreadful process of resetting a broken leg three days old. At the end of the operation we were all pretty limp.

"How long?" gasped Yank, opening his eyes.

"Three months; not a day less if you want that leg to be as good as ever," stated Dr. Rankin uncompromisingly.

Yank closed his eyes and groaned.

The doctor resumed his coat and picked up his beaver hat.

"What treatment?" I ventured to ask.

"I will inform the woman," replied the doctor. "These Californians are the best nurses in the world, once things are on a proper footing."

"Your fee, sir?" asked Johnny very formally, for the doctor's brusque manner had rubbed.

"One ounce," stated Dr. Rankin. "I shall direct the woman, and I shall return one week from to-day unless conditions change. In that case, summon me."

He pouched the gold dust that Johnny shook into the palm of his hand at a guess, bowed formally to each of us in turn, picked up his bag and departed, rigidly erect, the fine red dust crawling and eddying at his feet.

Then we held a council of war, all of us. Don Gaspar

announced his intention of returning to his rancho in the south.

"I have found the gold, and I have made fren's, and I have now enough," said he.

Bagsby, too, said he thought he would just ride down as far as Sutter's Fort, there to lay in a supply of powder and ball for a trip in the mountains.

"I kind of want to git up another b'ar fight," said he. "If I thought there was a ghost of a show to git them robbers for you boys, I'd stay and help you scout for them; but there ain't a show in the world. They've had a good three days' start."

After shaking hands with us again and again, and obtaining promises that we should all surely meet in San Francisco or Monterey, they mounted and took their departure in order to get well clear of the settlement before nightfall.

When they had gone Yank opened his eyes from the apparent sleep into which he had fallen.

"You fellows don't hang around here with me, I can tell you that," he stated. "I'm fixed all right. I want you to make arrangements with these people yere to keep me; tuck my gold under my piller, stack old Betsey up yere in the corner by me, and go about your business. You come out yere to dig gold, not to take keer of cripples."

'All right, Yank, we'll fix it somehow,' I agreed. "Now if you're all right, Johnny and I will just go and straighten out our camp things a little."

We were now, it will be remembered, without horses. Don Gaspar had unpacked our few belongings before departing. Johnny and I found a good camping place, then carried the stuff over on our backs. We cooked ourselves some food, lit pipes, and sat down to talk the situation over.

We got nowhere. As a matter of fact, we were both in the dead-water of reaction from hard, long-continued labour, and we could not bring ourselves to face with any enthusiasm the resuming of gold washing. Revulsion shook us at the mere thought of getting down in a hot, glaring ravine and moving heavy earth and rocks. Yet we had not made a fortune, nor much of a beginning at one, and neither of us was what is known as a quitter. We realized perfectly that we would go on gold mining.

"What we need is a recess," Johnny ended, "and I move we take it. Just let's camp here, and loaf for a few days or a week, and see how Yank gets along, and then we can go back to Porcupine."

As though this decision lifted a great weight, we sat back on our shoulder blades with a sigh of relief, and blew tobacco smoke straight up in the air for at least fifteen minutes. By the end of that time we, being young and restless, felt thoroughly refreshed.

"Let's go look this outfit over," suggested Johnny.

We gravitated naturally to the diggings, which were very much like those at Hangman's Gulch, except that they were rather more extensive, and branched out more into the tributary ravines. The men working there were, many of them, of a much better type than those we had seen in town; though even here was a large element of rough-looking, wild, reckless customers. We wandered about here and there, our hands in our pockets, a vast leisure filling our souls. With some of the more pleasant-appearing miners we conversed. They told us that the diggings were rich, good "ounce a day" diggings. We saw a good many cradles in use. It was easy to tell the old-timers from the riffraff of newcomers. A great many of the latter seemed to lack the steadiness of purpose characteristic of nearly all the first rush. They worked haphazardly, spasmodically, pulling and hauling against each other. Some should not have been working at all, for their eyes were sunken in their heads from illness.

"We've got to hustle now," they told us. "We can take a good rest when the rains stop work."

We noticed especially a marked change in demeanour among some of the groups. In the early part of the summer every man answered every man good-naturedly, except he happened to have a next day's head or some other sort of a personal grouch. Now many compact little groups of men worked quite apart. When addressed they merely scowled or looked sullen, evidently quite unwilling to fraternize with the chance-comer.

We loafed about here and there through the diggings, swapping remarks with the better disposed, until the men began to knock off work. Then we returned through the village.

Its street had begun to fill. Here, too, we could not but be struck by the subtle change that had come over the spirit of the people. All used to seem like the members of a big family, good-natured and approachable even when strangers. Now a slower acquaintance must precede familiarity. We seemed out of it because we did not know anybody, something we had not felt before in a mining camp. There was no hostility in this, not an iota; only now it had evidently become necessary to hold a man off a little until one knew something about him. People seemed, somehow, *watchful*, in spite of the surface air of good-nature and of boisterous spirits. We did not quite understand this at the moment, but we learned more about it later.

We sauntered along peering into the various buildings. The saloons were here more elaborate than at Hangman's, the gambling places larger, and with some slight attempt at San Francisco splendour. That is to say, there were large gilt-framed mirrors on the walls, nude pictures, and in some cases a stage for musical performers. One of the three stores was devoted entirely to clothing and "notions," to us a new departure in specialization. We were sadly in need of garments, so we entered, and were at once met by a very oily, suave specimen of the chosen people. When we had escaped from this robber's den we looked at each other in humorous dismay.

"Glad Yank don't need clothes, anyway," said Johnny.

We were, it will be remembered, out of provisions, so we entered also one of the general stores to lay in a small supply. The proprietor proved to be an old friend, Jones, the storekeeper at Hangman's.

"Which," said Johnny shrewdly, "is a sad commentary on the decline of the diggings at Hangman's."

Jones was evidently prosperous, and doing business on a much larger scale than at the old place; for in his commodious building were quantities of goods displayed and many barrels and boxes still unopened. He did not recognize us, of course; and we had to await the completion of a tale he was telling a group perched on the counters and on the boxes.

"Got a consignment of mixed goods from Mellin," he was saying, "and one of the barrels wasn't marked with anything I could make out. I knocked the top in, and chucked her out behind for spoiled beef. Certainly stunk like it. Well, sir, that barrel lay there for a good ten days; and then one day up drifted a Dutchman with a brogue on him thick enough to plant flag-poles in. 'How mooch,' says he 'is dot stoof?' 'What stuff?' says I. 'Dot stoof oudt behind.' 'I ain't got no stuff out behind What's eating you?' says I. Then he points out that spoiled beef. 'Good Lord!' says I, 'help yourself. I got a lot of nerve, but not enough to charge a man for anything that stinks like that beef. But you better let it alone; you'll get sick!' Well, sir, you wouldn't think there was any Dutchmen in the country, now would you? but they came to that stink like flies to molasses. Any time I'd look out the back door I'd see one or two nosing around that old spoiled beef. Then one day another old beer-belly sagged in. 'Say, you got any more barrels of dot sauerkraut?' he wants to know. 'That what?' I asks. 'Dot sauerkraut,' says he, 'like dot in the backyard. I gif you goot price for a whole barrel,' says he. And here I'd give away a whole barrel! I might've got a dollar a pound for the stuff. *I* don't know what it might be worth to a Dutchman."

He turned away to wait on us.

"And you wouldn't guess there was so many Dutchmen in the country!" he repeated.

We paid his terrible prices for our few necessities, and went out. The music was beginning to tune up from the gambling places and saloons. It reminded us of our Italian friend.

"Seems to me his place was right here where we are," puzzled Johnny. "Hanged if I don't believe this *is* the place; only they've stuck a veranda roof on it."

We turned into the entrance of the hotel, to find ourselves in the well-remembered long, low room wherein we had spent the evening a few months before. It was now furnished with a bar, the flimsy partitions had been knocked out, and evidently additions had been constructed beyond the various closed doors. The most conspicuous single thing was a huge bulletin board occupying one whole end. It was written over closely with hundreds and hundreds of names. Several men were laboriously spelling them out. This, we were given to understand, was a sort of register of the overland immigrants; and by its means many parties obtained first news of scattered members.

The man behind the bar looked vaguely familiar to me, but I could not place him.

"Where's the proprietor of this place?" I asked him.

He indicated a short, blowsy, truculent-looking individual who was, at the moment, staring out the window.

"There used to be an Italian ——" I began.

The barkeeper uttered a short barking laugh as he turned to attend to a customer.

"He found the climate bad for his heart — and sold out!" said he.

On the wall opposite was posted a number of printed and written handbills. We stopped idly to examine them. They had in general to do with lost property, stolen horses, and rewards for the apprehension of various individuals. One struck us in particular. It was issued by a citizens' committee of San Francisco, and announced a general reward for the capture of any member of the "Hounds."

"Looks as if they'd got tired of that gang down there," Johnny observed. "They were ruling the roost when we left. Do you know, I saw one of those fellows this afternoon — perhaps you remember him — a man with a queer sort of blue scar over one cheekbone. I swear I saw him in San Francisco. There's our chance to make some money, Jim."

The proprietor of the hotel turned to look at Johnny curiously, and several of the loafers drinking at the bar glanced in the direction of his clear young voice. We went on reading and enjoying the notices, some of which were very quaint. Suddenly the door burst open to admit a big man followed closely by a motley rabble. The leader was a red-faced, burly, whiskered individual, with a red beard and matted hair. As he turned I saw a star-shaped blue scar above his cheekbone.

"Where's the —— —— —— that is going to make some money out of arresting me?" he roared, swinging his huge form ostentatiously toward the centre of the room.

I confessed I was aghast, and completely at a loss.

A row was evidently unavoidable, and the odds were against us. Almost at the instant the door came open, Johnny, without waiting for hostile demonstration, jerked his Colt's revolvers from their holsters. With one bound he reached the centre of the room, and thrust the muzzles beneath the bully's nose. His black eyes were snapping.

"Shut up, you hound!" he said in a low, even voice. "I wouldn't condescend to make money out of your miserable carcass, except at a glue factory. And if you or your friends so much as wink an eyelid, I'll put you in shape for it."

Caught absolutely by surprise, the "Hound" stared fascinated into the pistol barrels, his jaw dropped, his face redder than ever, his eyes ridiculously protruding. I had recovered my wits and had backed against the bulletin board, a revolver in either hand, keeping an eye on the general company. Those who had burst in with the bully had stopped frozen in their tracks. The others were interested, but not particularly excited.

"I'm going to stay in this camp," Johnny advised crisply, "and I'm not going to be bothered by big bluffs like you. I warn you, and all like you, to let me alone and keep away from me. You stay in camp, or you can leave camp, just as you please, but I warn you that I shoot you next time I lay eyes on you. Now, about face! March!"

Johnny's voice had an edge of steel. The big man obeyed orders implicitly. He turned slowly, and sneaked out the door. His followers shambled toward the bar. Johnny passed them rather contemptuously under the review of his snapping eyes, and they shambled a trifle faster. Then, with elaborate nonchalance, we sauntered out.

"My Lord, Johnny!" I cried when we had reached the street, "that was fine! I didn't know you had it in you!"

"Damn the luck!" he cried, kicking a tin can. "Oh, *damn!*"

He muttered to himself a moment, then turned to me with humorous despair.

"What a stupid, useless mess!" he cried. "The minute that fellow came into the room I saw we were let in for a row; so I went at it quick before he had got organized. He didn't expect that. He thought he'd have to work us into it."

"It certainly got him," said I.

"But it just starts us all wrong here," complained Johnny. "We are marked men."

"We'll just have to look out for him a little. I don't believe he's really dangerous. He looks to me a lot like a bluffer."

"Oh, him!" said Johnny contemputously, "he doesn't worry me any. It's all the rest of them. I've practically challenged all the hard cases in camp, don't you see? I'm no longer an inconspicuous newcomer. Every tough character with any real nerve will want to tackle me now, just to try me out."

From the impulsive and unanalytical Johnny this was surprising enough, and my face must have showed it.

"I've seen it worked out in my part of the country," he explained sombrely. "I don't want to bother with that sort of thing. I'm a peaceable citizen. Now I've

THE BULLY

got to walk around on tiptoe all the time watching for trouble. Oh, *damn!*"

"If you're afraid —— " I began.

"I'm not afraid," said Johnny so simply that I believed him at once. "But I'm annoyed. And of course you recognized that barkeeper."

"I thought I'd seen him before, but I don't remember just where."

"He's one of those fellows we fired out of our canoe down at Chagres. You can bet he doesn't love us any!"

"You move along to Porcupine to-morrow," I suggested. "I can look after Yank all right. They won't bother me."

Johnny walked for some steps in silence.

"No, they won't bother you," he repeated slowly.

He thought for a moment, then he threw back his head. "But look here, Jim," he said briskly, "you forget. I told that fellow and his friends that I was going to live in this place. I can't leave now."

"Nonsense," said I. "What do you care for that gang?"

"It would look like running away. No, I certainly don't intend to leave now."

CHAPTER XXIX

THE CHALLENGE

We went out to see Yank, with the full intention of spending the evening and cheering him up. He was dozing, restless, waking and sleeping by fits and starts. We sat around in the awkward fashion peculiar to very young boys in the sickroom; and then, to our vast relief, were shoved out by Señora Moreña. With her we held a whispered conversation outside, and completed satisfactory arrangements for Yank's keep. She was a chuckling, easy-going, motherly sort of creature, and we were very lucky to have her. Then we returned in the gathering dusk to our camp under the trees across the way.

A man rose from a seat against a tree trunk.

"*Good* evenin', stranger," said he.

"Good evening," responded Johnny guardedly.

"You are the man who stuck up Scar-face Charley in Morton's place, ain't you?"

"What's that to you?" replied Johnny. "Are you a friend of his?"

His habitual air of young carelessness had fallen from him; his eye was steady and frosty, his face set in stern lines. Before my wondering eyes he had grown ten years older in the last six hours. The other was lounging toward us — a short, slight man, with flaxen moustache and eye-

272

brows, a colourless face, pale blue eyes, and a bald forehead from which the hat had been pushed back. He was
chewing a straw.

"Well, I was just inquirin' in a friendly sort of way,"
replied the newcomer peaceably.

"I don't know you," stated Johnny shortly, "nor
who you're friends to, nor your camp. I deny your right
to ask questions. Good night."

"Well, good night," agreed the other, still peaceable.
"I reckon I gather considerable about you, anyhow." He
turned away. "I had a notion from what I heard that
you was sort of picked on, and I dropped round, sort of
friendly like; but Lord love you! I don't care how many
of you desperadoes kill each other. Go to it, and good
riddance!" He cast his pale blue eyes on Johnny's rigid
figure. "Also, go to hell!" he remarked dispassionately.

Johnny stared at him puzzled.

"Hold on!" he called, after a moment. "Then you're
not a friend of this Hound?"

The stranger turned in slow surprise.

"Me? What are you talking about?" He looked from
one to the other of us, then returned the few steps he had
taken. "I believe you don't know me. I'm Randall,
Danny Randall."

"Yes?" puzzled Johnny.

"Of Sonoma," added Randall.

"I suppose I should know you, but I'm afraid I don't,"
confessed Johnny.

Randall turned back to the tree beneath which lay
our effects.

"I believe I'll just have a cup of coffee with you boys," said he.

We blew up the fire, scoured the frying pan, made ourselves food. Randall brought a pail of water. We all ate together, without much conversation; then lit our pipes and piled on dry wood to make a brighter friendship fire.

"Now, boys," said Randall, "I'm going to ask you some questions; and you can answer me or not, just as you please. Only I'll say, it isn't just curiosity."

Johnny, who was studying him covertly from beneath the shadow of his hat, nodded briefly, but said nothing.

"How long have you been in the mines?"

"Since March."

"Since March!" echoed Randall, as though a little bewildered at this reply. "Yet you never heard —— What camp?"

Johnny studied a while.

"Hangman's Gulch for six weeks," said he. "Then just prospecting."

"Where?"

"I don't believe I'll answer that question," replied Johnny slowly.

"But somewhere back in the hills?" persisted Randall.

"Somewhere back in the hills," agreed Johnny.

"Seems to me ——" I broke in, but Johnny silenced me with a gesture. He was watching Randall intently, and thinking hard.

"Then you have been out of it for three months or so. That explains it. Now I don't mind telling you I came up here this evening to size you up. I heard about your row with Scar-face Charley, and I wanted to see whether you were just another fighting desperado or an honest man. Well, I'm satisfied. I'm not going to ask you if you have much gold with you, for you wouldn't tell me; but if you have, keep it with you. If you don't, you'll lose it. Keep in the middle of the road, and out of dark places. This is a tough camp; but there are a lot of us good men, too, and my business is to get us all to know each other. Things are getting bad, and we've got to get together. That's why I came up to see you. Are you handy with a gun?" he asked abruptly.

"Fair," said Johnny.

"You need to be. Let's see if you are. Stand up. Try to get the draw on me. Now!"

Johnny reached for his pistol, but before his hand was fairly on the butt, Randall had thrust the muzzle of a small revolver beneath his nose. His pale blue eyes had lit with concentration, his bleached eyebrows were drawn together. For an instant the thought flashed across my mind that this was a genuine hold-up; and I am sure Johnny caught the same suspicion, for his figure stiffened. Then Randall dropped his hand.

"Very pretty," said Johnny coolly. "How did you do that? I didn't catch your motion."

"From the sleeve," said Randall. "It's difficult, but it's pretty, as you say; and if you learn to draw from the sleeve, I'll guarantee you'll get the draw on your man every time."

"Show me," said Johnny simply.

"That gun of yours is too big; it's a holster weapon. Here, take this."

He handed Johnny a beautifully balanced small Colt's revolver, engraved, silver-plated, with polished rosewood handles. This he showed Johnny how to stow away in the sleeve, how to arrange it, how to grasp it, and the exact motion in snatching it away.

"It takes practice, lots of it, and then more of it," said Randall. "It's worse than useless unless you get it just right. If you made a mistake at the wrong time, the other man would get you sure."

"Where can I get one of these?" asked Johnny.

"Good!" Randall approved his decision. "You see the necessity. You can't. But a derringer is about as good, and Jones has them for sale. Now as for your holster gun: the whole trick of quick drawing is to throw your right shoulder forward and *drag* the gun from the holster with one forward sweep. Don't lift it up and out. This way!" He snapped his hand past his hip and brought it away armed.

"Pretty," repeated Johnny.

"Don't waste much powder and ball shooting at a mark," advised Randall. "It looks nice to cut out the ace of hearts at ten yards, but it doesn't mean much. If you can shoot at all, you can shoot straight enough to hit a man at close range. Practise the draw." He turned to me. "You'd better practise, too. Every man's got to take care of himself these days. But you're not due for trouble same as your friend is."

"I'm obliged to you," said Johnny.

"You are not. Now it's up to you. I judged you

didn't know conditions here, and I thought it only right to warn you. There's lots of good fellows in this camp; and some of the hard cases are a pretty good sort. Just keep organized, that's all."

"Now I wonder who Danny Randall is!" speculated Johnny after our visitor had departed. "He talked as though we ought to know all about it. I'm going to find out the first fellow I get acquainted with."

Next morning we asked the Moreñas who was Danny Randall.

"*El diabolo*," replied Moreña shortly; and trudged obstinately away to his work without vouchsafing further information.

"Which is interesting, but indefinite," said Johnny.

We found Yank easier in body, and embarked on the sea of patience in which he was to float becalmed until his time was up. In reply to his inquiries as to our plans, we told him we were resting a few days, which was the truth. Then we went up to town and made two purchases; a small tent, and a derringer pistol. They cost us three hundred and fifty dollars. It was the quiet time of day; the miners had gone to work, and most of the gentlemen of leisure were not yet about. Nevertheless a dozen or so sat against the walls, smoking paper cigarettos. They all looked at us curiously; and several nodded at Johnny in a brief, tentative sort of fashion.

The rest of the day, and of several days following, we spent in putting up our tent, ditching it, arranging our cooking affairs, building rough seats, and generally making ourselves comfortable. We stretched these things to cover as long a space of time as possible, for we secretly dreaded tacing the resumption of the old grind, and postponed it as long as we could. A good deal of the time we spent at Yank's bedside, generally sitting silent and constrained, to the mutual discomfort of all three of us, I am sure. At odd intervals we practised conscientiously and solemnly at the "draw." We would stand facing each other, the nipples of our revolvers uncapped, and would, at the given word, see who could cover the other first. We took turns at giving the word. At first we were not far apart; but Johnny quickly passed me in skill. I am always somewhat clumsy, but my friend was naturally quick and keen at all games of skill or dexterity. He was the sort of man who could bowl, or play pool, or billiards, or anything else rather better than the average accustomed player the first time he tried. He turned card tricks deftly. At the end of our three days' loafing he caught me at the end of his pistol so regularly that there ceased to be any contest in it. I never did get the sleeve trick; but then, I never succeeded in fooling the merest infant with any of my attempts at legerdemain. Johnny could flip that little derringer out with a twist of his supple wrist as neatly as a snake darts its forked tongue. For ten minutes at a time he practised it, over and over, as regularly as well-oiled machinery.

"But that proves nothing as to how it would work out in real action," said Johnny thoughtfully.

The afternoon of the third day, while we were resting from the heat beneath the shade of our tree, we were approached by three men.

"Howdy, boys," said the first. "We hain't seen you around camp lately, and thought mebbe you'd flew."

"We are still here," replied Johnny with smooth politeness. "As you see, we have been fixing our quarters to stay here."

"Scar-face Charley is here, too," observed the spokesman, "and he wanted me to tell you that he is going to be at the Bella Union at eight this evenin', and he wants to know, will he see you? and to come heeled."

"Thank you, gentlemen," replied Johnny quietly. "If by accident you should happen to see the desperado in question — who, I assume, can be in no way your friend — I hope you will tell him that I, too, will be at the Bella Union at eight o'clock, and that I will come heeled."

"You'll be comin' alone?" said the man, "or p'rhaps yore friend ——"

"My friend, as you call him, is simply a miner, and has nothing to do with this," interrupted Johnny emphatically.

"I thank you, sir," said the spokesman, rising.

The other two, who had throughout said no word, followed his example.

"Do you know Danny Randall?" asked Johnny as they moved off.

If he had presented his derringer under their noses, they could not have stopped more suddenly. They stared at each other a moment.

"Is he a friend of yours?" inquired the spokesman after an uncertain moment.

"He likes fair play," said Johnny enigmatically.

The trio moved off in the direction of town.

"We don't know any more about Danny Randall than we did," observed Johnny, "but I tried a shot in the dark."

"Nevertheless," I told him, "I'm going to be there; and you want to make up your mind to just that."

"You will come, of course," agreed Johnny. "I suppose I cannot keep you from that. But Jim," he commanded earnestly, "you must swear to keep out of the row, unless it develops into a general one; and you must swear not to speak to me or make any sign no matter what happens. I must play a lone hand."

He was firm on this point; and in the end I gave my promise, to his evident relief.

"This is our visitors' day, evidently," he observed. "Here come two more men. One of them is the doctor; I'd know that hat two miles."

"The other is our friend Danny Randall," said I.

Dr. Rankin greeted us with a cordiality I had not suspected in him. Randall nodded in his usual diffident fashion, and slid into the oak shadow, where he squatted on his heels.

"About this Scar-face Charley," he said abruptly, "I hear he's issued his defi, and you've taken him up. Do you know anything about this sort of thing?"

"Not a bit," admitted Johnny frankly. "Is it a duel; and are you gentleman here to act as my seconds?"

"It is not," stated the downright doctor. "It's a bar-room murder and you cannot get around it; and I, for one, don't try. But now you're in for it, and you've got to go through with it."

"I intend to," said Johnny.

"It's not precisely that," objected Danny Randall. "for, d'ye see, he's sent you warning."

"It's about all the warning you'll get!" snorted the doctor.

"There's a sort of rule about it," persisted Randall. "And that's what I'm here to tell you. He'll try to come up on you suddenly, probably from behind; and he'll say 'draw and defend yourself,' and shoot you as soon after that as he can. You want to see him first, that's all."

"Thanks," said Johnny.

"And," exploded the doctor, "if you don't kill that fellow, by the Eternal, when you get a chance ——"

"You'll give him a pill, Doctor," interrupted Randall, with a little chuckle. "But look here," he said to Johnny, "after all, this sort of a mess isn't required of you. You say the word and I'll take on this Scar-face Charley and run him out of town. He's a good deal of a pest."

"Thank you," said Johnny stiffly; "I intend to paddle my own canoe."

Randall nodded.

"I don't know as we can help you any more," said he. "I just thought you ought to be on to the way it's done."

"I'm obliged to you," said Johnny warmly. "The only doubt in my mind was when I was privileged to open."

"I'd pot him through the window with a shotgun first chance I got," stated the doctor; "that sort of a ruffian is just like a mad dog."

"Of course you would, Doctor," said Randall with just the faintest suspicion of sarcasm in his voice. "Well, I guess we'll be toddling."

But I wanted some information, and I meant to have it.

"Who is this Scar-face Charley," I asked.

"Got me," replied Randall; "you fellows seemed to recognize him. Only he's one of the gang, undoubtedly."

"The gang?"

"Oh, the general run of hangers-on. Nobody knows how they live, but every one suspects. Some of them work, but not many. There are a heap of disappearances that no one knows anything about; and every once in a while a man is found drowned and floating; *floating* mind you!"

"What of that?" I asked; "drowned bodies usually float."

"There's no miner in these diggings but has gold enough in his belt to sink him. If a man floats, he's been robbed, and you can tie to that reasoning. And the fellows are all well mounted, and given to mysterious disappearances."

"In other words," broke in the doctor, "they are an organized band of cut-throats and highway robbers making this honest camp a headquarters."

"Pshaw, Doctor," said Randall, "that's by no means certain."

"It's certain enough," insisted the doctor.

"I should think the miners would drive them out," I said.

"Drive them out!" cried the doctor bitterly; "they're too busy, and their own toes haven't been trodden on, and they're too willing to let well enough alone so as not to be interrupted in their confounded digging for gold."

"They're not organized and they are quite justly unwilling to get in a row with that gang when they know they'd be killed," stated Randall quietly. "They're getting on 'well enough,' and they'll continue to be run by this lot of desperadoes until something desperate happens. They want to be let alone."

The doctor recovered his equanimity with an effort.

"They present the curious spectacle," said he thought-fully, "of the individual man in a new untrammelled liberty trying to escape his moral obligations to society. He escapes them for a while, but they are there; and in the end he must pay in violence."

Randall laughed and arose.

"If the doctor is going to begin that sort of thing, I'm going," said he.

Our visitors took their departure.

"Oh, Doctor, one moment!" I called; then, as he returned. "Tell me, who and what is Danny Randall?"

"Danny Randall," said the doctor, a humorous twinkle coming into his eyes, "is a gentleman of fortune."

"And now we know a lot more than we did before!" said Johnny, as we watched the receding figures.

CHAPTER XXX

THE FIGHT

We ate a very silent supper, washed our dishes methodically, and walked up to town. The Bella Union was the largest of the three gambling houses — a log and canvas structure some forty feet long by perhaps twenty wide. A bar extended across one end, and the gaming tables were arranged down the middle. A dozen oil lamps with reflectors furnished illumination.

All five tables were doing a brisk business; when we paused at the door for a preliminary survey, the bar was lined with drinkers, and groups of twos and threes were slowly sauntering here and there or conversing at the tops of their voices with many guffaws. The air was thick with tobacco smoke. Johnny stepped just inside the door, moved sideways, and so stood with his back to the wall. His keen eyes went from group to group slowly, resting for a moment in turn on each of the five impassive gamblers and their lookouts, on the two barkeepers, and then one by one on the men with whom the place was crowded. Following his, my glance recognized at a corner of the bar Danny Randall with five rough-looking miners. He caught my eye and nodded. No one else appeared to notice us, though I imagined the noise of the place sank and rose again at the first moment of our entrance.

"Jim," said Johnny to me quietly, "there's Danny Randall at the other end of the room. Go join him. I want you to leave me to play my own game."

I started to object.

"Please do as I say," insisted Johnny. "I can take care of myself unless there's a general row. In that case all my friends are better together."

Without further protest I left him, and edged my way to the little group at the end of the bar. Randall nodded to me as I came up, and motioned to the barkeeper to set me out a glass, but said nothing. Ours was the only lot away from the gaming tables not talking. We sipped our drink and watched Johnny.

After surveying coolly the room, Johnny advanced to the farther of the gambling tables, and began to play. His back was toward the entrance. The game was roulette, and Johnny tossed down his bets methodically, studying with apparent absorption each shift of the wheel. To all appearance he was intent on the game, and nothing else; and he talked and laughed with his neighbours and the dealer as though his spirit were quite carefree.

For ten minutes we watched. Then a huge figure appeared in the blackness of the doorway, slipped through, and instantly to one side, so that his back was to the wall. Scar-face Charley had arrived.

He surveyed the place as we had done, almost instantly caught sight of Johnny, and immediately began to make his way across the room through the crowds of loungers. Johnny was laying a bet, bending over the table, joking with the impassive dealer, his back turned to the door,

GOLD

totally oblivious of his enemy's approach. I started forward, instantly realized the hopelessness of either getting quickly through that crowd or of making myself heard, and leaned back, clutching the rail with both hands. Johnny was hesitating, his hand hovering uncertainly above the marked squares of the layout, in doubt exactly where to bet. Scar-face Charley shouldered his way through the loungers and reached the clear space immediately behind his unconscious victim. He stopped for an instant, squared his shoulders, and took one step forward. Johnny dropped his chips on the felt layout, contemplated his choice an instant — and suddenly whirled on his heel in a lightning about-face.

Although momentarily startled by this unexpected evidence that Johnny was not so far off guard as he had seemed, the desperado's hand dropped swiftly to the butt of his pistol. At the same instant Johnny's arm snapped forward in the familiar motion of drawing from the sleeve. The motion started clean and smooth, but half through, caught, dragged, halted. I gasped aloud, but had time for no more than that; Scar-face Charley's revolver was already on the leap. Then at last Johnny's derringer appeared, apparently as the result of a desperate effort. Almost with the motion, it barked, and the big man whirled to the floor, his pistol, already at half raise, clattering away. The whole episode from the beginning occupied the space of two eye-winks. Probably no one but myself and Danny Randall could have caught the slight hitch in Johnny's draw; and indeed I doubt if anybody saw whence he had snatched the derringer.

THE FIGHT

A complete silence fell. It could have lasted only an instant; but Johnny seized that instant.

"Has this man any friends here?" he asked clearly.

His head was back, and his snapping black eyes seemed to see everywhere at once.

No one answered or stirred. Johnny held them for perhaps ten seconds, then deliberately turned back to the table.

"That's my bet on the *even*," said he. "Let her roll!"

The gambler lifted his face, white in the brilliant illumina· tion directly over his head, and I thought to catch a flicker of something like admiration in his passionless eyes. Then with his left hand he spun the wheel.

The soft, dull whir and tiny clicking of the ball as it rebounded from the metal grooves struck across the tense stillness. As though this was the releasing signal, a roar of activity burst forth. Men all talked at once. The other tables and the bar were deserted, and everybody crowded down toward the lower end of the room. Danny Randall and his friends rushed determinedly to the centre of disturbance. Some men were carrying out Scar-face Charley. Others were talking excitedly. A little clear space surrounded the roulette table, at which, as may be imagined, Johnny was now the only player. Quite methodi- cally he laid three more bets.

"I think that's enough for now," he told the dealer pleasantly, and turned away.

"Hullo! Randall! hullo! Frank!" he greeted us. "I've just won three bets straight. Let's have a drink. Bring your friends," he told Randall.

We turned toward the bar and way was instantly made for us. Johnny poured himself a big drink of whiskey. A number of curious men, mere boys most of them, had crowded close after us, and were standing staring at Johnny with a curiosity they made slight attempt to conceal. Johnny suddenly turned to them, holding high his whiskey in a hand as steady as a rock.

"Here's to crime, boys!" he said, and drank it down at a gulp. Then he stood staring them uncomprisingly in the face, until they had slunk away. He called for and drank another whiskey, then abruptly moved toward the door.

"I think I'll go turn in," said he.

At the door he stopped.

"Good-night," he said to Randall and his friends, who had followed us. "No, I am obliged to you," he replied to a suggestion, "but I need no escort," and he said it so firmly that all but Randall went back.

"I'm going to your camp with you, whether you need an escort or not," said the latter.

Without a word Johnny walked away down the street, very straight. We hurried to catch up with him; and just as we did so he collapsed to the ground and was suddenly and violently sick. As I helped him to his feet, I could feel that his arm was trembling violently.

"Lord, fellows! I'm ashamed," he gasped a little hysterically. "I didn't know I had so little nerve!"

"Nerve!" suddenly roared Danny Randall; "confound your confounded impudence! If I ever hear you say another word like that, I'll put a head on you, if it's the last act of my life! You're the gamest little chicken in this roost, and I'll make you beg like a hound if you say you aren't!"

Johnny laughed a little uncertainly over this contradiction.

"Did I kill him?" he asked.

"No, worse luck; just bored him through the collarbone. That heavy little derringer ball knocked him out."

"I'm glad of that," said Johnny.

"Which I am *not*," stated Danny Randall with emphasis. "You ought to have killed him."

"Thanks to you I wasn't killed myself. I couldn't have hoped to get the draw on him with my holster gun. He is as quick as a snake."

"I thought you were going to bungle it," said Randall. "What was the matter?"

"Front sight caught at the edge of my sleeve. I had to tear it loose by main strength. I'm going to file it off. What's the use of a front sight at close range?"

I heaved a deep sigh.

"Well, I don't want ever to be so scared again," I confessed. "Will you tell me, by all that's holy, *why* you turned your back on the door?"

"Well," said Johnny seriously, "I wanted to get him close to me. If I had shown him that I'd seen him when he first came in the door, he'd have opened fire at once. And I'm a rotten shot. But I figured that if he thought I didn't see him, he'd come across the room to me."

"But he nearly got you by surprise."

"Oh, no," said Johnny; "I saw him all the time. I

got his reflection from the glass over that picture of the beautiful lady sitting on the Old Crow Whiskey barrel. That's why I picked out that table."

"My son," cried Danny Randall delightedly, "you're a true sport.   You've got a head, you have!"

"Well," said Johnny, "I figured I'd have to do *something;* I'm such a rotten shot."

CHAPTER XXXI

THE EXPRESS MESSENGER

We slept late the following morning, and awoke tired, as though we had been on a long journey.

"Now," said Johnny, when our after-breakfast pipes had been lit, "we've got to get together. There's two serious questions before the house: the first and most important is, who and what is Danny Randall?"

"I agree with you there," said I heartily.

"And the second is, what are we going to do with ourselves?"

"I'm going to begin mining," I stated.

"All right, old strong-arm; I am not. I'm dead sick of cricking my back and blistering my hands. It isn't my kind of work; and the only reason I ever thought it was is because the stuff we dig is called gold."

"You aren't going to lie down?" I cried incredulously.

"No, old sport, I'm not going to lie down. I came out here to make my fortune; but I don't know that I've got to dig gold to do that."

"What are you going to do?"

"That I don't know," confessed Johnny, "but I'll be able to inform you in a few days. I suppose you'll be going back to the Porcupine?"

"I don't know about that," said I seriously. "I don't

believe the Porcupine is any richer than these diggings, and it's mighty uncertain. I believe a man's more apt to keep what he gets here, and there's a lot more company, and —— "

"In other words, you're going to stick around old Yank or know the reason why!" interrupted Johnny with a little smile.

I flushed, hesitated, then blurted out: "Well, yes. I shouldn't be easy about him here by himself. It strikes me this is a tough camp, and almost anything's likely to happen."

"I feel the same way," confessed Johnny. "We're all partners. All right; 'stick' it is. We'll have to be mighty plausible to keep Yank quiet. That's agreed," he grinned. "Now I'm going up to town to find out about Danny Randall, and incidentally to look around for something to do. You're a good steady liar; you go over and talk to Yank."

We separated until noon. I had no great difficulty with Yank, either because I was, as Johnny said, a plausible liar, or because Yank was secretly glad to have us near. After visiting with him a while I took the axe and set about the construction of a cradle. Johnny returned near twelve o'clock to find me at this useful occupation.

"As to Danny Randall," he began at once, squatting near by: "Origin lost in mists of obscurity. First known in this country as guide to a party of overland immigrants before the gold discovery. One of the original Bear Flag revolutionists. Member of Fremont's raiders in the south. Showed up again at Sonoma and headed a dozen forays after the horse-thieving Indians and half-breeds in the San Joaquin. Seems now to follow the mines. Guaranteed the best shot with rifle or pistol in the state. Guaranteed the best courage and the quietest manners in the state. Very eminent and square in his profession. That's his entire history."

"What is his profession?" I asked.

"He runs the Bella Union."

"A gambler?" I cried, astonished.

"Just so — a square gambler."

I digested this in silence for a moment.

"Did you discover anything for yourself?" I asked at last.

"Best job ever invented," said Johnny triumphantly, "at three ounces a day; and I can't beat that at your beastly digging."

"Yes?" I urged.

"I invented it myself, too," went on Johnny proudly. "You remember what Randall — or the doctor — said about the robberies, and the bodies of the drowned men floating? Well, every man carries his dust around in a belt because he dare not do anything else with it. I do myself, and so do you; and you'll agree that it weighs like the mischief. So I went to Randall and I suggested that we start an express service to get the stuff out to bank with some good firm in San Francisco. He fell in with the idea in a minute. My first notion was that we take it right through to San Francisco ourselves; but he says he can make satisfactory arrangements to send it in from Sacramento. That's about sixty miles; and we'll call it a day's hard ride through this country, with a change of horses. So now I'm what you might call an express messenger — at three good ounces a day."

"But you'll be killed and robbed!" I cried.

Johnny's eyes were dancing.

"Think of the fun!" said he.

"You're a rotten shot," I reminded him.

"I'm to practise, under Danny Randall, from now until the first trip."

"When is that?"

"Do you think we'll advertise the date? Of course I'd tell you, Jim; but honestly I don't know yet."

Since the matter seemed settled, and Johnny delighted, I said no more. My cradle occupied me for three days longer. In that length of time Johnny banged away an immense quantity of ammunition, much of it under the personal supervision of Danny Randall. The latter had his own ideas as to the proper practice. He utterly refused to let Johnny shoot at a small mark or linger on his aim.

"It's only fairly accurate work you want, but quick," said he. "If you practise always getting hold of your revolver the same way, and squeeze the trigger instead of jerking it, you'll do. If you run against robbers it isn't going to be any target match."

When my cradle was finished, I went prospecting with a pan; and since this was that golden year 1849, and the diggings were neither crowded nor worked out, I soon found 'colour.' There I dragged my cradle, and set quite happily to work. Since I performed all my own labour, the process seemed slow to me after the quick results of trained co-operation; yet my cleanings at night averaged more than my share used to be under the partnership. So I fell into settled work, well content. A week later Johnny rode up on a spirited and beautiful horse, proud as could be over his mount.

He confided to me that it was one of the express horses; that the first trip would be very soon; and that if I desired to send out my own savings, I could do so. I was glad to do this, even though the rates were high; and we easily persuaded Yank of the advisability. Nobody anticipated any danger from this first trip, for the simple reason that few knew anything about it. Randall and his friends made up the amount that could be carried by the three men. For the first time I learned that Johnny had companions. They started from our own tent, a little after sundown. Indeed, they ate their supper with us, while their beautiful horses, head high, stared out into the growing darkness. One of the express riders was a slight, dark youth whom I had never seen before. In the other I was surprised to recognize Old Hickory Pine. He told me his people had "squatted" not far from Sacramento, but that he had come up into the hills on summons by Danny Randall. The fact impressed me anew as to Randall's wide knowledge, for the Pines had not been long in the country.

The trip went through without incident. Johnny returned four days later aglow with the joy of that adventurous ride through the dark. Robbers aside, I acknowledge I should not have liked that job. I am no horseman, and I confess that at full speed I am always uneasy as to how a four-hoofed animal is going successfully to plant all

four of them. And these three boys, for they were nothing
else, had to gallop the thirty miles of the road to Sacramento
that lay in the mountains before dawn caught them in the
defiles.

Johnny seemed to glory in it, however. Danny Randall
had arranged for a change of horses; and the three express
riders liked to dash up at full speed to the relay station,
fling themselves and their treasure bags from one beast
to the other, and be off again with the least possible
expenditure of time. The incoming animal had hardly
come to a stand before the fresh animal was off. There
could have been no real occasion for quite so much haste;
but they liked to do it. The trips were made at irregular
intervals; and the riders left camp at odd times. Indeed,
no hour of the twenty-four was unlikely to be that of their
start. Each boy carried fifty pounds of gold dust dis-
tributed in four pouches. This was a heavy weight, but
it was compensated for to some extent by the fact that
they rode very light saddles. Thus every trip the enormous
sum of thirty-five thousand dollars went out in charge of
the three.

The first half dozen journeys were more or less secret,
so that the express service did not become known to the
general public. Then the news inevitably leaked out.
Danny Randall thereupon openly received shipments
and gave receipts at the Bella Union. It seemed to me
only a matter of time before the express messengers should
be waylaid, for the treasure they carried was worth any
one's while. I spoke to Randall about it one day.

"If Amijo or Murietta or Dick Temple were in this

part of the country, I'd agree with you," said he seriously, "but they are not, and there's nobody in this lot of cheap desperadoes around here that has the nerve. Those three boys have a big reputation as fighters; their horses are good; they constantly vary their route and their times of starting; and Johnny in especial has a foxy head on him."

"The weak point is the place they change horses," said I.

Randall looked at me quickly, as though surprised.

"Why, that's true," said he; "not a doubt of it. But I've got five armed men there to look after just that. And another thing you must remember: they know that Danny Randall is running this show."

Certainly, thought I, Danny at least appreciates himself; and yet, after all, I do not think he in any way exaggerated the terror his name inspired.

CHAPTER XXXII

ITALIAN BAR

As now we are all settled down to our various occupations, Yank of patience, Johnny of delighted adventuring, and myself of dogged industry, it might be well to give you some sort of a notion of Italian Bar, as this new camp was called. I saw a great deal of it, more than I really wished, for out of working hours I much frequented it in the vague hope of keeping tabs on its activities for Johnny's sake.

It was situated on one of the main overland trails, and that was possibly the only reason its rich diggings had not been sooner discovered — it was too accessible! The hordes of immigrants dragged through the dusty main street, sometimes in an almost unending procession. More of them hereafter; they were in general a sad lot. Some of them were always encamped in the flats below town; and about one of the stores a number of them could be seen trying to screw their resolution up to paying the appalling prices for necessities. The majority had no spare money, and rarely any spirit left; and nobody paid much attention to them except to play practical jokes on them. Very few if any of this influx stopped at Italian Bar. Again it was too accessible. They had their vision fixed hypnotically on the West, and westward they would push until they bumped the Pacific Ocean. Of course a great many were no such dumb creatures, but were capable, self-reliant men who knew what they were about and where they were going. Nobody tried to play any practical jokes on them.

Of the regular population I suppose three fourths were engaged in gold washing. The miners did not differ from those of their class anywhere else; that is to say, they were of all nationalities, all classes of life, and all degrees of moral responsibility. They worked doggedly and fast in order to get as much done as possible before the seasonal rains. When night fell the most of them returned to their cabins and slept the sleep of the weary; with a weekly foray into town of a more or less lurid character. They had no time for much else, in their notion; and on that account were, probably unconsciously, the most selfish community I ever saw. There was a great deal of sickness, and many deaths, but unless a man had a partner or a friend to give him some care, he might die in his cabin for all the attention any one else would pay him. In the same spirit only direct personal interest would arouse in any of them the least indignation over the only too frequent killings and robberies.

"They found a man shot by the Upper Bend this morning," remarks one to his neighbour.

"That so? Who was he?" asks the other.

"Don' t know. Didn't hear," is the reply.

The barroom or street killings, which averaged in number at least two or three a week, while furnishing more excitement, aroused very little more real interest. Open and above-board homicides of that sort were always the result of differences of opinion. If the victim had a friend, the latter might go gunning for his pal's slayer; but nobody had enough personal friends to elevate any such row to the proportions of a general feud.

All inquests were set aside until Sunday. A rough and ready public meeting invariably brought in the same verdict — "justifiable self-defence." At these times, too, popular justice was dispensed, but carelessly and not at all in the spirit of the court presided over by John Semple at Hangman's Gulch. A general air of levity characterized these occasions, which might strike as swift and deadly a blow as a shaft of lightning, or might puff away as harmlessly as a summer zephyr. Many a time, until I learned philosophically to stay away, did my blood boil over the haphazard way these men had of disposing of some poor creature's destinies.

"Here's a Mex thief," observed the chair. "What do you want done with him?"

"Move we cut off his ears!" yelled a voice from the back of the crowd.

"Make it fifty lashes!" shouted another.

A wrangle at once started between the advocates of cropping and the whip. The crowd wearied of it.

"Let the —— —— —— go!" suggested some one.

And this motion was carried with acclamation. No evidence was offered or asked as to the extent of the man's guilt, or indeed if he was guilty at all!

The meeting had a grim sense of humour, and enjoyed nothing more than really elaborate foolery. Such as, for example, the celebrated case of Pio Chino's bronco.

Pio Chino was a *cargador* running a train of pack-mules into some back-country camp. His bell mare was an ancient white animal with long shaggy hair, ewe neck, bulging joints, a placid wall eye, the full complement of ribs, and an extraordinarily long Roman nose ending in a pendulous lip. Yet fifteen besotted mules thought her beautiful, and followed her slavishly, in which fact lay her only value. Now somebody, probably for a joke, "lifted" this ancient wreck from poor Chino on the ground that it had never been Chino's property anyway. Chino, with childlike faith in the dignity of institutions, brought the matter before the weekly court.

That body took charge with immense satisfaction. It appointed lawyers for the prosecution and the defence.

Prosecution started to submit Chino's claim.

Defence immediately objected on the ground that Chino, being a person of colour, was not qualified to testify against a white man.

This point was wrangled over with great relish for an hour or more. Then two solemn individuals were introduced as experts to decide whether Chino was a man of colour, or, as the prosecution passionately maintained, a noble, great-minded and patriotic California member of the Caucasian race.

"Gentlemen," the court addressed this pair, "is there any infallible method by which your science is able to distinguish between a nigger and a white man?"

"There is," answered one of the "experts."

"What?"

"The back teeth of a white man have small roots reaching

straight down," expounded the "expert" solemnly, "while those of a negro have roots branching in every direction."

"And how do you expect to determine this case?"

"By extracting one or more of the party's back teeth," announced the "expert" gravely, at the same time producing a huge pair of horseshoeing nippers.

Chino uttered a howl, but was violently restrained from bolting. He was understood to say that he didn't want that mare. I should not have been a bit surprised if they had carried the idea of extraction to a finish; but the counsel for defence interposed, waiving the point. He did not want the fun to come to that sort of a termination.

Prosecution then offered the evidence of Chino's brand. Now that old mare was branded from muzzle to tail, and on both sides. She must have been sold and resold four or five times for every year of her long and useful life. The network of brands was absolutely indecipherable.

"Shave her!" yelled some genius.

That idea caught hold. The entire gathering took an interest in the operation, which half a dozen men performed. They shaved that poor old mare from nose to the tip of her ratlike tail. Not even an eye-winker was left to her. She resembled nothing so much as one of the sluglike little Mexican hairless dogs we had seen on the Isthmus. The brands now showed plainly enough, but were as complicated as ever in appearance. Thunders of mock forensic oratory shook the air. I remember defence acknowledged that in that multiplicity of lines the figure of Chino's brand could be traced; but pointed to the stars of the heavens and the figures of their constellations to prove what could be done by a vivid imagination in evolving fancy patterns. By this time it was late, and court was adjourned until next week.

The following Sunday, after a tremendous legal battle, conducted with the relishing solemnity with which Americans like to take their fooling, it was decided to call in an expert on brands, and a certain California rancher ten miles distant was agreed upon.

"But," objected the defence, "he is a countryman of the complainant. However honest, he will nevertheless sympathize with his own blood. Before the case is put before him, he should view these brands as an unpredjudiced observer. I suggest that they be transcribed to paper and submitted to him without explanation."

This appealed to the crowd. The astonished mare was again led out, and careful drawings made of her most remarkable sides. Then the case was again adjourned one week.

On that day the Californian was on hand, very grave, very much dressed up, very flattered at being called as an expert in anything. The drawing was laid before him.

"Don Luis," said the court formally, "what do you, as expert, make of that?"

Don Luis bent his grave Spanish head over the document for some minutes. Then he turned it upside down and examined it again; sideways; the other end. When he looked up a little twinkle of humour lurked deep in his black eyes, but his face was solemn and ceremonious.

"Well, Don Luis," repeated the court, "what do you make of it?"

Señor," replied Don Luis courteously, "it looks to me like a most excellent map of Sonora."

When the crowd had quieted down after this, the court ordered the animal brought forth.

"May it please y'r honour, the critter got a chill and done died," announced the cadaverous Missourian, to whose care the animal had been confided.

"H'm," said the court. "Well, here's the court's decision in this case. Pio Chino fined one drink for taking up our valuable time; Abe Sellers fined one drink for claiming such an old crow-bait on any grounds; Sam is fined one drink for not putting a blanket on that mare." ("I only got one blanket myself!" cried the grieved Missourian.) "The fines must be paid in to the court at the close of this session."

Hugely tickled, the meeting arose. Pio Chino, to whom the tidings of his bell mare's demise was evidently news, stood the picture of dejected woe. His downcast figure attracted the careless attention of one of the men.

"Here boys!" he yelled, snatching off his hat. "This ain't so damn funny for Chino here!" He passed the hat among the crowd. They tossed in gold, good naturedly, abundantly, with a laugh. Nobody knows what amount was dumped into the astounded Chino's old sombrero; but the mare was certainly not worth over fifteen dollars. If some one had dragged Chino before that same gathering under unsupported accusation of any sort, it would as cheerfully and thoughtlessly have hung him.

Of the gambling places, one only — that conducted by Danny Randall and called the Bella Union — inspired any sort of confidence. The other two were frequented by a rough, insolent crew, given to sudden silences in presence of newcomers, good-humoured after a wild and disconcerting fashion, plunging heavily at the gaming tables and drinking as heavily at the bars. This is not to imply that any strong line of demarkation existed between the habitues of one or the other of these places. When an inhabitant of Italian Bar started out for relaxation, he visited everything there was to visit, and drifted impartially between Morton's, Randall's Bella Union, and the Empire. There was a good deal of noise and loud talk in any of them; and occasionally a pistol shot. This was generally a signal for most of the bystanders to break out through the doors and windows, and for the gayly inclined to shoot out the lights. The latter feat has often been cited admiringly as testifying to a high degree of marksmanship, but as a matter of fact the wind and concussion from the heavy revolver bullets were quite sufficient to put out any lamp to which the missiles passed reasonably close. Sometimes these affrays resulted in material for the Sunday inquests; but it is astonishing how easily men can miss each other at close range. Most of the shootings were the results of drunken quarrels. For that reason the professed gunmen were rarely involved. One who possessed an established reputation was let alone by the ordinary citizen; and most severely alone by the swaggering bullies, of whom there were not a few. These latter found prey for their queer stripe of vanity among the young, the weak, and the drunken. I do not hesitate to say that any man of determined character could keep out of trouble even in the worst days of the camp, provided he had no tempting wealth, attended to his own affairs, and maintained a quiet though resolute demeanour.

When in camp Johnny and his two companions shone as bright particular stars. They were only boys, and they had blossomed out in wonderful garments. Johnny had a Californian sombrero with steeple crown loaded with silver ornaments, and a pair of Spanish spurs heavily inlaid with the same metal, a Chinese scarf about his neck, and a short jacket embroidered with silver thread. But most astonishing of all was a large off-colour diamond set in a ring, through which he ran the ends of his scarf. Parenthetically, it was from this that he got his sobriquet of Diamond Jack. I had a good deal of fun laughing at Johnny, but he didn't mind.

"This diamond," he pointed out, "is just as good as gold dust, it's easier carried, and I can have some fun out of it."

I am afraid he and Old Hickory Pine and Cal Marsh did a bit of swaggering while in town. They took a day to the down trip, and jogged back in a day and a half, stopping in Sacramento only the extra half day. Then they rested with us one day, and were off the next. Thus they accomplished seven or eight trips in the month. Both Old and Cal had the reputation of being quick, accurate shots, although I have never seen them perform. As the three of them were absolutely inseparable they made a formidable combination that nothing but an organized gang would care to tackle. Consequently they swaggered as much as they pleased. At bottom they were good, clean, attractive boys, who were engaged in an adventure that was thrilling enough in sober reality, but which they loved to deck forth in further romance. They one and all assumed the stern, aloof, lofty pose of those whose affairs were too weighty to permit mingling with ordinary amusements. Their speech was laconic, their manners grave, their attitude self-contained. It was a good thing, I believe; for outside the fact that it kept them out of quarrels, it kept them also out of drinking and gambling.

I made many acquaintances of course, but only a few friends. The best of these were Dr. Rankin and Danny Randall. Strangely enough, these two were great pals. Danny had a little room back of the Bella Union furnished out with a round table, a dozen chairs, and a sofa. Here he loved to retire with his personal friends to sip drinks, smoke, and to discuss all sorts of matters. A little glass-less window gave into the Bella Union, and as the floor of the little room was raised a foot or so, Danny sat where he could see everything that went on. These gatherings varied in number, but never exceeded the capacity of the dozen chairs. I do not know how Danny had caused it to be understood that these were invitation affairs, but understood it was, and no one ever presumed to intrude unbidden into the little room. Danny selected his company as the fancy took him.

As to why he should so often have chosen me I must again confess ignorance. Perhaps because I was a good listener. If so, the third member of a very frequent triumvirate, Dr. Rankin, was invited for the opposite quality. The doctor was a great talker, an analyst of conditions, and a philosophical spectator. The most frequent theme of our talks was the prevalence of disorder. On this subject the doctor had very decided views.

"There is disorder because we shirk our duty as a community," he stated, "and we shirk our duty as a community because we believe in our hearts that we aren't a community. What does Jones or Smith or Robinson or anybody else really care for Italian Bar as a place; or, indeed, for California as a place? Not a tinker's damn! He came out here in the first place to make his pile, and in the second place to have a good time. He isn't dependent on any one's good opinion, as he used to be at home. He refuses to be bothered with responsibilities and he doesn't need to be. Why a pan miner needn't even speak to his next neighbour unless he wants to; and a cradle miner need bother only with his partners!"

"Miners' meetings have done some pretty good legislation," I pointed out.

"Legislation; yes!" cried the doctor. "Haven't you discovered that the American has a perfect genius for organization? Eight coal heavers on a desert island would in a week have a full list of officers, a code of laws, and would be wrangling over ridiculous parliamentary points of order in their meetings. That's just the trouble. The ease with which Americans can sketch out a state on paper is an anodyne to conscience. We get together and pass a lot of resolutions, and go away with a satisfied feeling that we've really done something."

"But I believe a camp like this may prove permanent," objected Randall.

"Exactly. And by that very fact a social obligation

comes into existence. Trouble is, every mother's son tries to escape it in his own case. What is every one's business is no one's business. Every fellow thinks he's got away from being bothered with such things. Sooner or later he'll find out he hasn't, and then he'll have to pay for his vacation."

"We never stood for much thieving at Hangman's Gulch," I interposed.

"What did you do?"

"We whipped and sent them about their business."

"To some other camp. You merely passed on your responsibility; you didn't settle it. Your whipping merely meant turning loose a revengeful and desperate man. Your various banishments merely meant your exchanging these fiends with the other camps. It's like scattering the coyotes that come around your fire."

"What would you do, Doctor?" asked Randall quietly; "we have no regular law."

"Why not? Why don't you adopt a little regular law? You need about three in this camp — against killing, against thievery, and against assault. Only enforce in every instance, as far as possible."

"You can't get this crowd to take time investigating the troubles of some man they never heard of."

"Exactly."

"And if they get too bad," said Danny, "we'll have to get the stranglers busy."

"Confound it, man!" roared Dr. Rankin, beating the table, "that's just what I've been trying to tell you. You ought not to care so much for punishing as for deterring.

Don't you know that it's a commonplace that it isn't the terrifying quality of the penalty that acts as a deterrent to crime, but it's the certainty of the penalty! If a horse thief knows that there's merely a chance the community will get mad enough to hang him, he'll take that chance in hopes this may not be the time. If, on the other hand, he knows that *every time* he steals a horse he's going to be caught and fined even, he thinks a long time before he steals it."

"All that's true, Doctor," said Danny, "as theory; but now I'm coming to bat with a little practice. Here's the camp of Italian Bar in the year 1849. What would you do?"

"Elect the proper officers and enforce the law," answered the doctor promptly.

"Who would you elect?"

"There are plenty of good men here."

"Name me any one who would take the job. The good men are all washing gold; and they're in a hurry to finish before the rains. I don't care who you're about to name — if anybody; this is about what he'd say: 'I can't afford to leave my claim; I didn't come out here to risk my life in that sort of a row; I am leaving for the city when the rains begin, and I don't know that I'll come back to Italian Bar next season!'"

"Make it worth their while. Pay them," insisted the doctor stoutly.

"And how's the money to pay them to be collected? You'd have to create the officers of a government — and pay *them*."

ITALIAN BAR

"Well, why not?"

"At the election, who would take interest to elect a decent man, even if you could get hold of one? Not the other decent men. They're too busy, and too little interested. But the desperadoes and hard characters would be very much interested in getting some of their own stripe in office. The chances are they would be coming back to Italian Bar next season, especially if they had the legal machinery for keeping themselves out of trouble. You'd simply put yourself in their power."

Dr. Rankin shook his head.

"Just the same, you'll see that I am right," he prophesied. "This illusion of freedom to the social obligation is only an illusion. It will have to be paid for with added violence and turmoil."

"Why, I believe you're right as to that, Doctor," agreed Danny, "but I've discovered that often in this world a man has to pay a high price for what he gets. In fact, sometimes it's very expedient to pay a high price."

"I can foresee a lot of violence before the thing is worked out."

At this point the doctor, to his manifest disgust, was summoned to attend to some patient.

"That all sounds interesting," said I to Danny Randall once we were alone, "but I don't exactly fit it in."

"It means," said Danny, "that some day Morton's gang will go a little too far, and we'll have to get together and string some of them up."

CHAPTER XXXIII
THE OVERLAND IMMIGRANTS

The overland immigrants never ceased to interest us. The illness, destitution, and suffering that obtained among these people has never been adequately depicted. For one outfit with healthy looking members and adequate cattle there were dozens conducted by hollow-eyed, gaunt men, drawn by few weak animals. Women trudged wearily, carrying children. And the tales they brought were terrible. They told us of thousands they had left behind in the great desert of the Humboldt Sink, fighting starvation, disease, and the loss of cattle. Women who had lost their husbands from the deadly cholera were staggering on without food or water, leading their children. The trail was lined with dead mules and cattle. Some said that five thousand had perished on the plains from cholera alone. In the middle of the desert, miles from anywhere, were the death camps, the wagons drawn in the usual circle, the dead animals tainting the air, every living human being crippled from scurvy and other diseases. There was no fodder for the cattle, and one man told us that he estimated, soberly, that three fourths of the draught animals on the plains must die.

"And then where will their owners be?"

The Indians were hostile and thieving. Most of the

ample provision that had been laid in had to be thrown away to lighten the loads for the enfeebled animals. Such immigrants as got through often arrived in an impoverished condition. Many of these on the route were reduced by starvation to living on the putrefied flesh of the dead animals along the road. This occasioned more sickness. The desert seemed interminable. At nightfall the struggling trains lay down exhausted with only the assurance of another scorching, burning day to follow. And when at last a few reached the Humboldt River, they found it almost impossible to ford — and the feed on the other side. In the distance showed the high forbidding ramparts of the Sierra Nevadas. A man named Delano told us that five men drowned themselves in the Humboldt River in one day out of sheer discouragement. Another man said he had saved the lives of his oxen by giving some Indians fifteen dollars to swim the river and float some grass across to him. The water of the Humboldt had a bad effect on horses, and great numbers died. The Indians stole others. The animals that remained were weak. The destruction of property was immense, for everything that could be spared was thrown away in order to lighten the loads. The road was lined with abandoned wagons, stoves, mining implements, clothes.

We were told these things over and over, heavily, in little snatches, by men too wearied and discouraged and beaten even to rejoice that they had come through alive. They were not interested in telling us, but they told, as though their minds were so full that they could not help it. I remember one evening when we were feeding at our camp the members of one of these trains, a charity every miner proffered nearly every day of the week. The party consisted of one wagon, a half dozen gaunt, dull-eyed oxen, two men, and a crushed-looking, tragic young woman. One of the men had in a crude way the gift of words.

He told of the crowds of people awaiting the new grass at Independence in Missouri, of the making up of the parties, the election of officers for the trip, the discussion of routes, the visiting, the campfires, the boundless hope.

"There were near twenty thousand people waiting for the grass," said our friend; a statement we thought exaggerated, but one which I have subsequently found to be not far from the truth.

By the middle of May the trail from the Missouri River to Fort Laramie was occupied by a continuous line of wagons.

"That was fine travelling," said the immigrant in the detached way of one who speaks of dead history. "There was grass and water; and the wagon seemed like a little house at night. Everybody was jolly. It didn't last long."

After Fort Laramie there were three hundred miles of plains, with little grass and less water.

"We thought that was a desert!" exclaimed the immigrant bitterly. "My God! Quite a lot turned back at Laramie. They were scared by the cholera that broke out, scared by the stories of the desert, scared by the Indians. They went back. I suppose they're well and hearty — and kicking themselves every gold report that goes back east."

The bright anticipations, the joy of the life, the romance of the journey all faded before the grim reality. The monotony of the plains, the barrenness of the desert, the toil of the mountains, the terrible heat, the dust, the rains, the sickness, the tragedy of deaths had flattened all buoyancy, and left in its stead only a sullen, dogged determination.

"There was lots of quarrelling, of course," said our narrator. "Everybody was on edge. There were fights, that we had to settle somehow, and bad feeling."

They had several minor skirmishes with Indians, lost from their party by disease, suffered considerable hardships and infinite toil.

"We thought we'd had a hard time," said our friend wonderingly. "Lord!"

At the very start of the journey they had begun to realize that they were overloaded, and had commenced to throw away superfluous goods. Several units of the party had even to abandon some of their wagons.

"We chucked everything we thought we could get along without. I know we spent all one day frying out bacon to get the grease before we threw it away. We used the grease for our axles."

They reached the head of the Humboldt. Until this point they had kept together, but now demoralization began. They had been told at Salt Lake City that they had but four hundred miles to go to Sacramento. Now they discovered that at the Humboldt they had still more than that distance to travel; and that before them lay the worst desert of all.

"Mind you," said our friend, "we had been travelling desperately. Our cattle had died one by one; and we had doubled up with our teams. We had starved for water until our beasts were ready to drop and our own tongues had swollen in our mouths, and were scared — *scared*, I tell you — scared!"

He moistened his lips slowly, and went on. "Sometimes we took two or three hours to go a mile, relaying back and forth. We were down to a fine point. It wasn't a question of keeping our property any more; it was a case of saving our lives. We'd abandoned a good half of our wagons already. When we got to the Humboldt and learned from a mountain man going the other way that the great desert was still before us, and when we had made a day or two's journey down the river toward the Sink, I tell you we lost our nerve — and our sense." He ruminated a few moments in silence. "My God! man!" he cried. "That trail! From about halfway down the river the carcasses of horses and oxen were so thick that I believe if they'd been laid in the road instead of alongside you could have walked the whole way without setting foot to ground!"

And then the river disappeared underground, and they had to face the crossing of the Sink itself.

"That was a real desert," the immigrant told us sombrely. "There were long white fields of alkali and drifts of ashes across them so soft that the cattle sank way to their bellies. They moaned and bellowed! Lord, how they moaned! And the dust rose up so thick you couldn't breathe, and the sun beat down so fierce you felt it like something heavy on your head. And how the place stunk with the dead beasts!"

The party's organization broke. The march became a rout. Everybody pushed on with what strength he had. No man, woman, or child could ride; the wagons were emptied of everything but the barest necessities. At every stop some animal fell in the traces, and was cut out of the yoke. When a wagon came to a stop, it was abandoned, the animals detached and driven forward.

Those who were still afoot were constantly besought by those who had been forced to a standstill.

"I saw one old man, his wife and his daughter, all walking along on foot," said the immigrant bitterly. "They were half knee deep in alkali, the sun was broiling hot, they had absolutely nothing. We couldn't help them. What earthly chance had they? I saw a wagon stalled, the animals lying dead in their yokes, all except one old ox. A woman and three children sat inside the wagon. She called to me that they hadn't had anything to eat for three days, and begged me to take the children. I couldn't. I could have stopped and died there with her, but I couldn't put another pound on my wagon and hope to get through. We were all walking alongside; even Sue, here."

The woman raised her tragic face.

"We left our baby there," she said; and stared back again into the coals of the fire.

"We made it," resumed the immigrant. "We got to the Truckee River somehow, and we rested there three days. I don't know what became of the rest of our train; dead perhaps."

We told him of the immigrant register or bulletin board at Morton's.

"I must look that over," said he. "I don't know how long it took us to cross the mountains. Those roads are terrible; and our cattle were weak. We were pretty near out of grub too. Most of the people have no food at all. Well, here we are! But there are thousands back of us. What are they going to do? And when the mountains fill with snow —— "

After the trio, well fed for the first time in months, had turned in, we sat talking about our fire. We were considerably subdued and sobered; for this was the first coherent account we had heard at first hand. Two things impressed us — the tragedy, the futility. The former aspect hit us all; the latter struck strongly at Old and Cal. Those youngsters, wise in the ways of the plains, were filled with sad surprise over the incompetence of it all.

"But thar ain't no manner of *use* in it!" cried Old. "They are just bullin' at it plumb regardless! They ain't handled their cattle right! They ain't picked their route right — why, the old Mormon trail down by the Carson Sink is better'n that death-trap across the Humboldt. And cut-offs! What license they all got chasin' every fool cut-off reported in? Most of 'em is all right fer pack-trains and all wrong fer wagons! Oh, Lord!"

"They don't know," said I, "poor devils, they don't know. They were raised on farms and in the cities."

Johnny had said nothing. His handsome face looked very sombre in the firelight.

"Jim," said he, "we're due for a trip to-night; but I

want you to promise me one thing — just keep these people here, and feed them up until we get back. Tell them I've got a job for them. Will you do it?"

I tried to pump Johnny as to his intentions, but could get nothing out of him; and so promised blindly. About two o'clock I was roused from my sleep by a soft moving about. Thrusting my head from the tent I made out the dim figures of our horsemen, mounted, and moving quietly away down the trail.

CHAPTER XXXIV

THE PRISONERS

I had no great difficulty in persuading the immigrants to rest over.

"To tell you the truth," the narrator confided to me, "I don't know where we're going. We have no money, We've got to get work somehow. I don't know now why we came."

His name, he told me, was George Woodruff; he had been a lawyer in a small Pennsylvania town; his total possessions were now represented by the remains of his ox team, his wagon, and the blankets in which he slept. The other man was his brother Albert, and the woman his sister-in-law.

"We started with four wagons and a fine fit-out of supplies," he told me — "food enough to last two years. This is what we have left. The cattle aren't in bad shape now though; and they are extra fine stock. Perhaps I can sell them for a little."

Two days passed. We arose the morning of the third to find that the oxen had strayed away during the night. Deciding they could not have wandered far, I went to my gold washing as usual, leaving Woodruff and his brother to hunt them up. About ten o'clock they came to my claim very much troubled.

"We can't find them anywhere," they told me, "and it doesn't seem natural that they should stray far; they are too tired."

I knocked off work, and returned with them to the flat, where we proceeded to look for tracks. The earth was too hard and tramped to show us much, and after a half hour of fruitless examination we returned to camp with the intention of eating something before starting out on a serious search. While thus engaged the express messengers rode up.

"Hullo!" said Johnny cheerfully. "Glad to hear you made such a good thing out of your cattle!"

He caught our stare of surprise, swung from his horse and advanced on us with three swift strides.

"You haven't sold them?" he exclaimed.

"We've been looking for them all the morning."

"Stolen, boys!" he cried to his companions. "Here's our job! Come on!"

He leaped on his horse in the headlong, graceful fashion the boys had cultivated at the relay station, and, followed by Cal and Old, dashed away.

We made nothing definite of this, though we had our surmises to exchange. As the boys had not returned an hour later, I resumed my digging while the Woodruffs went over to visit with Yank, who was now out of bed. Evening came, with no sign of our friends. We turned in at last.

Some time after midnight we were awakened by the shuffling and lowing of driven cattle, and went out into the moonlight to see our six oxen, just released from herding, plunging their noses thirstily into the little stream from the spring. Five figures on horseback sat motionless in the background behind them. When the cattle had finished drinking, the horsemen, riding in two couples and one single, turned them into the flat, and then came over to our camp.

After they had approached within plain sight we saw that the single horseman was Cal Marsh; and that Johnny and Old each led an animal on which a man was tied, his arms behind him, his feet shackled beneath the horse's barrel.

"Here, you fellows," said Johnny in a low voice, "just catch hold here and help with these birds."

The three descended rather wearily from their horses, the lead lines of which Cal held while the rest unshackled the prisoners and helped them to dismount. They were both known to me, one as the big desperado, Malone; and the other as the barkeeper at Morton's place, our old friend of Chagres days. The latter's head was roughly bound with a bloody cloth. Under Johnny's direction we tied them firmly. He issued his orders in a low-voiced, curt fashion that precluded anything but the most instant and silent obedience.

"There," said he at last, "they'll do. Chuck them inside where they'll be out of sight. Now about those two horses ——"

"I'll just run 'em up to the Dutchman's Flat and stake 'em out thar," interposed Old. "Thar ain't no one thar; and they won't be discovered."

"Well," conceded Johnny, "if your horse isn't too tired."

"She'll make it," replied Old confidently.

"Now for our horses," said Johnny. "Won't do to be

getting in at this time of night. It doesn't look natural. Don't believe we can get them to the stable without being spotted. Maybe you'd better stake them up there too. Can you walk back?"

"I reckon," said Old.

He tied the four led horses' together, mounted, took the lead rope from Cal, and rode off up the gulch.

Cal came to the fire and sat down. I was instantly struck by his ghastly appearance.

"Cal's bored through the shoulder," Johnny explained. "Now, Jim, you've got to go up and get Dr. Rankin. He lives at Barnes's hotel, you know. Barnes is all right; bring him down, too, if you happen to wake him up. Go around to Danny Randall's quietly and tell him we want to see him. He sleeps in that little back room. Throw some pebbles against the stovepipe; that'll wake him up. Look out he doesn't pot you. Don't let anybody see you if you can possibly help; and tell the others to slip out here quietly, too. Do you understand all that?"

"I see what I'm to do," I assented; "but let me in! What's it all about?"

"We met these men and three others driving Woodruff's oxen this morning," said Johnny rapidly. "Stopped and had quite a chat with them. They told what sounded like a straight story of having bought the oxen. I knew Woodruff wanted to sell. Didn't suppose they'd have the nerve to lift them right under our noses. Guess they hadn't an idea they'd meet us on the road. We were taking the lower trail just for a change. So as soon as we got the news from you, we went back, of course. They suspected trouble, and had turned off. Old and Cal are wonders at trailing. Came up with them just beyond Bitter Water, and monkeyed around quite a while before we got a favourable chance to tackle them. Then we took the cattle away and brought back these birds. That's all there was to it."

"You said five. Where are the other three?"

"Killed 'em," said Johnny briefly. "Now run along and do your job."

After some delay and difficulty I fulfilled my instructions, returning at last in company with Danny Randall, to find my friends sitting around the little fire, and Dr. Rankin engaged in bathing Cal's wound. Johnny was repeating his story, to which the others were listening attentively.

"I learned a little more of this sort of thing in Sacramento," he was concluding. "And I'd like to state this right here and now: practical jokes on these immigrants are poor taste as far as I am concerned from now on. That's my own private declaration of war."

"Let's take a look at your birds, Johnny," suggested Randall.

I brought out the prisoners and stacked them up against the trees. They gave us back look for look defiantly.

"You won't live a week after this," said the Morton man, whose name was Carhart, addressing Johnny.

"I'll just have a look at your head, my friend," said Dr. Rankin.

The man bent his head, and the doctor began to remove the bloody bandages.

"Question is," said Johnny, "what do we do with them?"

Danny was thinking hard.

"One of two things," said he at length: "We can string them up quietly, and leave them as a warning; or we can force matters to a showdown by calling a public meeting."

"Question is," said I, "whether we can get anybody with nerve enough to serve as officers of court, or, indeed, to testify as witnesses."

"You said a true word there," put in Carhart with an oath.

"I'll bear witness for one," offered Dr. Rankin, looking up from his work, "and on a good many things."

"Look out, damn you!" muttered Carhart.

"I've been called to a good many cases of gunshot wounds," continued the doctor steadily, "and I've kept quiet because I was given to understand that my life was worth nothing if I spoke."

"You'd better keep your mouth shut!" warned the bandit.

"Now," pursued the doctor, "I personally believe the time has come to assert ourselves. I'm in favour of serving notice on the whole lot, and cleaning up the mess once and for all. I believe there are more decent men than criminals in this camp, if you get them together."

"That's my idea," agreed Johnny heartily. "Get the camp together; I'll see every man in it and let Woodruff tell his tale, and then let Old or me tell ours."

"And I'll tell mine," said Dr. Rankin.

Danny Randall shook his head.

"They'll rise to it like men!" cried Johnny indignantly.

"Nobody but a murderer and cattle thief listening to that story could remain unmoved."

"Well," said Danny, "if you won't just quietly hang these fellows right now, try the other. I should string 'em up and shut their mouths. You're too early; it won't do."

CHAPTER XXXV

THE TRIAL

The meeting took place in the Bella Union, and the place was crowded to the doors. All the roughs in town were on hand, fully armed, swearing, swaggering, and brandishing their weapons. They had much to say by way of threat, for they did not hesitate to show their sympathies. As I looked upon their unexpected numbers and listened to their wild talk, I must confess that my heart failed me. Though they had not the advantage in numbers, they knew each other; were prepared to work together; were, in general, desperately courageous and reckless, and imbued with the greatest confidence. The decent miners, on the other hand, were practically unknown to each other; and, while brave enough and hardy enough, possessed neither the recklessness nor desperation of the others. I think our main weakness sprang from the selfish detachment that had prevented us from knowing whom to trust.

After preliminary organization a wrangle at once began as to the form of the trial. We held very strongly that we should continue our usual custom of open meeting; but Morton insisted with equal vehemence that the prisoners should have jury trial. The discussion grew very hot and confused. Pistols and knives were flourished. The chair put the matter to a vote, but was unable to decide from the yells and howls that answered the question which side had the preponderance. A rising vote was demanded.

"Won't they attempt a rescue?" I asked of Danny Randall, under cover of the pandemonium. "They could easily fight their way free."

He shook his head.

"That would mean outlawing themselves. They would rather get clear under some show of law. Then they figure to run the camp."

The vote was understood to favour a jury trial.

"That settles it," said Danny; "the poor damn fools."

"What do you mean?" I asked him.

"You'll see," said he.

In the selection of the jury we had the advantage. None of the roughs could get on the panel to hang the verdict, for the simple reason that they were all too well known. The miners cautiously refused to endorse any one whose general respectability was not known to them. I found myself one of those selected.

A slight barrier consisting of a pole thrown across one corner of the room set aside a jury box. We took our places therein. Men crowded to the pole, talking for our benefit, cursing steadily, and uttering the most frightful threats.

I am not going to describe that most turbulent afternoon. The details are unessential to the main point, which was our decision. Counsel was appointed by the court from among the numerous ex-lawyers. The man who took charge of the defence was from New York, and had served some ten years in the profession before the gold fever took him. I happen to know that he was a most sober-minded, steady individual, not at all in sympathy with the rougher elements; but, like most of his ilk, he speedily became so intensely interested in plying his profession that he forgot utterly the justice of the case. He defended the lawless element with all the tricks at his command. For that reason Woodruff was prevented from testifying at all, except as to his ownership of the cattle; so that the effect of his pathetic story was lost. Dr. Rankin had no chance to appear. This meeting should have marked the awakening of public spirit to law and order; and if all the elements of the case had been allowed to come before the decent part of the community in a common-sense fashion, I am quite sure it would have done so. But two lawyers got interested in tangling each other up with their technicalities, and the result was that the real significance of the occasion was lost to sight. The lawyer for the defence, pink and warm and happy, sat down quite pleased with his adroitness. A few of us, and the desperadoes, alone realized what it all meant.

We retired to Randall's little room to deliberate. Not a man of the twelve of us had the first doubt as to the guilt of the prisoners. We took a ballot. The result was eleven for acquittal and one for conviction. I had cast the one vote for conviction.

We argued the matter for three hours

"There's no doubt the men are guilty," said one. "That isn't the question. The question is, dare we declare it?"

"It amounts to announcing our own death sentence," argued another. "Those fellows would stand together, but who of the lot would stand by us? Why, we don't even know for sure who would be with us."

"This case ought never to have been tried by a jury," complained a third bitterly. "It ought to have been tried in a miners' court; and if it hadn't been for those soft heads who were strong for doing things 'regularly' instead of sensibly, we'd have had it done that way."

"Well," said an older man gravely, "I agree to that. I am going to be governed in my decision not by the merits of the case, but by the fact that I have a family back in the States. I consider my obligations to them greater than to this community."

I reasoned with them for a long time, bringing to bear all the arguments I had heard advanced at various times during our discussions in Danny Randall's back room. At last, seeing I could in no manner shake their resolution, I gave in. After all, I could not blame them. The case was to them only one of cattle stealing; they had no chance to realize that it was anything more. Without solicitation on my part they agreed to keep secret my opposition to the verdict of acquittal.

Our decision was greeted by wild yells and the discharge of pistols on the part of the rough element. The meeting broke up informally and in confusion. It would have been useless for the presiding officer to have attempted to dismiss court. The mob broke through en masse to congratulate the prisoners. Immediately the barkeepers were overwhelmed with work. Here and there I could see a small group of the honest men talking low-voiced, with many shakes of the head. Johnny, Old, and Cal, who had attended with his arm slung up, had their heads together in a corner. Danny Randall, who, it will be remembered, had not appeared publicly in any way, stood at his customary corner of the bar watching all that was going on. His gamblers were preparing to reopen the suspended games.

After conferring together a moment the three express messengers made their way slowly across the room to the bar. I could not see exactly what happened, but heard the sudden reverberations of several pistol shots. The lamps and glasses rattled with the concussion, the white smoke of the discharges eddied and rose. An immediate dead silence fell, except for the sounds made by the movements of those seeking safe places. Johnny and his two friends shoulder to shoulder backed slowly away toward the door. Johnny and Old presented each two pistols at the group around the bar, while Cal, a revolver in his well hand, swept the muzzle slowly from side to side. Nobody near the bar stirred. The express messengers backed to the door.

"Keep your heads inside," warned Johnny clearly. On the words they vanished.

Immediately pandemonium broke loose. The men along the bar immediately became very warlike; but none of those who brandished pistols tried to leave the building. From the swing and sway of the crowd, and the babel of yells, oaths, threats, and explanations I could make nothing. Danny Randall alone of all those in the room held his position unmoved. At last a clear way offered, so I went over to him.

"What's happened?" I shouted at him through the din.

Danny shrugged his shoulders.

"They killed Carhart and Malone," Danny replied curtly.

It seemed, I ascertained at last, that the three had advanced and opened fire on the two ex-prisoners without warning.

As soon as possible I made my escape and returned to our own camp. There I found the three of them seated smoking, their horses all saddled, standing near at hand.

"Are they coming our way?" asked Johnny instantly.

I told them that I had seen no indications of a mob.

"But why did you do it?" I cried. "It's an open challenge! They'll get you boys now sure!"

"That remains to be seen," said Johnny grimly. "But it was the only thing to do. If Carhart and Malone had ever been given time to report on our confab the other evening, you and Danny Randall and Dr. Rankin would have been marked men. Now no one knows of your connection with this matter."

"But they'll be after you —— "

"They were after us in any case," Johnny pointed out. "Don't deceive yourself there. Now you keep out of this and let us do it."

"I reckon we can handle this bunch," said Old.

"Lord! what a lot of jellyfish!" cried Johnny disgustedly. "Danny was right enough about them. But let me state right here and once again that practical jokes on immigrants are going to be mighty unhealthy here."

CHAPTER XXXVI

THE RULE OF THE LAWLESS

No concerted attempt was made by the roughs to avenge the execution of their comrades. Whether they realized that such an attempt would be likely to solidify the decent element, or whether that sort of warfare was not their habit, the afternoon and night wore away without trouble.

"Danger's over," announced Johnny the following morning.

"What next?" I asked.

"We'll go up to town," said Johnny.

This they proceeded to do, negativing absolutely my desire to accompany them.

"You stay out of this," said Johnny. "Go and wash gold as usual."

I was immensely relieved that afternoon when they returned safe and sound. Afterward I heard that they had coolly visited every saloon and gambling place, had stopped in each to chat with the barkeepers and gamblers, had spent the morning seated outside the Bella Union, and had been in no manner molested.

"They'll be all right as long as they stick together and keep in the open," Yank assured me. "That gang will sooner assassinate than fight."

333

GOLD

Although for the moment held in check by the resolute front presented by these three boys, the rough element showed that it considered it had won a great victory, and was now entitled to run the town. Members of the gang selected what goods they needed at any of the stores, making no pretence of payment. They swaggered boldly about the streets at all times, infested the better places such as the Bella Union, elbowed aside insolently any inoffensive citizen who might be in their way, and generally conducted themselves as though they owned the place. Robberies grew more frequent. The freighters were held up in broad daylight; rumours of returning miners being relieved of their dust drifted up from the lower country; mysterious disappearances increased in number. Hardly an attempt was made to conceal the fact that the organized gang that conducted these operations had its headquarters at Italian Bar. Strange men rode up in broad daylight, covered with red dust, to confer with Morton or one of the other resident blackguards. Mysteriously every desperado in the place began to lay fifty-dollar octagonal slugs on the gaming tables, product of some lower country atrocity.

The camp soon had a concrete illustration of the opinion the roughs held of themselves. It was reported quietly among a few of us that several of our number had been "marked" by the desperadoes. Two of these were Joe Thompson, who had acted as counsel for the prosecution in the late trial, and Tom Cleveland, who had presided, and presided well, over the court. Thompson kept one of the stores, while Cleveland was proprietor of the butcher shop. No overt threats were made, but we understood that somehow these men were to be put out of the way. Of course they were at once warned.

The human mind is certainly a queer piece of mechanism. It would seem that the most natural thing to have done, in the circumstances, would have been to dog these men's footsteps until an opportunity offered to assassinate them quietly. That is just what would have been done had the intended victims been less prominently in the public eye. The murder of court officials, however, was a very different matter from the finding of an unknown miner dead in his camp or along the trail. In the former case there could be no manner of doubt as to the perpetrators of the deed — the animus was too directly to be traced. And it is a matter for curious remark that in all early history, whether of California in the forties, or of Montana in the bloodier sixties, the desperadoes, no matter how strong they felt themselves or how arrogantly they ran the community, nevertheless must have felt a great uncertainty as to the actual power of the decent element. This is evidenced by the fact that they never worked openly. Though the identity of each of them as a robber and cut-throat was a matter of common knowledge, so that any miner could have made out a list of the members of any band, the fact was never formally admitted. And as long as it was not admitted, and as long as actual hard proof was lacking, it seemed to be part of the game that nothing could be done. Moral certainties did not count until some series of outrages resulted in mob action.

Now consider this situation, which seemed to me then as it seems to me now, most absurd in every way. Nobody else considered it so. Everybody knew that the rough element was out to "get" Thompson and Cleveland. Everybody, including both Thompson and Cleveland themselves, was pretty certain that they would not be quietly assassinated, the argument in that case being that the deed would be too apt to raise the community. Therefore it was pretty well understood that some sort of a quarrel or personal encounter would be used as an excuse. Personally I could not see that that would make much essential difference; but, as I said, the human mind is a curious piece of mechanism.

Among the occasional visitors to the camp was a man who called himself Harry Crawford. He was a man of perhaps twenty-five years, tall, rather slender, with a clear face and laughing blue eyes. Nothing in his appearance indicated the desperado; and yet we had long known him as one of the Morton gang. This man now took up his residence in camp; and we soon discovered that he was evidently the killer. The first afternoon he picked some sort of a petty quarrel with Thompson over a purchase, but cooled down instantly when unexpectedly confronted by a half dozen miners who came in at the opportune moment. A few days afterward in the slack time of the afternoon Thompson, while drinking at the bar of the Empire and conversing with a friend, was approached by a well-known sodden hanger-on of the saloons.

"What 'n hell you fellows talking about?" demanded this man impudently.

"None of your business," replied Thompson impatiently, for the man was a public nuisance, and besides was deep in Thompson's debt.

The man broke into foul oaths.

"I'll dare you to fight!" he cried in a furious passion.

Facing about, Thompson saw Crawford standing attentively among the listeners, and instantly comprehended the situation.

"You have the odds of me with a pistol," said Thompson, who notoriously had no skill with that weapon. "Why should I fight you?"

"Well, then," cried the man, "put up your fists; that'll show who is the best man!"

He snatched off his belt and laid it on the bar. Thompson did the same.

"Come on!" cried the challenger, backing away.

Thompson, thoroughly angry, reached over and slapped his antagonist. The latter promptly drew another revolver from beneath his coat, but before he could aim it Thompson jumped at his throat and disarmed him. At this moment Crawford interfered, apparently as peacemaker. Thompson was later told secretly by the barkeeper that the scheme was to lure him into a pistol fight in the street, when Crawford would be ready to shoot him as soon as the first shot was fired.

On the strength of his interference Crawford next pretended to friendship, and spent much of his time at Thompson's store. Thompson was in no way deceived. This state of affairs continued for two days. It terminated in the following manner: Crawford, sitting half on the counter, and talking with all the great charm of which he was master, led the subject to weapons.

"'This revolver of mine," said he, at the same time drawing

the weapon from its holster, "is one of the old navy model. You don't often see them nowadays. It has a double lock." He cocked it as though to illustrate his point, and the muzzle, as though by accident, swept toward the other man. He looked up from his affected close examination to find that Thompson had also drawn his weapon and that the barrel was pointing uncompromisingly in his direction.

For a moment the two stared each other in the eye. Then Crawford sheathed his pistol with an oath.

"What do you mean by that?" he cried.

"I mean," said Thompson firmly, "that I do not intend you shall get the advantage of me. You know my opinion of you and your gang. I shall not be shot by any of you, if I can help it."

Crawford withdrew quietly, but later in the day approached a big group of us, one of which was Thompson.

"There's a matter between you and me has got to be settled!" he cried.

"Well, I can't imagine what it is," replied Thompson. "I'm not aware that I've said or done anything to you that needs settlement."

"You needn't laugh!" replied Crawford, with a string of insulting oaths. "You're a coward; and if you're anything of a man you will step out of doors and have this out."

"I am, as you say, a coward," replied Thompson quietly, "and I see no reason for going out of doors to fight you or anybody else."

After blustering and swearing for a few moments Crawford withdrew. He made no attempt to fight, nor do I believe his outburst had any other purpose than to establish the purely personal character of the quarrel between Thompson and himself. At any rate, Thompson was next morning found murdered in his bunk, while Crawford had disappeared. I do not know whether Crawford had killed him or not; I think not.

About this time formal printed notices of some sort of election were posted on the bulletin board at Morton's place. At least they were said to have been posted, and were pointed out to all comers the day after election. Perhaps they were there all the time, as claimed, but nobody paid much attention to them. At any rate, we one day awoke to the fact that we were a full-fledged community, with regularly constituted court officers, duly qualified officials, and a sheriff. The sheriff was Morton, and the most worthy judges were other members of his gang!

This move tickled Danny Randall's sense of humour immensely.

"That's good head work," he said approvingly. "I didn't think Morton had it in him."

"It's time something was done to run that gang out of town," fumed Dr. Rankin.

"No; it is not time," denied Danny, "any more than it was time when you and Johnny and the rest of you had your celebrated jury trial."

"I'd like to know what you are driving at!" fretted the worthy doctor.

Danny Randall laughed in his gentle little fashion. I will confess that just at that time I was very decidedly wondering what Danny Randall was at. In fact, at moments. I was strongly inclined to doubt his affiliations. He seemed to stand in an absolutely neutral position, inclining to neither side.

Tom Cleveland was killed in the open street by one of the Empire hangers-on. The man was promptly arrested by Morton in his capacity of sheriff, and confined in chains. Morton, as sheriff, selected those who were to serve on the jury. I had the curiosity to attend the trial, expecting to assist at an uproarious farce. All the proceedings, on the contrary, were conducted with the greatest decorum, and with minute attention to legal formalities. The assassin, however, was acquitted.

From that time the outrages increased in number and in boldness. No man known to be possessed of any quantity of gold was safe. It was dangerous to walk alone after dark, to hunt alone in the mountains, to live alone. Every man carried his treasure about with him everywhere he went. No man dared raise his voice in criticism of the ruling powers, for it was pretty generally understood that such criticism meant death.

It would be supposed, naturally, by you in our modern and civilized days, that such a condition of affairs would cast a fear and gloom over the life of the community. Not at all. Men worked and played and gambled and drank and joked and carried on the light-hearted, jolly existence of the camps just about the same as ever. Outside a few principals like Morton and his immediate satellites, there was no accurate demarkation between the desperadoes and the miners. Indeed, no one was ever quite sure of where his next neighbour's sympathies lay. We all mingled together, joked, had a good time — and were exceedingly cautious. It was a polite community. Personal quarrels were the product of the moment, and generally settled at the moment or soon after. Enmities were matters for individual adjustment.

Randall's express messengers continued to make their irregular trips with the gold dust. They were never attacked, though they were convinced, and I think justly, that on numerous occasions they had only just escaped attack. Certainly the sums of money they carried were more than sufficient temptation to the bandits. They knew their country, however, and were full of Indian-like ruses, twists, doublings and turns which they employed with great gusto. How long they would have succeeded in eluding what I considered the inevitable, I do not know; but at this time occurred the events that I shall detail in the next chapter.

CHAPTER XXXVII

THE LAST STRAW

This is a chapter I hate to write; and therefore I shall get it over with as soon as possible.

Yank had progressed from his bunk to the bench outside, and from that to a slow hobbling about near the Moreña cabin. Two of the three months demanded by Dr. Rankin had passed. Yank's leg had been taken from the splint, and, by invoking the aid of stout canes, he succeeded in shifting around. But the trail to town was as yet too rough for him. Therefore a number of us were in the habit of spending our early evenings with him. We sat around the door, and smoked innumerable pipes, and talked sixty to the minute. Moreña had a guitar to the accompaniment of which he sang a number of plaintive and sweet-toned songs. Three or four of his countrymen occasionally came up from below. Then they, too, sang more plaintive songs; or played a strange game with especial cards which none of us "gringos" could ever fathom; or perhaps stepped a grave, formal sort of dance. Señora Moreña, the only woman, would sometimes join in this. She was a large woman, but extraordinarily light on her feet. In fact, as she swayed and balanced opposite her partner she reminded me of nothing so much as a balloon tugging gently at its string.

342

"But it ees good, the dance, eh, señores?" she always ended, her broad, kind face shining with pleasure.

We Americans reciprocated with a hoe-down or so, to jigging strains blasphemously evoked by one of our number from that gentle guitar; and perhaps a song or two. *Oh, Susannah!* was revived; and other old favourites; and we had also the innumerable verses of a brand-new favourite, local to the country. It had to do with the exploits and death of one Lame Jesse. I can recall only two of the many verses:

> "Lame Jesse was a hard old case;
> He never would repent.
> He ne'er was known to miss a meal —
> He never paid a cent!

> "Lame Jesse, too, like all the rest,
> He did to Death resign;
> And in his bloom went up the flume
> In the days of Forty-nine."

When the evening chill descended, which now was quite early, we scattered to our various occupations, leaving Yank to his rest.

One Sunday in the middle of October two men trudged into town leading each a pack-horse.

I was at the time talking to Barnes at his hotel, and saw them from a distance hitching their animals outside Morton's. They stayed there for some time, then came out, unhitched their horses, led them as far as the Empire, hesitated, finally again tied the beasts, and disappeared. In this manner they gradually worked along to the Bella

GOLD

Union, where at last I recognized them as McNally and Buck Barry, our comrades of the Porcupine. Of course I at once rushed over to see them.

I found them surrounded by a crowd to whom they were offering drinks free-handed. Both were already pretty drunk, but they knew me as soon as I entered the door, and surged toward me hands out.

"Well! well! well!" cried McNally delightedly. "And here's himself! And who'd have thought of seeing you here! I made sure you were in the valley and out of the country long since. And you're just in time! Make a name for it? Better call it whiskey straight. Drink to us, my boy! Come, join my friends! We're all friends here! Come on, and here's to luck, the best luck ever! We've got two horse-loads of gold out there — nothing but gold — and it all came from our old diggings. You ought to have stayed. We had no trouble. Bagsby was an old fool!" All the time he was dragging me along by the arm toward the crowd at the bar. Barry maintained an air of owlish gravity.

"Where's Missouri Jones?" I inquired; but I might as well have asked the stone mountains. McNally chattered on, excited, his blue eyes dancing, bragging over and over about his two horse-loads of gold.

The crowd took his whiskey, laughed with him, and tried shrewdly to pump him as to the location of his diggings. McNally gave them no satisfaction there; but even when most hilarious retained enough sense to put them off the track.

As will be imagined, I was most uneasy about the

344

whole proceeding, and tried quietly to draw the two men off.

"No, sir!" cried McNally, "not any! Jes' struck town, and am goin' to have a *time!*" in which determination he was cheered by all the bystanders. I did not know where to turn; Johnny was away on one of his trips, and Danny Randall was not to be found. Finally inspiration served me.

"Come down first and see Yank," I urged. "Poor old Yank is crippled and can't move."

That melted them at once. They untied their long-suffering animals, and we staggered off down the trail.

On the way down I tried, but in vain, to arouse them to a sense of danger.

"You've let everybody in town know you have a lot of dust," I pointed out.

McNally merely laughed recklessly.

"Good boys!" he cried; "wouldn't harm a fly!" and I could veer him to no other point of view. Barry agreed to everything, very solemn and very owlish.

We descended on Yank like a storm. I will say that McNally at any time was irresistible and irrepressible, but especially so in his cups. We laughed ourselves sick that afternoon. The Moreñas were enchanted. Under instructions, and amply supplied with dust, Moreña went to town and returned with various bottles. Señora Moreña cooked a fine supper. In the meantime, I, as apparently the only responsible member of the party, unsaddled the animals, and brought their burdens into the cabin. Although McNally's statement as to the loads consisting exclusively of gold was somewhat of an exaggeration, nevertheless the *cantinas* were very heavy. Not knowing what else to do with them, I thrust them under Yank's bunk.

The evening was lively, I will confess it, and under the influence of it my caution became hazy. Finally, when I at last made my way back to my own camp, I found myself vastly surprised to discover Yank hobbling along by my side. I don't know why he came with me, and I do not think he knew either. Probably force of habit. At any rate, we left the other four to sleep where they would. I remember we had some difficulty in finding places to lie.

The sun was high when we awoke. We were not feeling very fresh, to say the least; and we took some little time to get straightened around. Then we went down to the Moreña cabin.

I am not going to dwell on what we found there. All four of its inmates had been killed with buckshot, and the place ransacked from end to end. Apparently the first volley had killed our former partners and Señora Moreña as they lay. Moreña had staggered to his feet and halfway across the room.

The excitement caused by this frightful crime was intense. Every man quit work. A great crowd assembled. Morton as sheriff was very busy, and loud threats were uttered by his satellites as to the apprehension of the murderers. The temper of the crowd, however, was sullen. No man dared trust his neighbour, and yet every honest breast swelled with impotent indignation at this wholesale and unprovoked massacre. No clue was possible. Everybody remembered, of course, how broadcast and publicly the fact of the gold had been scattered. Nobody dared utter his suspicions, if he had any.

The victims were buried by a large concourse, that eddied and hesitated and muttered long after the graves had been filled in. Vaguely it was felt that the condition of affairs was intolerable; but no one knew how it was to be remedied. Nothing definite could be proved against any one, and yet I believe that every honest man knew to a moral certainty at least the captains and instigators of the various outrages. A leader could have raised an avenging mob — provided he could have survived the necessary ten minutes!

We scattered at last to our various occupations. I was too much upset to work, so I returned to where Yank was smoking over the fire. He had, as near as I can remember, said not one word since the discovery of the tragedy. On my approach he took his pipe from his mouth.

"Nothing done?" he inquired.

"Nothing," I replied. "What is there to be done?"

"Don't know," said he, replacing his pipe; then around the stem of it, "I was fond of those people."

"So was I," I agreed sincerely. "Have you thought what a lucky escape you yourself had?"

Yank nodded. We sat for a long time in silence. My thoughts turned slowly and sullenly in a heavy, impotent anger. A small bird chirped plaintively from the thicket near at hand. Except for the tinkle of our little stream and the muffled roar of the distant river, this was the only sound to strike across the dead black silence of the autumn night. So persistently did the bird utter its single call that at last it aroused even my downcast attention, so that I remarked on it carelessly to Yank. He came out of his brown study and raised his head.

"It's no bird, it's a human," he said, after listening a moment. "That's a signal. Go see what it is. Just wander out carelessly."

In the depths of the thicket I found a human figure crouched. It glided to me, and I made out dimly the squat form of Pete, Barnes's negro slave, from the hotel.

"Lo'*dee*, massa," whispered he, "done thought you nevah *would* come."

"What is it, Pete?" I asked in the same guarded tones.

"I done got somefin' to tell you. While I ketchin' a lil' bit of sleep 'longside that white trash Mo'ton's place, I done heah dey all plannin' to git out warrant for to arres' Massa Fairfax and Massa Pine and Massa Ma'sh for a-killin' dem men las' week; and I heah dem say dey gwine fer to gib dem trial, and if dey fight dey gwine done shoot 'em."

"That *is* serious news, Pete," said I. "Who were talking?" But Pete, who was already frightened half to death, grew suddenly cautious.

"I don' jest rightly know, sah," he said sullenly. "I couldn't tell. Jes' Massa Mo'ton. He say he gwine sw'ar in good big posse."

"I can believe that," said I thoughtfully. "Pete," I turned on him suddenly, "don't you know they'd skin you alive if they found out you'd been here?"

Pete was shaking violently, and at my words a strong

shudder went through his frame, and his teeth struck faintly together

"Why did you do it?"

"Massa Fairfax is quality sah," he replied with a certain dignity. "I jest a pore nigger, but I knows quality when I sees it, and I don't aim to have no pore white truck kill none of my folks if I can help it."

"Pete," said I, fully satisfied, "you are a good fellow Now get along back."

He disappeared before the words were fairly out of my mouth.

"Yank," I announced, returning to the fire, "I've got to go uptown. That was Pete, Barnes's nigger, to say that they've got out a legal warrant for the express messengers' arrest for that killing last week. Neat little scheme."

I found Danny Randall in his accustomed place. At a hint he sent for Dr. Rankin. To the two I unfolded the plot. Both listened in silence until I had quite finished. Then Danny leaped to his feet and hit the table with his closed fist.

"The fools!" he cried. "I gave them credit for more sense. Hit at Danny Randall's men, will they? Well, they'll find that Danny Randall can protect his own! Forgotten that little point, have they?"

The cool, impassive, mild little man had changed utterly. His teeth bared, the muscles of his cheeks tightened, two deep furrows appeared between his eyes, which sparkled and danced. From the most inoffensive looking creature possible to imagine he had become suddenly menacing and dangerous.

GOLD

"What do you intend, Randall?" asked Dr. Rankin. He was leaning slightly forward, and he spoke in a gentle voice, but his hand was clenched on the table, and his figure was rigid.

"Do?" repeated Randall fiercely; "why, run that gang out of town, of course!"

"I thought you said the time was not ripe?"

"We'll ripen it!" said Danny Randall.

CHAPTER XXXVIII

THE VIGILANTES

Danny Randall issued his orders as a general would. First he sent warning word to Cal Marsh, still nursing his shoulder. Through one of his barkeepers he caused to be called to his presence four men. Three of them were miners, the fourth a lookout at the Empire. He met them in his little room, quite openly, which, as I have explained, was in accordance with his usual custom. He detailed the exact situation in a few words.

"Now," he ended, "we get busy. Are you in?"

Each assented, with apparent deep satisfaction.

"Now," said he briskly, "Munroe, you go to the lower trail, near the big oak at the second crossing. Wait there. If the express messengers have not passed by to-morrow morning at ten o'clock, return here. If they do come by, stop them, and tell them to proceed by the cut-off to the place they know of, and to wait there for me. Understand?"

To each of the other four men he assigned a different watching on other trails, giving them the same instructions.

"Now git!" he finished.

After informing Yank of my projected absence, I waited at the appointed place until the appointed time, then returned to the Bella Union.

"That's all right," Danny greeted my report; "they came across the Hog's Back, and are now safely in hiding. Here," he gave me a slip of paper. "During the day contrive to see these men. Make it casual and easy, as though you just happened to see them. Chat a few minutes and tell them this: 'Danny Randall calls a secret miners' meeting at the upper horse flat at nine o'clock to-night. Slip up there without being seen.' Be sure to let them understand that it is *I* who am issuing the call. Get them to tell you whether they will or will not come."

I took the slip of paper and read over the half dozen names it contained. They were all known to me; so I nodded my comprehension and went out.

All the rest of the day I loafed about, chatting with dozens of people, among the others with Morton himself. That individual professed great zeal for law and order, and told of the wonderful things he, as sheriff, intended to accomplish. Among the lot I contrived to include the six men whose names were on my paper, and to deliver my message. I explained as far as I knew, and got from each a definite and emphatic promise to be present.

"It's time this thing was brought to a head," said one man. "If Danny Randall is taking hold of it, I enlist."

I returned to report these facts, received an indifferent nod, and, under further instruction, went quietly to camp to await the agreed hour.

We started up the trail about eight o'clock. Yank insisted that he was going, if he had to roll all the way; but after a little we simultaneously remembered that the

Moreñas had owned horses. One of these I caught, and on it Yank rode to the place of rendezvous.

The night was very black. After we had entered the woods its darkness seemed at first to hang in front of my eyes like a filmy curtain, so that I fairly groped, as one would when blindfolded. In the open a faint starlight helped us, but after we had entered the pines we had fairly to proceed by instinct. I remember feeling a shock of surprise once, when we skirted the river, at seeing plainly the whiteness of the rapids, as though the water were giving off a light of its own. Straight overhead were scattered patches of stars with misty abysses of blackness between them. Only after an interval did I appreciate that these apparent abysses were in reality the tops of trees!

We felt our way slowly, the soft muzzle of the horse at my shoulder. Gradually our pupils expanded to the utmost, so that we caught ghostly intimations of gray rocks, of dust patches, or seized the loom of a tree or the opening of a forest aisle. Luckily the trail was well marked. We had only to stick to it.

At the Flat Rock we were halted by a low-voiced command. I gave the password, as instructed by Danny Randall. This experience was once repeated, a little farther on. Then, as we neared the upper horse flat, we were stopped by a man who flashed a dark lantern in our faces, scrutinized us for a moment, shut off his light, and told us to go forward.

We found a small fire behind a screen of firs, and around or near it the figures of a dozen men. They stood silent and scattered a little apart from the firelight. We could not make out their features. From time to time other men came in, singly or in couples, until probably twenty-five were gathered. Then ensued a few moments of waiting. A sudden stir proclaimed fresh arrivals, and four newcomers strode briskly to the fire. As the light fell on them I recognized Randall and the three express riders.

Danny kicked together the fire until it flared.

"Somebody put some more wood on this," he said in his natural voice. "We've got to see each other."

In a moment the flames were leaping. I looked about me with considerable interest to see who of the camp had been summoned. I must confess to a few surprises, such as the gambler from the Empire, but in general the gathering consisted of those whom I should have characterized as solid citizens — Barnes, the hotel-keeper, Himmelwright, and men of his stripe. They were all armed, and all very grave and sober. Danny ran his eye over us one by one.

"Meeting come to order," he commanded briskly. "This is a Vigilante meeting. I hope you all realize what that means. There are just thirty of us here; and Morton's gang is probably a hundred strong when it is all together. We cannot fight them; but we can give the honest, decent men of this camp a chance to fight them. I myself believe the honest men will back us, and am willing to risk it. If any of you who are here now think differently, say so."

He paused, but no one spoke up.

"If anybody doesn't want to go into this, now is the time to back out. Just keep your mouths shut, that is all."

He paused again, but again no one moved.

"That's all right," observed Danny with satisfaction. He lifted a paper. "Listen to this: 'We the undersigned agree, as we are decent men, to stand by each other to the last, to avenge the death of any one of us, and to obey the orders of our leaders. And if we fail in this may God deny us mercy.' Boys," said Danny Randall earnestly, "this is serious. If we start this now, we've got to see it through. We are not much on Bible oaths, any one of us, but we must promise. Frank Munroe, step forward!"

I obeyed. The little man stared up into my eyes, and I will freely confess that never have I experienced quite the queer sensation it gave me. Danny Randall had become not only formidable, but great. He seemed to see through into the back of my mind. I braced myself as though to resist some strong physical force.

"Do you, Frank Munroe, subscribe to this document as a man of honour, so help you God?" he demanded.

"I do," I answered solemnly, and affixed my signature below that of Danny Randall. And queerly enough, as I stepped aside, I felt somehow that I had assisted at something sacred.

One by one Danny Randall called us forward and administered his simple oath. The fire leaped, and with it the mighty shadows. Outside the circle of light the tall pines and fir-trees watched us like a multitude standing witness. The men's faces were grave. There was about the roughest of them something noble, reflected from the earnest spirit of justice.

Randall had the plans all made, and he detailed them rapidly. We were to arrest four men only, and he named them — Morton, Scar-face Charley, who had recovered, a gambler named Catlin, and Jules, the proprietor of the Empire.

"Crawford is back in town," said some one.

"Make it five then," said Danny instantly.

We had a long discussion over all this. Many other names were suggested. Danny agreed that they were those of men guilty of the worst crimes, but maintained that the first thing to do was to get hold of the real leaders, the brains and motive power of the gang. The five first designated filled that description.

"Can we really prove anything against them?" asked some one.

"No," said Danny instantly, "we cannot. Does any one here think any of them guiltless? Consult your consciences, gentlemen. I agree with you that it is a fearful thing to take a man's life. Vote carefully. Consult your consciences."

We balloted at last on each name separately, and the five leaders were condemned to death.

Next came up the vital questions of ways and means. Many were in favour of a night surprise, and an immediate hanging before the desperadoes could be organized for defence. Danny had a hard time showing them good reasons against this course, but at last he succeeded.

"This must be done deliberately and publicly," he maintained. "Otherwise it fails of its effect. We've got to show the gang that the camp is against them; and that won't be done by hanging some of them secretly."

"Suppose the camp doesn't back us up?" queried a miner.

"Remember your oath, gentlemen," was Danny's only reply to this.

It was decided at last that five committees should be appointed to arrest each of the five men, that the prisoners should be confined in a certain isolated log cabin, and that the execution should take place in broad daylight. There remained only to apportion the committees. This was done, and at about two or three o'clock we quietly dispersed. I was instructed to coöperate with three of the miners in the arrest of Catlin.

With the members of my committee I returned to our own camp, there to await the appointed hour of seven. This had been selected for several reasons: it was daylight, the roughs would be at home, and the community, although afoot, would not yet have gone to work. While waiting we cooked ourselves some hot coffee and made some flap-jacks. The chill, gray time of day had come, the period of low vitality, and we shivered with the cold and with excitement. Nobody had much to say. We waited grimly for the time to pass.

About six o'clock Yank arose, seized his long rifle and departed for the log cabin that had been designated as the jail. His lameness had prevented him from being appointed on one of the arresting committees, but he had no intention of being left out. A half hour later we followed him into town.

It was a heavenly fall morning of the sort that only mountain California can produce. The camp was beginning to awaken to its normal activity. I remember wondering vaguely how it could be so calm and unconcerned. My heart was beating violently, and I had to clench my teeth tight to keep them from chattering. This was not fear, but a high tension of excitement. As we strolled past the Bella Union with what appearance of nonchalance we could muster, Danny Randall nodded at us from the doorway. By this we knew that Catlin was to be found at his own place.

CHAPTER XXXIX

THE VIGILANTES (*continued*)

Catlin dwelt in a detached room back of the Empire, together with one of the other professional gamblers. We lounged around the corner of the Empire building. The door of the cabin was shut. Outside we hung back, hesitating and a little uncertain. None of us was by nature or training a man of violence, and we experienced the reluctance of men about to plunge into cold water. Nobody was more than pardonably afraid, and of course we had every intention of seeing the affair through. Then suddenly in the actual face of the thing itself my excitement drained from me like a tide receding. My nerves steadied, my trembling stilled. Never had I felt more cool in my life. Drawing my revolver, I pushed open the door and entered the building.

Catlin was in the act of washing his face, and him I instantly covered with my weapon. His companion was still abed. On my entrance the latter had instinctively raised on his elbow, but immediately dropped back as he saw the figures of my companions darkening the door.

"Well, gentlemen?" demanded Catlin.

"You must come with us," I replied.

He showed no concern, but wiped carefully his face and hands.

"I will be ready in a minute," said he, throwing aside the towel, and rolling down his shirt sleeves. He advanced toward a bench on which his coat had been flung. "I'll be with you as soon as I can put on my coat."

I glanced toward that garment and saw the muzzle of a revolver peeping out from beneath it.

"I'll hand your coat to you," said I quickly. Catlin turned deadly pale, but spoke with his usual composure.

"What am I wanted for?" he inquired.

"For being a road agent, a thief, and an accessory to robberies and murders," I replied.

"I am innocent of all — as innocent as you are."

"There is no possibility of a mistake."

"What will you do with me?"

"Your sentence is death," I told him.

For a single instant his dark face lit up.

"You think so?" he flashed.

"Hurry!" urged one of my companions.

With one man on either side and another behind, revolvers drawn, we marched our prisoner in double-quick time past the rear of the stores and saloons to the agreed rendezvous. There we found Danny Randall and his committee with Morton. Within the next few moments, in rapid succession, appeared the others with Scar-face Charley, Crawford, and Jules.

The camp was already buzzing with excitement. Men poured out from the buildings into the streets like disturbed ants. Danny thrust his prisoners into the interior of the cabin, and drew us up in two lines outside. He impressed on us that we must keep the military formation, and that we were to allow no one to approach. Across the road about twenty yards away he himself laid a rope.

"That's the dead-line," he announced. "Now you keep the other side!"

In no time a mob of five hundred men had gathered. They surged restlessly to and fro. The flash of weapons was everywhere to be seen. Cries rent the air — demands, threats, oaths, and insults so numerous and so virulent that I must confess my heart failed me. At any instant I expected the mob to open fire; they could have swept us away with a single volley. To my excited imagination every man of that multitude looked a ruffian. We seemed alone against the community. I could not understand why they did not rush us and have it over with. Yet they hesitated. The fact of the matter is that the desperadoes had no cohesion, no leaders; and they knew what none of us knew — namely, that a good many of that crowd must be on our side. The roar and turmoil and heat of discussion, argument, and threat rose and fell. In one of the lulls an Irish voice yelled:

"Hang them!"

The words were greeted by a sullen assenting roar. Five hundred hands, each armed, were held aloft. This unanimity produced an instant silence.

"Hang who?" a truculent voice expressed the universal uncertainty.

"Hang the road agents!" yelled back the little Irishman defiantly.

"Bully for you, Irish; that took nerve!" muttered Johnny, at my elbow.

Fifty threats were hurled at the bold speaker, and the click of gunlocks preceded a surge in his direction. Then from the mob went up a sullen, formidable muttering of warning. No individual voice could be distinguished; but the total effect of dead resistance and determination could not be mistaken. Instantly, at the words so valiantly uttered, the spirit of cohesion had been born. The desperadoes checked in surprise. We had friends. How many or how strong no one could guess; but they were there, and in case of a battle they would fight.

On our side the line was a dead, grim silence. We stood, our weapons ready, rigidly at attention. Occasionally one or the other of us muttered a warning against those who showed symptoms of desiring to interfere.

In the meantime, three of our number had been proceeding methodically with the construction of a gallows. This was made by thrusting five small pine butts, about forty feet long, over a cross beam in the gable of the cabin and against the roof inside. Large drygoods boxes were placed beneath for the trap.

About this time Danny Randall, who had been superintending the construction, touched me on the shoulder.

"Fall back," he said quietly. "Now," he instructed several of us, after we had obeyed this command, "I want you to bring out the prisoners and hold them in plain view. In case of rescue or attempted escape, shoot them instantly. Don't hesitate."

"I should think they would be safer inside the cabin," I suggested.

"Sure," agreed Danny, "but I want them here for the moral effect."

We entered the cabin. The five prisoners were standing or sitting. Scar-face Charley was alternately blaspheming violently, upbraiding his companions, cursing his own luck, and uttering frightful threats against everybody who had anything to do with this. Crawford was watching him contemptuously and every once in a while advising him to "shut up!" Jules was alternately cursing and crying. Morton sat at one side quite calm and very alert. Catlin stared at the floor.

The moment we entered Catlin ran over to us and began to plead for his life. He, better than the rest, with the possible exception of Morton, seemed to realize the seriousness of his plight. From pleadings, which we received in silence, he changed to arguments concerning his innocence.

"It is useless," replied one of our men. "That affair is settled and cannot be changed. You are to be hanged. You cannot feel worse about it than I do; but I could not help it if I would."

Catlin stood for a moment as though overwhelmed; then he fell on his knees before us and began to plead rapidly.

"Not that!" he cried. "Anything but that! Do anything else you want to with me! Cut off my ears and cut out my tongue! Disable me in any way! You can certainly destroy my power for harm without taking my life! Gentlemen! I want to live for my wife — my poor absent wife! I want time to settle my affairs! O God! I am too wicked to die. I cannot go bloodstained and unforgiven into the presence of the Eternal! Only let me go, and I will leave the country forever!"

In the meantime Scar-face Charley and Crawford were cursing at us with an earnestness and steadiness that compelled our admiration.

"Oh, shut up, Catlin!" cried Crawford at last. "You're going to hell, and you know it; but I'll be there in time to open the gate for you."

"Don't make a fool of yourself," advised Charley; "there's no use being afraid to die."

Morton looked around at each of us in turn.

"I suppose you know you are proceeding against a regularly constituted officer of the law?" he reminded us. Receiving no reply, he beckoned me. "Can I speak to you alone a moment?" he asked.

"I will send for our leader," I replied.

"No," said he, "I want no leader. You'll do as well."

I approached him. In an anxious tone he asked:

"Is there any way of getting out of this scrape? Think well!"

"None," said I firmly. "You must die."

With revolvers drawn we marched them outside. A wild yell greeted their appearance. The cries were now mixed in sentiment. A hundred voices raised in opposition were cried down by twice as many more. "Hang 'em!" cried some. "No, no, banish them!" cried others. "Don't hang them!" and blood-curdling threats. A single shot would have brought on a pitched battle. Somehow eventually the tumult died down. Then Morton, who had been awaiting his chance, spoke up in a strong voice.

"I call on you in the name of the law to arrest and disperse these law-breakers."

"Where is Tom Cleveland?" spoke up a voice.

The appeal, which might otherwise have had its effect, was lost in the cries, accusations, and counter-accusations that arose like a babel. Morton made no further attempt. He better than any one realized, I think, the numerical superiority against him.

The preparations were at length completed. Danny Randall motioned us to lead forward the prisoners. Catlin struggled desperately, but the others walked steadily enough to take their places on the drygoods boxes.

"For God's sake, gentlemen," appealed Crawford in a loud tone of voice, "give me time to write home!"

"Ask him how much time he gave Tom Cleveland!" shouted a voice.

"If I'd only had a show," retorted Crawford, "if I'd known what you were after, you'd have had a gay time taking me."

There was some little delay in adjusting the cords.

"If you're going to hang me, get at it!" said Jules with an oath; "if not, I want you to tie a bandage on my finger; it's bleeding."

"Give me your coat, Catlin," said Crawford; "you never gave me anything yet; now's your chance."

Danny Randall broke in on this exchange.

"You are about to be executed," said he soberly. "If you have any dying requests to make, this is your last opportunity. They will be carefully heeded."

Scar-face Charley broke in with a rough laugh.

"How do I look, boys, with a halter around my neck?" he cried.

This grim effort was received in silence.

"Your time is very short," Danny reminded him.

"Well, then," said the desperado, "I want one more drink of whiskey before I die."

A species of uneasy consternation rippled over the crowd. Men glanced meaningly at each other, murmuring together. Some of the countenances expressed loathing, but more exhibited a surprised contempt. For a confused moment no one seemed to know quite what to do or what answer to make to so bestial a dying request. Danny broke the silence incisively.

"I promised them their requests would be carefully heeded," he said. "Give him the liquor."

Somebody passed up a flask. Charley raised it as high as he could, but was prevented by the rope from getting it quite to his lips.

"You ——" he yelled at the man who held the rope. "Slack off that rope and let a man take a parting drink, can't you?"

Amid a dead silence the rope was slacked away. Charley took a long drink, then hurled the half-emptied flask far out into the crowd.

To a question Crawford shook his head.

"I hope God Almighty will strike every one of you with forked lightning and that I shall meet you all in the lowest pit of hell!" he snarled.

Morton kept a stubborn and rather dignified silence.

Catlin alternately pleaded and wept. Jules answered Danny's question:

"Sure thing! Pull off my boots for me. I don't want it to get back to my old mother that I died with my boots on!"

In silence and gravely this ridiculous request was complied with. The crowd, very attentive, heaved and stirred. The desperadoes, shouldering their way here and there, were finding each other out, were gathering in little groups.

"They'll try a rescue!" whispered the man next to me.

"Men," Danny's voice rang out, clear and menacing, "do your duty!"

At the words, across the silence the click of gunlocks was heard as the Vigilantes levelled their weapons at the crowd. From my position near the condemned men I could see the shifting components of the mob freeze to immobility before the menace of those barrels. At the same instant the man who had been appointed executioner jerked the box from beneath Catlin's feet.

"There goes one to hell!" muttered Charley.

"I hope forked lightning will strike every strangling —" yelled Crawford. His speech was abruptly cut short as the box spun from under his feet.

"Kick away, old fellow!" said Scar-face Charley. "Me next! I'll be in hell with you in a minute! Every man for his principles! Hurrah for crime! Let her rip!" and without waiting for the executioner, he himself kicked the support away.

Morton died without a sign. Catlin, at the last, suddenly calmed, and met his fate bravely.

Before the lull resulting from the execution and the threat of the presented weapons could break, Danny Randall spoke up.

"Gentlemen!" he called clearly. "The roster of the Vigilantes is open. Such of you as please to join the association for the preservation of decency, law, and order in this camp can now do so."

The guard lowered their arms and moved to one side. The crowd swept forward. In the cabin the applicants were admitted a few at a time. Before noon we had four hundred men on our rolls. Some of the bolder roughs ventured a few threats, but were speedily overawed. The community had found itself, and was no longer afraid.

PART IV
THE LAW

CHAPTER XL

THE RAINS

No sooner had this radical clean-up of the body politic been consummated than the rains began. That means little to any but a Californian. To him it means everything. We were quite new to the climate and the conditions, so that the whole thing was a great surprise.

For a month past it had been threatening. The clouds gathered and piled and blackened until they seemed fairly on the point of bursting. One would not have given two cents for his chances of a dry skin were he to start on a journey across the street. Yet somehow nothing happened. Late in the afternoon, perhaps, the thunderous portents would thin. The diffused light would become stronger. Far down in the west bars of sunlight would strike. And by evening the stars shone brilliantly from a sky swept clear. After a dozen repetitions of this phenomenon we ceased to pay any attention to it. Somebody named it "high fog," which did well enough to differentiate it from a genuine rain-bringing cloud. Except for that peculiar gourd that looks exactly like a watermelon, these "high fogs" were the best imitation of a real thing I have ever seen. They came up like rain clouds, they looked precisely like rain clouds, they went through all the performances of rain clouds — except that never, never did they rain!

But the day of the Vigilante execution the sky little by little turned shimmering gray; so that the sun shining from it looked like silver; and the shadows of objects were diffused and pale. A tepid wind blew gently but steadily from the southeast. No clouds were visible at first; but imperceptibly, around the peaks, filmy veils formed seemingly out of the gray substance of the very sky itself. How these thickened and spread I did not see; but when I came out of the Bella Union, after a long and interesting evening of discussion, I found no stars; and, as I stood looking upward, a large warm drop splashed against my face.

Sometime during the night it began to rain in earnest. We were awakened by its steady drumming on the canvas of our tent.

"My Lord! but she sure is *raining!*" said Johnny across the roar of sound.

"Don't tech the canvas!" warned Old. "If you do, she'll leak like a spout where you teched her!"

"Thank heaven, that high fog scared us into ditching around the tent," said Cal fervently.

But our satisfaction was short lived. We had ditched the tent, to be sure, but we had badly underestimated the volume of a California downpour.

Before many minutes had passed Johnny gave a disgusted snort.

"I'm lying in a marsh!" he cried.

He struck a light, and we all saw the water trickling in a dozen little streams beneath the edge of the tent.

"We're going to be ruined!" cried Johnny comically.
He arose, and in doing so brushed his head violently
against the slanting canvas roof. Almost immediately
thereafter the rays of the lantern were reflected from tiny
beads of water, like a sweat, appearing as though by
magic at that spot. They swelled, gathered, hesitated,
then began to feel their way slowly down the dry canvas.
The trickle became a stream. A large drop fell straight
down. Another followed.

"Anybody need a drink?" inquired Cal.

"I'm sorry!" said Johnny contritely.

"You needn't be," I consoled him. "The whole thing
is going to leak, if this keeps up."

"What's the matter with going over to the Moreña
cabin?" queried Yank.

We hesitated a little. The events of the day had
affected us all more deeply than we liked to acknowledge;
and nobody but Yank much liked the idea of again entering
that blood-stained abode.

"We'd drown getting there," said Cal at last. "I move
some of you fellows with two good arms rustle out and
fix that ditch." He laughed. "Nothing like having a hole
in you to get out of work."

We took his advice, and managed to turn the flood,
though we got very wet in the process.

Then we returned to the tent, changed our clothes,
crept into our blankets, and wrapped ourselves close. The
spot brushed by Johnny's head dripped steadily. Otherwise our roof shed well. The rain roared straight down with
steady, deadly persistency.

GOLD

"She can't keep this up long, anyway; that's a comfort," muttered Johnny sleepily.

Couldn't she? All next morning that flood came down without the let-up of even a single moment. It had all the volume and violence of a black thunderstorm at its height; only the worst of the thunderstorm lasts but a few moments, while this showed no signs of ever intending to end. Our stout canvas continued to turn the worst of it, but a fine spray was driven through, to our great discomfort. We did not even attempt to build a fire, but sat around wrapped in our damp blankets.

Until about two of the afternoon the deluge continued. Our unique topic of conversation was the marvel of how it could keep it up! We could not imagine more water falling were every stream and lake in the mountains to be lifted to the heavens and poured down again.

"Where the devil does it all come from?" marvelled Old, again and again. "Don't seem like no resevoy, let alone clouds, could hold so much!"

"And where does it go to?" I supplemented.

"I reckon some of those plains people could tell you," surmised Yank shrewdly.

At two o'clock the downpour ceased as abruptly as though it had been turned off at a spigot. Inside of twenty minutes the clouds had broken, to show beyond them a dazzling blue sky. Intermittent flashes and bands of sunlight glittered on the wet trees and bushes or threw into relief the black bands of storm clouds near the horizon.

Immensely cheered, we threw aside our soggy blankets and sallied forth.

"Great Christmas!" cried Johnny, who was in the advance. "Talk about your mud!"

We did talk about it. It was the deepest, most tenacious, slipperiest, most adhesive mud any fiend ever imagined. We slid and floundered as though we had on skates; we accumulated balls of it underfoot; and we sank disconcertingly half-leg deep at every third step. Our first intention had been to go up to town; but we soon revised that, and went down to the Moreña cabin instead, with the idea of looking after the two horses. The beasts, very shaggy underneath and plastered above, stood humped up nose to tail. We looked into the cabin. The roof had leaked like a sieve; and the interior was dripping in a thousand places.

"Reckon even the tent was better after all," acknowledged Yank, looking with disfavour on the muddy floor.

We returned to the tent and made shift to get a fire going. After cooking some hot food, we felt better, and set about drying our blankets. In the cañon we could hear the river roaring away hollowly.

"I'll bet she's on the rampage!" said Old.

"I'll bet she's got my cradle and all of my tools!" I cried, struck with a sudden thought.

And then, about as we commenced to feel cheerful and contented again, the scattered black clouds began to close ranks. One by one the patches of blue sky narrowed and disappeared.

"Why!" cried Cal in astonishment, "I believe it's getting ready to rain again!"

GOLD

"Shucks!" replied Old, "It can't. There ain't no more rain."

Nevertheless there was, and plenty of it. We spent that second night shifting as little as possible so as not to touch a new cold place in our sodden blankets, while the waters roared down in almost a solid sheet.

This lasted the incredible period of four days! Nobody then knew anything about measuring rainfall; but, judging by later experience, I should say we must have had close to seven inches. There was not much we could do, except to get wetter and wetter, although we made shift to double up at night, and to use the extra blankets thus released to make a sort of double roof. This helped some.

The morning of the fifth day broke dazzlingly clear. The sky looked burnished as a blue jewel; the sunlight glittered like shimmering metal; distant objects stood out plain-cut, without atmosphere. For the first time we felt encouraged to dare that awful mud, and so slopped over to town.

We found the place fairly drowned out. No one, in his first year, thought of building for the weather. Barnes's hotel, the Empire and the Bella Union had come through without shipping a drop, for they had been erected by men with experience in the California climate; but almost everybody else had been leaked upon a-plenty. And the deep dust of the travel-worn overland road had turned into a morass beyond belief or description.

Our first intimation of a definite seasonal change came from our old friend Danny Randall, who hailed us at once when he saw us picking our way gingerly along the edge of the street. In answer to his summons we entered the Bella Union.

"I hope you boys weren't quite drowned out," he greeted us. "You don't look particularly careworn."

We exchanged the appropriate comments; then Danny came at once to business.

"Now I'm going to pay off you three boys," he told the express messengers, "and I want to know what you want. I can give you the dust, or I can give you an order on a San Francisco firm, just as you choose."

"Express business busted?" asked Johnny.

"It's quit for the season," Danny Randall told him, "like everything else. In two weeks at most there won't be a score of men left in Italian Bar." He observed our astonished incredulity, smiled, and continued: "You boys came from the East, where it rains and gets over it. But out here it doesn't get over it. Have you been down to look at the river? No? Well, you'd better take a look. There'll be no more bar mining done there for a while. And what's a mining camp without mining? Go talk to the men of '48. They'll tell you. The season is over, boys, until next spring; and you may just as well make up your minds to hike out now as later. What are you laughing at?" he asked Johnny.

"I was just thinking of our big Vigilante organization," he chuckled.

"I suppose it's true that mighty few of the same lot will ever get back to Italian Bar," agreed Danny, "but it's a good thing for whatever community they may hit next year."

GOLD

Johnny and Old elected to take their wages in dust; Cal decided on the order against the San Francisco firm. Then we wandered down to where we could overlook the bar itself.

The entire bed of the river was filled from rim to rim with a rolling brown flood. The bars, sand-spits, gravel-banks had all disappeared. Whole trees bobbed and sank and raised skeleton arms or tangled roots as they were swept along by the current or caught back by the eddies; and underneath the roar of the waters we heard the dull rumbling and crunching of boulders rolled beneath the flood. A crowd of men was watching in idle curiosity. We learned that all the cradles and most of the tools had been lost; and heard rumours of cabins or camps located too low having been swept away.

That evening we held a very serious discussion of our prospects and plans. Yank announced himself as fit to travel, and ready to do so, provided he could have a horse; the express messengers were out of a job; I had lost all my tools, and was heartily tired of gold washing, even had conditions permitted me to continue. Beside which, we were all feeling quite rich and prosperous. We had not made enormous fortunes as we had confidently anticipated when we left New York, but we were all possessed of good sums of money. Yank had the least, owing to the fact that he had been robbed of his Porcupine River product, and had been compelled for nearly three months to lie idle; but even he could count on a thousand dollars or so sent out from Hangman's Gulch. I had the most, for my digging had paid me better than had Johnny's express riding. But much of my share belonged of right to Talbot Ward.

Having once made up our minds to leave, we could not go too soon. A revulsion seized us. In two days the high winds that immediately sprang up from the west had dried the surface moisture. We said good-bye to all our friends — Danny Randall, Dr. Rankin, Barnes, and the few miners with whom we had become intimate. Danny was even then himself preparing to return to Sonoma as soon as the road should be open to wagons. Dr. Rankin intended to accompany him, ostensibly because he saw a fine professional opening at Sonoma, in reality because in his shy, hidden fashion he loved Danny.

Nobody objecting, we commandeered the two horses that had belonged to the Moreñas. One of them we packed with our few effects, and turned the other over to Yank. Thus, trudging afoot, Johnny and I saw our last of Italian Bar. Thirty years later I rode up there out of sheer curiosity. Most of the old cabins had fallen in. The Bella Union was a drear and draughty wreck. The Empire was used as a stable. Barnes's place and Morton's next door had burned down. Only three of the many houses were inhabited. In two of them dwelt old men, tending small gardens and orchards. I do not doubt they too were Forty-niners; but I did not stop. The place was full of too many ghosts.

CHAPTER XLI

WE GO OUT

We made our way out of the hills without adventure worth noting. The road was muddy, and a good deal washed. In fact, we had occasionally to do considerable manœuvring to find a way at all around the landslides from the hills above.

As we descended we came upon traces of the great exodus that was taking place from the hills. All the miners were moving out. We found discarded articles of camp equipment; we passed some people without any equipment at all. Sick men lay under bushes without covering, or staggered painfully down the muddy trails. Many were utterly without food. If it rained, as it did from frequent showers, they took it as cheerfully as they could. This army of the unsuccessful was a striking commentary on the luck of the mines.

Robbers most singularly lacked. I did not hear of a single case of violence in all the rather slow journey out. The explanation did not seem difficult, however. Those who travelled alone had nothing worth the taking; while those who possessed gold went in numbers too strong to be attacked. The road agents had gone straight to the larger cities. Nor, must I confess, did I see many examples of compassion to the unfortunate. In spite of the sentimental stories that have been told — with real enough basis in isolated fact, probably — the time was selfish. It was also, after eliminating the desperadoes and blacklegs, essentially honest. Thus one day we came upon a wagon apparently deserted by the roadside. On it was a rudely scrawled sign:

"Will some kind person stay by my wagon. I am in distress looking for my oxen. Please do not take anything, for I am poor, and the property is not mine."

Nothing had been touched, as near as I could make out. We travelled by easy stages, and by a roundabout route, both because the road was bad, and because we wanted to see the country. On our way we passed several other small camps. A great many Chinese had come in, and were engaged in scratching over the abandoned claims. In fact, one man told me that sometimes it was worth while to file on some of the abandoned claims just to sell them to these patient people! As we descended from the mountains we naturally came upon more and more worked-out claims. Some had evidently been abandoned in disgust by men with little stamina; but, sometimes, with a considerable humour. An effigy clad in regulation gambler's rig, including the white shirt, swayed and swung slowly above the merest surface diggings. Across the shirt front these words were written:

"My claim failed!"

And then below them:

*"Oh, Susannah! don't you cry for me!
I'm a-living dead in Californi-ee"* —

which was very bad as doggeral, but probably very accurate as to its author's state of mind.

One afternoon we turned off on a trail known to Old, and rode a few miles to where the Pine family had made its farm. We found the old man and his tall sons inhabiting a large two-roomed cabin situated on a flat. They had already surrounded a field with a fence made of split pickets and rails, and were working away with the tireless energy of the born axemen at enclosing still more. Their horses had been turned into ploughing; and from somewhere or other they had procured a cock and a dozen hens. Of these they were inordinately proud, and they took great pains to herd them in every night away from wildcats and other beasts. We stayed with them four days, and we had a fine time. Every man of them was keenly interested in the development of the valley and the discovery of its possibilities. We discussed apples, barley, peaches, apricots, ditches, irrigation, beans, hogs, and a hundred kindred topics, to Johnny's vast disgust. I had been raised on a New England farm; Yank had experienced agricultural vicissitudes in the new country west of the Alleghanies; and the Pines had scratched the surface of the earth in many localities. But this was a new climate and a new soil to all of us; and we had nothing to guide us. The subject was fascinating. Johnny was frankly bored with it all, but managed to have a good time hunting for the game with which the country abounded.

For a brief period Yank and I quite envied the lot of these pioneers who had a settled stake in the country.

"I wish I could go in for this sort of thing," said Yank.

"Why don't you?" urged old man Pine. "There's a flat just above us."

"How did you get hold of this land?" I inquired curiously.

"Just took it."

"Doesn't it belong to anybody?"

"It's part of one of these big Greaser ranchos," said Pine impatiently. "I made a good try to git to the bottom of it. One fellar says he owns it, and will sell; then comes another that says *he* owns it and won't sell. And so on. They don't nohow use this country, except a few cattle comes through once in a while. I got tired of monkeying with them and I came out here and squatted. If I owe anybody anything, they got to show me who it is. I don't believe none of them knows themselves who it really belongs to."

"I'd hate to put a lot of work into a place, and then have to move out," said I doubtfully.

"I'd like to see anybody move me out!" observed old man Pine grimly.

Farther up in the hills they were putting together the framework of a sawmill, working on it at odd times when the ranch itself did not demand attention. It was built of massive hewn timbers, raised into place with great difficulty. They had no machinery as yet, but would get that later out of their first farming profits.

"There ain't no hurry about it anyway," explained Pine, "for as yet there ain't no demand for lumber yereabouts."

"I should say not!" exploded Johnny with a derisive shriek of laughter, "unless you're going to sell it to the elks and coyotes!"

Pine turned toward him seriously.

"This is all good land yere," said he, "and they'll want lumber."

"It looks mighty good to me," said Yank.

"Well, why don't you settle?" urged Pine.

"And me with fifteen hundred good dollars?" replied Yank. "It ain't such an everlasting fortune; but it'll git me a place back home; and I've had my fun. This country is too far off. I'm going back home."

To this sentiment Johnny and I heartily agreed. It is a curious fact that not one man in ten thousand even contemplated the possibility of making California his permanent home. It was a place in which to get as rich as he could, and then to leave.

Nevertheless we left our backwoods friends reluctantly; and at the top of the hill we stopped our two horses to look back on the valley. It lay, with its brown, freshly upturned earth, its scattered broad oaks, its low wood-crowned knolls, as though asleep in the shimmering warm floods of golden sunshine. Through the still air we heard plainly the beat of an axe, and the low, drowsy clucking of hens. A peaceful and grateful feeling of settled permanence, to which the restless temporary life of mining camps had long left us strangers, filled us with the vague stirrings of envy.

The feeling soon passed. We marched cheerfully away, our hopes busy with what we would do when we reached New York. Johnny and I had accumulated very fair sums of money, in spite of our loss at the hands of the robbers, what with the takings at Hangman's Gulch.

what was left from the robbery, and Italian Bar. These sums did not constitute an enormous fortune, to be sure. There was nothing spectacular in our winnings; but they totalled about five times the amount we could have made at home; and they represented a very fair little stake with which to start life. We were young.

We found Sacramento under water. A sluggish, brown flood filled the town and spread far abroad over the flat countryside. Men were living in the second stories of such buildings as possessed second stories, and on the roofs of others. They were paddling about in all sorts of improvised boats and rafts. I saw one man keeping a precarious equilibrium in a baker's trough; and another sprawled out face down on an India rubber bed paddling overside with his hands.

We viewed these things from the thwarts of a boat which we hired for ten dollars. Our horses we had left outside of town on the highlands. Everywhere we passed men and shouted to them a cheery greeting. Everybody seemed optimistic and inclined to believe that the flood would soon go down.

"Anyway, she's killed the rats," one man shouted in answer to our call.

We grinned an appreciation of what we thought merely a facetious reply. Rats had not yet penetrated to the mines, so we did not know anything about them. Next day, in San Francisco, we began to apprehend the man's remark.

Thus we rowed cheerfully about, having a good time at the other fellow's expense. Suddenly Johnny, who was

steering, dropped his paddle with an exclamation. Yank
and I turned to see what had so struck him. Beyond the
trees that marked where the bank of the river ought to be
we saw two tall smokestacks belching forth a great volume
of black smoke.

"A steamer!" cried Yank.

"Yes, and a good big one!" I added.

We lay to our oars and soon drew alongside. She
proved to be a side wheeler, of fully seven hundred tons,
exactly like the craft we had often seen plying the Hudson.

"Now how do you suppose they got her out here?"
I marvelled.

She was almost completely surrounded by craft of all
descriptions; her decks were crowded. We read the name
McKim on her paddle boxes.

A man with an official cap appeared at the rail.

"Bound for San Francisco?" I called to him.

"Off in two minutes," he replied.

"What's the fare?"

"Forty dollars."

"Come on, boys," said I to my comrades, at the same
time seizing a dangling rope.

"Hold on!" cried Yank. "How about our two horses
and our blankets, and this boat?"

I cast my eye around, and discovered a boy of fourteen
or fifteen in the stern of a neat fisherman's dory a few
feet away.

"Here!" I called to him. "Do you want two good horses
and some blankets?"

"I ain't got any money."

"Don't need any. These are free. We're going down on this boat. You'll find the outfit under the big white oak two miles above the forks on the American. They're yours if you'll go get them."

"What do you want me to do?" he demanded suspiciously.

"Two things: return this boat to its owner — a man named Lilly who lives ——"

"I know the boat," the boy interrupted.

"The other is to be sure to go up to-day after those horses. They're picketed out."

"All right," agreed the boy, whose enthusiasm kindled as his belief in the genuineness of the offer was assured.

I seized a rope, swung myself up to the flat fender, and thence to the deck.

"Come on!" I called to Yank and Johnny, who were hesitating. "It'll cost more than those horses and blankets are worth to wait."

Thereupon they followed me. The boy made fast our boat to his own. Five minutes later we were dropping down the river.

"This is what I call real luxury," said Johnny, returning from an inspection of our craft. "There's a barroom, and a gambling layout, and velvet carpets and chairs, mirrors, a minstrel show, and all the fixings. Now who'd expect to run against a layout like this on the river?"

"What I'd like to know is how they got her out here," said I. "Look at her! She's a river boat. A six-foot wave ought to swamp her!"

We thought of a half dozen solutions, and dismissed

them all. The discussion, however, served its purpose in inflaming our curiosity.

"I'm going to find some one who knows," I announced at last.

This was not so easy. The captain was of course remote and haughty and inaccessible, and the other officers were too busy handling the ship and the swarming rough crowd to pay any attention to us. The crew were new hands. Finally, however, we found in the engine room a hard bitten individual with a short pipe and some leisure. To him we proffered our question.

"Sailed her," said he.

"Around the Horn?" I cried.

He looked at me a bitter instant.

"The sailing wasn't very good across the plains, *at that time*," said he.

Little by little we got his story. I am not a seafaring man, but it seems to me one of the most extraordinary feats of which I have ever heard. The lower decks of the *McKim* had been boarded up with heavy planks; some of her frailer gimcracks of superstructure had been dismantled, and then she had been sent under her own power on the long journey around the Horn. Think of it! A smooth-water river boat, light draught, top heavy, frail in construction, sent out to battle with the might of three oceans! However, she made it; and after her her sister ship, the *Senator*, and they made money for their owners, and I am glad of it. That certainly was a gallant enterprise!

She was on this trip jammed full of people, mostly

those returning from the mines. A trip on the *McKim* implied a certain amount of prosperity, so we were a jolly lot. The weather was fine, and a bright moon illuminated the swollen river. We had drinkers, songsters, debaters, gamblers, jokers, and a few inclined to be quarrelsome, all of which added to the variety of the occasion. I wandered around from one group to another, thoroughly enjoying myself, both out on deck and in the cabins. It might be added that there were no sleepers!

Along toward midnight, as I was leaning on the rail forward watching the effect of the moon on the water and the shower of sparks from the twin stacks against the sky, I was suddenly startled by the cry of "man overboard," and a rush toward the stern. I followed as quickly as I was able. The paddle wheels had been instantly reversed, and a half dozen sailors were busily lowering a boat. A crowd of men, alarmed by the trembling of the vessel as her way was checked, poured out from the cabins. The fact that I was already on deck gave me an advantageous post; so that I found myself near the stern rail.

"He was leaning against the rail," one was explaining excitedly, "and it give way, and in he went. He never came up!"

Everybody was watching eagerly the moonlit expanse of the river.

"I guess he's a goner," said a man after a few moments. "He ain't in sight nowhere."

"There he is!" cried a half dozen voices all at once.

A head shot into sight a few hundred yards astern, blowing the silvered water aside. The small boat, which was now afloat, immediately headed in his direction, and a moment later he was hauled aboard amid frantic cheers. The dripping victim of the accident clambered to the deck.

It was Johnny!

He was beside himself with excitement, sputtering with rage and uttering frantic threats against something or somebody. His eyes were wild, and he fairly frothed at the mouth. I seized him by the arm. He stared at me, then became coherent, though he still spluttered. Johnny was habitually so quietly reserved as far as emotions go that his present excitement was at first utterly incomprehensible.

It seemed that he had been leaning against the rail, watching the moonlight, when suddenly it had given way beneath his weight and he had fallen into the river.

"They had no business to have so weak a rail!" he cried bitterly.

"Well, you're here, all right," I said soothingly. "There's no great harm done."

"Oh, isn't there?" he snarled.

Then we learned how the weight of the gold around his waist had carried him down like a plummet; and we sensed a little of the desperate horror with which he had torn and struggled to free himself from that dreadful burden.

"I thought I'd burst!" said he.

And then he had torn off the belt, and had shot to the surface.

"It's down there," he said more calmly, "every confounded yellow grain of it." He laughed a little. "Broke!" said he. "No New York in mine!"

The crowd murmured sympathetically.

"Gol darn it, boys, it's rotten hard luck!" cried a big miner with some heat. "Who'll chip in?"

At the words Johnny recovered himself, and his customary ease of manner returned.

"Much obliged, boys," said he, "but I've still got my health. I don't need charity. Guess I've been doing the baby act; but I was damn mad at that rotten old rail. Anyway," he laughed, "there need nobody say in the future that there's no gold in the lower Sacramento. There is; I put it there myself."

The tall miner slowly stowed away his buckskin sack, looking keenly in Johnny's face

"Well, you'll have a drink, anyway," said he.

"Oh, hell, yes!" agreed Johnny, "I'll have a drink!"

CHAPTER XLII

SAN FRANCISCO AGAIN

We drew up to San Francisco early in the afternoon, and we were, to put it mildly, thoroughly astonished at the change in the place. To begin with, we now landed at a long wharf projecting from the foot of Sacramento Street instead of by lighter. This wharf was crowded by a miscellaneous mob, collected apparently with no other purpose than to view our arrival. Among them we saw many specialized types that had been lacking to the old city of a few months ago — sharp, keen, businesslike clerks whom one could not imagine at the rough work of the mines; loafers whom one could not imagine at any work at all; dissolute, hard-faced characters without the bold freedom of the road agents; young green-looking chaps who evidently had much to learn and who were exceedingly likely to pay their little fortunes, if not their lives, in the learning. On a hogshead at one side a street preacher was declaiming.

Johnny had by now quite recovered his spirits. I think he was helped greatly by the discovery that he still possessed his celebrated diamond.

"Not broke yet!" said he triumphantly. "You see I was a wise boy after all! Wish I had two of them!"

We disembarked, fought our way to one side, and discussed our plans.

"Hock the diamond first," said Johnny, who resolutely refused to borrow from me; "then hair-cut, shave, bath, buy some more clothes, grub, drink, and hunt up Talbot and see what he's done with the dust we sent down from Hangman's."

That program seemed good. We strolled toward shore, with full intention of putting it into immediate execution. "Immediate" proved to be a relative term; there was too much to see.

First we stopped for a moment to hear what the preacher had to say. He was a tall, lank man with fine but rather fanatical features, dressed in a long black coat, his glossy head bare. In spite of the numerous counter-attractions he had a crowd; and he was holding it.

"You're standing on a whiskey barrel!" called some one; and the crowd yelled with delight.

"True, my friend," retorted the preacher with undaunted good nature, "and I'll venture to say this is the first time a whiskey barrel has ever been appropriated to so useful a purpose. The critter in it will do no harm if it is kept underfoot. Never let it get above your feet!"

A boat runner, a squat, humorous-faced negro with flashing teeth and a ready flow of language, evidently a known and appreciated character, mounted the head of a pile at some little distance and began to hold forth in a deep voice on the advantages of some sort of an excursion on the bay. A portion of the preacher's crowd began to drift in the direction of the new attraction.

"Ho! ho! ho!" cried the preacher suddenly in tremendous volume. "Ho! All ye who want to go to heaven, now's your time! A splendid line of celestial steamers will run for a few days from San Francisco to the port of Glory, a country every way superior to California, having in it the richest gold diggings ever discovered, the very streets of the city being paved with gold. In that country are oceans of lager beer and drinks of every kind, all free; pretty women also, and pleasures of endless variety exceeding the dreams of Mohammed as far as the brightness of the meridian sun exceeds the dim twinkle of the glowworm! Program for the voyage: embarkation amid the melody of the best band in the world; that music that so attracted you this morning not to be mentioned in comparison. Appropriate entertainments for each week day, to be announced daily. Each Sunday to be celebrated, first, with a grand feast, closing with a rich profusion of beer, champagne, good old port, whiskey punch, brandy smashes, Tom and Jerry, etc. Second, a game of cards. Third, a grand ball in upper saloon. Fourth, a dog fight. Fifth, a theatrical performance in the evening. If I could truthfully publish such an ad as that I think about two sermons would convert this city."

The crowd had all turned back to him, laughing good-humouredly. The preacher stretched out his long bony arm, and held forth. His talk was against gambling, and it had, I am afraid, but little real effect. Nevertheless he was listened to; and at the end of his talk everybody contributed something to a collection.

At the land end of the wharf we ran into the most extraordinary collection of vehicles apparently in an inextricable tangle, that was further complicated by the fact

that most of the horses were only half broken. They
kicked and reared, their drivers lashed and swore, the
wagons clashed together. There seemed no possible way
out of the mess; and yet somehow the wagons seemed to get
loaded and to draw out into the clear. Occasionally
the drivers were inclined to abandon their craft and do
battle with the loaded ends of their whips; but always a
peacemaker descended upon them in the person of a large
voluble individual in whom I recognized my former friend
and employer, John McGlynn. Evidently John had no
longer a monopoly of the teaming business; but, as evidently, what he said went with this wild bunch.

Most of the wagons were loading goods brought from
the interiors of storehouses alongside the approach to the
wharf. In these storehouses we recognized the hulls
of ships, but so shored up, dismantled, and cut into by doors
and stories that of their original appearance only their
general shapes remained. There was a great number of
these storehouses along the shore, some of them being quite
built about by piles and platforms, while two were actually
inland several hundred feet. I read the name *Niantic*
on the stern of one of them; and found it to have acquired
in the landward side a square false front. It was at that
time used as a hotel.

"Looks as if they'd taken hold of Talbot's idea hard,"
observed Yank.

"Say!" cried Johnny, "will one of you drinking men
kindly take a look and inform me if I've gone wrong?"

This remark was called forth by the discovery, as we
neared the shore, of hordes of rats. They were large,

fat, saucy rats; and they strolled about in broad daylight as if they owned the place. They sat upright on sacks of grain; they scampered across the sidewalks; they scuttled from behind boxes; they rustled and squeaked and fought and played in countless droves. The ground seemed alive with them. It was a most astonishing sight.

"And will you look at that dog!" cried Yank disgustedly.

Across an open doorway, blinking in the sun, lay a good-looking fox terrier. His nose was laid between his paws, and within two yards of that nose a large brown rat disported itself with a crust of bread.

"My Lord!" cried Johnny, his sporting blood aboil. "Here, pup, sic 'em! sic 'em!" He indicated the game urgently. The fox terrier rolled up one eye, wagged his stub tail — but did not even raise his nose.

"No use," observed the dog's owner, who had appeared in the doorway.

"What's the matter with him?" demanded Johnny indignantly; "is he sick?"

"No, he ain't sick," replied the owner sadly; "but he ain't got no use for rats. I bought him for damn near his weight in gold dust when the *Panama* came in last month. He was the best ratter you ever see. I reckon he must've killed a million rats the first week. But, Lord! he got sick of rats. I reckon a rat could go right up and pull his whiskers now, and he'd never mind."

We condoled with the *blasé* dog, and moved on.

"Same old mud," observed Yank.

The place was full of new buildings, some of them

quite elaborate two-story structures of brick; and elevated plank sidewalks had taken the place of the old makeshifts. Although the Plaza was still the centre of town, the streets immediately off it had gained considerable dignity and importance. There were many clothing stores, nearly all kept by Jews, and a number of new saloons and gambling houses. As we were picking our way along we ran into an old acquaintance in the person of the captain of the *Panama*. He recognized us at once, and we drew up for a chat. After we had exchanged first news Johnny asked him if he knew of a place where a fair price could be raised on the diamond.

"Why, the jewellery store is your ticket, of course," replied the captain.

"So there's a jewellery store, too!" cried Johnny.

"And a good one," supplemented the captain. "Come along; I'll take you to it."

It *was* a good one, and carried a large stock of rings, chains, pins, clocks, watches, and speaking trumpets. The latter two items were the most prominent, for there were hundreds of watches, and apparently thousands of speaking trumpets. They stood in rows on the shelves, and depended in ranks from hooks and nails. Most of them were of silver or of silver gilt; and they were plain, chased, engraved, hammered, or repoussé, with always an ample space for inscription. After Johnny had concluded a satisfactory arrangement for his diamond, I remarked on the preponderance of speaking trumpets. The man grinned rather maliciously at our captain.

"They are a very favourite article for presentation

by grateful passengers after a successful sea trip," he said smoothly.

At this our captain exploded.

"Are they?" he boomed. "I should think they were! I've got a dozen of the confounded things; and as I've just got in from a trip, I'm expecting another any minute. Good Lord!" he cried as a group of men turned in at the door. "Here come some of my passengers now. Come along, let's get out of this!"

He dragged us out a back door into a very muddy back alley, whence we floundered to dry land with some difficulty.

"That was a narrow escape!" he cried, wiping his brow. "Let's go get a drink. I know the best place."

He led us to a very ornate saloon whose chief attraction was the fact that its ceiling was supported on glass pillars! We duly admired this marvel; and then wandered over to the polished mahogany bar, where we were joined by the half dozen loafers who had been lounging around the place. These men did not exactly join us, but they stood expectantly near. Nor were they disappointed.

"Come, let's all take a drink, boys!" cried the captain heartily.

They named and tossed off their liquor, and then without a word of farewell or thanks shambled back to their roosting places.

"What's the matter, Billy?" demanded the captain, looking about curiously. "Where's your usual crowd?"

"They're all down at the Verandah," replied the bar-keeper, passing a cloth over the satiny wood of the bar. "Dorgan's got a girl tending bar. Pays her some ungodly wages; and he's getting all the crowd. He'd better make the most of it while it lasts. She won't stay a week."

"Why not?" I asked curiously.

"Married; sure," replied the barkeeper briefly.

"And the glass pillars will always be here; eh, Billy?" suggested the captain. "Nevertheless I believe we'll just wander down and look her over."

"Sure," said Billy indifferently; "that's where all the rest are."

The Verandah, situated on the Plaza, was crowded to the doors. Behind the bar slaved a half dozen busy drink-mixers. The girl, and a very pretty girl she was, passed the drinks over the counter, and took in the dust.

"She's straight," observed the captain sagaciously, after inspection; "if she wasn't there wouldn't be such a gang. The other sort is plenty enough."

We did not try to get near the bar, but after a few moments regained the street. The captain said farewell; and we hunted up, by his direction, the New York Tonsorial Emporium. There we had five dollars' worth of various things done to us; after which we bought new clothes. The old ones we threw out into the street along with a vast collection of others contributed by our predecessors.

"Now," said Johnny, "I feel like a new man. And before we go any farther I have a little duty to perform."

"Which is?"

"Another drink at the sign of the Glass Pillars, or whatever they call the place."

"We don't want anything more to drink just now," I protested.

"Oblige me in this one treat," said Johnny in his best manner.

We entered the Arcade, as the bar was called. At once the loafers moved forward. Johnny turned to them with an engaging air of friendliness.

"Come on, boys, let's all take a drink!" he cried.

The glasses were poured. Johnny raised his. The others followed suit. Then all drained them simultaneously and set down the empty glasses.

"And now," went on Johnny in the same cheerful, friendly tone, "let's all pay for them!"

The loafers stared at him a moment. One growled menacingly, but fell silent under his clear glance. One or two others forced a laugh. Under Johnny's compelling eye they all paid. Billy, behind the bar, watched with sardonic amusement. When Johnny proffered his dust, the barkeeper thrust it back.

"My treat here," said he briefly.

"But ——" objected Johnny.

"It's a privilege."

"If you put it that way, I thank you, sir," said Johnny in his grandest manner; and we walked out. "Those bums made me tired," was his only comment to us. "Now let's go hunt up Talbot. I'll bet my extinct toothbrush that he's a well-known citizen around here."

Johnny's extinct toothbrush was perfectly safe. The first man of whom we inquired told us where our friend lived, and added the gratuitous information that the Ward Block was nearing completion. We looked up the hotel, a new one on Montgomery Street. The clerk spoke with respect of Talbot, and told us we would probably find him at one of the several places of business he mentioned, or at the Ward Block. We thanked him, and went direct to the Ward Block first. All of us confessed to a great desire to see that building.

It was to be a three-story brick structure, and was situated at one corner of the Plaza. We gazed upon it with appropriate awe, for we were accustomed to logs and canvas; and to some extent we were able to realize what imported bricks and the laying of them meant. The foreman told us that Talbot had gone out "Mission way" with Sam Brannan and some others to look at some property, and would not be back until late.

Johnny and I spent the rest of the afternoon wandering about. Yank retired to the soft chairs of one of the numerous gambling places. His broken leg would not stand so much tramping.

We had lots of fun, and many interesting minor adventures and encounters, none of which has any particular bearing here. The town had spread. Most of the houses were of the flimsied description. Many people were still living in tents. The latter flopped and tugged in the strong wind. Some men had merely little cot tents, just big enough to cover the bed. An owner of one of these claimed stoutly that they were better than big tents.

"They don't get blowed away by the wind, and they re fine to sleep under," he asserted, "and a man cooks outside, anyway."

"How about when it rains?" I asked him.

"Then I go down to the Verandah or the Arcade or

Dennison's Exchange and stay there till she quits," said he.

In the evening, as Talbot had not yet returned, we wandered from one place of amusement to another. The gambling places were more numerous, more elaborate, more important than ever. Beside the usual rough-looking miners and labourers, who were in the great majority, there were small groups of substantial, grave, important looking men conferring. I noticed again the contrast with the mining-camp gambling halls in the matter of noise; here nothing was heard but the clink of coin or the dull thud of gold dust, a low murmur of conversation, or an occasional full-voiced exclamation.

Johnny, who could never resist the tables, was soon laying very small stakes on *monte*. After a time I tired of the close air and heavy smoke, and slipped away. The lower part of the town was impossible on account of the mud, so I made my way out along the edge of the hills. The moon was sailing overhead. The shadows of the hills hung deep in the hollows; and, abroad, a wide landscape slept in the unearthly radiance. A thousand thousand cheerful frogs piped up a chorus against the brooding moon-stillness they could not quite break. After the glare of the Arcade and the feverish hum and bustle of the busy new city, this still peace was almost overpowering. I felt, somehow, that I dared not give way to it all at once, but must admit its influence trickle by trickle until my spirit had become a little accustomed. Thus gradually I dropped into a reverie. The toil, excitement, strain, striving of the past eight or nine months fell swiftly into the background. I relaxed; and in the calm of the relaxation for the first time old memories found room.

How long I had tramped, lost in this dreaming, I did not know; but at some point I must have turned back, for I came to somewhere near the end of Sacramento Street — if it could be said to have an end — to find the moon far up toward the zenith. A man overtook me, walking rapidly; I caught the gleam of a watch chain, and on a sudden impulse I turned toward him.

"Can you tell me what time it is?" I asked.

The man extended his watch in the moonlight, and silently pointed to its face — with the muzzle of a revolver!

"Half-past twelve," said he.

"Good Lord!" I cried with a shout of laughter. "Do you take me for a robber, Talbot?"

CHAPTER XLIII

THE GOLDEN WEB

He thrust away his watch and the pistol and with a shout of joy seized both my hands.

"Well! well! well! well!" he cried over and over again. "But I *am* glad to see you! I'd no idea where you were or what you were doing! Why couldn't you write a man occasionally?"

"I don't know," said I, rather blankly. "I don't believe it ever occurred to us we *could* write."

"Where are the others? Are they with you?"

"We'll look them up," said I.

Together we walked away, arm in arm. Talbot had not changed, except that he had discarded his miner's rig, and was now dressed in a rather quiet cloth suit, a small soft hat, and a blue flannel shirt. The trousers he had tucked into the tops of his boots. I thought the loose, neat costume very becoming to him. After a dozen swift inquiries as to our welfare, he plunged headlong into enthusiasms as to the town.

"It's the greatest city in the world!" he cried; then catching my expression, he added, "or it's going to be. Think of it, Frank! A year ago it had less than a thousand people, and now we have at least forty thousand. The new Commercial Wharf is nearly half a mile long and cost us a hundred and fifty thousand dollars, but we raised the money in ten minutes! We're going to build two more. And Sam Brannan and a lot of us are talking of putting down plank roads. Think what that will mean! And there's no limit to what we can do in real estate! Just knock down a few of these hills to the north ——"

He stopped, for I was laughing.

"Why not drain the bay?" I suggested. "There's a plenty of land down there."

"Well," said Talbot in a calmer manner, "we won't quite do that. But we'll put some of those sand hills into the edge of the bay. You wait and see. If you want to make money, you just buy some of those water-front lots. You'll wake up some morning to find you're a mile inland."

I laughed again; but just the other day, in this year 1899, I rode in a street car where fifty years ago great ships had lain at anchor.

We discovered Johnny and Yank, and pounded each other's backs, and had drinks, and generally worked off our high spirits. Then we adjourned to a corner, lit cigars — a tremendous luxury for us miners — and plunged into recital. Talbot listened to us attentively, his eyes bright with interest, occasionally breaking in on the narrator to ask one of the others to supplement some too modestly worded statement.

"Well!" he sighed when we had finished. "You boys have certainly had a time! What an experience! You'll never forget it!" He brooded a while. "I suppose the world will never see its like again. It was the chance of a lifetime. I'd like — no I wouldn't! I've lived, too. Well, now for the partnership. As I understand it, for the Hangman's Gulch end of it, we have, all told, about five thousand dollars — at any rate, that was the amount McClellan sent down to me."

"That's it," said I.

"And the Porcupine Flat venture was a bad loss?"

"The robbers cleaned us out there except for what we sent you," I agreed regretfully.

"Since which time Yank has been out of it completely?"

"Haven't made a cent since," acknowledged Yank cheerfully, "and I owe something to Frank, here, for my keep. Thought I had about fifteen hundred dollars, but I guess I ain't."

"At Italian Bar," went on Talbot, "how much did you make?"

"Doesn't matter what I made," interposed Johnny, "for, as Frank told you, it's all at the bottom of the Sacramento River."

"I did pretty well," said I, and pulled out two hundred and sixteen ounces.

"About three thousand dollars," computed Talbot. "You're the plutocrat, all right. Well, I've done pretty well with this end of the partnership, too. I think — but I guess we'd better take a fresh day to it. It must be ungodly late. Good Lord, yes! Three o'clock!"

Nobody would have thought so. The place seemed nearly as full as ever. We accompanied Talbot to his hotel, where he managed, after some difficulty, to procure us a cot apiece.

Our sleep was short; and in spite of our youth and the vitality we had stored in the healthy life of the hills we felt dragged out and tired. Five hours' sleep in two days is not enough. I was up a few minutes before the rest; and I sat in front of the hotel basking in the sun like a lizard. The let-down from the toil and excitement of the past months still held me. I thought with lazy satisfaction of the two thousand-odd dollars which was my share of our partnership. It was a small sum, to be sure; but, then, I had never in my life made more than twelve dollars a week, and this had cost me nothing. Now that definitely I had dropped overboard my hopes of a big strike, I unexpectedly found that I had dropped with them a certain feeling of pride and responsibility as well. As long as I had been in the mining business I had vaguely felt it incumbent on me to do as well as the rest, were that physically possible. I was out of the mining business. As I now looked at it, I had been mighty well paid for an exciting and interesting vacation. I would go back to New York at a cost of two or three hundred dollars, and find some good opening for my capital and ability.

Talbot appeared last, fresh and smiling. Breakfast finished, he took us all with him to the new brick building. After some business we adjourned once more to the Arcade. There Talbot made his report.

I wish I could remember it, and repeat it to you verbatim. It was worth it. But I cannot; and the most I can do is to try to convey to you the sense of that scene — we three tanned, weather-beaten outlanders listening open-mouthed to the keen, competent, self-assured magician

who before our eyes spun his glittering fabric. Talbot
Ward had seized upon the varied possibilities of the new
city. The earnings on his first scheme — the ship storehouses, and the rental of the brick building on Montgomery
Street, you will remember — amounted net, the first
month, I believe, to some six thousand dollars. With his
share of this money he had laid narrow margins on a
dozen options. Day by day, week by week, his operations
extended. He was in wharves, sand lots, shore lots, lighter-
ing, plank roads, a new hotel. Day after day, week after
week, he had turned these things over, and at each turn
money had dropped out. Sometimes the plaything proved
empty, and then Talbot had promptly thrown it away,
apparently without afterthought or regret. I remember
some of the details of one deal:

"It looked to me," said Talbot, "that somebody ought
to make a good thing in flour, the way things were going.
It all comes from South America just now, so enough
capital ought to be able to control the supply. I got
together four of the big men here and we agreed with the
agents to take not less than a hundred and fifty thousand
barrels nor more than two hundred thousand barrels at
fourteen dollars. Each firm agreed to take seven hundred
thousand dollars' worth; and each agreed to forfeit one
hundred thousand dollars for failure to comply. Flour
could be held to twenty-five to thirty dollars a barrel;
so there was a good thing."

"I should think so," I agreed. "Where did you come in?"

"Percentage of the profits. They took and sold quite
a heap of flour at this rate — sixty thousand barrels to be

exact — on which there was a net profit of seven hundred thousand dollars. Then one of those freak things happened that knocked us all silly. Flour just dropped down out of sight. Why? Manipulation. They've got a smart lot out here. The mines had flour enough for the time being; and the only thing that held the price up was the uncertainty of just where the flour was coming from in the future. Well, the other crowd satisfied that uncertainty, and our flour dropped from about twenty-five dollars down to eight! We had sold sixty thousand barrels, and we had ninety thousand to take on our contract, on each one of which we were due to lose six dollars. And the other fellows were sitting back chuckling and waiting for us to unload cheap flour."

"What was there to do?"

Talbot laughed. "I told our crowd that I had always been taught that when a thing was hot, to drop it before I got burned. If each firm paid its forfeit it would cost us four hundred thousand dollars. If we sold all the flour contracted for at the present price, we stood to lose nearer six hundred thousand. So we simply paid our forfeits, threw over the contract, and were three hundred thousand ahead."

"But was that fair to the flour people?" I asked doubtfully.

"Fair?" retorted Talbot. "What in thunder did they put the forfeit clause in for if it wasn't expected we might use it?"

As fast as he acquired a dollar, he invested it in a new chance, until his interests extended from the Presidio to the waterfront of the inner bay. These interests were strange odds and ends. He and a man with his own given name, Talbot H. Green, had title in much of what is now Harbour View — that is to say, they would have clear title as soon as they had paid heavy mortgages. His shares in the Commercial Wharf lay in the safes of a banking house, and the dollars he had raised on them were valiantly doing duty in holding at bay a pressing debt on precariously held waterfront equities. Talbot mentioned glibly sums that reduced even the most successful mining to a child's game. The richest strike we had heard rumoured never yielded the half of what our friend had tossed into a single deal. Our own pitiful thousands were beggarly by comparison, insignificant, not worth considering.

Of all the varied and far-extending affairs the Ward Block was the flower. Talbot owned options, equities, properties, shares in all the varied and numerous activities of the new city; but each and every one of them he held subject to payments which at the present time he could by no possibility make. Mortgages and loans had sucked every immediately productive dollar; and those dollars that remained were locked tight away from their owner until such time as he might gain possession of a golden key. This did not worry him.

"They are properties that are bound to rise in value," he told us. "In fact, they are going up every minute we sit here talking. They are futures."

Among other pieces, Talbot had been able to buy the lot on the Plaza where now the Ward Block was going up. He paid a percentage down, and gave a mortgage for the rest. Now all the money he could squeeze from all his other interests he was putting into the structure. That is why I rather fancifully alluded to the Ward Block as the flower of all Talbot's activities.

"Building is the one thing you have to pay cash for throughout," said Talbot regretfully. "Labour and materials demand gold. But I see my way clear; and a first-class, well-appointed business block in this town right now is worth more than the United States mint. That's cash coming in for you — regularly every month. It will pay from the start four of five times the amount necessary to keep everything else afloat. Jim Reckett has taken the entire lower floor at thirty thousand. The offices up-stairs will pay from a thousand a month up and they are every one rented in advance. Once we get our rents coming in, the strain is relieved. I can begin to take up my mortgages and loans, and once that is begun we are on the road to Millionaireville."

Once more he recapitulated his affairs — the land on the Plaza two hundred thousand; the building eighty thousand; the Harbour View lands anything they might rise to, but nearly a quarter million now; ten thousand par value of the wharf stock already paying dividends; real estate here and there and everywhere in the path of the city's growth; shares in a new hotel that must soon touch par; the plank road — as we jotted down the figures, and the magic total grew, such trifling little affairs as gold mines dropped quite below the horizon. We stared at Talbot fascinated.

And then for the first time we learned that the five

thousand dollars we had sent down from Hangman's Gulch, and the sum left from the robbery, was not slumbering in some banker's safe, but had been sent dancing with the other dollars at Talbot's command.

"I didn't know just what you fellows intended," said he, "but we were partners up there at the mines, and I concluded it would be all right. You didn't mean ——"

"Sure not!" broke in Johnny heartily. "You're welcome to mine."

"Same here," agreed Yank and I.

And then Talbot let us see that he considered us to that extent partners in the business.

"I have the date it arrived," he told us, "and I know just how much actual capital I had myself at that time. So I'm computing your shares in the venture on that basis. It comes to about one tenth apiece for Yank and Johnny. Frank and I have an agreement already."

Johnny stared at the paper on which the totals had been pencilled.

"Not any!" he protested vehemently. "It isn't fair! You've made this thing by sheer genius, and it isn't fair for me to take a tenth of it on the strength of a measly little consignment of gold dust. You give me your note for a thousand dollars — or whatever the sum is — at interest, if you want to, and that's all that is coming to me."

"I feel the same," said Yank.

"Boys," argued Talbot earnestly, "that doesn't go. That five thousand saved me. It came at a time when I had to have money or go down. I had been to every bank, to every firm, to every man in town, and I couldn't raise ten cents more. If you refuse this thing, you will be doing something that ——"

"Oh, hush up, Tal!" broke in Johnny gruffly; "if that's how you feel ——"

"It is."

"It is now," said Johnny firmly, " 10:30 A. M., but I'm going to have bubbles. If you fellows don't want me all drunk and dressed up, you've got to help me drink them."

CHAPTER XLIV
PLUTOCRATS!

We felt very elated — and rather small. Talbot had alone and without, so to speak, moving from his tracks, made a fortune, while we, after going through many hardships, adventures, and hard work, had returned almost penniless. One of our first tasks was to convince Talbot of the injustice to himself in giving us shares based on a proportionate money investment. We made him see, after a while, that his own genius counted for something in the matter. He then agreed, but reluctantly, to reduce our shares to a twentieth each, and included me in this, despite our previous agreement. If we had adhered to that, my proportion would have been nearer a fortieth.

This having been decided — after considerable argument — we settled down to wait for the completion of the Ward Block. Once the rents from that structure should begin to come in, it was agreed we should take out ready money enough to return East. The remainder, less Talbot's expenses, would of course have to go back into releasing all the other interests. The formal opening had been arranged for the first of January.

In the meantime we loafed magnificently, and lived on my money. Now that our futures were all assured, Yank and Johnny condescended to temporary loans. Occasionally we could help Talbot in some of the details of his varied businesses, but most of the time we idled. I do think we deserved a rest.

Our favourite occupation was that of reviewing our property. To this end we took long tramps over the hills, hunting painstakingly for obscure corner stakes or monuments that marked some one of our numerous lots. On them we would gaze solemnly, although in no manner did they differ from all the other sage-brush hill country about them. In a week we knew accurately every piece of property belonging to Our Interests, and we had listed every other more intangible equity or asset. One of Johnny's favourite feats was to march Yank and me up to a bar, face us, and interrogate us according to an invariable formula. We must have presented a comical sight — I with my great bulk and round, fresh face alongside the solemn, lank, and leathery Yank; both of us drawn up at attention, and solemn as prairie dogs.

"How much is one twentieth of two thousand thousand?" inquired Johnny.

"One hundred thousand," Yank and I chorused.

"Is that a plutocrat?" demanded Johnny cryptically.

"It is!" we cried.

Our sense of our own financial importance being thus refreshed, we advanced in rigid military formation to the bar and took our drinks. Two million dollars was the amount we had chosen as representing the value of Our Interests. In deciding upon this figure we considered ourselves very moderate in refusing to add probable future increment. It might also be added that we equally neglected to deduct present liabilities. Nobody ever guessed what this mysterious performance of ours meant, but every one came to expect it and to be amused by it. In a mild way we and our fool monkeyshines came to be a well-known institution.

Having nothing else to do, we entered heartily into the life and pleasures of the place, and we met many of the leading citizens. Some of them have since become historical personages. Talbot was hand in glove with most of them, and in and out of dozens of their schemes. There was David Broderick, a secretive, dignified, square-cut, bulldog sort of a man, just making his beginning in a career that was to go far. I remember he was then principally engaged in manufacturing gold coins and slugs and buying real estate.* His great political rival, Dr. Gwin the Southerner, I also met; and Talbot H. Green, then and for some time later, one of the most liked and respected of men, but whose private scandal followed him from the East and ruined him; and Sam Brannan, of course, the ex-elder of the Mormons; and Jim Reckett, the gambler; and W. T. Coleman, later known as Old Vigilante, and a hundred others. These were strong, forceful men, and their company was always interesting. They had ideas on all current topics, and they did not hesitate to express those ideas. We thus learned something of the community in which we had been living so long.

We heard of the political difficulties attendant on the

---

* Broderick actually manufactured coins with face value of $5 and $10 containing but $4 and $8 worth of gold. The inscription on them was simply that of the date, the location, and the value. They passed everywhere because they were more convenient than dust, and it was realized that only the last holders could lose.

jumble of military and unauthorized civil rule; of the convention at Monterey in September, with its bitterly contested boundary disputes; of the great and mooted question as to whether California should be "slave" or "free"; of the doubt and uncertainty as to the status of California-made law pending some action by the Federal Congress; of how the Federal Congress, with masterly inactivity and probably some slight skittishness as to mingling in the slavery argument, had adjourned without doing anything at all! So California had to take her choice of remaining under military governorship or going ahead and taking a chance on having her acts ratified later. She choose the latter course. San José was selected as the capital. Nobody wanted to serve in the new legislature; men hadn't time. There was the greatest difficulty in getting assemblymen. The result was that, with few exceptions, the first legislature of fifty-two members was composed of cheap professional politicians from the South, and useless citizens from elsewhere. This body was then in session. It was invariably referred to as "The Legislature of the Thousand Drinks." I heard discussed numberless schemes for its control for this or that purpose; many of them, it seemed to me, rather unscrupulous.

These big men of the city talked of other things besides politics. From them I heard of the state of commercial affairs, with its system of consignments and auctions, its rumours of fleet clipper ships, its corners of the market, its gluttings with unforeseen cargoes of unexpected vessels, and all the other complex and delicate adjustments and changes that made business so fascinating and so uncertain. All these men were filled with a great optimism and an abiding enthusiasm for the future. They talked of plank roads, of sewers, of schools, churches, hospitals, pavements, fills, the razing of hills, wharves, public buildings, water systems; and they talked of them so soberly and in such concrete terms of accomplishment that the imagination was tricked into accepting them as solid facts. Often I have gone forth from listening to one of these earnest discussions to look about me on that windswept, sandblown, flimsy, dirty, sprawling camp they called a city, with its half dozen "magnificent" brick buildings that any New England village could duplicate, and have laughed wildly until the tears came, over the absurdity of it. I was young. I did not know that a city is not bricks but men, is not fact but the vitality of a living ideal.

There were, of course, many other men than those I have named, and of varied temperaments and beliefs. Some of them were heard of later in the history of the state. Terry, James King of William, Stephen J. Field, General Richardson were some of those whose names I remember. They were, in general, frank and open in manner, ready to offer or take a joke, and on terms of good-natured comradeship with each other; and yet somehow I always felt behind it all a watchful reservation. This was indefinable, but it indubitably existed. The effect on me was an instinct that these men would remain good-natured, laughing, joking, intimate, just as long as nothing happened to make them otherwise. They were a pack, hunting in full cry the same quarry; but were one of them to fall out, the rest would sweep on without a backward glance. As an individual human being no one of them was in reality important to any other. They pursued the same aims, by much the same methods, and they could sometimes make use of each other to the advantage of both. In the meantime, since they as the prominent men of a mixed community must possess qualities in common, they found each other mutually agreeable. Many called themselves friends; but I much doubt if the friendship that would render aid at a sacrifice was very common. Every man played his own game.

In the town outside we made many other acquaintances, of all classes of society. In 1849 no social stigma, or very little, attached to any open association. Gamblers were respectable citizens, provided they ran straight games. The fair and frail sisterhood was well represented. It was nothing against a man, either in the public eye or actually, to be seen talking, walking, or riding with one of these ladies; for every one knew them. There were now a good many decent women in town, living mainly with their husbands and children very quietly among the sandhills on the edges of the town. One saw little of them unless he took the trouble to search them out. We did so, and thus struck up acquaintance with a half dozen very pleasant households, where occasionally my New England heart was gladdened by a genuine homebaked New England pie. These people had children and religious beliefs; and for the one and the other they had organized churches and schools, both of which were well attended. Furthermore, such institutions were contributed to by many of the business men who never entered their doors. This respectable life was stronger than is generally known. It was quiet and in the background, and under the deep shadow cast by the glaring light of downtown, but it was growing in solidity and strength.

Among the others we came across the preacher we had seen holding forth on the wharf. He was engaged, with the assistance of two men of the Methodist persuasion, in building a church. The three had themselves cut and hewed the timbers. Mr. Taylor, for that was his name, explained to me that, having no money, that seemed the the only way to get a church. He showed us his own place, a little shack not unlike the others, but enclosed, and planted with red geraniums, nasturtiums and other bright things.

"As far as I know," he told us with pride, "that is the first garden in San Francisco."

In the backyard he had enclosed three chickens — two hens and a cock.

"I paid eighteen dollars for them," said he.

We looked at each other in startled astonishment. The sum appeared a trifle extravagant considering the just-acknowledged impecuniosity of the church. He caught the glance.

"Boys," he said quaintly, "San Francisco is a very lonesome place for the godly. The hosts of sin are very strong, and the faithful are very few. Mortal flesh is weak; and mortal spirit is prone to black discouragement. When I bought those chickens I bought eighteen dollars' worth of hope. Somehow Sunday morning seems more like the Sabbath with them clicking around sleepy and lazy and full of sun."

We liked him so much that we turned to at odd times and helped him with his carpenter work. While thus engaged he confided to us his intention to preach against the gambling the next Sunday in the Plaza. We stopped hammering to consider this.

"I shouldn't, if I were you," said I. "The gamblers own the Plaza; they are respected by the bulk of the community; and they won't stand any nonsense. They none of them think anything of shooting a man in their places. I don't think they will stand for it. I am afraid you will be roughly handled."

"More likely shot," put in Johnny bluntly.

"Well, well, boys, we'll see," said Taylor easily.

Nor could we move him, in spite of the fact that, as we came to see his intention was real, we urged very earnestly against it.

"Well, if you will, you will," Johnny conceded at last, with a sigh. "We'll see what we can do to get you a fair show."

"Now that is just what I don't want you to do," begged the old man earnestly. "I want no vain contention and strife. If the Lord desires that I preach to these sinners, He will protect me."

In the end he extorted from us a reluctant promise not to mingle in the affair.

"He's just *looking* for trouble," muttered Johnny, "and there's no doubt he'll find it. The gamblers aren't going to stand for a man's cussing 'em outright on their own doorsteps — and I don't know as I blame them. Gambling isn't such a terrible, black, unforgivable sin as I see it."

"That's because you're ahead of the game, Johnny," drawled Yank.

"Just the same the old fool is wrong," persisted Johnny, "and he's as obstinate as a mule, and he makes me mad clean through. Nevertheless he's a good old sort, and I'd hate to see him hurt."

The news spread abroad, and there was much speculation as to what would happen. In general the sentiment was hostile to the preacher. It was considered an unwarrantable interference with freedom for any man to attempt to dictate the conduct of another. Everybody agreed that religion was all right; but by religion they meant some vague utterance of platitudes. On the appointed Sunday a very large crowd gathered in the Plaza. Nobody knew just what the gamblers intended to do about it. Those competent citizens were as close mouthed as ever. But it was understood that no nonsense was to be permitted, and that this annoying question must be settled at once and fully. As one man expressed it:

"We'll have these fellows caterwauling all over the place if we don't shut down on them right sharp off quick."

Taylor arrived about ten o'clock and proceeded briskly to the pork barrel that had been rolled out to serve as a pulpit. He faced a lowering, hostile mob.

"Gentlemen," said he, "if some means of communication existed by which the United States could this morning know that street preaching was to be attempted in the streets of San Francisco, the morning papers, badly informed as to the temper and disposition of the people of this new country, would feel themselves fully justified in predicting riot, if not actual bloodshed. Furthermore, I do not doubt that the greater dailies would hold their forms open to report the tragedy when news of it should come in. But we of the West know better than that. We know ourselves rough and ready, but we know ourselves also to be lovers of fair play. We know that, even though we may not agree with a man, we are willing to afford him a fair hearing. And as for rioting or bloodshed, we can afford to smile rather than become angry at such wide misconception of our decency and sense of fair dealing."

Having in this skilful fashion drawn the venom from the fangs of the mob, he went directly ahead at his sermon, hammering boldly on his major thesis. He finished in a respectful silence, closed his Bible with a snap, and strode away through the lane the crowd opened for him.

Truth to tell, there was much in the sermon. Gambling, although considered one of the respectable amusements, undoubtedly did a great deal of harm. Men dropped their last cents at the tables. I remember one young business man who had sold out his share in his firm for ten thousand dollars in cash and three notes for five thousand each. He had every intention of taking this little fortune back to his family in the East, but he began gambling. First, he lost his ten thousand dollars in cash. This took him just two days. After vacillating another day, he staked one of the notes, at a discount, of course. This he lost.

GOLD

A second note followed the first; and everybody confidently expected that the third would disappear in the same fashion. But Jim Reckett, who was a very good sort, took this man aside, and gave him a good talking-to.

"You confounded fool," said he, "you're barred from my tables. My advice to you is to go to your old partners, tell them what an ass you've made of yourself, and ask them to let you have a few thousand on that last note. And then you leave on to-day's Panama steamer. And, say, if they won't do it, you come to me."

The young fellow took this advice.

The Panama steamers were crowded to the rail. Indeed, the exodus was almost as brisk as the immigration, just at this time of year. A moderate proportion of those going out had been successful, but the great majority were disappointed. They were tired, and discouraged, and homesick; and their minds were obsessed with the one idea — to get back. We who remained saw them go with considerable envy, and perhaps a good deal of inner satisfaction that soon we were to follow. Of the thousands who were remaining in California, those who had definitely and permanently cast their lot with the country were lost in the crowd. The rest intended to stay another year, two years, perhaps even three; but then each expected to go back.

CHAPTER XLV

THE CATASTROPHE

So things went along for a month. Christmas drew near. Every joint in town was preparing for a big celebration, and we were fully in the mood to take part in it. The Ward Block was finished. From top to bottom it had been swept and cleared. Crowds came every day to admire the varnish, the glass, the fireplaces, the high plastered walls; to sniff the clean new smell of it. Everybody admitted it to be the finest building in the city. Yank, Johnny, and I spent most of our time proudly showing people around, pointing out the offices the various firms intended to occupy. Downstairs Jim Reckett was already installing some of the splendours that were to make the transplanted El Dorado the most gorgeous gambling place in town. Here the public was not admitted. The grand opening, on New Year's day, was not thus to lose its finest savour.

On Christmas eve we went to bed, strangely enough, very early. All the rest of the town was celebrating, but we had been busy moving furniture and fixtures, had worked late in order to finish the job, and were very tired. By this time we were so hardened that we could sleep through any sort of a racket, so the row going on below and on both sides did not bother us a bit. I, personally, fell immediately into a deep slumber.

GOLD

The first intimation of trouble came to me in my sleep. I dreamed we were back on the Porcupine, and that the stream was in flood. I could distinctly hear the roar of it, as it swept by; and I remember Johnny and myself were trying desperately to climb a big pine tree in order to get above the encroaching waters. A wind sprang up and shook the pine violently. I came slowly to waking consciousness, the dream fading into reality. Yank was standing by my cot, shaking me by the shoulder. He was fully dressed, and carried his long rifle.

"Get up!" he told me. "There's a big fire one or two doors away, and it's headed this way."

Then I realized that the roar of the flames had induced my dream.

I hastily slipped on my clothes and buckled my gold belt around my waist. The fire was humming away in a steady crescendo, punctuated by confused shouts of many men. Light flickered redly through the cracks of the loosely constructed hotel building. I found Johnny awaiting me at the door.

"It's a hummer," he said; "started in Denison's Exchange. They say three men have been killed."

The Plaza was black with men, their faces red with the light of the flames. A volunteer crew were busily darting in and out of the adjacent buildings, carrying out all sorts of articles and dumping them in the square.

"There's no water nearer than the bay," an acquaintance shouted in our ears. "There ain't much to do. She'll burn herself out in a few minutes."

The three buildings were already gutted. A sheet

of fire sucked straight upward in the still air, as steadily as a candle flame, and almost as unwavering. It was a grand and beautiful spectacle. The flimsy structures went like paper. Talbot saw us standing at a little elevation, and forced his way to us.

"It will die down in five minutes," said he. "What do you bet on Warren's place? Do you think she'll go?"

"It's mighty hot all around there," said I doubtfully.

"Yes, but the flames are going straight up; and, as you say, it will begin to die down pretty soon," put in Johnny.

"The walls are smoking a little," commented a bystander judicially.

"She's a fine old bonfire, anyway," said Talbot.

Fifteen or twenty men were trying to help Warren's place resist the heat. They had blankets and pails of water, and were attempting to interpose these feeble defences at the points most severely attacked. Each man stood it as long as he could, then rushed out to cool his reddened face.

"Reminds me of the way I used to pop corn when I was a kid," grinned a miner. "I wouldn't care for that job."

"Just the same, they'll save it," observed Talbot judicially.

Almost coincident with his words a long-drawn *a-ah!* burst from the crowd. A wandering gust of wind came in from the ocean. For the briefest instant the tall straight column of flame bent gracefully before it, then came upright again as it passed. In that instant it licked across the side wall of Warren's place, and immediately Warren's place burst into flame.

"Hard luck!" commented Talbot.

The firefighters swarmed out like bees from a disturbed hive.

"Our hotel next," said Johnny.

"That's safe enough; there's a wide lot between," I observed.

A fresh crew of firefighters took the place of the others — namely, those personally interested in saving the hotel.

"Lucky the night is so still," said Talbot.

We watched Warren's place burn with all the half guilty joy of those who are sorry; but who are glad to be there if it has to happen. Suddenly Talbot threw up his head.

"Feel that breeze?" he cried.

"Suction into the fire," suggested Johnny.

But Talbot shook his head impatiently, trying to peer through the glare into the sky.

It was a very gentle breeze from the direction of the ocean. I could barely feel it on my cheek, and it was not strong enough as yet to affect in the slightest the upward-roaring column of flame. For a moment I was inclined to agree with Johnny that it was simply a current of air induced by the conflagration. But now an uneasy motion began to take place in the crowd. Men elbowed their way here and there, met, conferred, gathered in knots. In less than a minute Talbot signalled us. We made our way to where he was standing with Sam Brannan, Casey, Green, and a few others.

"Thank God the wind is from the northwest," Talbot said fervently. "The Ward Block is safely to windward, and we don't need to worry about that, anyway. But it is a wind, and it's freshening. We've got to do something to stop this fire."

As though to emphasize the need for some sort of action, a second and stronger puff of wind sent whirling aloft a shower of sparks and brands.

We started at double quick in the direction of the flimsy small structures between the old El Dorado and the Parker House. Some men, after a moment, brought ropes and axes. We began to tear down the shanties.

But before we had been at work five minutes, the fire began to run. The wind from the sea increased. Blazing pieces of wood flew through the air like arrows. Flames stooped in their stride, and licked up their prey, and went on rejoicing. Structures one minute dark and cold and still burst with startling suddenness and completeness into rioting conflagration. Our little beginning of a defence was attacked and captured before we had had time to perfect it. The half dozen shanties we had pulled to the ground merely furnished piled fuel. Somewhat demoralized, we fell back, and tried, rather vaguely, to draw a second line of defence. The smoke and sparks suffocated and overwhelmed us, and the following flames leaped upon us as from behind an ambush. Some few men continued gropingly to try to do something, but the most of us were only too glad to get out where we could catch a breath.

Almost immediately, however, we were hurried back by frantic merchants.

"Save the goods!" was the cry.

We laboured like slaves, carrying merchandise, fixtures, furniture, anything and everything from the darkened interiors of buildings to the open spaces. I worked as I had never worked before, and not once did I know whose property I thus saved. At first I groped in the darkness, seizing what I could; then gradually, like the glow of a red dawn, a strange light grew, showing dimly and ruddily the half-guessed features of the place. It glowed, this light, increasing in power as heating metal slowly turns red. And then the flames licked through; and dripping with sweat, I abandoned that place to its enemy.

All sense of time and all sense of locality were lost. The world was a strange world of deep, concealing shadows and strong, revealing glares, and a mist of smoke, and hurrying, shouting, excited multitudes. Sometimes I found myself in queer little temporary eddies of stillness, where a certain calm and leisure seemed to have been insulated. Then for a brief moment or so I rested. Occasionally I would find myself with some stranger, and we would exchange brief exclamatory remarks.

"Whole city is going!"

"Looks like it."

"Hear a roof fell in and killed twenty men."

"Probably exaggerated."

"Probably. Don't catch me under no falling roofs! When she gets afire, I get out."

"Same here."

"Well, I suppose we ought to try to do *something*."

"Suppose so."

And we would go at it again.

At the end of two or three hours — no man can guess time in such a situation — the fire stopped advancing. I suppose the wind must have changed, though at the time I did not notice it. At any rate, I found myself in the gray dawn looking rather stupidly at a row of the frailest kind of canvas and scantling houses which the fire had sheared cleanly in two, and wondering why in thunder the rest of them hadn't burned!

A dense pall of smoke hung over the city, and streamed away to the south and east. In the burned district all sense of location had been lost. Where before had been well-known landmarks now lay a flat desert. The fire had burned fiercely and completely, and, in lack of food, had died down to almost nothing. A few wisps of smoke still rose, a few coals glowed, but beside them nothing remained to indicate even the laying out of the former plan. Only over across a dead acreage of ashes rose here and there the remains of isolated brick walls. They looked, through the eddying mists and smoke, like ancient ruins, separated by wide spaces.

I gazed dully across the waste area, taking deep breaths, resting, my mind numb. Then gradually it was borne in on me that the Plaza itself looked rather more empty-sided than it should. A cold hand gripped my heart. I began to skirt the smouldering embers of the shanties and wooden warehouses, trying to follow where the streets had been. Men were prowling about everywhere, blackened by smoke, their clothing torn and burned.

"Can you make out where Higgins's store was?" one of them hailed me. "I had a little shanty next door, and some gold dust. Figure I might pan it out of the ashes, if I could only find the place."

I had no time to help him, and left him prowling around seeking for a landmark.

The Plaza was full of people. I made my way to the northerly corner, and, pushing a passage through the bystanders, contemplated three jagged, tottering brick walls, a heap of smouldering débris, and a twisted tangle of iron work. This represented all that remained of the Ward Block. The change of wind that had saved the shanties had destroyed our fortune!

CHAPTER XLVI

THE VISION

Within ten hours men were at work rebuilding. Within ten days the burned area was all rebuilt. It took us just about the former period of time to determine that we would be unable to save anything from the wreck; and about the latter period for the general public to find it out.

Talbot made desperate efforts for a foothold, and in succession interviewed all the big men. They were sorry but they were firm. Each had been hard hit by the fire; each had himself to cover; each was forced by circumstances to grasp every advantage. Again, they were sorry.

"Yes, they are!" cried Talbot; "they just reach out and grab what ought to be my profits! Well, it's the game. I'd do the same myself.'

By that night we knew that Talbot had lost every piece of property he owned — or thought he owned. The destruction of the Ward Block swept away every cent of income, with the exception of the dividends from the Wharf Company stock. These latter could not begin to meet the obligations of interest and agreed payments on the other property.

The state of affairs became commonly known in about ten days simply because, in those rapid times, obligations were never made nor money lent for longer periods than one month. At the end of each thirty days they had to be renewed. Naturally Talbot could not renew them.

We knew all that long in advance, and we faced the situation with some humour.

"Well, boys," said Talbot, "here we are. About a year ago, as I remember it, our assets were a bundle of newspapers and less than a hundred dollars. Haven't even got a newspaper now, but I reckon among us we could just about scrape up the hundred dollars."

"I've got nearer twenty-seven hundred in my belt," I pointed out.

An embarrassed silence fell for a moment; then Talbot spoke up, picking his words very carefully.

"We've talked that over, Frank," said he, "and we've come to the conclusion that you must keep that and go home, just as you planned to do. You're the only man of us who has managed to keep what he has made. Johnny falls overboard and leaves his in the bottom of the Sacramento; Yank gets himself busted in a road-agent row; I — I — well, I blow soap bubbles! You've kept at it, steady and strong and reliable, and you deserve your good luck. You shouldn't lose the fruits of your labour because we, each in our manner, have been assorted fools."

I listened to this speech with growing indignation; and at its conclusion I rose up full of what I considered righteous anger. My temper is very slow to rouse, but when once it wakes, it takes possession of me.

"Look here, you fellows!" I cried, very red in the

face, they tell me. "You answer me a few questions. **Are** we or are we not partners? Are we or are we not friends? Do you or do you not consider me a low-lived, white-livered, mangy, good-for-nothing yellow pup? Why, confound your pusillanimous souls, what do you mean by talking to me in that fashion? For just about two cents I'd bust your fool necks for you — every one of you!" I glared vindictively at them. "Do you suppose I'd make any such proposition to any of you — to ask you to sneak off like a whipped cur leaving me to take the ——"

"Hold on, Frank," interposed Talbot soothingly. "I didn't mean ——"

"Didn't you?" I cried. "Well, what in hell did you mean? Weren't you trying to make me out a quitter?" I had succeeded in working loose my heavy gold belt, and I dashed it on the table in front of them. "There! Now you send for some gold scales, right now, and you divide that up! Right here! Damn it all, boys," I ended, with what to a cynical bystander would have seemed rather a funny slump into the pathetic, "I thought we were all real friends! You've hurt my feelings!"

It was very young, and very ridiculous — and perhaps (I can say it from the vantage of fifty years) just a little touching. At any rate, when I had finished, my comrades were looking in all directions, and Talbot cleared his throat a number of times before he replied.

"Why, Frank," he said gently, at last, "of course we'll take it — we never dreamed — of course — it was stupid of us, I'll admit. Naturally, I see just how you feel ——"

"It comes to about seven hundred apiece, don't it?" drawled Yank.

The commonplace remark saved the situation from bathos, as I am now certain shrewd old Yank knew it would.

"What are you going to do with your shares, boys?" asked Talbot after a while. "Going back home, or mining? Speak up, Yank."

Yank spat accurately out the open window.

"I've been figgering," he replied. "And when you come right down to it, what's the use of going back? Ain't it just an idee we got that it's the proper thing to do? What's the matter with this country, anyway — barring mining?"

"Barring mining?" echoed Talbot.

"To hell with mining!" said Yank; "it's all right for a vacation, but it ain't noways a white man's stiddy work. Well, we had our vacation."

"Then you're not going back to the mines?"

"Not any!" stated Yank emphatically.

"Nor home?"

"No."

"What then?"

"I'm going to take up a farm up thar whar the Pine boys is settled, and I'm going to enjoy life reasonable. Thar's good soil, and thar's water; thar's pleasant prospects, and lots of game and fish. What more does a man want? And what makes me sick is that it's been thar all the time and it's only just this minute I've come to see it."

"Mines for you, Johnny, or home?" asked Talbot.

"Me, home?" cried Johnny; "why ——" he checked himself, and added more quietly. "No, I'm not going home. There's nothing there for me but a good time, when you come right down to it. And mines? It strikes me that fresh gold is easy to get, but almighty hard to keep."

"You never said a truer word than that, Johnny," I put in.

"Besides which, I quit mining some time ago, as you remember," went on Johnny, "due to an artistic aversion to hard work," he added.

"Any plans?" asked Talbot.

"I think I'll just drift up to Sonoma and talk things over with Danny Randall," replied Johnny vaguely. "He had some sort of an idea of extending this express service next year."

"And you?" Talbot turned to me.

"I," said I, firmly, "am going to turn over my share in a business partnership with you; and in the meantime I expect to get a job driving team with John McGlynn for enough to pay the board bill while you rustle. And that goes!" I added warningly.

"Thank you, Frank," replied Talbot, and I thought I saw his bright eye dim. He held silent for a moment. "Do you know," he said suddenly, "I believe we're on the right track. It isn't the gold. That is a bait, a glittering bait, that attracts the world to these shores. It's the country. The gold brings them, and out of the hordes that come, some, like us, will stick. And after the gold is dug and scattered and all but forgotten, we will find that we have fallen heirs to an empire."

NOTE

The author desires fully to acknowledge his indebtedness to the following writers, from whose books he has drawn freely, both for historical fact, incidents, and the spirit of the times:

Tuthill — History of California.
Foster — The Gold Regions of California.
Stillman — Seeking the Golden Fleece.
Taylor — El Dorado.
Delano — Life on the Plains.
Shinn — Mining Camps.
Brooks — Four Months Among the Gold Finders.
Johnson — Sights in the Gold Region and Scenes by the Way.
Bostwicks — Three Years in California.
Shaw — Ramblings in California.
Hittell — History of San Francisco.
Bates — Four Years on the Pacific Coast.
Taylor — California Life Illustrated.
Marryatt — Mountains and Molehills.
James — The Heroes of California.
Hunt — California the Golden.
Haskins — The Argonauts of California.
Bell — Reminiscences of a Ranger.
Royce — California.
Eldredge — Beginnings of San Francisco.
Langford — Vigilante Days and Ways.

I-2